STEVE BRAKER
AFRICAN JINN

A WILLIAM BRODY

ACTION THRILLER

Table of Contents

Chapter One 1
Chapter Two 17
Chapter three 39
Chapter Four...47
Chapter five 57
Chapter Six..69
Chapter Seven 77
Chapter Eight 87
Chapter Nine...97
Chapter Ten 107
Chapter Eleven 113
Chapter Twelve...137
Chapter Thirteen 145
Chapter Fourteen 159
Chapter Fifteen...177
Chapter Sixteen 187
Chapter Seventeen 205
Chapter Eighteen 213
Chapter Nineteen 217
Chapter Twenty 231
Chapter Twenty-One 233
Songo Songo 241
Epilogue 253

Copyright 2023 by Steve Braker Books

All rights are reserved. No part of this book may be reproduced, scanned, photocopied, or made available in any format whatsoever, or distributed in any printed or electronic form without express written permission in contract form. As an indie author I would appreciate it if you did not participate in or encourage piracy of copyrighted material in violation of the author's rights. Please support the artist by purchasing only authorized editions.

African Jinn is a work of fiction. Names, characters, and incidents are either the product of the authors imagination or are used fictitiously. Any resemblance to an actual person or persons, alive or dead, businesses, companies, corporations, and any other entity is entirely coincidental.

Most of the locations herein are fictional or are used fictitiously as a point of reference. However, I live on the coast of East Africa and have spent most of the last twenty years plying the coastline. In the interest of entertainment, I have tried to describe some of the main towns as cities as accurately as possible to give the reader a real feel for the location. Shukran is not a real dhow but similar to many I have sailed along the coast. I have tried my best to convey the language, culture, and attitude of the people of the East African Coast.

PREFACE

Dear Reader

As an indie author, this series of books has been such a pleasure to write. I love trying to convey how I truly feel about my life in Africa, the encounters I have, the people I meet, and the culture.

To this end, I must especially thank my ever-patient wife Pauline, who continuously gives me ideas on the history, culture, and language of East Africa. Without her encyclopedic brain, I would have been lost many years ago.

In African Jinn, I wanted to bring out the juxtaposition between a Western way of thinking against the ages-old African culture and religion. I spent many months studying the darker sides of the Koran to get a feel for my African Jinn. I even interviewed several people who had either met the Jinn or actually kept one in their house!

The Swahili people are very aware of the spirit's presence and will often alter their lives to accommodate the Jinn. A black dog, cat, or snake are all considered very special animals, as they are known to be Jinn.

When I first arrived in Kenya in 2000 and decided to live in an area called Montomondoni in the middle of nowhere; the first piece of advice that was given to me was, *"Buy yourself some black dogs!"* I have also seen grown men change direction and take a much longer route rather than walk past a black kitten in the street.

African Jinn has been a voyage of discovery for me, and I sincerely hope you enjoy the read.

If, when you have finished the book, you are in a position to write a review on Amazon, I will be eternally grateful.

Tutaonana baadaye, Steve.

Chapter One
Living the Dream

The crisp early morning breeze cooled Brody's face. A bright golden orb was just beginning to show its shimmering tip on the horizon to the east, throwing shards of golden light into the clouds above. He reached up and ran his fingers through a ragged, unkempt beard smothering his jawline and flowing up and along his ruddy cheeks. Lank, uncut hair gritty with salt fell almost to his shoulders. His old sergeant major would have had a heart attack if he saw him now. The dark-stained, polished, teak deck felt moist and slippery beneath his bare feet from the morning dew just forming as the night moved from a cool pleasurable temperature through to a humid, sweltering day. The midnight blue of the night sky was being washed back into infinity. The last few stragglers of stars fighting against the glory of the sun blinked one last time before the day began. Brody felt exhilarated at the beauty of nature at this time of day. A new beginning. The world was fresh. Anything could happen.

To his port, China cups rattled in their hardwood box as Hassan started preparing the morning coffee. The jiko, a small brazier, was lit. The long black fingers of charcoal soon glowed red; the smell of burning trees filled the salt-laden air. An ancient, polished, mvule coffee grinder with a brass, filigree handle appeared from one of the lockers. A measured hand full of the best Kenyan beans was poured reverently into its grinding chamber. A few seconds later, Brody could smell the earthy coffee granules as they were ground to just the right consistency. Hassan took the art of making Arabic coffee very seriously; it was more a ceremony than a task. A few minutes later, Brody was handed a white China mug of steaming black coffee, laden with sugar the way the Swahilis love to take it.

Hassan went back to his jiko and moved on to the second part of his morning ritual. Another locker was opened to show a bright orange

Tupperware box. Hassan opened the box and carefully removed a handful of dough. He gazed at it with the eye of a keen watchmaker, then slammed it down on a scarred slice of a bamba coffee tree. He worked the dough with practiced hands to get exactly the right texture. A sufuria, a black cast-iron cooking pot, was placed on the hot charcoal, and fresh golden-brown coconut oil was added from a glass bottle. As soon as the oil started bubbling, triangles of rolled dough were slid into the hot oil. They bobbed and floated around for a few minutes then Hassan carefully ladled them out and set them on a white ceramic plate. As they cooled, he sprinkled a good dose of brown sugar and some local dark honey over the hot fried cakes known as kaimati. Brody loved his morning routine of coffee and sweet sugary cakes. It was a luxury he had gotten used to over the years, and one he would sorely miss if taken away.

Shukran rose and fell with the gentle swells of the Indian Ocean. A pod of bottlenose dolphins came to play with the bow wash, spinning and flipping out of the water in front of the boat. The smaller ones in the group plunged into the depths and then hurtled toward the surface, leaping into the air. Brody imagined he could almost hear their shouts and cheers of laughter, like young children playing on the beach. He wiggled his hip against the long wooden tiller to keep *Shukran* on course heading directly toward the rising sun.
"Hassan?"
"Yes, Boss."
"Can you call Gumbao, the wind's coming up. We should raise the sail and turn his baby off."
Hassan wandered over to a hatch in the deck, lifted it, and shouted into the hold. "Old man, we need your muscles on deck."
A grizzly, white-haired African appeared with a huge smile, showing two teeth missing from his upper and lower jaw. "I'm not your old man, kid," Gumbao said with a gruff smile. "Why can't you hoist the sail? Or are your dainty cooking fingers too precious for real work?"
Hassan laughed at his old friend, passing him a plate of steaming kaimati and a cup of fresh coffee. "No, I just enjoy watching you struggle with the sails while I man the tiller." Brody smiled at the banter. His two

best friends—his crew—were always at it. Hassan was a devout Muslim who prayed five times every day. Gumbao, by comparison, was a ruffian, of no fixed address, who lived life to the fullest and never had a care for tomorrow.

"Hassan, come take the tiller," Brody said. "Gumbao, we need the exercise—this will get our blood pumping, and your baby needs a rest!"

Shukran was an old, fat-bellied dhow that had plied the coast of East Africa for more than fifty years. She had sunk and been refloated on more than one occasion. The dhows that roamed the coast of Africa are always in a state of repair. They are kept afloat and sailing only with daily maintenance. *Shukran* had come under Brody's care a few years ago when he had helped save some young girls from slavery in Somalia. Since then, he had lived aboard her with his only two friends in the world. Brody was proud of his ship. Having spent years in the Special Boat Service working for Her Majesty's government he had spent many hours on boats of all shapes and sizes. When he was presented with *Shukran* he fell in love, and since then had spent every available dollar making sure she was as good as could be. The deck teak was polished to a high shine, and the brass and stainless steel were clean, without a hint of corrosion. The mast, or al-sari, was a solid, hardwood tree trunk Hassan had found in the forests north of Lamu. She was a wonderful ship, at just over fifty feet long. *Shukran* was a displacement hull, which meant she could only manage about eight knots with a good wind and the engine going, but his life was not about speed or getting anywhere, so they usually cruised along at a leisurely four to six knots.

The sailing rig on a dhow is called a lateen rig. The boom is hoisted to the top of the mast and the sail flows out underneath tied to a point in the stern where the captain can control the angle of the sail to the wind. When Brody had renovated *Shukran,* he had kept her as close to original as possible, there were no electrical winches or fancy pulleys. The wooden pulley blocks were made from teak painstakingly carved by Gumbao, they had little wooden wheels inside pasted with shark liver oil to keep them moving.

"Gumbao," Brody said, "untie the mast from the roof cleat, and let's get this beast up!" Brody loved pulling the sail up; it was a workout in itself. The stiff, five-ply hawser woven rope was full of salt and hard in his calloused hands.

When Gumbao was ready, they each grabbed the rope and started heaving. The heavy wooden boom with the sail wrapped tightly below it slowly dragged itself up the mast. Brody shouted, "Hassan, bring us into the wind!"

Shukran sluggishly answered the push of the tiller and dragged herself around facing northeast into the Kaskazi monsoon. Brody and Gumbao hauled on the line, jumping up as far as they could to grab the rope then using their combined weight to haul the boom up the mast inch by inch.

After twenty long minutes of swearing and sweating the boom finally hit the tip of the mast. The front of the boom was still attached to the bow, so it now made a triangle, the classic shape of a sailing dhow.

"Tie her off to the port cleat," shouted Brody, over his shoulder, as he dashed forward to make sure the bottom of the boom was securely tied to the bow. Gumbao grabbed the long sheet for the sail and walked it back to Hassan. "Ready when you are, Captain," he said, as he handed the line to Hassan. Hassan leaned into the tiller, pushing *Shukran* away from the wind. As he did, he pulled the sheet, ripping the coconut fronds holding the sail in place. Sluggishly at first, but as the palm fronds broke, the sail flapped and billowed, dragging Hassan forward as the wind filled the sail. Brody stepped in and helped Hassan loop the sheet around the Samson post on the starboard side of the dhow and pull it tight. *Shukran* felt the wind in her bright white sail and heeled over, bringing her onto a broad reach heading back toward the rising sun.

Hassan said, "Old man, you can turn off that engine now."

And suddenly there was peace. A peace only a sailor knows, when the engine is turned off the ocean is surprisingly quiet. *Shukran* was pushed through the light ocean swells at four knots; all that could be heard was the wash of the falling waves as they gently broke on the bow. It was a sudden and dramatic change that all seamen relish.

"Gumbao, let's get the lines out, there might be a wahoo or dorado we can add to the catch," said Brody as he looked at the row of six stout wooden cases lined up on the deck. "You really think we can fill them all with fish in one night?"

"Boss, if we hit the tuna shoals just right, and we can keep hauling them in, they will keep coming."

Hassan called from the stern, "Mzee, don't you think all that ice will melt long before we get to the rips?"

"Ah boy, you're always full of the negative. Half will melt leaving room for the fish."

"The ice and crates cost us four hundred dollars," said Brody. "How many tuna do we need to catch to make a profit?"

Gumbao looked at his two partners in crime as if he were looking at children. "Boss, I've done this trip so many times I cannot count. We bought the crates and the ice this morning at the quay in Kiwayu. We are lucky as *Shukran* has a big sail so we can move faster than the other boats and carry more fish. All we have to do is hit the rip currents out at about the fifty-mile mark and find a shoal of tuna. Then we throw in the hooks and pull them in all night if we have to. Once the crates are full, we turn and head for Kismayo …"

"As in Kismayo in Somalia?" Brody interjected.

"Yes, Boss, as in that one. But you have no problem, you look like all the other Arab traders. Since we left Lamu a month ago, you haven't shaved or had a haircut. You look more like a local than a local! We can rub some of Hassan's henna into your beard, then you will look like a real Swahili, mzee."

Brody thought to himself this was very true. They had sailed to Lamu and provisioned, then headed north toward the border of Somalia. The area was totally untouched; not a living soul for one hundred miles in all directions. The coastline was beautifully rugged and broken with many small inlets all covered with mangrove forests. The land behind the barren coast was a massive game reserve used as a buffer between Somalia and Kenya. The place was full of herds of elephants, buffalo, and zebra with prides of lions and packs of hyenas roaming around like street gangs looking for an easy mark. A real wilderness. Brody had decided to go off-grid and live on the ocean and the long white sandy beaches. He speared coral trout, Spanish mackerel, jobfish, and the occasional big-eyed tuna in the crystal-clear waters along the coast. Once they had enough fish for a few days, Hassan would steer *Shukran* back toward the coast and find one of the multitudes of tiny inlets amongst the tangled, sunken roots of the mangrove trees with their green, effervescent leaves.

Invariably just behind the mangroves, they would find a soft white sandy beach that had never been touched by humans. A quick climb up a coconut tree would provide the much-needed hydration for the day. Then Hassan would cook some sweet potatoes and fish over an open grill. When the fish ran out, they would just rinse and repeat on another beach. Life was idyllic, and Brody was more at peace with himself than he had ever been. The nightmares had almost stopped. The days had merged into weeks. Brody had not worn a shirt or had shoes on his feet for as long as he could remember. His life was simple and carefree. As long as there were fish and coconuts he was prepared to stay as long as he could.

A few nights earlier, as they had sat around the fire, Gumbao had come up with the plan of making some much-needed cash. It was simple, just go out to the rips fifty miles offshore, catch the fish, and take them to Kismayo where the markets were always wanting. Passport control along the East African coast was more of a preference than a requirement, so a quick hop over into Somalia was not an issue. Brody had visited Kismayo many years ago as a soldier on a deadly raid that changed his life, but that was a long time ago, and he was a different man now.

Gumbao broke into his thoughts, "Anyway, Boss, it will be a quick in and out. I know the guys on the quay. We'll sell the crates from the boat to a fish dealer and then be on our way at least five hundred dollars better off. There's nothing that can go wrong."

"Sure, Gumbao, nothing ever goes wrong with our plans!" said Brody with a wry grin on his face. "But for now, let's concentrate on getting those crates filled with fish."

Shukran sailed on a broad reach, cruising along at four knots. Soon they lost sight of land and were alone in the vast open ocean. The day was long and hot on the deck of the dhow. Gumbao sat on the stern rail, always watching his fishing lures bouncing on the surface, like a wounded fish, about fifty yards behind the boat. Brody lay on the stern cushions in the shade, content to doze in the early afternoon sun. His life was perfect, not a worry to concern him. Around noon, as Hassan was starting to doze on the tiller, one of the reels suddenly started screaming as the line was ripped from the spool. Brody was on his feet in a second and lunged for the fishing rod as the line raced away. Gumbao moved like a leopard jumping from a tree onto an innocent dik-dik, and plucked the second rod from its holder, reeling in the lure to stop any chance of a tangle.

Brody felt the strength of the fish on the rod. He watched the line strip off the reel as he tentatively slid the brake lever forward while easing the rod up—then down; the fish slowed and turned. The line dipped into the ocean. Brody held his breath; the moment of truth was upon him. He had to jerk the line up, which would either jam the barbed hook into the hard upper palate of the fish's mouth—known as setting the hook—or break the line and set the monster free. He jerked the rod up with all of his strength. Then he waited.

Sweat poured into his eyes as the seconds seemed to hang in the air in front of him. He turned to Gumbao, who just nodded sagely. Then the rod was almost yanked out of his grip as the fish turned in the water column and raced for the bottom. The fight was on! It was a contest of the ages, between man and beast. Brody fought for a yard of line and the great ocean creature fought to take that yard right back. The line went as taut as a piano string as the fish made a small gain, taking a few precious yards off the reel. Then as he felt the line slacken, Brody jerked the rod up and gained a few yards. The fish was undeterred and valiantly fought to escape, diving for the depths. Brody stood on the stern of *Shukran*, his body glistening with sweat, his biceps taut and strained as he pulled the rod once again. The fish battled for thirty minutes before it started to wane. Brody felt the give in the line and started reeling as fast as he could.

Gumbao shouted, "Boss, you better get it on board before the bull sharks sense it's weak. If they catch it, you'll only see the head!"

Hassan laughed, "Old man, I thought this was an easy five hundred?"

"Shut up, boy. This is only the beginning; by morning you'll have found out what a real day's work is."

Brody heaved on the line, sensing it second by second. When he felt it was close to its breaking point, he would gently release the brake, teasing the giant fish toward the boat. If he became impatient and pulled too hard the line would break and the fish would head for the bottom once again.

"Hassan, bring us into the wind—this bugger is ready to become part of the crew." Hassan pushed the tiller and *Shukran* slowly responded. Once the wind left the sails, he dashed to the side rails with Gumbao to wait for the fish.

Brody hauled on the line and the fish broke the surface. Gumbao yelled, "Boss, it's a yellowfin tuna; about eighty kilos, I would say."

The exhausted fish flapped on the surface as Brody dragged it over to the side of the boat. Gumbao yelled, "Pass the flying gaff, we need to hook it quickly."

Hassan passed the long rope with a twelve-inch barbed hook at the end. Gumbao reached out as far as he could and threw the long hook into the side of the fish. The tuna suddenly came back to life and raced for the depths, but Gumbao had the rope attached to the hook firmly tied off to a bollard on the handrail of *Shukran*. Hassan and Gumbao hauled the fish to the side of the boat and the three of them manhandled the huge fish onto the deck.

Within minutes, Gumbao was working on the animal with a razor-sharp filleting knife. "Boss, we can't put this in the boxes, we'll have to chop it up. It's a good omen—these fish swim in shoals. I'm sure by morning the crates will be full."

"All I want right now is a cold beer," said Brody.

"Sorry, Boss, you drank the last one about two weeks ago. All we have is water, and it's warm!"

Brody sank down onto the cushions in the stern as Hassan pushed the tiller, bringing them back into the wind and on the way to the rips.

When the deck was tidied, and the blood had been rinsed into the ocean it was nearing dusk. One box was almost half full of huge chunks of fish, which boded well for their venture.

As night was beginning to fall, Gumbao stood at the bow, staring into the distance. "We have about an hour to go. You see the swells are changing, that's the beginning of the rips. The water gets shallow out here and acts differently. The fish love it and come up near the surface to eat. That's when we grab 'em!"

Brody was exhausted already and had been dozing on the cushions. He couldn't believe the energy Gumbao could put into a project. It seemed endless. It reminded him of his old soldier days when they marched all night then had to dig in and be ready for an unseen enemy who were fresh and waiting for them.

Shukran started to feel the swells change under her keel and began rising and falling into the ocean. Hassan said, "Boss, we're about here. We need the sonar to make sure we can see where the fish are."

Brody turned on the Lowrance HDS-10 combined depth sounder and GPS. He had also bought a three-kilowatt transducer to allow them to see the ocean floor at over one thousand feet. The unit came with side-scan sonar, which was ideal to spot shoals of fish near the surface. The machine beeped twice as it located the satellites in the sky above them; then a large, yellow map appeared on the left of the fourteen-inch screen and a deep blue rectangle on the right with a black line at the top. As the transducer started sending its signal, a depth line appeared from the gloom of the blue screen. Suddenly the bottom came into view at sixty feet, which was incredibly shallow.

Gumbao was looking over his shoulder and said, "Perfect, Boss, we've hit the shelf. You watch, in a few miles the bottom will just drop away as we come to the North Kenya Banks where the water just goes down forever."

Brody set the depth alarm to five hundred feet then went to the bow of *Shukran* to study the water. The sun had set in the west, and they were waiting for the moon to rise in the east. The water ahead was calm, but different. The waves were running at angles to each other as if they could not decide which way to go. The oily water moved as if a serpent was swimming underneath. It looked beautiful in the fading light. The slight breeze of the evening blew across the water all the way from India. The sound of the ocean flowing under the keel was mesmerizing; a time to meditate on life.

Half an hour later, just as the half-moon started dragging itself out of the ocean in front of them, the alarm on the depth sounder started bleating into the peace of the night. Gumbao ran over to the screen. "Come on, Boss, we need the lines ready and out. This is local fishing; we don't use the rods. Put your gloves on and take a hand reel. Just throw it over the back and let out about sixty feet of line. The lures will do the work. Hassan, you watch that depth sounder and get us as close to the edge as you can. When you see a load of fish, yell, so we can start jigging the lines."

"We are on it now," shouted Hassan, "and I can see small shoals of fish on the screen but nothing big."

"Don't worry, boy, those are the baitfish, they're there for our tuna to eat. Keep on them, circle if you have to, but keep the small fish in sight."

Hassan yelped, "Inshallah, they're coming, the monsters from below. I can see them on the machine, and they're big. Guys, get ready!"

Thirty seconds later, Gumbao grunted as his arm was almost pulled out of the socket. "We're on. I have my first fish. Boss, get ready, yours will go soon."

Gumbao expertly hauled the line in, hand over hand, letting it fall at his feet in huge circles to keep it from tangling. He grappled with the leader then reached over the stern and pulled two yellowfin tuna into the boat. Within seconds they had their throats cut. Bright red blood spilled onto the deck. He re-baited the hooks and threw them back over the stern.

Brody watched the old man in awe as he handled the fish and the lines. His hands seemed to be everywhere at once. The fish flapped across the deck and into the gunnels.

"Just leave them till this shoal has passed, then we'll tidy up, but for now concentrate on getting the fish on the deck."

Brody's line went next. The force of the tuna hitting the hooks dragged him across the deck. Before he could react, the heavy-grade fishing line started running through his fingers; it was only the thick gloves that saved him from a serious burn.

"I'm on!" he shouted. He grasped the line and wound one turn around his fist and started walking back across the deck.

"No messing, Boss, we just haul them in. Each one is a few dollars in our pocket. So, no playing around!"

Brody pulled and staggered ten good feet, then ran forward, hauling the line in. The lines had six hooks each and he knew he had more than one tuna pulling for the bottom. The sun had left them a while ago. Thankfully a half-moon glowed silver in the night giving them enough light to work by.

Soon Brody was sweating more than he had earlier. His back and thighs were screaming for a rest, but he had to get the line in and put the fish on the deck. He grappled with the thick monofilament, pulling it in hand over hand. There was none of the finesse that Gumbao had shown, his line was just chucked on the floor in a big pile. Brody fought the fish for ten minutes, finally dragging the flapping tuna over the gunwale onto the deck. The fish were still writhing and wiggling when Hassan passed him another fresh line. "Boss, no time to lose. Here's a new baited line, get it in the water—we don't know how long the fish will stay."

Brody looked at Hassan with tired dismay, "Shit, man! This is bloody hard work. I don't know how I'm going to keep up with Gumbao."

Gumbao looked up from cutting the tuna's throats so the deep red blood could pump out, keeping the pink flesh from going red. "Boss, this is real fishing, we're here for the cash!"

Brody threw his line in the water and let it run back behind the boat. Within seconds it was almost ripped out of his hand as another shoal of tuna passed under the boat. Brody set his jaw and tightened his grip. It was going to be a long night!

Hassan expertly kept *Shukran* crisscrossing between the deep water and the shallow reef all night. His eyes were either on the depth finder looking for the strange, green-shaped fish that would appear from the depths or when the shoal of tuna hit the surface, he would steer *Shukran* into the center of the boiling feeding frenzy.

Gumbao looked like he was just having fun. He would throw the line twenty feet behind the boat then jerk it a few times and start pulling. Invariably, he would haul in one or two fish. Then with a shake of the line, he would dislodge the fish onto the deck and pick another line and send it back over the stern; he was like a machine.

Brody, on the other hand, was a newbie and knew it. The experience reminded him of his early days when he had joined the

Marines. Everything was difficult and went wrong. His line was always getting tangled and pulling the fish onboard took twice as long as Gumbao. As a soldier, he had always been competitive and saw this as a competition between him and his good friend, but before two hours were gone, he knew he was an amateur up against an Olympic athlete. Then he relaxed and started having fun.

"How many boxes are full?" Brody shouted to Gumbao.

"Boss, full or not, don't even think about it, just keep pulling the samaki in. We'll worry about the boxes in the morning."

Brody took the hint and went back in earnest to his task of throwing the hook into the seething mass of feeding fish, waiting for a few seconds for the baited hooks to sink into the gloom. Then a quick jerk and the bright stainless-steel hooks would glint in the darkness and the smell of the bait would drive the tuna crazy. Another few seconds and the line would streak out of his hands. Then the long pull, dragging the five- and six-pound tuna up to the surface and throwing them on the deck.

Then either Hassan or Gumbao would dash forward and slit the throats of the fish. By the time Brody had brought another round of fish to the deck the bleeding tuna would have been stowed in the ice and Hassan or Gumbao would be back at their stations.

The night dragged on as exhaustion set in. Every bone in Brody's body was aching. More than once his feet lost their footing on the slippery deck covered in fish blood and guts and he was sent sprawling across the floor, but there was nothing for it, just get back up and throw the line and pull the fish.

At around four a.m. The fish suddenly disappeared. One second the water was boiling in the darkness with a massive ball of feeding fish. Dark silvery shapes leaped out of the water. Then it was gone, as if nothing had ever been there. Suddenly, all they could hear was the hum of *Shukran*'s engine as she purred along through the night.

Gumbao said, "Go around, Hassan, see if you can find them."

Hassan pushed *Shukran*'s tiller hard over and the dhow sluggishly moved in a long circle, finally coming back to where they had started. They plied up and down the line, staring at the depth sounder, waiting in silence, blood and gore mixed with sweat dripping from their bodies. They expected an explosion at any moment. But none came. After thirty minutes of trawling back and forth over the drop-off, Gumbao finally said, "That's it. They've gone for now. But it's fine, I think we have enough to fill the boxes and head to the market."

Brody felt so relieved. He had not worked this hard in years. He was about to fall onto the cushions in the stern of *Shukran* when Gumbao said, "Boss, before we can stop, we need to finish bleeding and gutting and then wash the decks and ourselves. You look like you've been slashing goats in an abattoir all night."

It was another hour before Brody threw a large bucket over the side and pulled up some fresh clean seawater. He lifted the bucket over his head and let the cold, salty water flow over his battered body. Then he scrubbed at his skin, getting all of the blood out of his fingernails, hair, and beard. He could taste the coppery fish blood in his mouth. He felt like he had been bathing in blood and guts all night like some sick horror movie.

Hassan was still manning the tiller, holding *Shukran* on a course back toward the mainland. He said, "Boss, you take a nap. I'll take the first shift and wake you in a couple of hours."

Brody said, "Thanks, man, I'm absolutely knackered, that's about as hard as I have worked since I got to Kenya."

Hassan laughed, "I know, Boss, Gumbao is already asleep."

Shukran sailed silently into the night, heading for the mainland some forty-five miles away. Hassan stood next to the tiller. Whenever he was on night watch he always stood up to ward off the dreaded dozing. The splash of the water against the hull was mesmerizing, a sound he had been used to since he was a child. It was said by the old men of his village in Pemba that the noise was made by the Jinn, mystical creatures that lured sailors to their death. His father had taken him out on the boats before he could walk. He would sit in the small dugout canoe called an ingalawa and watch his father stand on the bow and throw his net long and wide into the shimmering ocean. Then as if by magic he would scoop up hundreds of tiny silver sardines. As the morning wore on the boat would fill with the wriggling mass of silver and white fish. His dad would say, "Son, these fish come all the way from the south. They swim thousands of miles just to come and help us eat. Allah is good in all things and always provides."

Shukran plowed on into the darkness; there was no other light anywhere in the ocean. The swells gently picked her up and then placed her gently down on the far side of the wave. Hassan loved this time of the night. As a Swahili, he preferred the night more than the day. It was a time to think and wonder at what was around him. He knew all of the stars in the sky. The North Star was easy to find—the brightest in the sky and the best to navigate by. But the planet Jupiter was also a good guide, and Orion's Belt plus many others. His grandfather had sat with him on the beach back in Pemba when he had managed to buy his first fishing boat. The old man spent hours with Hassan, explaining how to get home if he was blown away from the islands. Fishing on the western side of Pemba was fine, as it was a shallow channel and then the mainland. However, once you went for the bigger fish at Ras Kingomasha, then you were dealing with the ocean for real and could be swept out to sea.

His grandfather said, "Son, you listen to me, and you will always be able to get home. The ocean is a good friend that provides for us, but she is a cruel mistress to boot. If you get lost, you must know the stars as the ocean is forever. Allah made it for us to feast on. But be incredibly careful, there are devils and genies out there too that can drag you out to sea and you will never return. Inshallah, we are all safe and well."

Hassan was a very good Muslim. He prayed five times every day without fail. He loved his God and could never imagine a time when he would forsake him. Although he now worked with two infidels, he felt close to them, and he knew his God was looking over them as much as he helped Hassan. His friend Gumbao was a lost soul, gone forever, there was no way of bringing him back, so all Hassan could do was look after him and keep him in his thoughts and prayers. Mr. Brody was different: they had met a few years back when the stranger arrived on Pemba Island looking for a place to dive. It was obvious from the outset that the dark brooding man did not want the normal tourist trips and tricks. So, Hassan had set the young man up in a small shack on the beach, no posh hotels. Then he had taken him diving in the mornings and left him to drink in the afternoons. He knew his new friend was troubled, his eyes were flat and bleak, and he had very little to say. When things went wrong, he would go into a rage, almost losing his temper. But Hassan had liked the man, as he was honest and humble. Over the years, as they had gotten to know each other, Brody had loosened up and now smiled and laughed, and he never lost his cool. But there was still a coldness in his eyes, a place that could not be reached. Sometimes when they were all asleep on the boat, he could hear Brody muttering in his sleep. He would toss and turn on his mat as if he was fighting demons.

A noise on the starboard bow brought Hassan back to the present. He watched as a pod of dolphins jumped in the darkness, like gray and white ghosts rising from the ocean only to return with a small splash. These were the genies his grandfather had spoken about. They were good and bad. Some saved sailors in the ocean and others took them to their deaths.

The day was just about to start, and he kicked Brody gently on the foot. "Boss it's time to wake up. I've to pray, then I'll make coffee before I sleep."

"Fine, I'm awake, you go and pray I'll take over the tiller."

Brody dragged himself up and shook off the night. A cold bucket of seawater sat on the deck next to the side rail. He grabbed the bucket and sloshed the water over his head bringing him back to the land of the living. Once he was refreshed, he wandered over to the tiller, unhooked the rope they called the autopilot and pushed *Shukran* more toward the land. She heeled slightly as the wind hit her sails then gently evened out and came onto her new course. Brody watched Hassan prepare. He washed his hands and his feet carefully, then he got the fancy little Allah compass out of his pocket, so he knew where Mecca was. Then he carefully placed his mat in exactly the right position. Once everything was set and correct, he bowed his head and brought his hands up to his chin muttering some words in Arabic, then squat down to kneel and press his forehead on the mat. The prayers only lasted for a few minutes, but they were essential to Hassan. Brody felt little about God. He had seen way too much of life's evil to ever believe in such things. The day in Somalia when he had been forced to kill kids holding AK-47s was the last he had thought about a greater being. He loved the ocean and all it gave him, but as far as he was concerned it was all a freak of nature. Millions of years of evolution playing out in front of him. He had no place for a God in his life.

Chapter Two
Kismayo

Gumbao stood on the deck, appraising Brody. "Kid, I think he needs more henna in his beard. You Swahilis love that stuff. I don't think it's orange enough."

"Old man, what do you know about our ways? You're just a ruffian that lived in the streets of Mombasa Old Town."

"Shut up, boy. I grew up with you lot. I'm a proud Luo and know how things should be."

"Guys," Brody interjected. "I think the beard is fine. This kanzu makes me look more like a tramp than a trader."

Brody was dressed to look like an Arab trader. With his straggly uncut hair, and now-orange beard, along with the teak color of his face and arms, he could easily pass as the crew of one of the dhows that plied the coast from Mozambique to the Horn of Africa.

Hassan said, "Just make sure you keep your mouth shut. Your Kiswahili is okay but not in the markets and towns. We all speak Sheng, which is a mixture of all the coastal languages. Just nod and I'll jump in."

"Don't worry, Boss, I know the people on the wharf in Kismayo—we'll be in and out in a couple of hours. No problem," said Gumbao with his ever-present smile.

"What's the town like?" asked Brody.

"It's small and really dusty, Boss. The harbor is very old. The Sultan of Zanzibar first opened it way back when. Then the English had it for a while, as usual. Then it went to the Somalis and then to the Al-Shabaab, who have it now."

"Isn't that really dangerous, then?" asked Brody.

"Ah, Boss, we're all coastal traders here. Just out to make a living. No one takes much notice of a dhow or two coming in and out. Especially when we have some fresh fish to sell."

Hassan butted in and said, "The harbor is way out of town, we'll have to get a bike in. It's a bit of a ride, but I need some supplies and charcoal for the jiko. Boss, you can come with me, but you must not talk. The Al-Shabaab are everywhere, they have religious police that make sure everyone is following the Koran. If they catch you then we're in shit."

Brody wanted to tell them that he had actually been just north of Kismayo many years ago when he was in the Special Boat Service. He had been sent to capture a particularly noisy cleric that was threatening to bring hell to the western world. If the Somalis knew he was around and grabbed him, it would be a lot more than a bit of shit. But he figured it would be fine. That was a long time ago, and he had to admit his disguise was very good—as long as he kept his mouth shut.

Kismayo had a well-marked channel, even the Lowrance HDS-10 had the approach lines clearly drawn on the map. The English had done an excellent job. Hassan expertly maneuvered *Shukran* through the channel toward the long spit of land that jutted out at almost right angles to the beach. This made a huge natural harbor. As soon as *Shukran* was inside the spit of land Hassan carefully turned her one hundred and eighty degrees, so she was pointing back the way they had come and then eased her up to the ancient blocks of the harbor wall. The place was busy with fish buyers and sellers, and charcoal merchants selling huge sacks of the burned wood. Even cows were being unloaded in stained, torn slings from a massive wooden dhow that was moored further along the pier.

"This place is so busy. I thought they were at war with the west and just about everyone else," said Brody.

Gumbao said, "Boss, war or no war you gotta eat, and to eat you need money. The Al-Shabaab turn a blind eye to us as they need the food. We'll be in and out before you know it. Now you and Hassan head into town. He knows it well; I think he has a cousin or an uncle that will help you. Me, I'm going to sell this fish and make us a cool five hundred dollars."

Brody and Hassan jumped off the deck and onto the old stone harbor wall. As usual, after so long at sea Brody still felt the movement of the ship below him and swayed from side to side. Hassan laughed, "Boss, you have been out too long!"

Hassan gently pushed Brody behind him, "Boss, you just look stupid. I'll do all the talking. We're heading to town to visit my uncle. He'll help us with some supplies, and he is family, so I have to say hi."

Hassan walked into the dense crowd of people all jostling and pushing to get their wares on a ship or off a ship. Everyone was shouting at once in Somali, Arabic, Kiswahili, and many other languages Brody could not make out. But business was being done, and goods were moving from A to B. Brody was shocked to see this much commerce in a town that was virtually under siege from the western military forces and even Kenya was building an attack force with its eye on this well-placed strategic port.

A man pushed Brody aside as he was heading for the edge of the dock. He had a wad of dollars in his hand and was shouting at a captain who stood above them on the deck of his dhow. Brody momentarily lost sight of Hassan as he weaved in and out of the people, but he pushed back at the angry man who looked at him and spat a stream of words in what Brody guessed was Somali. Brody nodded and smiled then ducked behind the man and went after Hassan. His heart was pumping as the last thing he wanted was to be recognized as a muzungu.

Brody broke through the dense crowd on the edge of the dock and looked for Hassan. Immediately he saw four men leaning against a wall smoking cigarettes. Each man had a scratched and worn AK-47 with a long banana magazine clicked into place. They were deep in conversation and ignored him as they watched the crowd.

Hassan touched his arm, "Boss, don't stare at them, they're the religious police. They're watching for infidels or people who are not following their Koran. No radios or TV here, Boss. And women are not allowed out unless their husbands, older brothers, or uncles will walk with them. Let's go, I've found a bike to take us to town."

Brody followed his friend away from the men with the guns and the crowd at the dock toward a group of guys standing next to dilapidated bicycles. Hassan started talking to them in a language Brody did not understand, and before long a note was exchanged, and two men readied their big black bikes for the journey. Hassan whispered, "These are black mambas, the old bikes the British bought when they ran the place. The design has stayed the same forever."

On the back of the black mamba was an ancient seat with a coarse mat on the top. Brody hitched up his long kanzu, exposing the sandals made from old car tires, and climbed on. The man pushed off and started pedaling toward the town. The spit of land jutted out about three-quarters of a mile from the mainland and was only about the width of a single-lane road. They joined a procession of bikes, all either heading into town or back out toward the harbor. Brody settled in and watched the world go by. This was a strange place indeed. First, there were no women at all, not a girl child or woman anywhere on the journey. The men looked hard and withered. They all dressed similarly to Brody in long kanzus, mostly of dull browns and greys. Everyone wore either a small pillbox hat on their head, or had a checkered cloth looped around like a turban trying to combat the furnace of a sun beating down on them. The area was all bright white sand which reflected the heat and made the day almost unbearable. The smell of sweat started to engulf Brody's nose as the man pushing the pedals around began to feel the heat of the late morning.

Hassan looked across at Brody and said in Kiswahili, "We must rush, the Imam will be calling us soon, and everyone has to stop and pray. No one is allowed to work during prayers. We all must attend the mosque."

Brody nodded his understanding.

On the quay, Gumbao was busy trying to create an impromptu auction to get as much for his fish as he could. There was a great deal of interest as the fish were obviously fresh, but other boats had come into the harbor earlier selling tuna, so the market had already absorbed almost as much as it could take. Gumbao saw a tall, aloof man standing slightly to the side of the group. He walked over to him. "Sir, you look like you need some fish?"

The man nodded and answered in Somali, a rough language that always sounded like everything was an argument. Gumbao understood Somali, as he had plied this coast for years. "This tuna is fresh. You can eat it now or dry it and take it home, where you will get good money."

A man jostled Gumbao's arm, telling him, "But old man, I need some fish, too."

Gumbao was about to tell the second guy to back off then remembered the Arabic way: everyone can talk at any time. There is no interfering, you just blurt everything out and then negotiate until someone comes up with the cash. He said, "No problem. How many boxes are you taking?"

The second guy replied, "Not a whole box, I need like twenty fishes."

"Ah, I'm selling per crate only. No splitting."

A third man spoke up, "Look, old man, the fish came earlier—you are lucky to get anything now. We will take everything off you for three hundred dollars American cash. Right now."

"No chance," said Gumbao, "this is quality fish caught last night. I want two thousand dollars for the lot. First come first served."

The taller Somali pushed the second guy out of the way, "Two thousand dollars is too much. I can give you six hundred for all right now. What do you want dollars or Kenya shillings?"

Gumbao knew a lot of Kenyan shillings were forged in Somalia. "I'll only take dollars, good American ones that I sit here and check before you take. The best I can do is eighteen hundred dollars for all. You will pay more if I divide the crates. Look the ice is melting and you know it's a good deal."

The man who had been pushed out of the way raised his arm as he used the other elbow to get to the front of the group. "That's still too high, old man, All I have is eight hundred—here, take it right now," he said as he tried to push the grubby dollars into Gumbao's hand.

"I need double that before I part with one fish."

Another fat, sweating man pushed into the front of the group. He had a brown, stained kanzu with a tear in the collar and a dirty red scarf wrapped around his head. "Fisherman, I will take all the boxes from you for nine hundred dollars. That is the best offer you have had, and a better one you will not see on this dock. Take it!" He reached out his hand to shake Gumbao's. But Gumbao was holding out for the last one hundred dollars.

He shouted to the crowd, "This man is offering nine hundred—who will give me fifteen?"

A shout from the back of the crowd confirmed an offer of nine hundred and fifty.

Gumbao thought to himself, *Almost there.*

He knew he had to be quick, as the Imam would start calling the loyal Muslims to prayer very soon. Once they went to pray, they would conspire against him and come back with a terrible offer, so time was against him now, but he smiled at the rough-looking group and said, "I have nine hundred and fifty, anyone give me a round thousand and I'm done with this?"

The tall Somali guy from the beginning stepped out of the crowd with a handful of bills and said, "Here count this; it's one thousand even."

Gumbao heard the first call of the cleric for the morning prayer, he knew this was the time to bow out gracefully, and he had made the one thousand anyway, so he grabbed the cash and started counting it.

The tall Somali said, "You will come to pray, then we will unload the catch?"

Gumbao was no Muslim, but he decided the safest place to be right now was beside the tall Somali, so he nodded in agreement.

The men with the machine guns had started walking up and down the quay, shouting at everyone to go to prayer. All the men turned as one and headed toward the quayside where there were large stone overhangs that had been changed into prayer rooms, so the men did not have to rush back to town.

A hosepipe ran from the roof into a large blue plastic barrel. The men all lined up and washed their hands, feet, and faces then moved into the shade of the overhanging rock. Gumbao followed, stuffing the now-counted notes into his pocket. He had the basics of praying and knew all about the washing of his feet and hands and face, but the prayers themselves were beyond him.

The Somali man stood next to him; he was keen to stay near his money until the deal was finalized. "Fisherman, I will show you what to do. You are no Muslim—I can see that from a mile away, but those men with the guns want us all in here and to pray to Allah, so as they have the guns this is what we shall do."

Gumbao nodded his agreement and walked dutifully behind his new host to the back of the room in a darker corner away from the cleric and the men with the AKs. "Now just follow me and do as I do. This will all be over in ten minutes. Allah does not want to interfere with trade and business too much," The tall man said with a wry smile.

Brody was in the same predicament in the small-town square of Kismayo. They had arrived on the bicycles just as the cleric had started to chant his prayers from the tower of the mosque. It was amazing to Brody how the people were affected. Everyone just stopped what they were doing and headed toward the mosque. They were like robots; it was as if a switch had been flipped in their heads as they all rushed to pray. The boda boda men turned and rode straight to the entrance and parked their bikes. Hassan jumped off his bike and came over to Brody. "We have to join them and pray, everyone here is either a Muslim or an infidel and you don't want to be the last one."

Brody whispered back in English, "I don't have a clue what to do in there."

"Don't worry," said Hassan, "I'll lead you."

The two men did the same as Gumbao had done and filed into the mosque. Hassan was an expert and felt completely at ease, but Brody didn't know what he was doing and just blindly followed his friend through the ritual of the prayers. By the time the ten minutes were over, Brody was convinced everyone in the mosque was staring at him. As the seconds slowly ticked past, he expected to feel the muzzle of an AK pushed into his back. His mind was awash with the thoughts of stinking jails and pictures of him on TV as an infidel who had abused the Koran or worse still a grainy video of some cleric with a huge sword standing over him chanting in Arabic. Sweat was running down his spine as he wished the time away. Hassan nudged Brody with his elbow and nodded toward the door. Brody had been so absorbed in his own personal nightmare he had not seen the other men filing back toward the door and freedom.

Brody and Hassan emerged into the burning day to find the two boda boda men waiting for them to finish the ride to Hassan's uncle's house. The streets were dusty, with long concrete buildings along each side. Once, many years ago, the road had been tarmacked but now it was just a collection of deep potholes and rutted tracks running around them showing the safest route for bicycles. Brody sat on the back of his black mamba and watched the world go by. The shops on either side of the road were just long metal doors painted in a variety of dull colors. Most of the doors were folded back to reveal a brown wooden counter at the front, with a man in a kanzu leaning on it, and behind him the wares he was selling. There was no blaring music, like in Mombasa, or televisions or ladies parading up and down in high heels and short skirts. This place was sullen and sad; the Al-Shabaab had removed all life. Everyone seemed to be looking over their shoulders and hurrying off to be somewhere else. After five minutes, Hassan asked the boda boda riders to stop and they dismounted. Then Hassan started walking toward a narrow alley between two shops. As soon as they were out of earshot, Hassan said, "My uncle owns these two shops, and lives in the back with his three wives and seven children. They have been here for many years. I hope he remembers me."

Hassan bashed on a large black metal door and shouted, "Hodi. Hodi."

A few minutes later, a woman slid a small metal plate back in the center of the door and peered out, asking in Kiswahili, "Who is it—we are eating, you can come back later?"

Hassan replied, "I'm Hassan from Pemba. I would like to see my uncle Hashan Mohamed if he is home?"

The lady retreated and slid the small door closed. Hassan looked at Brody. "It has been years since I met my uncle, I hope he's here."

Just as they were starting to get worried the door opened and a small, fat man stepped out into the sunlight. He looked Hassan up and down then smiled broadly, "You look just like your father did when he was your age."

Hassan held his hand out to shake but his uncle just enveloped him in a hug. "Come, boy, and bring your guest, we have just sat down to lunch," his uncle said. "You must sit with us and eat. Who is your Arabic friend?"

Brody shuffled his feet and responded, "Hujambo, mzee, ninaitwa Brody." *Hello, sir, my name is Brody.*

Hashan looked at Brody with a smile, then a laugh. "You will have to do better than that, muzungu, to fool anyone around here. That Kiswahili is nice, but not really for Kismayo!"

Hassan spoke up. "Uncle, this is my friend Brody, we live on his dhow. We didn't want him recognized as a muzungu here, so I dressed him up like an Arab trader."

"The look is good," said Hashan, "but the accent is awful, he sounds like a missionary. Remember those that used to come to the island all Kiswahili sanifu, we could never understand what they were saying."

"We are teaching him, uncle."

"If he is your friend then he is my friend. Come and meet the family."

The house was on two floors behind the shops that Hashan had built and run for many years. There was a kitchen, which was full of chattering women in bui buis all sitting on the floor around a large metal plate piled with rice. They all had hands full of rice and a piece of fish with some greens. Hashan led them through the throng of women and into the back room which had a flight of stairs leading up to the second floor. Hashan pointed at the stairs, "That is for the children and the women, I live down here to get some peace!"

The rooms on the ground floor were sparsely furnished. There was only one long wooden trestle chair, like a pew from a church, along one wall. The floor had some brown and green cushions scattered around and a thick Persian rug. Hashan sat on the floor and asked, "Brody, are you O.K. sitting on the floor? We do not use the chairs. They are only for visitors."

"I'm good," said Brody, settling down on the rug.

"Uncle," said Hassan, "How is life in Kismayo now the Al-Shabaab has taken over? The last time I was here you had the Ugandans and the Kenyans helping you?"

"That was the Amisom, The African Union Mission in Somalia. They are still here, but the Al-Shabaaba have chased them away from this region. The fighting in the streets was pretty bad for a couple of weeks. Now there is an uneasy peace as long as the Al-Shabaab don't do anything stupid like a suicide bomb, then they leave each other alone."

"Are you safe here, uncle?"

"Ah boy, where is safe, I have my business. I sell to the locals and make enough money to get by. There are a lot of Somalis that live outside of the country these days and they send back money for their family. Smuggling money is a thriving business! I have two small boats that head to Lamu every month. My guys pick up a sack of money from a shop in Lamu town and bring it here. The religious police are as hungry as everyone else, so they do not notice me bringing in the cash. I then distribute it to the families and take my fair share. All is good and Allah always provides."

Hassan mumbled, "Alhamdulillah." *Praise be to God.*

"Now, let's eat. I hope you like fish. We have not had any meat in a month or so."

Two ladies filed out of the kitchen carrying a large tray each, and a bowl of water. Hashan said, "This is my second wife, Kamaria, she has a face as round as the moon!" The young girl blushed. She was covered head to foot in a black bui bui—even her face was partially covered—only her pretty brown, oval eyes could be seen.

She knelt in front of Brody and carefully laid the bowl in front of his knees. Brody just stared. He did not know what to do and felt embarrassed that a young lady would be kneeling in front of him.

Hashan said, "If you want to act like a good Muslim man you have to learn a bit about our society! She wants you to wash your hands. Hold them out for her to help you."

Brody gingerly held out his hands as Kamaria took them and poured water over them, then soaped and rinsed and dried his hands. Brody was both surprised and shocked that a woman would be so subservient, but all he could do was follow along as he was in another man's house in a town full of Al-Shabaaba.

Kamaria went around all the men and washed and dried their hands. Then she stood back, and her sister wife came forward.

Hashan said, with a broad smile on his face, "This is my youngest wife, number three. Her name is Hediye, a true gift to a man of my age."

Hediye laid two large metal plates in front of the three men. The first had a substantial portion of boiled white rice, the second had a whole silver king mackerel that had been fried then placed in a sauce of tomatoes and chilies.

"My friends, eat until you are full, the rice is courtesy of our wonderful saviors, the soldiers of Amisom!"

Brody and Hassan didn't need to be asked twice and dug into the lovely meal, using their hands as the women had done in the kitchen. When the meal was over, Kamaria came back with her bowl and water and washed everyone's hands.

Then coffee was served in a copper filigree pot that looked like it was a hundred years old. Brody sat with his back against a cushion, feeling very satisfied. "Hashan," he said, "if I wanted to pick up some essentials for the boat and our trip back to Kenya, can you tell me of any good shops with stock? I noticed as we were coming in the shops are not exactly full of stuff."

"We still live a day-to-day life here, Brody. Most of the things come in on a dhow and are sold on the docks. But if you go back to the main road and turn to the left there are a couple of dukas along the road that keep some stock. You should find something."

Brody wrapped his scarf around his head assumed the slightly bent-over stance of an elderly mzee Swahili trader and wandered out to the road. He turned left and walked slowly down the dusty road. He soon found what Hashan had been talking about, a row of slightly better-kept shops that looked more like garages with big heavy metal doors painted black. As the shops were open, the doors were folded back against the wall, revealing a dark interior. There was no music or bright attention-seeking signs. Just deafening silence. Brody walked into the first shop to have a look around. An old man was asleep on the floor. The shelves had a few bags of rice, some tins of tomatoes, exercise books, pencils, and a stack of meticulously kept Korans. Brody didn't want to bother the old man, so he crept back out to the street. The next shop looked much better; this man obviously had connections. The door was open but only halfway. A young man with a bright white kanzu and a red kufi hat sat behind a worn but clean wooden counter. The man said, "Salaam Alekum."

Brody replied, "Alekum Salaam."

The young man carried on in either Somali or Arabic, Brody was not quite sure, so he tried his Kiswahili to see if it would work. He said, "Pole, sielewi." *Sorry, I don't understand.*

The man immediately turned to Kiswahili as if it was his mother tongue and blurted out, "Jambo Rafiki, unataka nini?" *Hello, my friend, what do you want?*

Brody was still stuck as he knew his Kiswahili would not last long, so he tried another tack: "Unaelewa Kiingreza, rafiki?" *Do you understand English, my friend?*

The man switched again like magic. "I speak a little, bwana. I used to live in Lamu many years ago when the tourists were around."

Relieved, Brody said, "Great. I just came in on a dhow to sell some fish. I'm leaving in an hour or so, and I was looking for some supplies."

"Well, you have come to the right place, but do not speak English when you are out on the road, the religious police will want to talk to you very quickly."

"I'll be careful."

"So, what do you want? We get the rations from the Amisom soldiers. They have a—what do you call it? A back door, where we can collect sacks of rice and tins of food. Sometimes we even get meat, but not so much lately. It's strange—we usually pay in charcoal; they don't want money. But who cares as long as we get the supplies, the world keeps turning. Allah is great in all things." The man waved behind him, and Brody immediately noticed he only had a stump at the end of his right arm.

Brody looked away quickly, not wanting to embarrass the young man.

"Don't worry, my friend, I am used to this now," the man said, waving his stump in the air.

"What happened?" asked Brody.

"When I came back from Lamu many years ago, I was a young and stupid boy. I thought the world was there for me to use and abuse. Those tourists from the west just drink and smoke bhang. The world is easy for them. I forgot I was a good Muslim from Kismayo and took on the ways of the devil. I arrived here with no job and no family. My father had died in a bombing and my mother was shot accidentally when the Amisom came in and started searching. So, I had no one. I hunted around for food, and I was sleeping on the docks and in the mosque. But the hunger became too bad. I tried to pray and quell my evil thoughts, but my stomach said different things to me. One afternoon it was too much for a weak man such as myself. I had not eaten for three days. I just could not stop myself, the Shetani was in me and took me to the market. I crept up on a stall and took a bunch of bananas then ran like the wind up into the sand dunes behind town. The man minding his stall did not even notice. I sat above the town looking down on my world and ate every single banana. It was strange to me, I felt both happy and sad. I knew I had committed a mortal sin, and Allah was watching. But because I was from the den of infidels in Lamu, I just didn't care.

"The next day, I was braver and took a goat's head from the grill. Ah, the Shetani in me loved it, I sucked the eyes and chewed on the tongue. Bwana, there is nothing like the sweet taste of goat. But as the days went on, I became worse and worse. I was taking from everyone. Before a week was gone, I was arrested by the religious police with the big guns.

"They took me to the cleric in the mosque in town and told him what I had been doing. The cleric just looked at me and said, 'You have sinned against Allah. You know what our Koran says of such things. And you know the punishment. We take your right hand.' And so, it was done. Outside in the square the men tied me to a post and laid my arm on a stone then chopped it off. That was it, the cleric sent me medicine and bandages, and he also got me this job, which I am very grateful for. And I am lucky I still have the left." He waved his left hand at Brody with a smile.

"All is good, and Allah has his ways. I can still work and look after my young family, and the devil will never enter my heart again."

Brody was shocked at the barbarity of the sentence for such a crime. He had studied the laws of Sharia when he was in the army and understood the absolute law of the cleric and the types of sentences handed down, but to actually meet someone who had suffered at the hands of these people was a different sensation. And to see the man had accepted his fate and gone along with it all and thanked the cleric in the end for saving his soul. Brody could not come to terms with this type of behavior from a so-called God or savior. He could not understand—if there was something bigger and wiser than all of us, then surely they should be merciful. It was beyond his thinking. He decided he would stay with his ways of believing in himself and his skills to get by, and not rely on a not-so-lenient friend in the sky.

Brody asked, "Do you have any tinned stuff from Amisom? When I was in the army, I loved the tinned peaches."

"No problem, sir," said the shopkeeper, "we have tinned peaches, pineapple, and some of that milk that is thick and very sweet."

"Great, I'll take four cans of each. It'll bring back memories of long ago. How much?"

"Do you have twenty dollars?"

Brody handed over the money without a word. It had crossed his mind to just give a one-hundred-dollar bill, but that would look like sympathy and this man was proud.

Back on the street, it was hot, the sun charred the bare earth and anything it was exposed to. Brody felt his scalp start to burn through the turban Hassan had made for him. He wandered around a little more, carrying his packages in the brown paper bag the man had given him. Finally, he turned back up at Hashan's door and knocked. "Ah you have returned," said Hashan. "Just in time, we have finished sorting out our family affairs, and I've written a letter to Hassan's father."

Hassan said, "Uncle, we must go now. I'm sure Gumbao has sold the fish and is waiting for us. We need to catch the outgoing tide and be gone before dark."

"Of course, boy. You go with Allah's blessings. Here is a sack of rice and one of flour with some millet and beans and I have thrown in a couple of coconuts for the sauce. Enjoy."

They walked back along the silent street and headed toward the mosque to collect some boda boda riders to take them back to *Shukran*. The walk was long and extremely hot. After five minutes Brody took the heavy sack from Hassan to share the load. They were both sweating from the sun as they approached the glaring, bright-white mosque.

Brody said quietly, "These bloody kanzus are like ladies' dresses, and they are so hot. I can't wait to get my shorts back on and get rid of this turban."

Hassan smiled, "Boss, you get used to it, and we need protection from the sun. We are either hot or burned."

Under the shade of an ancient mango tree stood a few boda boda men with their bicycles waiting for the afternoon prayer to start. Then they might get some business taking men out to the port or back home to their wives. Hassan walked up to the nearest man and asked, "How much to take us back out to our boat on the quay?"

The man looked at them both and said, "Fifty cents each, in American."

"O.K., we can go."

Brody walked over to the nearest bike and smiled at the man, then pulled up his kanzu and raised his leg to get on the backseat. The man holding the bike spat on the floor and said, "I don't carry infidels anywhere. Get another bike."

Brody didn't understand the language, but he got the message loud and clear from the body language so stepped back in surprise.

Hassan jumped in, "No problem. We can take another."

The man who had spat said, "'No one carries him. He's filth." Then he looked at Brody and shouted, "Come look. We have a muzungu infidel here who dares to visit our country."

Two men who had been sitting in the shade awning of the mosque suddenly stood up, picked their AK-47s from the table in front of them, and started walking toward the boda boda stand.

"I think we should go," said Hassan.

Brody was already backing away. His brain was on alert as his eyes assessed the dangers and looked for possible exits. "Down that alley over there," he said out of the corner of his mouth.

The two men backed away as quickly as they could. The boda boda man shouted, "Come quickly, they're getting away. An infidel and another, they are running away."

The boda boda man reached out to grab Brody, but he twisted and pushed the man away. "Let's get the fuck out of here," he said to Hassan in a forced whisper.

They jogged away toward a narrow alley that led into the backstreets of Kismayo. The town was built like most coastal towns of the region. The front houses were large with a wide road and shops but just behind was a twisting maze of narrow streets strewn with rubbish and piles of dirt and sand. Brody jogged to the end of the first alley and turned left then a quick right. He was still lugging the sack and his paper bag of goodies, so the going was tough. Hassan said, "Boss, the police are still following us they are speeding up."

"Shit, how do we get back to *Shukran*?"

"We need to lose these guys first, then we can make a plan to escape. That causeway is a no-go now. They'll easily spot us."

Brody took another turn to the right and then a left. The streets were becoming narrower and narrower. The high white walls towered above them. Brody heard a shout, followed by another, and knew they had not lost the men. "Quick, in here," he motioned to an ancient wooden door that had been left ajar.

They hurried inside and found themselves in a cool corridor with a smooth stone floor and high ceilings. To their right was a flight of winding stairs. Brody said, "This way, maybe we can get to the roof."

Hassan dodged in front of Brody and started racing up the stairs, Brody followed with his sack, the weight becoming more and more of a nuisance. Hassan hit the top step, as the door below was smashed back against its old brass hinges. "We have to move fast, Boss, or they'll grab us. Then we are in so much trouble."

Brody did not have to be told twice. He picked up the pace, jogging across a stone balcony and then followed Hassan out onto a wide, expansive, flat roof. Suddenly, they heard a scream. A tall, slim woman was grabbing a robe from the back of a chair. She had been sunning herself on the roof in private and now was exposed to two men. "Shit," said Brody, "this is not going well."

"Boss, jam that door shut, we need some time." Hassan ran around the rooftop looking for a way out. "We have to jump down to that lower level then cross those roofs. If we manage that we can try and make it out the back of town."

Brody dropped his bags and dragged a heavy wooden table over to the door. The lady was cowering in the corner. They could both hear shouting from the street below and heavy footsteps on the stairs. "We gotta go, man," said Brody.

They raced over to the far corner of the building. Brody said, "You go first."

Hassan took a few steps back then ran forward and launched himself over the six-foot gap between the buildings. He landed safely on the lower roof. Brody threw the sack over first then hitched his kanzu up and leaped across the open space. As he was flying through the air, he could hear the rat-a-tat-tat of an AK and the wood splitting from the jammed door.

He landed and parachute-rolled across the lower floor. Hassan was already up and carrying the sack toward the far end of the roof. Brody raced after him, taking the sack again and rushing to the roof's edge. When they looked over it seemed impossible. The space was way too big to jump. "Come, this way," said Hassan, as he jumped over a low wall and ran across another flat roof. The religious police had broken the door down and were standing above them, shouting in Somali and trying to get the people on the street below to enter the chase. Hassan and Brody ran across another roof and back into a dark stairwell that came out on the floor below and opened onto a balcony. "We have to jump across," said Brody. He took three steps back then launched himself across the void onto the balcony opposite, crashing through the wooden doors into a room full of children. Hassan followed him in and started apologizing to the kids. Brody was on his feet and grabbed the sack as he strode across the room and into another corridor. He heard a door smash below him and more footsteps on the stairs. "Shit man, this is serious, we have to find a way out of this building and it ain't going down."

Hassan pointed up toward another flight of stairs with a thick, carved, wooden door at the top. "This way." He led Brody up the short flight of stairs and pushed on the door, which creaked loudly but opened. He then launched himself through the space with Brody on his heels. They turned and slammed the door shut behind them. Hassan lifted a wood plank from the ground and slid it across between two braces on the door. "That will stop them for a while, but we need to get out of here and away from these people."

They looked out across the wide expanse of open roofs leading to a sandy hill behind. "If we can make it to the sand dunes, we'll probably be safe," said Brody.

They rushed across the roof between wooden stakes that had been set in the floor with long washing lines draped between them. When they reached the roof edge it was easy to climb to the second roof, but the shouts from below were still loud, and people on other rooftops were giving the police directions. "We have to get off the roof, we're too visible," said Brody.

They dodged around a turret and headed further inland.

Hassan said, "Boss, the buildings are running out, we'll have nowhere to go soon."

"Don't worry, I have a plan. If we can just get a bit more distance between us and those policemen."

They raced across another wide, white, stone roof and down a short flight of stairs. Brody turned as a man charged him from another room. Brody grabbed him and threw him down the second flight of stairs. "This way!" he shouted. They headed further into the house, turning left and right. They came to another flight of stairs heading down to the second floor. Brody took the steps three at a time, even though he was still lugging the sack. He slid on the smooth concrete floor and his kanzu wrapped itself around his legs, sending him tumbling across the polished surface. He got to his feet and saw another set of narrow steps leading down again. Hassan had already seen them and rushed down into the darkness. They found a door at the bottom that opened into a beautifully manicured, rectangular garden with a small fountain in the center. An old man was sitting on the left-hand side of the garden on a small, round, wooden stool. He wore a beautiful white kanzu and leather sandals on his feet. He was reading from the Koran and running beads through his fingers. Brody thought to himself, *Shit, now we're in trouble.*

The man looked up and put his finger to his lips, then waved toward the corner of the garden where a tree hung low onto the raked gravel. Brody looked at Hassan and whispered, "I don't think we have any choice."

They pushed through the weeping willow-like branches of the tree and stood in the cool darkness, hidden from the outside world. A few seconds later, the wooden door banged open, and two men ran into the garden. The man in the kanzu stood and said, "How can I help you, gentlemen?"

The men looked surprised, "The infidel came this way. Did you see him?"

"No one has come to interrupt my studies. Other than you."

"Mzee, are you sure? We were told he was Christian, and we have to arrest him."

"We are arresting all Christians now?"

"Yes, mzee, all non-Muslims must be punished."

"Well young men, you know me. I am a well-respected senior cleric here in Kismayo; I have studied the Koran for more than forty years. So you know I follow exactly what was written and no other word."

"Yes, mzee," the men said in unison, now realizing whom they were talking to.

"I have not seen a Christian, so you can leave me to my studies."

The men backed out, not quite sure what to believe, but they knew not to question the authority of such a man, as he was known through the town.

Brody and Hassan watched in amazement from under the tree as the two religious police backed out of the door. The man sat down and started reading again as if nothing had happened, and he was alone. Brody started to step out of his hiding place, but the man raised his fingers ever so slightly which stopped Brody in his tracks. After a full twenty minutes had passed, the old man in the kanzu stood up and walked over to the tree. "Would you like to join me for tea?" he asked them. "You must be exhausted racing around in the midday sun like that."

Brody nodded.

"Good. Follow me."

They entered the house through the same wooden door, then climbed the steps. The old man walked slowly, but he was in good health with a fine head of silver hair. He opened a door and said, "Please come in, this is my study." The man walked across to his desk and picked a silver bell, which he rang. A few seconds later another man entered from a side door. Brody jumped to his feet, ready to fight or run. "Don't worry, my friend," said the cleric, "this man works for me. He is very discreet. Please sit and calm down. You are safe in my home."

The old man sat at his desk with his fingers steepled in front of him and his eyes closed. They all stayed in silence for what felt like an age. "You young men have managed to get yourselves into quite a mess here. It will take a bit of unraveling."

"Thanks so much for saving us," said Brody.

"I've not saved you yet. I think we should hold off on the gushing thanks until your necks are truly out of the noose."

After a gentle knock on the door, the green tea was served in white porcelain cups with no handles, the way the Chinese drink it. Brody asked, "Who are you, Sir?"

"I am an Ulama. We are a class of Mullah and spend our lives training in the ways of the Koran and theology. My great grandfather was given this house by the Sultan of Zanzibar when he first took this area as part of his sultanate. My family has lived and studied here ever since. Before that, we were in Oman where my lineage can be traced back almost as far as the Prophet himself. Praise be to Allah."

Hassan gasped. This man was incredibly important in the Muslim culture, a man to be revered. He said, "Ulama, I am honored to meet you. This is a very special day for me."

The Ulama said, "As you know, my boy, we are all equal before God. I am just trying my best to learn and pass on what I have learned to the next generation. Currently, though, we are having trying times." He looked at Brody, "You may not know, but the Muslim religion is not the same as the Christian one in that we have no pope or priests or anything of that kind. It is truly clear in the Koran that every good Muslim has his own access to God and needs no intermediary. However, this can lead to challenges, as any good Muslim can also take the prayers at any mosque as long as he is of good character. In recent years this has led to many issues within our religion that have twisted and hurt the true message of Allah. If any good Muslim can lead a prayer, he can also push his own agenda, and times are not the same as they were. Some agendas are not truly following the ways of the Koran, but merely an interpretation of the words. My fellow students and I try extremely hard to gently push back and give anyone who cares to listen to our interpretation of the true word. Which my young man, does not agree with killing Christians or anyone from other races or religions, hence my helping hand to you two."

Brody sat quietly for a moment. "Sir, firstly, thank you so much for helping us. I am not a Christian or of any real faith, but I know a good man when I see one."

"I follow the law of Sharia and no other," said the Ulama, "and nowhere in the Sharia law does it say we kill infidels or anyone else, for that matter. The Koran preaches peace and piety in all things. But now we have a challenge. How do we get you out of here and back to your boat and safety?"

"You know of our boat?" said Hassan.

"Everyone knows about the shiny polished dhow that arrived on the early tide! Do you think the man you left on the boat has sold his fish yet?"

"That's Gumbao, Sir. I am pretty sure he is very worried about where his crew are by now. Especially after the shots were fired."

"I will send my man there to assure him you are fine. We will tell him to leave as if nothing has happened and wait offshore."

"Thank you, Ulama, we are very appreciative, but can you help us get back to our boat?" said Hassan.

The Ulama said, "I know a man who leaves here in the early evening and heads for parts unknown, then returns with a big sack of cash to help the local community. We will summon him and ask if he can help. Now enjoy your tea, he will be here in a few moments."

Hassan blushed as his uncle Hashan entered the Ulama's rooms. "Uncle, I am so sorry we brought all of this on your town. We meant no harm. We were just coming to visit you and your family then leave as quick as we could ..."

Hashan said, "Son, it was not your fault. This new group of Al-Shabb are not reading the Koran as it should be read. The cleric at the mosque is becoming increasingly insular in his thoughts, and the youngsters follow like sheep to the slaughter. This is not the way of a Muslim. Every good Muslim should have his own brain and talk to God himself."

The Ulama's man came back as the blood-red sun was beginning to set on the sandy hills behind Kismayo. It spread an eerie glow across the sun-bleached, windswept dunes. "Sir, I spoke to the old man on the boat," the man said. "He is going to wait three miles offshore, due east of the entrance."

Hashan clapped his hands, "Perfect. We can leave as soon as it's dark and the last prayer has been called."

Brody listened to the final prayers from the corner of a back alley about two hundred yards from the mosque. Hashan had attended the final prayer to make sure everything was still O.K. He came walking casually back through the town as if he owned it. Then he ducked down a side alley and came up behind Brody and Hassan. "All is well. They are sure you managed to get out into the dunes and headed down the coast back toward Kenya. It is common for people to walk to Lamu from here."

"Will they be watching the beach?" asked Brody.

"They are always patrolling the streets and the beach to make sure we are good Muslims," Hashan said with a smile. "But we have our ways."

Two hours later, Brody and Hassan army-crawled across the rough sand and stones heading toward the water's edge. To their left was an ocean-going canoe about thirty-five feet long with a fifty-five horsepower Yamaha outboard engine. Currently, the boat sat on the beach, but four young men and two policemen were sliding it into the water. Hashan stood with his men on the pebbles. He shouted, "Come, let's get going, we have a long way to go."

One of the policemen said, "Mzee, why are you going this time? That is unusual?"

"I have a big shipment and need to meet my people in Lamu. Don't worry, it won't affect your share. This time I will bring you something special for your family."

The policeman grinned, his bright white teeth showing in the moonlight.

Hashan said, "We must be going." As he waded out into the shallow water to board the boat.

The boys pushed the canoe further out into the gentle waves of the warm Indian Ocean. Hassan tapped Brody on the shoulder. "Come on, they're leaving. We have to swim out to meet them."

They both slid like eels into the shallow inky water behind a few rocks on the edge of the beach. Then took huge lungfuls of air and ducked beneath the surface. Brody swam using long, deep breaststrokes, keeping himself under the water. The darkness enveloped the two as they swam along the gently sloping sandy bottom. Brody kept going until he felt his ears pop, which meant he must have been about six feet underwater. He carefully rose to the surface, just allowing the crown of his head and eyes to appear. They had swum about twenty or thirty yards offshore and the long canoe was off to their left. Hashan had stalled the engine as planned and was busy trying to get it started again. Brody and Hassan swam in front of the canoe and signaled to Hashan. He saw them and let the engine start. Hands reached out of the darkness and grabbed Hassan and Brody as the boat started to move forward. With a simple quick flip both men were hauled over the side and thrown into the bottom of the boat.

"Well, boys, that was a great plan, well-played, even if I do say so myself. Another hour and you'll be safe and sound on your shiny dhow."

Chapter three
Kiywau

Brody sat cross-legged on the polished teak deck of *Shukran*. Hassan had been working on his charcoal jiko for the last two hours as they sailed at two knots out toward the horizon. After boarding in the middle of the night, they had decided to head directly offshore with a slight heading to the south to cross into Kenya at some point.

Hassan had prepared some fresh beans in coconut sauce, known *as* maharagwe, and was now preparing chapati. After cracking one of the coconuts his uncle had given him, he carefully poured the milk into a tin cup, then held the nut in his hand and expertly hit it with a panga, splitting it into two halves. A grater was produced with a long metal serrated edge. Hassan carefully grated all the meat of the coconut onto a plate on the deck. Then he was ready to make the chapati. Some coconut milk was used instead of water to make the flour. When the dough was ready, it was rolled out and the ground coconut was added along with some oil. When the mixture had been thoroughly kneaded together it was slapped down onto a circular wooden board and rolled flat to the size of a dinner plate. Next, a half-inch-thick, round steel plate, called a karai ya chapati, was put to heat on the jiko. When it was hot, the flat dough circles were placed one at a time to cook on the pan then piled on a separate plate to keep warm.

Gumbao and Brody sat with one eye on the ocean, but the other firmly on the last few chapatis cooking on the hot karai ya chapati. Their mouths had been watering for the last hour at the wonderful smells created from this one jiko burner.

Gumbao said, "Boy, we're starving. When's the food ready?"

"Ah, old man, just wait, another ten minutes."

The day had been long and idle as *Shukran* had meandered east and south away from Kismayo. They had not seen another boat since Uncle Hashan had dropped them off around midnight. The swells under the hull could hardly be felt as *Shukran* plowed on into the day. Brody looked up into the endless blue above him, a few hungry seagulls were circling above. They had smelled Hassan's cooking and were keen to take part in the feast.

"How did we do with the fish sales?" asked Brody.

"As always, Boss, I came through. The plan went off without a hitch on my side," Gumbao said with a smile. "In and out just like I said. And a cool one thousand dollars in our pockets. If you hadn't stirred up those police guys, we could have done it daily for a week and made over two K. But five hundred is enough for now. I'll come up with a new plan. Now I think we both need a drink, and Lamu is calling. My wife there is probably lonely and missing her man!"

Brody said, "That sounds like another brilliant idea. I just want to swing by one of my marked dive sites on the way. I have one cylinder of air left and it would be a waste to go to Lamu without using it."

"Which site?" asked Hassan.

"I've been thinking of the wreck near Kiwayu—we could pop in and see Jack on the way and maybe grab a drink," said Brody.

Brody got up and went to the Lowrance HDS-10 Chartplotter and started scrolling around looking for the dive site. "It's about ninety-five miles from here on a heading of two hundred and forty-four degrees. That's almost downwind. If we set the sails now before lunch, we should pick the afternoon breeze and be there this time tomorrow then carry on to Kiwayu and Lamu."

"Sounds like a plan, Boss, let's reset the sails and get moving."

Brody heaved on the tiller and *Shukran* slowly altered course, bringing the compass point around to the two-hundred-and-forty-degree mark. He then tied off the tiller and helped Gumbao trim the sail across the bow of the boat, bringing her to a point of sail known as running. After setting and resetting the sails three or four times, Brody and Gumbao were satisfied and settled back into their cushions on the deck of *Shukran* and looked at the feast that was in front of them.

Brody took a full chapati and tore it in half then dipped and scooped out the beans in coconut sauce. He wrapped the chapati and took a huge bite. The sauce dribbled into his orange beard and dripped onto the deck.

"Boss, now you look like a real Swahili trader. If we could only get the accent right, we could go back to Kismayo," laughed Gumbao.

After swallowing his first chapati and wiping his beard, Brody said, "No chance, man. That place is off-limits for us for now. You're going to have to come up with a much safer plan next time."

They ate their lunch, sat in the shade of the awning, and let *Shukran* do all of the work. The swells were behind them now, lifting *Shukran* and pushing her forward through the water.

After lunch, Brody said, "And now for tinned peaches and cream." He stood and went to the sack that he had carried across the roofs of Kismayo and dug out three Amison tins. "Here," he said, "time for some pure sweetness. A real soldier's heaven." The three men divided the rich tinned peaches and poured the thick condensed milk over the top, then enjoyed the dessert as the sun slowly climbed higher in the sky and the waves and wind passed them by.

Full bellies and the rocking of the boat soon put most of the crew asleep. Hassan had agreed to sit the first watch and kept an eye out for any other boats, but nothing came into sight. The afternoon wore on to the evening as the miles were ever so slowly eaten up by *Shukran*. Gumbao took the first dog watch and ran some lines from the stern of the dhow, but he was not lucky. When Brody rose at eight p.m. to take over from Gumbao he was refreshed and feeling ready for his watch. "Did you catch anything?"

"No, Boss, they're not hungry, but I'll leave them out, if a line goes just give me a shout and I'll come help."

Soon the crew were in the routine of their four-hour watches and spent the time between either sleeping or lounging on the deck. Hassan was always busy with his jiko, keeping hot coffee and sweet cakes coming. He would then leave a flask for the night watch.

At noon of the following day, Brody could see that the marker he had put for the dive site was coming into view on the Chartplotter. The Simambaya Ledges situated about two miles offshore were a ridge of mountains under the ocean. The depths varied from one hundred and fifty feet to twenty depending on the area, but none broke the surface. A storm many years ago had claimed the life of a steel coastal cargo ship. Brody had come across the story in Lamu and tracked the ship down to the Simambaya Ledges. After a few days of searching, he had found the old wreck, but he had not been able to dive on her because she had settled at around the sixty-foot mark, and his tanks had been dry. But now he had one full twelve-liter tank and was ready to give it a go.

Hassan expertly maneuvered *Shukran* to the northern edge of Simambaya Ledges. The reef ran for a further seven nautical miles to the south, lying roughly parallel to the coast. Although at the four-mile line, the name of the ledge changed to Arlett's Ledge, but it was the same string. Today, Brody was only concerned with the northern mile and a half, which was where the old coaster's engine had failed. She had been pushed inshore over the top of the sunken mountain range. The reef had been her final undoing as the razor-sharp coral had ripped through her hull. The crew all scrambled for shore, but the freighter drifted back out to sea, finally sinking on Simambaya Ledges. Now all that was left was a rusting hulk and an engine block all lying sixty feet below the water.

Brody meticulously prepared his diving equipment. In the Special Boat Service, he had dived all over the world and in most conditions imaginable from under the ice caps to close to a volcano. The training had been drilled into him from the very first dive he had ever taken. Always check and recheck your equipment. Never rely on another person—it's your air!—and once underwater, always breathe.

Brody set his B.C.D. (buoyancy control device) on the deck and attached the twelve-liter cylinder to the straps on the back. He then carefully attached the first stage to the tank valve. This piece of equipment would reduce the air from tank pressure to ambient pressure, allowing him to breathe easily. He held his pressure gauge, turned away from him, and twisted the black knob on the top of the tank. All the hoses went tight in his hands. The pressure read two hundred and twenty bar, which was a full tank of air. Depending on his depth this would last up to an hour. He then picked up the second stage and put it in his mouth and sucked several deep breaths of air as he watched the gauge. Everything was in order. Next Brody donned his three-millimeter wetsuit. Water removed heat twenty times faster than air and seeing as Brody had been in the tropics for several years now, he felt the cold very quickly.

Gumbao said, "Boss, stand on the edge, and I'll pick the tank up. Have you got your weights on?"

"Yes, all done. I'll use three kilos today. That should help on my safety stop."

Brody flopped his fins across the deck and stood on the side of *Shukran* while Hassan held her about one hundred yards down current of where they thought the wreck was. This gave Brody ample time to submerge and get to the bottom before the current pushed him past the wreck.

Gumbao patted Brody on the shoulder, "All ready, Boss, you're good to go."

Brody put his mask on, then took the hose attached to his B.C.D. and blew several breaths into the jacket to inflate the side wings and give him more buoyancy when he hit the water. He then nodded to Gumbao and took a giant stride off the side of the boat. He immediately surfaced and waved at Gumbao who was already looking worried. Then he was gone.

Gumbao said, "Boy, keep an eye on his bubbles. The current is going south, so we should be able to keep an eye on him."

"No worries, I can see the bubbles. We should just circle here for a while and keep watch."

Brody looked around him as he plunged into the warm water. He felt an immediate sensation of calm flow through his body. This was where he loved to be. The water seeped into his wetsuit and gave him the chills before it was heated by his body, then trapped inside to keep him warm. He noticed the long silver shape of a wahoo as it came toward the splash, hopefully looking for an easy meal. Brody took a deep breath from the regulator in his mouth and slowly exhaled fully pushing all the air out of his trachea. Then he slowly and lazily inhaled like a Buddha starting to meditate. Once he was satisfied all of his gear was working, he lifted the hose on his B.C.D. and pressed a button to expel the air and so decrease his buoyancy. As is always the case, nothing happened for a couple of seconds, then he felt the pressure increase in his mask as he slowly descended into the depths. He felt the mask go tight on his face and blew out through his nose to equalize the pressure. Then he put his head down and started finning toward the bottom.

Directly below him was a beautiful untouched reef; the corals were verdant and lush like a wild meadow in the spring. Some long tendrils of soft coral thrust themselves up toward the light and were gently wafting in the current, enjoying the rays of the sun. Below them were the hard corals. What looked like a huge grey boulder sat in a sandy patch directly below him. It had thick, rough ridges about one inch high covering its surface. The rock looked like a human brain had been removed from its skull and laid carefully on the bottom of the ocean. It was home to a group of iridescent blue cleaner shrimps that danced across the surface, waiting for a larger fish or a ray to come in and have its gills cleaned of mites and critters that loved to hop on for a ride. Brody finned gently, noting the southerly current on his compass. Ahead of him was a long sliver of a ridge smothered in a multitude of corals, all fighting for a space. The colors were amazing, from deep yellow and orange through to greens and blues, it was like a crazy Jackson Pollock painting full of color. It seemed like it was all a big mess, but each creature was living its best life, fighting for space and something to eat. Brody lay in the water, like an astronaut on a spacewalk, about six feet above the sand, and watched everything around him. It was like a busy metropolis at rush hour, everything had a place to go and something to do. As his eyes adjusted to the mayhem in front of him, he started to spot small differences in color and light. An octopus's tentacles with brown-grey suckers were slowly emerging from a crevice. Soon an eye appeared, then the rest of the diaphanous creature followed and walked across the bottom, blowing up small sand jets as it went in search of a soft-shelled crab.

Brody looked up and could just make out the hull of *Shukran* some sixty feet above him. He checked his air pressure, which was just under two hundred bar. At this depth, he could have a leisurely fifty-minute dive and still have plenty for his safety stop.

He finned across the reef to the edge of the drop-off and looked down into the dark abyss. A white-tipped reef shark circled in the deeper water; these sharks mostly fed at night so were not interested in him right now. As they have to keep swimming their whole lives, resting in an updraft was like an eagle effortlessly soaring on the thermals next to a cliff edge.

Brody turned and realigned himself with the reef. From his research, the old coaster was about one hundred and fifty yards further along the ridge. He let the current take him along the edge of the reef. After about fifty yards he angled himself more toward the center of the underwater ledge. The visibility was about twenty yards, but he still almost missed the rising rusted hulk of the old freighter. It was as if the ship had been attacked by a gang of psychedelic street artists. What was left of the hull was covered from stem to stern in beautiful corals both soft and hard. A multitude of different fish swam in and out of the many holes in the rusting hulk. At the far end, in the gloom, Brody could clearly see the engine sitting on what was left of the struts that used to hold the ship together. The reef had completely taken over the old ship and turned it into a wonderful garden of Eden, where all types of life slithered, swam, and crawled. A bright white sea anemone blossomed against the red rust of the steel, its long white fingers floating in the current; dancing between the poisonous fingers were a pair of *Nemo* fish guarding their symbiotic relationship and laying their eggs. Brody swam over the top of the bow rail and sank into what used to be the hold of the ship. There were rusted piles of chain and some almost unrecognizable winches encased in bright red and green corals. A dark-brown African grouper with its lightly spotted skin and iridescent blue fin tips swam around the hull then darted through a hole into the ocean. Brody was in awe at his luck in finding an absolutely pristine reef where probably no one had ever been before. To his left were ten or twelve barracuda moving across the reef, always on the lookout for a meal. Brody headed toward the engine block, which sat stoically at the stern of the freighter. He planned to hang around and watch the world go by then head for the surface. As he reached the rusted steel block, he looked up and saw a mass of fish above him. They looked like skipjack tuna, the ones that get tinned with olive oil. They were swimming around left and right, then they would race up toward the surface then back down. It looked totally erratic until Brody saw out of the corner of his eye a long, sleek shape come racing through the water. The fish was about nine feet long and had a black menacing beak protruding from its mouth like a gruesome extended lower lip which had been transformed over the ages. The fish glinted like silver in the rays of the sun from the surface, bright blue stripes ran down its sides. Its black, ridged dorsal fin stood straight in the water. When Brody looked closer, he could see several of these shadows racing around the fish like sheepdogs herding them together into a tight ball. The skipjacks were panicked and swam up and down in the water trying to escape from the predators. Once the larger marlin had pushed and cajoled the fish into an ever-tighter group one of them would swim into the shoal, waving its head around using the long spike to slap the fish and knock them unconscious. Then one of the others would come in and swallow the lifeless baitfish in one go. Brody was enthralled by the action above him and laid back on the top of the engine block watching the life-and-death scene play out in front of him. The marlin raced around the skipjacks batting them and snapping them up for a full two or three minutes. Then the fish managed to find a hole in their attack and streamed off into deeper water.

    Brody looked at his dive watch, he had been down for almost fifty-five minutes, and it was time to go before the nitrogen started building in his body. He was also thinking of the next stop on his journey. A visit to Jack's place was always an adventure—usually ending with a hangover. He took three deep breaths from the regulator then carefully removed it from his mouth, grabbed the hose to the B.C.D. then blew out the air, filling the inflatable wings to give him some more buoyancy. Then he finned a little and headed for the fifteen-foot safety stop before coming to the surface. *Shukran* was just in sight through the blurry gloom. He smiled. His friends were always there for him through thick and thin. They were probably the best people he had ever met, even including his days in the army. Good skins, as his army mates would say, meaning the best of people who could be relied on and would never let you down.

Chapter Four
Jack's Place

Shukran sailed on majestically, moving through the ocean, never in a hurry. The wind filled the single lateen sail pushing her at a steady four knots south toward the islands of Kiwayu. Brody loved this area as it was totally devoid of human life. A large area of land had been designated as a nature reserve called Dodori, in the late '70s. It had been hoped this area would improve tourism in Kenya, but the Al-Shabaab had put an end to that by raiding the few parties of tourists that had entered the reserve. Now it was just an empty space filled with wildlife left to their own devices. Even poachers feared the Al-Shabaab so would not enter. The Dodori Creek flowed through the reserve and into the ocean. It was one of the last places in Africa that the dugong still lived freely. In times gone past, the mariners that lay anchor in Dodori Creek swore they were surrounded by mermaids all singing in the night as the long, inquisitive, seal-like creatures would swim around them. Brody longed to head into the creek and find these gentle animals, but he decided his thirst was more important on this occasion!

Hassan shouted, "Hey look, there are elephants on the beach."

Brody grabbed his binoculars and focused on the shining white sand. "There's a whole herd of them, even some babies. Some are in the water swimming!" he shouted.

Hassan said, "This area is wild, Boss. The animals rule here. But there are some people that live alone in the forest. They are called the Aweer. When the government comes, they throw stones at them, and fire arrows then run away and hide. But my cousin in Lamu went to see them once. He said they were magical and could talk to the birds. He said he once went into the forest with a group of kids, and they started whistling at the trees. He didn't know what was happening and thought they had all smoked some bhang. But after a while, there was another whistle coming back from the trees and the kids all ran through the forest looking for the sound. He said, 'We charged around all over the place looking up into the branches.' My cousin didn't know what to look for and was just following along. After a while one of the kids pointed up into a tall tree and whistled and waited. After a couple of seconds, a whistle was returned, and he moved closer and whistled again. It took another ten minutes to find the little brightly colored bird sitting on a high branch. Some kids ran off into the forest and others started searching around the base of the tree and the roots, picking up loose branches. Soon they had a pile of wood and leaves and lit a fire under the tree. Two of the older boys tied T-shirts around their faces to stop the smoke and climbed the tree amongst shouts and hoots from the waiting boys below. It was not long before the older boys started shouting as well and then huge chunks of brown husk came falling down. The younger boys grabbed it and put it in their mouths. My cousin was given a big chunk and held it in his hand as a golden syrup poured onto his fingers. He said it was the best honey he had ever eaten. He even brought some back in a jar and gave it to my aunt."

Brody laughed, "That's an amazing story, man. We should come back this way one day and go see them. I would love to see that bird and eat that sweet honey."

"Boss, they would probably all run and hide if they saw a white man. You are like juju."

"What's juju?"

"It's black magic, Boss. The people in the forest believe in magic and spirits. They would think you were one and hightail it as soon as they saw you."

Brody laughed, he had been in many places where he was the only white man around and felt the stares and watched as the kids either ran away or came up to him, intrigued at the new stranger. They would stroke his arms to feel the hairs and sometimes even pinch him to see if he was real.

Shukran carried them further south toward Kiwayu and the run of islands that make up the Lamu archipelago at a sedate speed of three knots. They would not reach the island until the following day. By Brody's reconning it would be around lunchtime, which was perfect, he had quite a thirst going, and he needed a drink.

The lazy afternoon passed into a clear moonless night filled with the Milky Way. Everyone took their turn on watch then found a corner of the deck to sleep. As the sun came up, they were only a few miles from the Kiwayu cut-in, or *malango,* as it is known in Kiswahili.

"This malango is tricky, Boss. There's a big rock right in the middle of it. You have to come at it at an angle, then you're O.K."

"Hassan, have you done the entrance before?" said Brody.

"Yes, Boss, but today there is swell coming in and the tide is going out so there'll be a current across the entrance. And the wind is picking up. We should try and get through as quickly as possible before the current gets too strong, and we can't enter."

"O.K., Gumbao, stick the engine on, we can motor the last few miles—it'll be quicker. I'll go and get the sail down and stowed."

"Sawa, Boss."

Brody loosened the sheet that held the corner of the lateen sail to the stern Samson post. Then when the material started to deflate, he took the sheet and ran toward the bow, jumping up to grab the corner of the now-flapping sail and started wrapping it in his arms. As he got closer to the bow the amount of sailcloth he was carrying almost knocked him overboard, but he managed to get his feet back under him as he bundled and rolled the thirty-foot-long piece of material as best he could. The last and most risky part of the job was standing right on the pitching bow and tightly rolling the sail along the length of the boom, which was at a forty-five-degree angle to the ship. Brody braced his legs on either side of *Shukran's* bow and pulled the sail down and rolled it at the same time. Finally, he was able to pull in the last ends and tie the bottom of the sail to the boom to hold all of the material in place. This was quite an operation, but Brody loved the thrill of fighting with the sail and keeping his balance in this very precarious position. More than once he had misjudged the operation and ended up in the ocean with *Shukran* passing him by.

By the time Brody got back to the stern, the engine was purring away, and Hassan was lining them up with the entrance.

"Boss, we get one go at this, and it has to be dead-on," said Hassan.

Brody replied, "We're in your hands, my friend, I'm sure you'll do fine."

"Keep that engine running, old man!" Hassan shouted down the hatch to Gumbao in the hold.

A reply came from the hole, "Don't you worry about me and my engine, kid, just make sure you get us through the gap. I don't like swimming."

Hassan gripped the tiller and pushed it slightly to starboard. Then he jumped up on the stern seats to get a better view.

"Boss, the swells are already breaking on the rock in the middle."

"Just keep cool, Hassan and do your best, that's all we ask. You're the best sailor among us—if you can't do the gap, then no one can. So just go for it!"

"Sawa, Boss." Hassan jumped down from the stern seat and put himself just in front of the tiller. He held it with his right hand and gently nudged it back to port.

As a fat-bellied dhow, *Shukran* was not the nimblest of boats. These types of maneuvers made Brody sweat as he always thought they had overreached on any mark or buoy, but Hassan was an expert and knew his boat and its ways better than his own mother.

As *Shukran* slowly approached the entrance the swells started to increase. Then waves began to break on either side of them as they lined themselves up in the channel. Hassan kept a firm grip on the tiller, pushing it to port and starboard as they started to get nearer and nearer to the rock.

"Boss, I have to head straight for the rock, and just before we hit it, I turn hard to port. Go to the bow and count me down. Let me know how far away we are."

Brody ran forward and jumped onto the bowsprit. The rock stood about eight feet above the water. It was black with age and covered with sharp oysters and green algae. If Hassan judged this wrong and they hit the rock, that would be the end of his beloved boat.

"It's forty feet away," he shouted.

"O.K., let me know when we are twenty-five feet, then hold on for the turn."

Brody nodded and held onto the line leading from the bowsprit to the top of the mast. Then he started counting down in his head.

Hassan shouted, "Old man, when I shout again, give her full speed."

"Hakuna shida," answered Gumbao. *No problem* in Kiswahili.

Brody measured the distance in his head and held his arm aloft when they reached about thirty feet then watched as *Shukran* ate up the space. When he guessed they were twenty-five feet away, he dropped his arm and shouted, "Now, Hassan!"

Brody watched as Hassan pushed the tiller as far to starboard as he could. Then he heard the engine revs increase to full power and he was almost thrown off the bow as *Shukran* pivoted in the water, fighting against the current and the waves. A large swell came in off the ocean and broke over the rock, sending a shower of water over Brody and pushing the dhow dangerously close to disaster. But Hassan had control and pushed harder on the tiller. Then he shouted, "More power, old man!"

The engine screamed for a moment as Gumbao pushed it for all it was worth. Brody stood on the bowsprit, leaning forward, wishing his boat to complete the turn. He was soaked from head to foot from the spray of the waves breaking over the boulder.

Shukran kept turning as another wave came in to break on the rock. It picked up the dhow and rolled it to the left. Hassan had seen the wave coming and expertly surfed his boat along the length of the wave, missing the rock by ten feet and pushing them into the entrance. Brody leaped off the bow and ran along the deck, keeping the rock in his view as it passed them by.

"I've said it before, and I'll say it again. You are the finest skipper I have ever had the pleasure to sail with, Hassan. Bloody good job. Now I'm going to get drunk!"

Hassan smiled and shouted, "Old man, reduce the power back to normal, we're almost inside."

Shukran entered the curved lagoon with a long white protected beach on the landward side. The water was crystal clear with small outcrops of coral laying on virgin sand. A myriad of reef fish swam around the corals and darted across the sand, keeping away from the predators hiding in crevices and holes. Brody was amazed at the gin-like water in this hidden paradise. Just inside the entrance and to the left was a rickety wooden jetty that had seen better days. Alongside were a couple of ingalawas, boats made from a single trunk of a tree with an outrigger attached for ocean fishing. A group of fishermen were stood on the jetty and waved Hassan over.

Shukran came alongside, ropes were thrown then the engine was switched off. Hassan busied himself with tidying up the boat as Gumbao did his usual checks on the engine.

Brody said, "It's bloody hot here out of the wind." Then he dived off the side of *Shukran*, surfacing twenty feet away and broke into a freestyle stroke toward the beach. He powered through the water, enjoying the stretching and pulling of his muscles. The water was a warm twenty-eight degrees centigrade, which did little to cool him off, but the water flowing over his skin felt good, cleaning all the dry salt from his hair and beard. Every fifth stroke his head twisted, and he took a fresh gulp of air. The swim took him ten minutes. He was just starting to feel the acid buildup in his muscles when he realized he was in shallow water and was able to stand. In front of him was an untouched, brilliant white beach. The translucent water lapped against the soft sand. Tiny white shells made a line, like soldiers defending a bulwark, showing the high tide mark. Standing in knee-high water, further along the beach, he saw a portly man with a straw hat on his head and a cigarette sticking out of his mouth. Brody waded toward him.

"Hi, Jack, how's the going?"

The man stood and looked at him for a few seconds, his face was golden brown with deep creases of wisdom around his eyes. His smile was that of a man who had no problems in the world. His white shirt was unbuttoned to the waist, his brown safari shorts were worn, old, and stained with oil. His feet were bare. "My boy, you're back! It's been a long time. You're going to have to tell me all your stories."

Brody said, "We've been cruising along the coast, just living the dream, you know how it is?"

"Me, I live the dream every day. My biggest worry is will the beer be cold enough," said Jack.

"Is it beer o'clock yet?" asked Brody.

Jack looked up at the sun, "Well the sun is past the yardarm somewhere, so I guess it's beer o'clock here. This sun is bloody hot too. I'm thinking I'm dehydrated, which is dangerous for a man of my age."

"Well then, we ought to get you into the shade and rehydrate you," said Brody.

Jack wandered behind the bar, "There's no staff yet, they're all cleaning the rooms, so I'll be mother."

Brody accepted an ice-cold Tusker. "No worries from me, Jack, as long as they stay this cold." He took a long draft from the bottle then put it down on the polished, reclaimed-hardwood bar that stretched the length of the restaurant. The whole structure was no more than ten feet from the high watermark. Above them the roof was made from palm fronds which let the breeze in but kept the sun out. Jack grabbed a dozen bottles from the freezer and dumped them into a cooler box. Then he poured a bag of ice over the top. "There, that should do for an hour or so. Now where have you been and what have you been up to?"

Brody sat on a tall wooden barstool and regaled Jack with his latest adventures along the coast. When they got to Kismayo Jack's eyebrows raised. "What's the situation in the town?" he asked.

"It's very depressed. The Al-Shabaab has a real vice-like grip on the locals. Everyone is scared shitless of the thugs."

"You know that was a beautiful town twenty or thirty years ago. I used to go up there often to get supplies. It was easier than Lamu or Mombasa."

"It's certainly changed, but the people are resilient and seem to be getting by."

"Religion always makes a bloody mess of things, in my opinion. Just leave everyone alone to get on with their own lives. That's what I say," said Jack.

Brody nodded and held up his empty bottle.

"You have a thirst on you, my boy, we better mix it up a bit. How about a dark and stormy?"

Brody loved the mix of ginger ale and dark rum. "Sounds like a bloody good idea."

"How's business in these parts?" asked Brody.

"Well, you know, I've been here for nearly fifty years now, so it's pretty stable."

"Fifty years!" exclaimed Brody.

"Yes, I came here from England before independence. I landed as a young boy with my father in Mombasa port. We came on a steamer from Liverpool. The trip took us nearly a month and stopped in Gibraltar. It was a great adventure. My dad was a Bible salesman. He worked for a company called Allan's, they're based in Scotland. They're still there today, but they are bigger now. My dad was what we called a door-to-door salesman, but he went from church-to-church. Those Bibles were lovely, all leather-bound, proper cured calfskin and stitched together, not glued like the cheap stuff.

"We arrived on the steamer with four huge packing cases. It was a fantastic adventure for a young thirteen-year-old boy. We stayed in Mombasa for about a week, but my dad thought up-country would be better for him, so he bought us first-class tickets on the train. It was amazing—back in the day the train travelled right through what is now Tsavo Game Park. I spent hours gazing out of the windows watching thousands of elephants, giraffes, gazelles, and buffalo, all sorts of animals, as the old steam engine slowly puffed its way along the track. When we arrived in Nairobi, my dad decided we should set up shop at the Norfolk Hotel, the best place in town. He took a suite in the hotel and started courting the local church officials. After a few weeks he rented a townhouse, as business was going well. Then he realized I was not in school; I was just running around Nairobi getting myself into trouble. So, he asked around, and found a school up near the Ugandan border in a town near Busia. The place was run by a priest called Father Duncan who had purchased a lot of Bibles from my dad and offered him a good deal. The place was called Maseno School and was deep in the bush. My dad said it was for the sons of the chiefs from all over Kenya, so a great place for me to meet people. I went back to the Nairobi railhead and boarded the train to Kisumu. My dad gave me ten pounds and shook my hand.

"He said, 'Be good my son. See you in a few months.' That was it. I was off. It took two days to get to Kisumu where I was met by a priest with a bullock cart and journeyed another four days through the bush. We camped at night under the stars. The priest was called Father Henry and loved his life as a missionary. He told me stories all day long, then in the evening we lit a huge fire to keep the animals away and ate dik dik freshly roasted on the fire. Do you want a refill, Brody?"

"Thanks, another dark and stormy and a beer." Brody loved listening to the old-timers of Kenya—the stories were unbelievable. "What was Maseno School like?"

"It was great for a young Turk like me. The place was right in the bush, we had wildebeest walking just ten yards from the dorms. We studied in the morning then did woodwork and farming in the afternoon. We even hunted for our own meat. I had been good with a small rifle in Old Blighty shooting rabbits and pheasants, but this was the real deal. I joined the shooting team and was soon out on the savannah dropping gazelles and dik dik left and right. I became a real deadeye shot, the best in the school. I stayed there for four years straight, the best years of my life. My dad would pass by once a year to pay the fees and see me as he traveled to Uganda. Just after my eighteenth birthday, a group of elders came to the school and asked for someone to help them. An old lion had started taking their goats and sheep. This happened from time to time, the older lions would get kicked out of the pride by a new young buck then wander around starving to death. It was much easier to grab a goat from a pen than try running down some super-fit gazelle. The problem with this was the lion then came close to the homestead and didn't know the difference between a goat and a small child, which was even easier to grab. This old beast had taken a young boy and a girl from the same homestead. As soon as I heard, I volunteered to go with them and shoot the lion. This was a first for me, but as a young lad the sky's the limit. The head priest gave me a bag of food and a rifle with twenty rounds. I left the school and was taken on a six-day walk through the bush. We ended up at a place called Asembo, right on the shores of Lake Victoria. I was introduced to a young man who was to show me where the old *Simba* lived. He took me out into the bush, we seemed to wander aimlessly around until we came to a range of broken hills full of huge lumps of granite all balanced one on top of the other. We clambered about for most of the afternoon, climbing up boulders the size of a London bus. As dusk was starting to fall, the tracker noticed footprints in a sandy stretch. Then he picked up some spores and smelled it. After that we walked very slowly, I held my rifle cocked and ready to go. An hour or so later, when it was completely dark, we came across a bluff of rocks with a dark hole in the middle. My new friend pointed to the hole and said, 'Atunya, atunya.' This I guessed was where my quarry lay. I set up camp in an acacia bush about one hundred yards from the hole and waited all night. We dared not build a fire as we wanted to surprise the old guy. The next day, I sat in the tree until I couldn't feel my arse anymore. I would jump down and run around the camp trying to get the circulation back in my legs. Then I would go back up the tree and watch. My tracker friend brought me some meat and water but mostly I was on my own. It took three days, I had actually fallen asleep on my perch in the acacia tree. The young boy helping me had returned with my meal, and was much more vigilant and noticed the old simba on a ridge above us. He threw a rock which bounced off my head and woke me up. I thought I had been attacked and almost fell out of the tree. The old simba sniffed the air, but we were downwind so he couldn't smell us. His old myopic eyes studied the terrain but I am sure he was almost blind. Then he settled down on a boulder and watched the sun go down as if he knew this was his last night on earth. As the sun was finally setting, he ambled among the boulders toward his lair. He wasn't fierce at all, he actually looked sad and lonely as he walked into my sights. When the moment came, I didn't want to pull the trigger, but he had caused trouble and needed to go. So I lined my sights just behind his front shoulder blade so the bullet would pierce his heart. I took a deep breath and gently squeezed the trigger. That was it. My first lion. Anyway, my friend, the cooler box is empty, do you mind popping behind the bar and grabbing a few more beers? That story has given me a terrible thirst."

Chapter five
Baobab Tree

Gumbao was happily seated on the wide wooden stern rail of *Shukran*. He had managed to get three gourds of mnazi, fermented coconut juice, and had already finished one gourd and was busily guzzling the second. The stink of the rotting coconut pervaded the whole boat, which was annoying Hassan.

"I'm heading to the village to get some supplies," Hassan said in a humph.

Gumbao knew the alcohol annoyed the young man but was way past caring. "Ah boy, you should stay with me. We can drink the last one together," he laughed.

"I would never touch that evil stuff, it only rots your brain. I'm going to do something useful."

Hassan marched off, climbing a set of steep steps cut into the sandhill. When he reached the top, his clothes were soaked through, and his eyes were stinging from the sweat. Working and living on a boat was physical, but he did not get much cardio as it was usually his upper body that was tested. So, a walk up what amounted to a steep sand dune had exhausted him.

Hassan sat on the top of the dune some two hundred feet above the ocean to catch his breath. He looked east toward the horizon. The sun was setting behind him, randomly throwing oranges and reds across the sky, tainting the edges of the cumulus clouds floating in the light winds. The ocean sat calmly at his feet. It looked sinister and oily in the fading light. The darkness would fall quickly as they were so close to the equator where every day was twelve hours long. There were hardly any whitecaps on the ocean as it laid out before him, a quiet serene site that went on forever.

Once he had got his breath back, he headed along the top of the dune toward the village of Kiwayu. The island was only about three miles long and less than a mile wide. The mainland could just be seen in the distance as lights were flicked on against the gathering dusk. Hassan felt happy and content with his life. He enjoyed the adventures he had with Brody and really did not ask for anything more. As he walked the half-mile to the small village, he smiled to himself, he had been lucky on that day back in Pemba when Allah had blessed him and brought the strange soldier to his home. He was idly daydreaming about the last few years and how life had been so much fun. His mind had wandered so much, he almost missed the black snake lying on the path. The creature was gleaming the last rays of the sun. He almost stepped on it, but it moved at the last moment, allowing Hassan to jump back:

He instantly knew it was a black-necked spitting cobra, one of the most dangerous snakes in Kenya. As a child he had been warned about these vicious creatures, which spit venom into the eyes of their prey causing excruciating pain and blindness. Hassan felt rooted to the spot as the snake's black, shiny head rose from the ground, and spread its neck in the classic cobra-striking pose. The snake's body lay tensed and coiled on the warm sandy path. The creature seemed to hover, its head dancing left and right, its forked tongue flicking the evening air. It stared at Hassan with unblinking, black-sapphire eyes. The cobra seemed to be taking a measure of the creature that had dared to ruin the last rays of the sun. Hassan knew not to move. The cobra was not frightened at all; Hassan could see some sort of understanding in the creature's eyes. Then it twisted on itself and disappeared into the grass. He knew these snakes lived all over Kenya; his grandmother had been blinded a few years back when she was cleaning her house and one had taken up residence under a couch. But this one seemed different: it was not afraid, it looked as if it owned the island.

Hassan wandered down the sandy path and into the outskirts of the rustic fishing village. As with all such settlements along the coast, he felt right at home. There was a good chance he would be related to someone, and they would offer him some supplies and a bed for the night.

As he passed the outskirts of the village, he saw a light coming from a small hovel and thought he would start his search for a relative there. The hut was made of stone, which was unusual, the houses in this part of the country were normally made with mud walls and a coconut palm roof. It was set back from the track and away from the beach. An enormous grey baobab tree loomed next to the hut; its girth must have been forty feet. The majestic tree had probably watched over the town for hundreds if not thousands of years. Its long, bare, knurled branches stretched up into the blackness of the night like arms reaching up to the stars. In the darkness, Hassan could just make out the bulbs of fruit hanging on the extended branches. He fondly remembered climbing trees like this when he was a kid and pulling off the fruit, then smashing the hard cases and eating the seeds. His mouth filled with saliva as he remembered the taste of the sour-sweet kernels.

The door to the hovel was open, the interior was lit by the flicker of a dim oil lamp. Hassan stood back from the entrance and said, "Hodi, Hodi?" the traditional Kiswahili version of hello.

Then there was silence. He ventured one step closer and said in a louder voice, "Hodi, hodi?"

There was a shuffling from inside the hut then a weak voice said, "So, you've come to visit at last?"

Hassan immediately thought the person inside had mistaken him for someone else. He said, "No, I'm not from around here. My name is Hassan Alakija. I'm looking for my relatives. I've just arrived by boat."

There was more shuffling inside the hut, then the lamp rose off the floor and a withered old hand with skin as black as the night came into view. "I know who you are. I've been sitting waiting patiently for you."

"How could you know I was coming to the village? I only decided a few minutes ago."

"You were always going to come to see me, that was written as all things are. You just don't know how to listen and read."

Hassan was shocked, he knew that he had only decided to come to the village because Gumbao was getting drunk. Now this old hag was telling him it was all written down somewhere. He decided the old lady must be mad, as the hut was well outside the edge of the village. The people had probably put her here as she was a nuisance. He was going to be polite but get out of there and meet up with his relatives.

"Look, old lady. I've just come to find my uncle and aunt in the village. I will not bother you anymore. Could you direct me to the right house?"

The oil lantern flickered again and moved toward him. As the light grew, he was able to make out the shape of an old, emaciated woman about four feet tall. She stood on legs that looked like matchsticks. Her joints seemed swollen with age, or she was just so skinny they bulged out from the frail muscles. She had long white hair covering a weathered, black face. He could hardly make out her mouth and eyes as her skin was so creased with wrinkles. She opened her toothless mouth, and said, "You walk with the muzungu who saved those girls up here a while ago. He is a troubled man but has a good heart. I see him in my dreams, and you are there too."

Hassan was shocked she knew so much about him.

The old woman took a silver box out of her shawl. It was about three inches long, two wide, and one deep. Its polished surface shone in the moonlight. She opened the lid and rubbed her finger on a black substance inside then quickly sucked her finger and rubbed her gums. "You don't know, but you were sent here tonight."

She picked a carved wooden pole from behind the door and used it as a cane. The old crone hobbled out into the moonlight, with remarkable speed for what looked like a broken body. She wandered toward the trunk of the baobab tree. "This is my miti ya mburu, you know. There has always been one of us here watching, and listening, and reading. We don't have books or pages, we read life. The tree tells me everything I need to know. She stopped under the tree and whistled then waited. A few seconds later a scruffy dog appeared at the side of the clearing. It looked as old and decrepit as the woman, but it was jet black and its fur was immaculate. Hassan did not like dogs much, the elders had always warned them that bad spirits could easily take up residence in a dog. He backed away from the house. The old woman laughed, "Alakija, what is wrong with you? We are not here to harm you, or you would have been bitten on your walk. The dog is my friend, he comes and sits with me in the evenings. You don't have to worry as long as you are a good guest."

Hassan had heard about these old ladies that guarded baobab trees. They were harmless mystics and usually a bit mad. The village would look after them and occasionally ask them for a good fishing season or for a lost soul to be returned. But this old lady had intrigued him by knowing about Brody.

However, his friend Gumbao had managed to get free drinks in all the bars they had visited over the last three years by recounting the story of how they had managed to save some young schoolgirls from his village in Pemba. Gumbao had told the story so many times he had become the hero and Brody's part was mostly forgotten. So it was probably common knowledge in this part of the world.

The old woman was looking up at Hassan with glazed, milky, cataract eyes. She smiled again and with lightning speed reached into her shawl and produced the box, took a rub of the black substance, and then it was gone again.

Hassan said, "Old woman, what's in the box? Some kind of magic?"

She grinned, "That's my tobacco. Do you have any? What I have to say is worth a lot to you."

"No, sorry, I only have a few shillings for supplies."

"That will do. Hand over the money, and I will tell you something important that my friends in the trees have told me. If you think it is rubbish, then I will give you your money back."

Hassan was brought up to be polite, especially to mzee, or older people, but he knew a con when he saw one. He thought about it for a moment then gave the old woman a one-hundred-shilling note. "That's all I have. Take it, you're welcome."

"You have more than that, but I don't care. It's enough for me. All I need is my tobacco and some salt. I don't have teeth anymore, so I can't eat meat. The girls bring me soft fish and beans—tastes like shit, but I'm old and can't complain."

Hassan smiled, "You can buy some meat with the money and suck the juices out and give the rest to your dog."

The old woman cackled in the night. "The last time I ate meat I had gas for weeks. I couldn't stay in my house it smelled so bad, and the dog is so old he can't chew for shit."

"Do you know if anyone lives in the village by the name of Alakija?" asked Hassan.

"Aye, they live there, your people are all along this coast. One of the old families."

Hassan was impressed by this new piece of information, but again his family had been fishing for generations. They had spread all along the East African coast. It was rare for him to enter a town or village and not have a cousin or uncle living there. The Swahili were travelers, traders, and fishermen who followed the currents and were blown by the wind along the edge of the African continent ending up all the way from the horn to the island of Madagascar.

"It was nice to meet you and thanks for the info on my family, but I must be going now," said Hassan.

"You don't want the story I have to tell? The one the tree has told me?"

Hassan knew he could not get away, so he settled in for what he hoped would be a short story. "O.K., old lady, tell me what the tree has told you."

"Are you as stupid as you look! It's not really the tree, you know that, right? My miti ya Mburu only protects the spirits that live up high in the branches. They eat the fruit to stay strong. There are many of them all around here all the way to Mafi Island and beyond. The Jinn talk to each other and send messages through the trees and the spirits come to me when I sleep here at the foot of the miti and they whisper in my ear."

"So, what have they told you about me?" said Hassan.

"Lad, it is not about you, it is about the Alakija clan. You are conceited if you thought they would talk about just you." The old lady cackled. "Now sit and listen, you will learn something very important."

Hassan sat on the ground with his back against the ancient trunk. His sticky wet shirt was turning cold as the heat was leached from the ground by the hungry night. "O.K., old lady, I'm all ears."

The withered old woman settled in beside him, adjusting herself so she could gaze up at the branches of her mburu. Her old dog nuzzled up against her and laid down with his head on her lap. "Three nights ago, we were here sleeping as usual. It's too hot in that stone prison, so I usually come here and rest where it is cooler. When I am fast asleep the Jinn climb down from the tree and whisper in my ear. I get all sorts of information about the dirty things the villagers are up to. You know we have an interloper from Somalia, he lives in the new house with a metal roof. But I know he beats his wife, so I tell the Jinn to make his business bad for a year, so he will learn or just go away. That's the usual stuff I hear. But the other night I was fast asleep, and your face came into my dreams. Then I saw your muzungu swimming in the ocean like a fish. He was under the water, far down in the depths where the sharks live. He was fighting a fish that was as big as you and probably weighed more. I have never seen such an animal. He struggled with the creature and seemed to be fighting for his life. He was cut and bleeding and too deep to survive. No person should go and live with the fish, they must stay on the surface. The big grey sharks came out of the ocean, like the ones they bring on the beach here, and started attacking him. Then my dream was finished, but he must have died; no man can live through that. It was awful. Next, I saw your father and mother on the beach in Pemba, they were holding each other as a man in a bright white kanzu shouted at them. He held a young girl. The doctor."

Hassan gasped at this, "The doctor?"

"Yes, and don't interrupt."

"What did the doctor look like?"

"She was a young girl, very beautiful with long black hair down past her shoulders. She couldn't be related to you, as you are short and ugly. Do you know who she is?"

"That could be my sister. She is training to be a doctor in Dar. She comes on the new ferry to see my mum and dad every month."

"Well, she won't be doing that anymore. The man in the kanzu dragged her off to a big white boat and took her away. All your mum and dad could do was watch. I'll tell you he is protected by the bad ones. I could see them around him. My friends in the trees are the good ones, but there is always an opposite to everything."

Hassan didn't want to believe the story, but the old woman had rattled him. His collar was damp, and his spine was tingling. "Is there anything more, Nyanya?"

"Nothing. They told me you would come tonight, and I must tell you what I saw."

Hassan stood up, he felt shaky on his feet. This old lady had been able to see too much. He had to get to his uncle's house now and see if he could get in touch with his family.

"Asante Sana, mzee," he said and stumbled off into the night.

His uncle was sitting outside his hut repairing an old gill net under the light of the moon, with the help of an oil lamp perched on a box beside him. The flame flickered in the slight breeze, sending zephyrs of black smoke up into the night. He looked up as he heard Hassan approach. "So you have finally arrived," he said with a smile. "That old woman has been hassling me for days about you and your muzungu pet."

"I met her," Hassan said. "She told me my sister has been taken away by a man in a white kanzu."

"She told me the same thing yesterday," said Hassan's uncle. "I asked around, but no one had seen or heard from you in over a month."

"We were north of here out of contact. My friend enjoys living in the bush."

"Very strange, but you can never tell with a muzungu. They catch fish then put them back in the ocean! Have you ever heard of such madness?"

"Do you believe the old hag?"

Hassan's uncle said, "We have to call, there's a telephone on the next island, at the doctor's house. If we go now, we'll be there in about an hour. My boat is down on the beach. If we rush, we can get to it before the tide is gone."

Hassan forgot his tiredness and ran for the beach with his uncle.

They landed under the light of a half-moon on a deserted beach in what looked like the middle of nowhere. Hassan's uncle had expertly captained the boat through the shoals. They had only hit one sandbar as the tide dropped. This had set them back twenty nervous minutes as Hassan had to jump out and push the boat back into deeper water.

Hassan's uncle strode off across the beach hitching his kikoi above his knees as he marched toward a sand dune. Hassan raced after him. When they reached the top of the dune, they looked down onto another village that looked exactly the same as the one they had left an hour ago. A lone bark crashed through the night air as a dog spotted the newcomers. Hassan ran down into the village looking for the clinic. A black dog ran at his heels barking and yelping. He raced along the sandy track that was the main street. An old lady was sat outside her house resting in the cool of the night. She looked up as Hassan approached. "Jambo, Habari ya usiku?" Hassan said. *Hello, how is the night?*

She replied, "Niko sawa, asante." *It's fine, thanks.*

"Ninataka daktari, yuko wapi?" said Hassan. *I want the doctor, where is he?*

The old lady pointed to a lone lightbulb at the end of the street. "Enda pale." *Go there.*

Hassan rushed off toward the light, all he could think of was his beloved sister. She was the clever one. The one in the family who everyone knew would make something of herself and be able to look after their parents when they were old. He could not bear to think she had been taken by some rich man in a white boat. His imagination was running riot—she could be in the U.S. already or even worse, in Dubai. He couldn't stop thinking about all the terrible things that happen to Muslim girls in his country. By the time he reached the door, his poor sister was already lost to him, and he was almost in tears.

Hassan hammered on the black metal door as his uncle came running up. "Be quiet!" he stage-whispered. "This is a small town. We don't want to wake everyone."

"But I need to find out about my family. What if my sister has been taken? What will I do? My mum and dad will be devastated."

His uncle replied, "Don't think too much. That old woman doesn't always get it right. You know she licks that tobacco and smokes bhang!"

The door opened and a young man with unruly black hair and a thin, wispy beard looked down on them from the doorway. "What's the problem? Why have you come so late at night?"

"I'm Hassan Alakija from Pemba. The old lady on Kiwayu has said something has happened to my family. I need to use your phone to call them."

The doctor looked confused as he thought through what this young man was saying, then said, "O.K., my friend, come in. The phone is in my office, in the back, where the light is on. Go ahead and make your call."

Hassan rushed through the dark concrete clinic to the rear. The doctor's office was about ten feet square, not even big enough for a prison cell. It had bare, grey, concrete walls and floor, and in the center was an old school desk with papers scattered across it. Behind the desk was a white plastic chair like the ones you see in restaurants; in fact on closer inspection there were two chairs piled on top of each other. One had the front legs broken and the other had one back leg missing. Hassan strode across the room to the telephone hanging on the wall.

He picked up the receiver and dialed the only number he knew, as it was the only phone on the island of Pemba, and it belonged to the chief.

After ten rings he heard a sleepy voice come on the other end. "Hello, who is this calling at such a late hour? I was asleep."

Hassan said, "This is Hassan Alakija, I'm sorry for the late call, but I have heard some bad news about home and wanted to know the truth."

"Hassan, I am so glad you called. We have been looking for you. Call back in ten minutes, I think it is better your father talks to you."

Hassan hung up the phone and felt even worse. He had not been there when his family had needed him, he had been playing with a muzungu and having fun. He pictured himself laughing and joking with Brody as his family went through some kind of hell.

The ten minutes slowly ticked past. Hassan stood next to the phone as his uncle and the doctor stood out in the corridor whispering to each other. The white plastic clock on the wall finally clicked to show ten minutes was up and Hassan grabbed the phone and feverishly dialed the number. Then listened to the everlasting clicks and clunks as the call was connected. When the other end was picked up, he instantly recognized his father's voice: "Hassan, you have called. Where are you?"

"Father, I'm in Kiwayu right now. What has happened?"

"You must come as quick as you can. Zainab has been taken. I could do nothing, she was bewitched and just got on the boat to leave."

Hassan was dumbfounded; it took him a moment to get his voice back. "Father, I'm coming. I'll sort all of this out. We are two, maybe three days away. Just wait. I will be there as soon as I can. Has Jamal, the village elder, done anything?"

"Jamal has already tried to call the police, but this man is a tigiri, rich in many ways, we cannot get to him."

"Don't worry, Father, I will find a way to get Zainab back. I'm coming. See you soon." Hassan hung up and looked at the phone for several seconds. His head was spinning. The old lady had known the truth; she must have some second sight. His hands were shaking and his shirt was soaked as he turned to face his uncle. "Uncle, can you take me back to my boat, it is moored near Kiwayu Lodge on the jetty."

"My son, you look awful, maybe we could go home, then you can leave in the morning? I am sure the problem can wait."

Hassan uncharacteristically shouted at his uncle, "Uncle, I must go now and get on my way. My family needs me. Please take me as quickly as you can back to my boat."

Hassan's uncle was shocked. Swahilis rarely raised their voices. He said, "Just follow me, there is a shortcut through the mangroves. We can be there in thirty minutes."

Chapter Six
Pemba

The sky had a slight tinge of pink in the east. The grey water was glowing and shimmering as if it were waiting for the rays of the sun to climb above the edge of the earth and bring life. *Shukran* rode through the waves, pushing herself to the limit, heading south toward *Pemba*. Her bow wave churned the peaceful waters into a white, frothing mass. The dhow seemed to feel the impatience of the man holding the tiller. Droplets of spray sprang from the waves and hung in the rigging, waiting for the sun to come and pull them into the sky.

Hassan stood alone at the wheel with a grim look of determination on his face. His sister was gone, the golden child. Zainab was the clever one in the family. From an early age, everyone had known she was meant for better than the island of Pemba. She excelled at school and was given a scholarship to the mainland. This was unusual in itself: As she was a poor Muslim girl, scholarships were usually saved for the politicians' children. After several months in the boarding school in Dar es Salaam, the tutors had been so impressed they put her forward for a government accelerated-learning program. Zainab graduated at seventeen, a full year earlier than all the other students. She was accepted into the University of Dar es Salaam to study medicine. That was three years ago. Since then, she had been returning to Pemba for holidays and some weekends. But now she was gone, and he did not know what to do.

Hassan heard a groan from the pillows in the stern. Then a tousled head appeared. Hassan smiled, despite himself. "Morning, Boss."

"What the fuck. Hassan. What has happened? Why are we at sea?" Brody's head felt like the top had been unscrewed and a hand grenade had been carefully placed inside with the pin removed, waiting for him to move so it could do its damage.

Hassan said, "We're heading to Pemba."

Brody tried to stand, but it was too early. His head started reeling and he flopped back on the cushions. "I think I had a few too many last night," he mumbled into the cushions.

Hassan couldn't help himself. "Boss, I found you sitting in the shallows as the tide was coming in. You were slapping the water and watching those flashy lights that appear when you splash. It took me ages to get you to even stand up. You said, 'Nature is so beautiful,' or something—I can't remember, it was all gibberish. Do you remember anything?"

"I remember the dark and stormies, but that was before the sun went down. Then we went out to the beach and had some food and a couple of bottles of wine. After that, it's a blank. Where is Gumbao?"

"He's asleep in the hold. That madafu wine made him stink like rotten coconuts. I don't know why you people drink at all," Hassan said in disgust.

Brody slowly climbed to his feet and immediately felt a wave of nausea flow from his toes to his head. He just made it to the running rail and threw up over the side.

Hassan shouted, "There's a bucket of water, but you need more than that. We're sailing nonstop to Pemba, and I'll need you on shift in an hour."

Brody staggered back from the gunnels. His eyes felt like they were full of sand and his head had a full-blown military band playing "God Save the Queen" at full volume, a song he had always hated.

Hassan laughed, "Eh Boss, you know the cure."

Brody staggered to the port stern rail and found the loop of rope Hassan had laid out for him. He scanned the ocean with his bloodshot eyes for any likely fins, but it was empty and almost glasslike. He carefully looped the rope around his middle and tightened it, then stood on the stern of *Shukran* and just stepped off.

The free fall was short, about twelve feet. He hit the cool water and sank. His body reacted to the new environment by convulsing, making him want to throw up again, but he controlled the feeling and let himself sink. This was the cure. After a few seconds of sinking into the depths, the rope went tight as *Shukran* plied on her way and he was dragged to the surface, coughing and choking. Although the dhow was only going about eight miles an hour, he felt like he was being dragged at three times that speed. His head was plunged into the water time and time again. When *Shukran* went over a wave, he was dragged above the water to catch a breath only to be pulled back under again. The first few minutes were agony as his throat and nose filled with water and he fought to stay on the surface. Gradually, his hangover was pushed away by the rush of adrenaline flowing into his system, and he managed to get control and lie back and enjoy the ride. The cool water was exhilarating as it flowed over him, waking him up and testing all of his senses. He even turned on his back and let the water stream over his shoulders and down to his feet. After a few minutes, he felt a lot better and the need for coffee was making itself known. Brody turned in the water to face *Shukran* and started pulling himself along the rope. Hassan had not even looked over his shoulder all the time he had been in the water. It took another twenty minutes of dragging himself along hand over hand to reach the metal stern ladder hanging off the back of *Shukran*. Brody finally climbed on board and flopped back onto the cushions. "Shit, that always sorts out the booze. I'm knackered now but will be good in ten. Any chance of a coffee, Hassan?"

An hour later Brody looked like a different man. He stood at the tiller with his fourth cup of hot, black, sweet Arabian coffee in his hand. Next to him was a half-eaten plate of mahamry with a bowl of beans in a coconut sauce.

"So, what's the big rush to get to Pemba?"

Hassan looked up from his pots and pans. "My sister has been taken by some rich guy from Unguja and I need to get her back for uni."

"Where the hell is Unguja?"

"That's what we call Zanzibar. That island is full of witches and genies. My dad said Zainab was bewitched and taken there in a big white boat." Hassan had decided not to mention the part of the story where Brody had drowned, or about his chat with the old woman.

"How did you find out?" asked Brody.

"I was in the town last night and I decided to give my parents a call. They had been looking for me for a week or so. They're really upset, we have to go and see what we can do."

"No worries, my friend, we are in this together. Whatever I can do, I will." Brody only knew that his friend was in trouble. That's all the information he needed. Hassan's family had been very kind to him when he had first landed on Pemba. He still remembered the delicious fish pilau Hassan's mother had served him. He had become one of the family and had spent many hours sitting out front of their small house in Pemba chatting with his father and even Zainab.

The wind had picked up as the morning had passed and was now blowing at about seven knots. "Hassan, where's Gumbao? We can put the sail up and get some more speed. We'll have to tack, but if we head offshore one big run and we should be able to get to Pemba."

Hassan lifted the hatch to the hold and shouted, "Eh, you old drunk, we've work to do. You can't sleep all day."

A few minutes later Gumbao's grizzled head appeared, and a strong smell of rotting coconuts followed him up and onto the deck. "I was checking the engine, boy. You shouldn't disrespect your elders, you know."

"Man, you stink," said Brody.

"Ah, Boss, that's the supplies in the hold. I was going through them and some of the boy's coconut oil must have spilled on me."

"Yeah, sure. There's a bucket at the stern. Can you get the spilled oil off you quick before I throw up my breakfast?"

Gumbao grinned. "Eh, Boss, your eyes don't look so good. You got an infection?"

"Shut up, Gumbao! My eyes are fine, I must've gotten some grit in them yesterday."

"Sawa, Boss, give me five minutes and we can get the sail up."

As soon as the sail was up, Brody set a course east-southeast, heading out into the ocean. It was not a direct line to Pemba, but the wind would bring them up to their maximum sailing speed of eight knots. Once they were halfway between their current location and Pemba they could tack back toward the mainland. According to his math, they would reach the island early the following morning. As soon as the sails had been set there was not a great deal to do. *Shukran* was on course, the tiller was tied off so they could all sit and relax. The morning turned into afternoon, and then the sun started to set in the west. At six p.m. Hassan said, "It's time, Boss, we need to tack and head back toward Pemba."

Brody and Gumbao got to their feet and stretched out their limbs like overhung Olympic athletes.

"Hassan, take us up into wind, and Gumbao, get ready to untie the sheet when I give you some slack," said Brody.

He hauled on the sheet, pulling the sail in toward the center of the dhow, giving Gumbao some working room. As soon as Gumbao felt ready he released the rope.

Brody shouted, "Now, Hassan, quickly into the wind!"

Shukran began to slowly react to the tiller and pulled herself back into the wind. As she did, Brody grabbed the sail and started rolling it in his hands, pulling the material down toward the deck as he moved quickly forward. It was hard to keep his feet as *Shukran* started heaving and dropping as she came head-on to the wind.

"You need a hand?" asked Gumbao.

"No, I'm good. Get ready to receive the sheet when we roll the mast.

Brody staggered forward, pulling the sail as hard as he could and rolling it tightly along the length of the boom.

"Are you ready?" he shouted as he started stepping onto the bow of *Shukran*. This was the risky part of tacking, where everything could go wrong.

Brody grabbed the end of the boom with the sail wrapped tightly along its length. He then braced himself and stood on the bow as far out as he could get and faced back to the stern. The mast was heavy and waving around wildly. Brody wrestled it into his arms, then started heaving it back and forth. The top of the boom banged against the top of the mast and almost threw Brody into the sea, but he held on. On the second attempt, he rolled the top of the boom against the ridge in the top of the mast, and it almost rolled over. Then, at the last second, his strength gave out and it fell back to the starboard. With a final rush of adrenaline Brody braced his legs on the outermost part of the bow—he was now hanging over the water. If he fell, he would probably be dragged under the keel and chopped by the propeller. He heaved and rolled the boom, which banged hard against the top of the mast. Brody gave it one last roll and push and thankfully it lifted over the top and rolled onto the port side. Gumbao was there in a flash and grabbed the sheet then hurried back toward the stern. Brody dodged the flapping sail and leaped down onto the deck. By the time he had recovered his breath, they were on a new heading of south-southwest back toward Pemba Island. It would only be a matter of hours before they could find out the truth about Zainab.

Brody sat on the bow of *Shukran* and watched the water break against the old wooden ship. He loved this time of day as the darkness set in and the stars all came out to play. This far off the coast of East Africa there was no light pollution. The dhow was in complete darkness, but no one needed a light to get around. All the crew could put a hand on any piece of equipment in pitch darkness. A splash to starboard signaled the arrival of a pod of dolphins enjoying the bow wave as they played in the dark water.

Hassan said, "Those dolphins love to play with the boats at night. We believe they never sleep."

"You're probably right about that," said Brody.

"I'm very worried about my sister and what has happened. On our island we have witches and genies, but they leave us alone. There are a few of the old ones that go out into the bush and talk with them or give them food. But most of us stay clear. We're modern, those days are gone," said Hassan.

"I'm sure there is nothing to it, my friend. People can't be bewitched or whatever your father said. It's all just people playing games. That guy probably drugged her and took her away. We'll go along and have a chat with him and sort it all out."

"Boss, I don't think it will be as easy as that. The genies have power on some of the islands. The man who took her is a tigiri, that means a rich man. No one knows how his family got rich. The Swahili tribe is small, so everyone knows everyone's business. This man comes from an old family that is powerful and always has been."

"There is always a logical reason, Hassan," said Brody with a smile on his face.

"You don't believe in such things?" asked Hassan.

"Where I come from everything is explained with science. We look at a problem and work through it then find a solution. That tigiri in Unguja sounds like a silly rich kid that has more money than sense. We'll go and have a chat with him. I'm not worried. I'm sure he will see reason once we get him in a room on his own."

"Boss, I'm not so sure. When I was home the last time when you were resting after Tanga I heard about him. They say he feeds the genies and keeps them in his house. Once that happens then the genies take over. The man becomes very powerful, but the genies become much hungrier and need more to keep them happy. They always want the clever, beautiful people—genies are like us—but Allah made them bow to Adam, so they are always jealous. They promise riches and wealth, but whoever deals with them must always bow to them. It is what they need to survive. They will suck her spirit until she is dead."

"You are being way overdramatic, mate," said Brody. "This is just a silly misunderstanding. You know me, I won't let anything happen to Zainab. Just think about it logically. There's nothing out there, just you and me and nature," Brody laughed. "There's no such thing as genies and spirits. It's all just old people trying to hold onto some power and keep you youngsters in line."

"Boss, I hope you're right."

"Leave it to me, Hassan. I've got this. We'll go see your mum and dad then head over to Zanzibar and sort this out in five minutes."

Another splash on the port bow made them both jump. Brody said, "Go get some sleep. We'll reach Pemba in a few hours, just around daybreak. I'll take this watch. You will want to be fresh to speak to your parents."

Chapter Seven
The Island

As the sun was starting to rise and the tide was beginning to fall, *Shukran* sailed through the cut in the Pemba reef. Brody and Gumbao brought the sail down and tied the boom to the top of the stern sunshade as Hassan started the engine for the hour-long cruise though the lagoon to Hassan's village. Hassan stood at the tiller, expertly guiding *Shukran* between the shallows, making sure to skirt the blocks of reef and sandbars. The day was beginning, the sun was up and starting to burn the moisture from the polished wooden planks. It was going to be a hot day. Gumbao stood on the bow of the dhow, watching for unseen sandbars or large rocks that could ground *Shukran*. Brody sat at the stern in the shade and watched his friend Hassan.

"What do you really think has happened to your sister?" Brody asked.

Hassan stayed silent for a long time. He was not sure how much this muzungu could understand of the Swahili ways. "Boss, my sister was taken by a rich man from Zanzibar. All I know so far is that the island has a lot of genies, and some are dangerous. I told you last night."

"But Hassan," Brody said condescendingly, "surely a man of your age and experience does not believe in old wives' tales?"

"Boss, those old wives' tales sometimes have some truth in them. We can't explain everything that happens to us."

"My friend, everything can be explained with science or logic. I live by those rules, or I would always be jumping at shadows in the dark."

"But Boss, you have not seen what the genies can do."

"So, what do these genies look like?"

"They are spoken about in the Koran, Boss. We humans can't see them, but we can feel them. We were made from clay, and the Jinn were made from the smokeless fire."

"What, so not only are they genies but they are ghosts as well," Brody scoffed.

"No, Boss, the Koran says they are the same as us. They are born and die, but we can't see them. They are just jealous of humans and want to take our cleverest and most beautiful and suck their lives away. But some are good and some are bad, just like us."

"Hassan, I respect your religion, but come on, you're a grown man. Do you believe in Santa Claus too!"

"Who is Santa Claus?" said Hassan, bewildered.

"You see," said Brody, "that's my point exactly. In the Western world, we have a guy who only comes out on Christmas Eve. He travels all over the world and delivers presents to little children. When I was a kid, I would go to bed on Christmas Eve and wake up to some presents that had miraculously appeared overnight."

"And you believed that this Santa Claus brought them to you!" said Hassan.

"Absolutely, until I was around ten years old. Then I decided to stay awake and catch this old man and see if I could choose the presents I wanted. I went to bed early. When my mum came to check on me, I hid my head in the pillow and started snoring. She tucked me in and closed the door. As soon as she was gone, I leaped out of bed and went to the door. I slowly opened the door and peered out onto the landing. I was amazed as I watched my mum and dad come out of their bedroom carrying all of the presents for Christmas. That was it, my bubble burst, there was no such person as Santa Claus. I grew up on that night and realized it is all explainable."

"Boss, but that sounds stupid. How did this man break into your house anyway? That is nothing like this situation. The Jinn are real. they live in the baobab trees, and they feed off humans if they can."

"Now who is being ridiculous, Hassan. And they are invisible. Sounds like another Santa Claus to me."

"No, Boss, genies are clever, they lay in wait for a weak person to come along then they invade their body and will live inside them until they are removed, or the person dies. My grandmother told me she could feel them, and they would sit on a path to the beach and wait for a young child to come along and then invade their body. Once they are in, it's almost impossible to get them out."

"That sounds like some sort of folk story to keep children in their place and stop them running down to the beach."

Hassan raised his voice. "Boss, you muzungus don't understand our ways. You come from a plastic world where you think you understand how everything works! This is my problem and my sister's. I know you don't understand, and you can stay on *Shukran* or just drop me off. But I know what has happened and if it is a genie then I have probably lost my sister forever."

Brody realized he had overstepped the mark. "Hassan, I'm with you on this. You can look at it your way and I will look at it in my way. But I can guarantee you one thing. We will look for and find your sister and if anyone gets in our way, I will deal with them, Jinn or no Jinn."

Hassan looked down. "I know, Boss, it's just that my sister is the one in our family that is going places. We can't lose her, if this tigiri has taken her to Zanzibar and locked her up somewhere, we will never find her. And I can't say that to my mum and dad, they will die of sadness."

"Don't worry, my friend. Zainab is like a sister to me. I won't let anything happen to her. Just tell your parents we are on the case and there is nothing to worry about."

As *Shukran* pulled up alongside the quay next to Hassan's village Gumbao and Brody jumped off with the docking lines and made the dhow safe. By the time they had tied the lines Hassan was already running along the wharf to find his mum and dad.

Brody called out to Gumbao, "You stay here with the boat. I'll follow Hassan and find out what's going on."

Brody walked along the sandy path from the wharf toward the center of the village. He knew where Hassan's family lived, as he had spent some time there back when he had first come to East Africa. The mud-built house was set slightly back from the track in a small garden with banana trees growing around the border. Brody could smell the sweet, almost sickly, scent of the ripe mangoes above his head. Old, gnarled tree branches bent down to him, laden with the delicious, bright yellow fruit almost begging him to pick one and bite into the sweet flesh. But he was not in the mood for a fruit salad, he had to sort this mess out and get Zainab back to her family.

Hassan's father was standing on the front porch of their home. Brody remembered him as a man who had lived a tough but very healthy life. The Alakijas mostly lived on fresh fish from the ocean and fruits and vegetables from the garden or the local farms. Raahim had spent his life on the ocean, just like most of the men who lived in the village. He was lean and strong with a nut-brown face and wise eyes that stared into the distance. Brody remembered a happy man who was always looking on the bright side of life, but that had all changed. Now an old man with stooped shoulders and dark rings around his eyes greeted Brody. He looked as if he had aged thirty years since the last time they had met. Brody approached Raahim and said respectfully, "Salaam alaikum, Baba na Hassan."

"As salaam alaikum, rafiki yangu," Raahim replied.

Brody's Kiswahili was only really good enough for short conversations and greetings, so he switched to English to understand Hassan's father more easily.

"How is your wife, mzee?" Brody asked.

"She is not well, my friend. These things do not happen to us. We are good Muslims. I pray five times every single day and fast for Ramadan. I work for my family and do no one any harm. How could this terrible thing have fallen on us?"

Hassan's mother, Farhana, appeared behind Raahim. "My son!" she exclaimed. "Come in and sit. We have sweet, black Swahili tea and fresh chapatis. My husband, why are you being so rude to our visitor? He must be hungry and tired."

Brody was ushered into the small three-room house. Hassan was already sitting on a cushion which was on a rug on the floor. In front of him was a massive pile of steaming chapatis and a copper pot full of tea.

"Now sit and eat, then we will talk," said Farhana.

Brody knew better than to argue, so he sat and ate the delicious chapatis and drank two cups of sweet cinnamon tea before Farhana would settle so they could talk.

When the plates were cleared Raahim spoke up: "Hassan, I have been trying to find you for almost two weeks. I called everyone I knew along the coast, but you were nowhere to be found. I thought you had disappeared too."

Hassan looked down at his hands. "Father, we were north of here, near Somalia. I feel terrible that I was not here when you needed me. I came as soon as I spoke to uncle in Kiwayu."

"No matter," said Farhana, "you are here now, and you have brought my second son with you." She looked at Brody.

"Can you tell us what happened?" asked Hassan.

"It was so strange," said Raahim, taking over the story. "Zainab had returned from Dar for a short break. She comes as often as she can—she always brings such wonderful gifts, I don't know how she gets the money. But she says the city people love our sandals and kangas, so she takes them to sell to help with the fees. She also plaits hair and paints henna for the rich girls."

"Yes, Father, but can you tell us what happened and how she disappeared?"

"Hush my boy, I am getting to the story. This time when Zainab arrived, she was different. Not as happy as before. Not the young child that used to chase the chickens around the garden. I asked her what was wrong, and she said, 'It's nothing, Baba. Don't worry about me.' But I knew she wasn't right. I'm sure something happened in Dar. Those big cities are always full of bad omens and evil people."

"O.K., Baba, I understand. What happened next? How did she disappear, as you are saying?"

Raahim continued. "It was just a normal day at first. One of those hot ones we get at this time of year before the rains come. Mama had been in the garden all day digging so the ground would be ready for planting, and I had gone out in the boat early in the morning. We let Zainab sleep, as she works so hard in Dar and needs her rest. When I arrived back home from my fishing all was great, Zainab was up, and Mama had cooked us a wonderful lunch. After lunch, we sat out front and ate mangoes fresh from the tree. That is when I heard some people shouting about a big boat that had just pulled into the jetty.

"I wanted to go and see what all the excitement was about, so I headed down to the beach. The boat was beautiful, my son. It shone in the afternoon sun. I have never seen such a thing. We all gathered around the dock and looked at it. The sides were bright white and smooth. No nails or screws. The top was blue like the sky with shiny metal parts sticking out here and there. On the very top, a man in a long white kanzu sat at a table with his friends. They were all laughing and joking. The man in charge was tall with dark hair. He had a ring on his finger that glittered in the sun and a golden watch that dangled from his arm. The other men were dressed the same. The group sat on the boat for the whole afternoon just drinking and chatting. After some hours, the captain came down to shoo us away, but we caught him and asked him questions: 'Who are these men?' and 'Why are they here?' The captain said the boat belonged to Tariq bin Thuwaini, who is one of the richest people in Tanzania. We just sat and admired the beautiful boat. Then as the sun was going down it pulled away from the jetty and raced off toward the cut. We just thought they had come to see our village and now were gone."

"What happened next?" asked Hassan.

"In the morning of the following day, I headed out fishing. As I was going toward the cut in the reef, I saw the boat anchored alongside a small island about halfway between our village and the entrance. The men were driving jet skis around in big circles—the chop almost turned my boat over.

"When I arrived back home from fishing, I found Mama and Zainab in the house. Zainab was sitting on this mat, and she was crying. I asked, 'What is wrong, my girl?' but she would not tell me. This went on until I became angry. A daughter cannot defy her father, so I shouted, 'You must tell us why you are crying and won't go outside?' This seemed to sober her up a bit. She said, 'Dad, something awful has happened in Dar.'

"I asked, 'What, my girl?'

"Zainab sniffed once more, then she told me her story. It went something like this: 'Dad, it was not my fault. You know I work in Dar to get extra money to pay for my food and stuff. I never want to be a burden to the family. Well, for the last three months, I have been plaiting the rich girls' hair. I usually meet them in uni, and we find a quiet corner to sit, and I do such beautiful plaits the girls love them. They pay me two thousand shillings for just a couple of hours' work—it's good money. One day, this quiet Arab girl called Nawal asked me if I could do her nails and henna. I have painted a few girls in uni with henna paint on their arms and legs. I agreed, then she asked if I could come to her home to do the work. I don't normally agree to this, as I do not want to travel outside of the uni—it can be dangerous late in the evening. But the girl said she would make sure I was safe and even send a driver to pick me up. I thought this was amazing, I was really getting to meet the wealthy people of Dar es Salaam and I could get loads of business from her family, maybe even stop asking you for money.

"'The day came and I was met outside the gates by a big black Toyota car that I had to climb into. Dad, it was luxury, the seats were cool brown leather, and the driver was dressed in a black uniform and even wore a cap. I travelled across town like a queen looking out at the passing streets. Soon the driver turned into old town Dar. The streets are so narrow there the car mirrors were almost touching the walls. People had to step into doorways as the driver maneuvered his way through the winding streets. We had to stop when a mkokoteni handcart blocked the way. The driver leaned out of his window and shouted at the kibarua to move his load so we could pass. I felt very important. "'Then we arrived at a big golden gate with swirls of metal along the top, it looked beautiful. The driver spoke into a box and the gate swung open. Inside was a square turning place for the car and a huge white building.'

"'Dad,' she said, 'it looked like a mosque, it was so big with white walls glowing in the sun and balconies all around. The driver opened my door, and I was greeted by my school friend.'

"'I spent the day plaiting her hair and chatting. My friend had maids that brought us fresh pastries and cinnamon tea. The evening came very quickly, so I prepared to leave, but Nawal asked me if I could just do some long plaits on her sister. She said she would pay me an extra 1,000 shillings! Nawal took me across the big house and up a set of stairs to a different balcony. She reached above the door and took a key then looked at me. She said, "Do not be scared, my sister is a little odd but nothing to worry about and she loves to look pretty." Nawal slid the key into the lock and opened the door. Inside the room was dark and smelled of dust and damp. My skin felt prickly as I peered into the darkness. Then I sensed more than saw a lump on the bed in the middle of the room. It moved then groaned, "Who is there?" Nawal said. "Don't worry, Sister, it's only me. I have brought someone to make you look pretty."'

"'The voice under the covers said, "Truly, to make me look pretty?"'

"'"Yes," said Nawal as she walked across the room to the bed. "Now sit up and let's make your hair."'

"'Dad, I swear sweat was running between my shoulder blades when I crossed the room. It felt so odd, the room was so cold. The girl in the bed was about my age, but her face was grey like she had never seen the sun and her arms were like matchsticks. I sat on the damp sheets and plaited the girl's hair as quickly as I could. I did not want the 1,000 shillings anymore, it all felt just totally strange. As I was finishing, we heard steps outside, then the door was slammed open and a big man in a white kanzu stood in the doorway blocking the light. He said, "Nawal, what have you done? Why is there a stranger in this room?"'

"'Nawal stammered and looked at the floor with tears in her eyes. "But I was only helping. She needs to feel pretty sometimes, my brother."'

"'The man stamped his feet and then strode across the room and grabbed my arm and pulled me out onto the balcony. Then he shook his fist in my face. All I can remember is his big gold watch hanging from his arm. "Nawal should never have brought you here. Now you have seen what cannot be unseen. They know you now and will want more. You have been cursed by my stupid sister. Run from here and never come back!"'

"'I almost fell down the stairs as he chased me out of the house and onto the street. I was all alone and lost in Dar old town. It took me three hours to get back to my room. Dad, I was so scared—I have never been treated like that, and now the man is here on that big boat.'

"That was all Zainab would say about the matter," said Raahim.

"What happened next?" asked Hassan.

"Early the next morning I went off fishing as usual as the sun was coming up. I went the usual route and noticed the big boat was gone. But I didn't think anything of it. When I got home that evening, I asked Mama if she had seen Zainab. Mama said her room door had been closed all day and she thought she was working on her uni stuff. I went to the door and knocked but there was no answer. Then I became angry and pounded on the door. Mama came running and asked me what was wrong. By this time I could not control my fear and anger and kicked the locked door until it broke."

"Was she inside?" asked Hassan.

"There was no one, but the door had been locked from the inside. She must have climbed out of the window. This behavior is not like Zainab at all. We called all of the village together and no one had seen her. Then we searched all night long, but she was nowhere to be seen. That was two weeks ago; we have heard nothing since."

Brody looked up from the ground with a furrowed brow. "Have you called the university in Dar and asked if she has turned up?"

"Yes, we did that after one day. But they said they haven't seen her and her term starts tomorrow," said Raahim.

"We have searched everywhere on the island, the chief has called Dar and even Unguja looking for her, but no one has seen or heard from her," said Farhana.

"All we can do is assume this boat and the owner had something to do with it all. It definitely upset Zainab when she heard about it. And then her disappearance so soon after they left the wharf. But how do we track it down?" said Brody.

Raahim said, "Another fisherman said he saw it heading toward Unguja on the day they left, but by now it could be anywhere."

"Well, that's settled then," said Brody. "We head to Zanzibar as our first point then we break a few heads and see where we go from there. Don't worry, Raahim, I will follow this big white boat until I find her. She is not lost, we will get her back."

Brody and Hassan ran back to *Shukran* and jumped aboard. Brody shouted, "Gumbao, we're heading out right now."

"Boss, the tide is low—we might hit a bomma or a sandbar if we leave now."

"We'll deal with that as it comes. We have to get to Zanzibar as fast as we can. The trail is already nearly two weeks old. There is no time to lose."

Hassan had already untied *Shukran* from the wharf as Gumbao jumped down into the engine room and started the old Yanmar engine.

Brody was on the tiller. As soon as Gumbao put them in gear he spun the wheel and pushed *Shukran* off the wharf into deeper water.

Chapter Eight
Unguja

Shukran sailed steadily on a course of almost dead-south. Her bow gently plowed through the small swell that had built up when they had left Pemba Channel. The huge white sail billowed in front of them, catching the ten-knot wind that blew all the way from the hot plains of India. Brody's mind was spinning, so many thoughts coming and going. He had tried to settle and get a nap, but as soon as his head touched the pillow an image of Zainab came to mind. When he had first arrived on Pemba Island she had been keen to learn English, and he had been very happy to sit and explain the little he knew about grammar and vocabulary. She had often joked with him and mimicked the way he spoke. Before the first day was over she was saying, "Alright, mate," in a full cockney accent.

They would often walk along the beach in the afternoon, Brody wracking his brain to sound a bit more intelligent. For some reason he was desperate to impress this beautiful young lady. He thought it was probably because she was so quick to learn and clearly way more intelligent than he was. She would ask him questions about grammar that he had no clue how to answer. When this happened, which was often, he would blush and say, "That's just how we say it in England." Then Zainab would burst out laughing and say indignantly, "Did you even go to school?" Brody would push her in the shoulder, and she would punch him back, then run off down the beach shouting, "Help, help! The stupid muzungu is after me!" Brody would chase her along the beach, but she was so quick he could never catch her.

The crew were either sitting or standing on the deck, looking toward the diamond-like lights blinking in the distance, everyone in their own world.
"We'll be there at first light, Boss. Do you have any plans?" asked Hassan.

"What we need most is to find out more about that boat—when it came to Zanzibar, and if it's still hanging around. Gumbao, can you wander around the harbor and ask? See what you can find out. I'll go to the harbor master and see if he will give me any info. Hassan, you go into town and see if you can find an uncle. See if they are staying on the island or have left—and if they have left, when."

The ocean was still dark as *Shukran* gently nosed into the exposed harbor of Stone Town. The long, scarred, ancient sea wall was full of dhows and ferries all loading or unloading goods or people. *Shukran* pushed her way between a much larger wooden dhow with a Mozambique flag flying at her rear. The captain scowled down on *Shukran* as she nudged her way toward the harbor wall. Gumbao shouted at a smaller dhow on their starboard side and roughly shoved at it with a long wooden pole, gouging a space between the boats. *Shukran*'s shining deck and polished stainless steel looked totally out of place in this working harbor.

Men carried 100kg sacks of rice and flour on their backs as they climbed steep gangplanks to load the holds of the boats. Brody looked up as a shout rang out across the wharf. He watched a group of porters surrounding a crate that had been expertly dropped on one corner, splitting it wide open and spilling its contents onto the wharf. The men reached into their robes and produced long, black, eight-inch dhow nails that had been sharpened like a razor. The men grabbed at a slew of tins that had fallen onto the dock side. Brody realized they were family-size cans of meat pies; he could clearly see the advertisement on the brightly colored tins. One man grabbed a tin and expertly slid his sharpened dhow nail around the top then scooped the entire raw pie out and swallowed it whole. He reached for a second and was going for a third when a whistle sounded and the men quickly broke up, picked up their sacks from the ground and started trudging to the gangplank.

The whole area was a mass of moving humans and animals. Braying bullocks were being dragged onto narrow planks of wood. Then they were cajoled onto a boat, one man pushing and three pulling a beast by the silver ring attached to its nose.

The day was already hot when Gumbao said, "O.K., Boss, I've locked everything away. We should be fine for the day. I'm paying this kid to watch the boat, he wants two hundred bob."

"Fine," said Brody, "we'll need to come up with a better solution for security if we're here more than a day. Hassan, can you try and find someone to help with that?"

"Sawa, Boss, I'm on it. I'm sure one of my family needs some cash."

Brody wandered along the wharf and into the warehouse area where he had been told the harbor master had an office. He trudged around for more than an hour before he came across a metal shed with no windows. A sign hung loosely on a piece of string from a hook banged into the wood above the door. Brody paused, then knocked on the door and said, "Hodi, hodi." A voice that sounded like gravel answered with a rough "Karibu."

Brody entered the dark office and found a huge polished wooden desk that looked handmade. It was surrounded by a multitude of packing cases, some with their lids peeled back to reveal bottles of spirits and fancy perfumes. Behind the desk, basking in the air blowing from an enormous air-conditioning unit that hummed loudly in the background, was a very fat, sweaty man. His greasy smile said everything Brody needed to know. This was a very corrupt man in a position of power. Whatever Brody wanted would cost money, the only question was how much.

Brody started in faltering Kiswahili, "Jambo, rafiki, habari ya kazi?" *Hello, my friend, how is work?*

The man sat forward and looked at the fresh meat that had been delivered to his door. Brody could see the math running in his head. The man's smile broadened as a few ideas tracked their way across his brow, then he said, "Sir, we are not friends, nor ever will be. You have come to search me out for some information or a service which I am happy to provide."

Brody said, "I'm looking for a friend of mine. He has a big white fiberglass boat, something that many people can sleep on. Have you seen such a boat?"

"I'm the harbor master, I see all the boats that pass through here. I might have seen that boat—what is your interest?"

Brody knew he had to be careful with this man as his sole purpose in life was lifting money from other people's pockets, and by the size of his waist he was damn good at it. "I'm trying to meet with the owner of the boat. I heard he is selling."

The leather desk chair squealed in pain as the man adjusted his girth to get a better look at Brody. He slid a drawer of his desk open and removed a box of Cuban cigars, then diligently chose one and rolled it next to his ear, all the time staring at Brody. When he was satisfied, he picked a cigar cutter from his desk and sliced off the end. Then he put the cigar in his mouth and reached for an enormous golden lighter set into what was supposed to be a diamond the size of someone's fist. He sucked and puffed, making sure Brody could see just how rich and important he was. Brody watched the charade knowing he was being told just how much this was going to cost.

The dim office had no windows, as the business conducted there should have no prying eyes. "You are a scruffy muzungu who just arrived on a shiny dhow, and you want to buy a million-dollar boat?" the man scoffed as he blew smoke rings.

Brody tasted the coppery blood as he bit down on his tongue. "I'm looking on behalf of a man who is coming to Tanzania. Do you know if I could hire the boat for, say, a month?"

"That man does not need to hire out his boat," said the harbor master.

"Can I at least have his name, so I can ask him myself," asked Brody.

"Let me think, the boat might have been here, but it has left now. I will need to check my records before I can be certain of the dates. That could take a week or so. Can you wait?"

Brody felt the sweat trickle down his spine. He hated the corruption, even when he was asking a simple question, but he took a deep breath. "Do you think you could get me the information a bit quicker? Maybe I can go buy you a soda while you look."

The harbor master's sickly smile picked slightly at the corners, and he brushed a piece of imaginary thread off his immaculately ironed shirt. "I don't drink soda, only Chivas these days. You go into Stone Town and find a hotel, they sell liquor. Bring me back a bottle, and I will have had time to find the information."

Brody let himself smile. The room was full of booze, cigarettes, perfume and god knows what but this man just wanted more. "O.K., sir, I will be back in about an hour."

The harbor master waved at Brody for him to leave.

Brody wandered out of the office and back to the street. He knew Zanzibar was a strict Muslim city so no alcohol would be sold openly. The locals only tolerated the muzungu holiday makers having a drink, so all alcohol was sold in the hotels at exorbitant prices. As he wandered past the Arab Fort built after the Portuguese were chased from the island in 1699, a waft of hot air smelling of cooking meat seemed to engulf him. Across the paved road was an old man sitting under a brightly covered beach umbrella with a charcoal brazier and a palm frond. The brazier was sizzling with skewers of meat. Fat was spitting off the hot coals. The man expertly wafted the warm air out and into any passing person. Brody walked over to the old man. "Bei gani, mzee?" Brody asked.

The man said, "Piece moja, ni mia moja."

Brody took two one-hundred-shilling notes out of his pocket and picked up two sticks of meat.

The man said, "Unataka soda?"

Brody thought about it for a second, then said, "Baridi?"

"Undio, ni baridi sana."

Brody lifted the lid of the cooler box and sorted through the bottles until he came to a Sprite. "Nataka hii."

"Sawa, lete shilingi kumi."

Brody gave him a ten-shilling coin then opened the bottle and sat on the edge of the stone wall overlooking the fort. When he was finished, he gave the bottle back to the old man and continued on his way.

Brody arrived at the main hotel in Stone Town, the one used for tourists and businesses alike. It was an old colonial affair with a pair of huge white elephant tusks marking the main entrance. Photos adorned the entrance, showing the years of Arab and British rule in the area. The paint on the walls was yellow and fading. Brody strode into the foyer and immediately felt cool air blowing from the high ceiling fan. A man with a white turban and a red sash was standing in the doorway. He frowned at Brody as he entered. He asked, "Are you lost, sir?"

Brody looked down at his stained board shorts and rubber sandals and knew exactly what the man meant, but he was in no mood to entertain the snobbish remark. He stared at the man and said, "Where's the bar?"

Brody strode up to the bar and slapped a hundred-dollar bill down, which got the barman's attention. Although it was still way before the sun would cross the yard arm, Brody was thirsty and wanted service. He said, "Bring me a cold beer and a dark and stormy."

"Right away, sir, ice in the dark and stormy?"

"Absolutely," Brody smiled. "It's just too bloody hot out there, and I have had a hell of day."

"Of course, sir. Coming right up."

Brody cleared half of the beer straight from the bottle just after it was placed on the polished, dark mvule bar. "Bring me another beer, this one seems to have run out," he said.

After three beers Brody was feeling better. He made himself comfortable on an old wooden barstool and surveyed the area. The place was old but still looked opulent. The years had taken away some of the sheen. He could imagine the trades that had been done at the bar and in the dining room. Slaves and spices changing hands, fortunes being made and lost.

The barman approached, as all barmen do, holding a glass in one hand and a bright white cloth in the other. He grinned at Brody, and said, "You are new around here? I've never seen you before. Are you on holiday?"

Brody said, "I'm looking for a man that owns a big white boat that was moored here in the harbor a few days ago. Have you seen it?"

"That boat is famous, bwana, it belongs to the Thuwaini family. They own most of Zanzibar."

"Thanks, man. Do you know where they went from here?"

"No, bwana, they are the tigiri, the rich of the island for generations, they come and go as they please. I've no idea where the boat went. It's beautiful, though. I served drinks onboard once and it is like a palace. There are rooms downstairs and a kitchen and showers and everything. I did not believe such a boat even existed in this world."

"Do you know the boat's name?"

"It had two names if I can remember. We all laughed, it is called a Sunseeker, but here the sun is everywhere all day everyday so why chase something that is all around us!" The barman laughed at his own joke.

"Thanks, do you remember the second name?" said Brody. "Can I have another beer before I go, and how much is a bottle of Chivas?"

"The second name I forget, it was something in Kiswahili but written in English. I cannot remember. But everyone knows the ship, it comes here often. If you hang around for a week or so I am sure they will return."

Brody took a pull of his beer. "I would love nothing more than that, but I'm in a bit of a hurry."

The barman presented Brody with a quart bottle of Chivas whisky and said, "This is two hundred dollars, bwana."

"Bloody hell," said Brody under his breath. "O.K. Fine, bring me the bill."

Brody left the hotel with a brown paper bag under his arm, trying to look as if he was not carrying contraband.

He walked as quickly as he could back through Stone Town and into the commercial area of the port. He felt a prickling on the back of his neck but put it down to nerves. The streets began to narrow as he entered the older part of town, the cobbles under his sandals were rough and broken in parts. Soon he was dodging pushcarts and donkeys all trying to make a business in the maze of Stone Town. The sun was directly above, but only a few of the rays managed to fight their way into the cramped, narrow streets. His mind was fixed on getting back to the harbor master as soon as possible to get the info so they could get on their way. Consequently, he was not as attentive as he usually was. A man seemed to accidentally bump into him, pushing him up against a wall. Brody recovered quickly and turned to confront the man, but there was no one there. He started to move more quickly, as the crowd seemed to increase around him. Brody felt the need to keep moving and wanted to push through the crowd. His throat started to constrict as he pushed forward. A man pushing a handcart seemed to drive it straight at him, so he darted down a smaller side alley. The alley was lined with huge, wooden doors with brass ornamental spikes and strange, gargoyle-like faces carved into the ancient hardwood. Brody looked up toward the sun to get his bearings back and felt a hard push on his back. He was not ready, so he went sprawling across the floor, just managing to save the bottle. He rolled instinctively across the cobblestones and ended up in a puddle of water. He quickly jumped to his feet, but again there was no one there. Brody stood for a second with his back to the wall, panting, trying to get his mind to work properly and his heartbeat under control. After a few minutes he checked his surroundings and headed back toward the port. He moved as quickly as he could along the now-empty alleys then came out onto a larger street that was thronging with people. He dodged amongst the traders and started making his way back toward the port offices. His heart had stopped pounding in his head and he felt better. He felt odd, though, as if he was being watched at every turn. He passed an old lady sitting on the floor dressed in an old bui bui, with only her eyes showing. He could have sworn her eyes were on fire, and he was feeling the heat.

Brody broke into a trot as he came to a clearer area, then had to turn again as another handcart blocked the street right in front of him. He jogged into the side street, which had clothes hanging from lines but was eerily quiet compared to the main drag. He pushed through damp, brightly colored hanging clothes, and rushed for the exit. As he reached the opening another cart was roughly pushed across the entrance, so Brody turned to go back the way he had come. Instinct was kicking in. His army brain was taking over. This was a classic case of disorientation before, he assumed, an attack would come. All he could think of was someone had seen him go into the bar and now wanted to mug this silly muzungu who was walking around Stone Town half drunk.

He pushed through the hanging clothes and was immediately hit on the back of the head with what felt like a fist. Brody curled and rolled as he hit the floor, holding the whisky close to his chest to keep the bottle safe. He came up in a fighting stance, ready to face his attacker. But again, there was no one there. He stood for a second, surrounded by the laundry, not able to see more than a few feet in either direction.

A big man in a black kanzu stepped out of the shadows on his left. He had a turban wrapped around his head with a large golden medallion in the center. His dark eyes settled on Brody. Another man appeared on his right, as if he had been standing there the whole time. He was dressed the same and was about six feet tall and built like a Norseman. Brody faced the two men: "What the fuck do you two want?"

The men just looked at him. Brody turned to move away from them and noticed another man behind him dressed the same way. "You better move out of my way right now before anyone gets hurt," Brody said.

The first man drew a long sword from beneath his kanzu and moved toward Brody. The first slash came at a lightning speed and Brody had to swing his whole body backward or he would have been cut in half. The man from behind started moving in, but Brody was in fight mode now and knew what to do. He took a risk and turned from the attacking man in front and in one swift step moved close enough to the man behind to smell the garlic on his breath. The man was taken off guard by the sudden move, so Brody was able to swing his head in the way he had been trained and smash the guy's nose. He yelped and fell backward, grabbing at his bloody and broken face. Brody took the chance and grabbed the man's sword arm, wrenching the blade from his grip. He then swiftly kicked him in the groin.

Brody spun to take on the attacker from the front, but the square was empty. Only the clothes fluttered in the light breeze from the street. He spun on his toes and realized the whole place was empty again, as if nothing had happened. Even the man with the broken nose was gone. Brody stood in the silence for a few seconds, gathering his thoughts. He stuffed the sword into a trash can and headed back the way he had come. Just before he came out onto the main street heading to the harbor a child grabbed his hand, then another until there were six street urchins surrounding him. They held his hands and even clung to his leg as if they did not want him to move. Brody struggled to get away but did not want to seem too rough with the kids. As he gently untangled his hands from theirs a young girl of about sixteen walked up to him. She had dark brown oval eyes and flawless skin the color of coffee. She stood in bare feet on the cobbled stones, her ragged clothes hanging from her slim frame, but it was her eyes that held Brody. They were burning so bright there was an iridescent form to them like a cat's. She did not smile, but looked Brody straight in the eyes and said, "You are not wanted here. You must leave or you will suffer."

As soon as she was done, the kids let go of Brody and disappeared into the crowd and the girl seemed to vanish. The crowd came back, pushing and jostling. Suddenly there was a shout from a man pushing a cart and Brody had to jump out of the way. All was back to normal as if nothing had happened. But now everything had changed. Someone knew he was in Zanzibar, and they did not like it.

Chapter Nine
Stone Town

Gumbao and Brody sat at the stern of *Shukran* waiting for Hassan. Brody had decided to return to the dhow before anything else sinister happened to him. When he arrived, Gumbao was waiting for him. "Boss, you look worse than usual. What happened?"

"I think someone wanted to mug me," he replied.

"This place is full of thieves, that's why the tourists all head up north to the sandy beaches and posh hotels."

"Did you find anything?" Brody asked.

"Well, the boat was here, that's for sure, but it left a few days ago. The family that owns it are big people in Tanzania. They have a house in Stone Town, but the guys I talked to said it's rarely used. Always locked up. No one goes in or out except a few servants and cleaners."

"That's something, at least," said Brody. "We'll wait for Hassan then go and scout it out. Maybe we can get some ideas about the whereabouts of the owners."

Hassan returned an hour later from his uncle's house. He had an old man with him. "This is my uncle Sayyid. He has a stall in the market, and a house in Stone Town," said Hassan.

After the usual handshakes were complete, Brody asked, "Mzee Sayyid, do you know anything about the Thuwaini family?"

The old man thought for a few moments, then said, "They're tigiri in these parts. They own most of Stone Town and a load of Dar, they even have a mansion out in the forest. But they are very private. They come and go as they please on the island. I'm just a trader in the market."

"What about their big white boat?" asked Brody.

"I've seen it here many times. They come in and get supplies, the captain even came to the shop once to buy some spices for the kitchen. I think it was here a few days ago but has gone now. I would not go looking for those people if I were you. They are powerful and rich."

Hassan butted into the conversation, "Boss, Sayyid said he can look after *Shukran* while we have a look around."

"O.K.," said Brody. "Sounds like a plan."

Hassan spent five minutes showing Sayyid around *Shukran* then they left for the town.

As they strolled along the narrow streets Brody was getting more and more frustrated. He had not mentioned the weird encounter with the guys with swords to the others, and he did not even want to think about the young girl and her words of warning. Whatever was ahead of them, he would face to make sure he got Zainab back safely. But the back of his neck kept tingling as if people were staring at him.

The town was slowing down as afternoon passed through to evening. All the fish had been sold, and the tourists had either moved to the hotel bars or were headed back to the beautiful sandy beaches further along the coast. Hassan made some discreet enquiries about the Thuwainis' house, then led them along the twisting lanes across Stone Town to a quieter area where the properties looked much more expensive.

"We better look for a place to hole up, so we can see what's going on in the house," said Brody.

Hassan said, "We can find a place on that building site. It looks like it is not in use right now. They have gone up to the second floor so we can sit up high and watch."

"I'm hungry," said Gumbao. "I'll go and get us some food and a drink,"

An hour later they were sitting on the second floor of the deserted, partially built house, munching on beef samosas and drinking coke. Hassan asked, "How long do we sit here?"

Brody shrugged his shoulders, "We can't wait long, we don't even know if Zainab is actually with these people. We have no proof."

"I say we just wait till it's dark then go and have a look inside. It doesn't look guarded at all, and no one has come or gone for the last hour," said Gumbao.

"Good idea. I agree. If Zainab is around, then we need to find her quick. If these people have nothing to do with it, then we need to move on to plan B."

"What's plan B?" asked Hassan.

Brody looked off into the distance, "I've no bloody idea. But something will crop up, it always does."

"You stay here as lookout, Hassan, me and Brody will go have a poke around. I know this kind of house. When I was a kid, I used to get inside them all the time. We'll just have a quick look around—nobody'll know."

Hassan waited up in his aerie watching the others as they snuck down and out of the building site and around to the big house.

Brody asked, "How're we getting in?"

"Over the wall," said Gumbao. "If we go around the side, down that dark alley, we should be able to be up and over the wall in a few seconds."

"Do you think there'll be any alarms or guards?"

"I doubt it. These people are rich and arrogant. They know no one will come inside their house. But we should be careful. There might be a servant or two just left to keep the place clean."

They turned into the next alley and walked along the side of the house. This part of town was much quieter than where Brody had been earlier in the day. There were no handcarts or street vendors. Gumbao motioned to a narrow alley that led behind the main house. There were bare white plastered walls on either side stretching up into the early evening sky. Brody's shoulders brushed both walls as he peered into the gloom, "This looks like as good a place as any," he said.

They walked about twenty feet into the alley where they would not be spotted from the street. Then Brody braced his back against one wall and placed his feet on the other. He managed to shuffle his butt up a couple of feet then followed with his feet. After a couple of minutes, he was at the top of the surrounding wall of the compound. Gumbao copied him and soon they were both peering over the wall into the back garden of the Thuwainis' house. Brody said, "It all looks clear, not a light or a sound. What do you think?"

"Looks good to me. We'll find out when we get in the garden."

"Any chance of dogs?"

"Ah, Boss, the Swahili and Arabs don't like dogs much. I doubt if there's any here."

Hassan sat in his vantage point staring at the house. There were no lights or movement, but the hairs on the back of his neck were prickling. He angrily wiped at his damp forehead as the minutes passed by. He could not put his finger on the problem, but he felt a presence around him that was not good. He had begun to feel this way as they had walked toward the house. It was as if he should not be there, like when he was a kid and listened in on his parents' conversations. Hassan shook his head with frustration. This was their only lead; his home had been searched thoroughly, there was no way his sister could still be there—even if she was playing a game and hiding, she would have appeared by now. And the big white boat had left at exactly the same time as Zainab had gone missing. This had to be the place. But as much as he wanted to feel they would find Zainab inside the ominous dark building, he also knew it was very unlikely. The whole house was silent like the grave. Not even a cat wandering around the garden. He was not even sure why he had been left to stand guard, he had no way of contacting Brody or Gumbao. He sat back on his haunches and took the last samosa from the brown bag next to him. He ate in silent despair, wondering what was going to happen to them and how they could possibly find his sister. He prayed that Brody would find something, anything, in the house that would help.

Brody leaped off the wall and down into the perfectly manicured miniature garden. He landed softly on a well-cut lawn and quickly darted off toward some bushes at the rear of the house. Gumbao followed him stealthily over the wall and behind the bushes. "Still looks quiet," whispered Brody.

"My bet would be to go around the side and look for a servants' entrance. They're usually left unlocked; people here are careless."

"How do you know all of this?" Brody asked.

"As a kid I was often hungry. This place is the same as Old Town in Mombasa. I would sneak into houses like this and grab what I could and get out. Sometimes I was lucky, other times I got caught. But one thing I learned is: the servants are lazy."

"Fair enough. You lead the way."

The house looked as if it had been carved from a single block of limestone then carefully set down in the small compound, which was only about 300 feet square. The building would not have looked out of place in Old Town, Lamu, or Kismayo. The limestone walls rose straight out of the ground. The windows had carved wooden shutters and brass locks. On the second and third floors small balconies, with black, wrought-iron guardrails, stretched out into the growing gloom. Brody felt the cool dampness of the limestone blocks as he crept along behind Gumbao. They reached a couple of steps that ran up to an ornately carved, double wooden door. Gumbao took the steps two at a time. When he reached the door, he gently pushed it, and it creaked open into what looked like a corridor.

Brody followed as Gumbao slipped inside. The place smelled musty and felt empty. Brody's bare feet felt the chill from the polished terrazzo floor. The whitewashed walls seemed to glow and let off enough light to navigate their way.

Gumbao whispered, "You go left, and I'll go right. We meet back here in twenty minutes."

Brody nodded and headed off along the corridor. He came out into a hallway at the bottom of a flight of white marble steps that led to the upper floors. Brody figured that Gumbao would probably deal with the ground floor, so he gingerly climbed the stairs to the first floor. At the top of the first flight another corridor led off into the darkness. Everything was still, not a movement, no light penetrated from the outside at this level. Brody felt a trickle of sweat run down his spine as he climbed the next flight of stone steps. He was getting déjà vu, his neck prickled just like earlier in the day in Stone Town market. The next floor was an exact replica of the first and just as dark and quiet. He decided he would go to the top then come down and clear each floor. Brody ran up the last flight of steps which led out onto the flat roof of the house. He slid back the ornate brass lock and walked out onto the expansive rooftop. A polished teak pagoda occupied the center of the roof. Brody walked over to it and peered inside. The place looked empty and desolate, just a few scattered magazines from times gone by lay on the benches. He heard a faint squeal above him and sensed something dropping from above. He instinctively ducked out of the way as a colony of fruit bats flew above his head. They continued to squeal at each other as they lazily flapped off into the night. Brody took a minute to recover, then noticed Hassan on the opposite building and waved. Brody walked around the tiled roof looking out over the twinkling lights of Stone Town. This lead was not getting them anywhere. The house seemed empty; it looked as if the place was rarely used. He walked back inside and descended to the lower floor and started clearing the rooms. They were all bedrooms with high four-poster beds, all immaculate. Ready for the owners to take up residence. The floor below was much the same, polished floors and marble bathrooms.

Brody came down to the first floor and decided to check the rooms. He noticed this level had a different design, there were more doors than the other floors. He moved along the corridor carefully avoiding the cut glass vases set on carved wooden tables.

Then he felt the prickly sensation along his spine again. His body immediately froze in the darkness as a glaze of sweat covered his body. His stomach seemed to clench, and his head spun. He shook his head trying to get some clarity and without thinking stepped back into the shadows. He needed a minute to compose himself. He shut his eyes and tried to focus his foggy mind. *What the fuck is happening here?* was all he could think. After a couple of silent minutes standing in the darkness, he slowly moved out in the hallway again and continued on his way. The first room was much smaller than all the others he had investigated; it also smelled of age. The furniture was very old and threadbare. He moved around the room, not able to shake the feelings he was having. It was weird, he was sure he was being watched, just like earlier in the day. But there was no one around. He moved through the second and third rooms which were much the same. Then he came to the final door. He reached for the handle but immediately jerked his hand away, it was stone cold to the touch. He thought to himself, *Shit, man, I'm going crazy. This place has spooked me.* He reached out for the handle again and it was fine. He blinked in the darkness; this was worse than clearing a house full of hostiles in Afghanistan. Something was off, his senses were screaming to just walk away and leave the place. He could honestly tell Hassan that there was nothing in the house. But he had to know what was behind this door. What if he found a clue, or a message, or even Zainab? He had to look. The heavy, brass door handle groaned as he pushed it down. The door slowly opened in front of him, and he walked into the dark room. He immediately felt a breeze on his face and saw that the doors to the balcony were open. Brody kept an eye on the balcony, as he scanned the rest of the room. There were full-length mirrors along one wall. The bed was enormous, bigger than a king-size. Deep gouges had been scratched into the dark wood of the headboard. Then he noticed the chain wrapped around the solid poles of the four-poster bed and the manacles laying on the white pillows.

 Brody heart almost came out of his chest as he heard a footstep on the balcony. He ducked down by the side of the bed, trying not to be seen. His head was spinning, this was all too weird. He was sure that Hassan's stories had gotten into his mind and was fucking with his brain. Then he heard the child's voice again, "Why are you hiding? I saw you and the old man come in."

 Brody stood up, he was blushing and felt stupid. "Who are you?" he said to the girl from the market.

 "I told you before, you are not wanted here, and you must leave."

 "I can't. I'm looking for my friend, and I think the man who owns this house knows something."

 "The family that has this property knows many things about many people, but they never tell. I am the watcher of this house and Stone Town. You must leave, I've never spoken to a muzungu before, but I've heard you are stubborn. This is your last warning. We do not want attention, but we will not expose ourselves to the likes of you. Our ways are the old ways, you will not understand. Now take your friends and leave. The next time the men with the swords will not be as lenient."

Brody looked across at the pretty young girl, she had fine aquiline features, and a straight nose. Her shoulder-length, curly hair was as black as a raven's wing. Her eyes were the color of a clear blue sky on a summer's day and as deep as the ocean. She was standing in front of him without any fear. Her body was relaxed and still as if facing this white man intruding into what might be her house was completely normal. "I must find my friend. Can I speak to the man that owns the big white boat?"

"Never. He will not speak with you. If your friend is with him then forget all about her. She will never return."

"How do you know it is a girl?" asked Brody.

The young girl looked slightly crestfallen at Brody's remark. "You are trying to trick me," she blurted out.

"If you know it's a girl, then you probably know who I mean. She is a pretty girl from Pemba called Zainab. She was living in Dar. Going to the university. You must know her, tell me where she is?"

"I know nothing of any girl. I cannot say anything, or I will be cast out."

"What the hell do you mean, cast out?"

"Listen to me, you dumb muzungu. You have to go now. The men with swords have been called and are coming to kill you. No one is allowed to meet the Thuwainis. If you try, you will die."

"I can deal with a few men with swords. I'm going to find Zainab, whoever gets in my way."

Brody could see the young girl was exasperated, but he sensed she wanted to help him. "Listen, just tell me what you know, and I'm out of here. I can see you are a decent person. If they are holding you against your will, I can help you."

The young girl's eyes seemed to glow as her anger rose, "Muzungu, you can't help me. I was born to this. You will surely die before you help your friend, but you look like you will not give up. So go look in the forest, your friend may be there. Now leave this place and never come back. If you dare to return here, the men with the swords will slice you to pieces." The girl turned and went back to the balcony. Brody followed, but there was no one there. Then he heard a shout from the floor below. "Come quick, we've got company!"

Brody launched himself down the stairs three at a time, lost his footing and sprawled prostrate across the marble floor. He looked up from the ground to see Gumbao with his shoulder against the main door. "These guys want to come in real bad."

Brody said, "Can you hold them?"

"No chance, there must be three or four of them. They'll be through in a couple of seconds."

Brody ran to the door and put his back against it to help Gumbao. "What's your plan."

"Fucked if I know," whispered Brody as the door shifted another couple of inches, "If I'm right, we do not want to mess with these guys."

Gumbao took a risk and grabbed a polished hardwood writing table that was next to the door. He slid it up tight under the single handle and said, "Push. If we can close the door, we'll get enough time to go out the back."

Brody braced himself and shoved the door, closing it enough for Gumbao to force the writing table into place. "Run!" shouted Gumbao.

They both dashed back through the house sliding on the polished floor and crashing into furniture. Brody got to the back door first and burst through. He instinctively dodged to the right as he sensed a threat on his left. The blade clanged against the stone steps a couple of inches from his bare left foot. Brody spun around to face the man wielding the sword. The Arab was dressed in black from head to toe, the medallion set in his turban glowed in the moonlight. He raised the sword again to bring it down on Brody's shoulder as Gumbao came racing out of the door and smashed into him, sending the man and his sword into the far wall. Brody stepped forward and punched him in the throat before he could recover. "Let's get the fuck out of here!"

The two men ran across the lawn and were up and over the wall in seconds. Brody landed next to Gumbao, and they raced along the dark alley. As they reached the end a bright yellow tuk-tuk appeared in front of them. Hassan shouted, "Jump in, we've got to get out of here."

Brody and Gumbao piled into the back of the three-wheeled vehicle as Hassan gunned the tiny engine and took them down the alleys and streets heading downhill toward the harbor.

Brody untangled himself from Gumbao and got his breath back. "Those guys were the same as the ones that tried to mug me earlier."

Hassan looked over his shoulder. "You never told us that?"

"I thought it was just some guys trying to get my wallet."

"Those men are not your normal muggers," said Gumbao. "We were lucky they only had one guy at the rear, or we would have been chopped to pieces."

"What did they look like?" asked Hassan.

"Like they work for bloody Walt Disney," answered Brody.

"Who is Walt Disney?"

"He makes movies. Those guys looked like extras from a movie about Aladdin and the Forty Thieves," replied Brody. "I've never seen anything like it."

"Boss, I told you these are the Jinn, they're sending people after us. We must be careful. They know who we are and where we are," said Hassan.

"That's rubbish, Hassan. This rich guy just likes living like a fucking lord of the manor. He makes them dress up and parade around just to make his dick feel longer. I punched one and he went down like a sack of potatoes."

Hassan went back to his driving as they slowed for the main market, which was dark and empty. He stopped the little yellow vehicle and parked it next to some others that were chained up for the night. "I'll leave some money for the owner. I'm sure he'll not mind us borrowing his taxi," said Hassan as they walked off into the darkness.

Chapter Ten
Ituri, Democratic Republic of Congo

They approached *Shukran* in the early morning light and could hear the gentle snores of Hassan's uncle. Brody was brooding, this whole situation was getting out of hand. He was a simple soldier. All the way through his training he had been taught to look, listen, and understand. Everything he had ever come across had been explained. Now this young girl appearing from nowhere had given him the willies. He knew she could have easily climbed up to the balcony then come in through the doors to make an entrance. Hell, she said she was the guardian or housekeeper of the house, so she would know any secret routes or passages. His senses were telling him this was all just smoke and mirrors. There must be a logical explanation for the two encounters with the swordmen and the young girl.

The whole charade reminded him of the time he was deployed in the Congo. He was in the Special Boat Squadron at the time. The higher-ups had ordered his team into the jungle to hunt down a particularly nasty militia whose head man was known as Kakwavu. His squad had wandered around the interior, always two steps behind the gang. After several weeks of living off food from a bag then shitting in the same bag to keep their trail to a minimum, they had caught up with the ruthless gang.

Brody and his team sat in the jungle and watched as small children, girls, and young men were brutalized by these thugs. It was as if there was no humanity left in them. They would cut a child's arm off as soon as pick up a beer. But Brody's squad was ordered to watch and wait until Kakwavu appeared; only then could they order in a strike.

One morning, the team were in their respective haunts, watching the camp wake up. One of the guys whispered through his mic, "What the fuck's that noise? Over."

They all listened, and finally heard what seemed to be a trumpet being blown in the distance. The squad hunkered down a little lower and slid back a few more feet into the undergrowth, as the blasts on the trumpet grew louder and louder.

After another twenty minutes, a man appeared in the clearing. He was wearing a black suit jacket, white shirt, a bow tie, and a pair of brown, torn cargo shorts. He also had an AK hanging from his shoulder. In his hand was a brightly polished trumpet that shone in the morning sun. He stood to the side of the track and proceeded to blare out random notes. This went on for a few minutes, then a long procession of strangely dressed people started to walk into the clearing. Brody lay amongst the exposed routes of a massive okoume tree; he had been there so long he was partially covered in enormous green and brown leaves. He watched as this pantomime played out in front of him. The people in the procession all wore ball gowns or dress shirts, some were wearing top hats, others had sprays of feathers wrapped around their heads. Brody watched in awe as the people walked into the clearing and created a circle. Then the trumpet stopped its cacophony of untuned notes and silence fell on the jungle. Brody tapped his mic, "This is where it gets interesting, guys. Keep your fingers on your triggers."

"Roger that" was repeated into his ear three times.

"Dobo, do you have the laser pointer set up?" whispered Brody.

"Yes, Boss, all ready to paint this pantomime pink. Over."

"Stay chilly. It looks like our wait is over, over."

As he finished speaking a final group of people started entering the clearing, they were dressed in bright white pantaloon trousers, small tight waistcoat jackets and had turbans on their heads. Each man carried an eight-foot pike with a deadly polished spike on the end. Brody counted twenty-five men, all dressed the same. The next man to enter was obviously the big boss. He had a headdress carved from the skull of a massive silverback gorilla. The shining, silver-black-and-white coat of the beast sparkled in the early morning sun as it hung over his shoulders and down his back, almost reaching the floor. Wrapped around his left arm was a four-foot-long forest cobra. The snake's head was raised above the man's clenched fist. It swung from left to right as if it were sizing up the humans around it. The man flaunted the animal in front of the followers, walking up to them to see if they would flinch. One young lady, dressed in a pink floral dress that would not have been out of place at Royal Ascot on Gold Cup Day, made the mistake of backing away. The head man lunged forward with his left arm and the snake lashed out at the girl's face. She laughed, then cried in fear as two pricks of blood appeared on her cheek. The crowd loved the show and cheered as the poor young lady fell to her knees and started vomiting, then convulsing on the floor as the deadly snake's venom took effect.

Kakwavu waved the snake around in the air which seemed to be a signal for silence. He stood at the entrance to the camp and waited.

Brody click his mic, "Dave, take Colin and penetrate the village. We need as many of those kids saved as possible before the air strike hits. Over."

"I'm on it. Over," was Dave's reply.

Brody continued to watch this weird show in front of him. Kakwavu had been given a megaphone and was now speaking to his followers. "You see this snake. It is truly the worst snake in the jungle. It kills with no fear. It strikes as it pleases. Just like us. We strike fear into the government and soldiers alike. But the snake cannot bite the mighty Kakwavu. I am immune to its venom, as I am immune to all venom the jungle can throw at me. I have taken the towns of Ituri as my own. I am invincible, the gods they smile on me as I am a true leader for freedom. Bullets they pass through me. I am untouchable by the government invaders. No one can harm you if you follow me into battle. I am the chosen one. I have been blessed by the gods to run the whole of Ituri and will do so regardless of the government. They can send their soldiers and their guns and bullets, but nothing can harm Kakwavu. I am here to stay. You, my soldiers, will follow me from this place and we will take more towns and more villages until the whole of Ituri is our land. Our chosen land, as we are the chosen people of God. When you go into battle just know the bullets cannot harm you, as I am here. I am watching you like a good father and will stand my own body in front of the guns and the lead will bounce from my chest."

Brody pressed his mic, "Dave how are you doing? We need to shut this guy up. Over."

"We are on the final huts, about two minutes. Everyone is listening to this lunatic, so we've had the place to ourselves. Over."

"Paint the silly fucker, Dobo. Over."

"O.K., Boss, I am painting the target now. Over."

Brody changed frequencies and called into command based in Juba, South Sudan. "This is Jungle One. Over."

"Juba Three reading loud and clear."

"Juba Three, we are painting the target. Come in hot and heavy."

"That's a go, Jungle One. Thirty seconds to target."

Brody went back to the local frequency, "Guys, thirty seconds until the big boom."

Brody counted down in his head as he watched Kakwavu continue his despotic speech. Then the place evaporated in front of him. There was a huge orange flash as the missile landed among Kakwavu's followers. There were no screams, no shouting or yelling, just an enormous explosion that rocked the ground and sent Brody and his team deeper into their redoubts trying to avoid the blowback that was about to hit the jungle.

When it was all over Brody crept into the clearing. There were body parts scattered all around, mostly burnt. Some were up in the trees; others had been thrown hundreds of feet away. There were no signs Brody could find of Kakwavu. He had been at the center of the explosion. No god had saved him, the snake was gone up in flames too. This man was just as mortal as any other. He had made the mistake of killing a diplomat a few months ago and since then he was a walking dead man. He was not able to dodge bullets or control snakes. The man was just an evil human that deserved to die. The innocent people that had surrounded him had gone up in smoke too. The poor girl who had been bitten by the snake was vaporized. If there was a god at play here, then Brody wanted nothing to do with him. Everything was plain and simple: you are born, you live, and then one day you die and rot in a hole.

"Boss, what you thinking about?" asked Hassan.

"Nothing, really. This is just all smoke and mirrors, we have nothing to fear here. I've seen loads of these types of people pretending to be something they're not. We'll go to this forest and get some bloody answers."

"Don't be so sure. Those men turning up at the house. That was weird, and why were they dressed like that? I saw them from the building site. They just materialized out of the darkness."

"That's just your imagination playing tricks on you. This is all just an act to keep people scared. Let's get some food and then head over to the forest later. Can your uncle look after *Shukran* while we're gone?"

"I'll speak to him. But I'm sure we can find someone."

Chapter Eleven
Masingini Forest, Zanzibar

"Uncle, you're too old to watch *Shukran*," said Hassan. "We probably won't be back until tomorrow, or maybe even another day."

Sayyid's bright smile lit his face as he said, "No. My boy! It gives me peace from those noisy women and kids."

"But uncle, won't you get cold here all night long?"

"Not at all," said Sayyid happily. "Aya will come after prayers and bring my meal. She's a good wife, the first one is always the best. Amina, now, she is trouble."

"Who's Amina?" asked Hassan.

Sayyid settled into the cushion at the back of *Shukran*, ready to tell his story, "Is there any of that fine coffee around and maybe a nip for the night?" Hassan gave the old man a bright yellow mug of coffee and dashed a generous dose of whiskey on top. "That should keep out the cold. Now what of your wives?"

"Amina is my second wife," Sayyid said proudly. "Allah says four is a good number, but I stopped at three. I am not a greedy man," he chuckled at his own joke. "And three is all I need. Amina is good with the kids: she is kind and caring. She will look after them while Aya comes to bring me food. Aya is better here, she does not chat like Amina. We can sit and be peaceful. She is good to sleep with under the stars, and she has a nice soft round body which will keep me warm. Then in the morning, we will wake and pray. Then she will make me some of your wonderful coffee."

"Uncle, how many kids do you have now?"

Sayyid took a gulp of his extra-strong coffee. "This is good stuff, make sure you leave it where I can find it. I have seven, two with Aya, three with Amina, and two with Amal. They are good kids. You know now the government has said they all must go to school. Not just Madrassa, but a real school; even the girls! My eldest girl is nearly sixteen now. She goes to school then Madrassa then she works in the spice shop. She says she will take over from me. Alma says the world is changing and we have to keep up or we will lose out. I have sold spices for fifty years, it's a simple life. I buy huge sacks from the dhows. I put the spices into small bags and sell them. She says this is the past, and we must look to the future. Alma says we have to get techno-savvy and sell on a net. I told her we are not fishermen; how can we sell our turmeric and black pepper on a net? Alma says everyone does it now. We can sell to the Americans in America direct from my small shop in Stone Town. I don't understand. We sell small packets of spice in the government market, the one where the tourists go. They buy a tiny packet, just a kichko moja, *one spoon*. I don't know why, but they love to go into the dusty hot market and buy these small things. If they just walked into Stone Town and came to my real shop, they could buy a sack of turmeric for the same as the tiny packet. Tourists, I never understand." Sayyid stopped and looked down at the water lapping against the hull of *Shukran*. When he looked up the sparkle had left his eyes. "I'm too old to buy a net, but Alma says she can just do it on her computer, so I must let her go.

"When I was young, my sisters never even went to school. They stayed in the house until they were twelve years old then got married and went to have children and serve their husbands."

"Uncle, the times are changing. We live in a different world now. My sister is training to be a doctor in Dar. She is much cleverer than me, and she will earn more than all of our family together. Imagine, I will have to ask my sister for a loan!"

"So, you see, my boy, I am happy here sitting on *Shukran*. The stars are bright, and my dinner will arrive soon. I can feel the waves lapping against the old wood I can trust. I would rather be here than in the house with all those shouting kids, or having Alma talk to me about the net. You go, and Allah will be with you watching. I'm sure you will find Zainab out there and bring her home safe."

"O.K., uncle, we'll be back as soon as we can. You stay safe and warm. And don't touch that bottle too much!"

A fully laden dala dala was at the curbside as the trio made their way up from the docks. The Toyota van had seen better days. The orange mural along the side depicted a Swahili rock group in full swing. The driver was obviously a fan of the group as he was blaring some disco music from the two massive speakers in the back of the battered van. Hassan jumped in the front seat, squeezing next to another passenger. The driver asked, "Where you going?"

Hassan replied, "You can drop us off at the Masingini junction."

"Is that all three of you?"

"Yes. How much?"

"Two hundred, seeing as one of you is a muzungu."

Hassan sighed and handed over the cash. Then he turned to Gumbao and Brody and said, "You get in the back, we're about to leave."

Brody squeezed into the fourteen-passenger vehicle that was currently holding at least eighteen people plus luggage, and a baby goat that kept braying at everyone from below the seat. A fat lady seated next to the door frowned at him but nudged her enormous behind along the seat a fraction, giving Brody enough space to rest one cheek. Gumbao had forced himself deeper into the dala dala and was now wedged between two children. He sat back, relaxed, and lit a cigarette. The vehicle sat in the same spot for another twenty minutes, the driver blaring the horn and the conductor running around trying to gather more passengers or goods going north along the coast road. Finally, the conductor jumped into the van and squeezed the door closed, then banged his fist on the door which was the signal for the driver to head off. The dala dala crunched into gear and lurched off along the tarmac road heading for Nungwi on the most northerly tip of the island.

Brody was dozing when he heard the conductor slap his hand on the roof of the dala dala, signaling the driver to pull over. Hassan turned in his seat and said, "This is us."

Gumbao unceremoniously clambered over sweaty people and boxes then nimbly jumped out of the van. Brody, who was near the door, almost fell out as the large woman regained her space on the seat.

"We walk along this track for about a mile, then we'll be in the forest for real," said Hassan.

Gumbao grumbled, then took the crumpled pack of cigarettes from his pocket and lit up. "Can we get any food or drink around here?"

Hassan answered, "I don't know. It looks pretty empty along this road. Maybe when we get a bit further in. We'll need to ask someone anyway."

They walked along the track beside the dense forest in silence. The dark trees seemed somehow foreboding, even menacing, just mutely staring at them as if to say, *Come on in. I dare you.*

After ten sweaty minutes of walking, they came to several mud huts with palm frond-thatched roofs. Gumbao disappeared for a few minutes then his head poked out between two of the huts. "Come, there's food and drink here. We can ask our questions while we get our bellies full."

Brody ducked as he entered the larger mud hut at the back of the small village. His eyes immediately started watering from the smoke in the air. Gumbao had already made himself at home at a rickety bench made from bamboo, and he had a clay cup in his hand. "Boss, you want some mnazi?"

"I'll only take one cup, that fermented coconut juice is lethal."

"Ah boss, one cup just keeps you warm at night," Gumbao said as he swallowed the remains of his first drink and signaled for another round.

Hassan poked his head inside the smoky bar. "I'll go and see what I can find out."

Brody took his clay cup of the yellowish liquid, held his breath then swallowed. The sweet, slightly rotting smell of coconut burned as it slid down his throat. He almost gagged.

Gumbao laughed, "Man, you just have to get the first few down, then it's easy!"

"Fuck that," said Brody. "Don't they have any beer?"

"I'll ask," said Gumbao, as he waived the waitress over.

The young lady that presented herself as the bar lady was not really that interested in her career. She sauntered over to the bamboo table, sliding her feet across the mud floor. She was dressed in tight jeans and a short cutoff T-shirt with the words "I'm a Virgin" emblazoned on the front. Brody raised his eyebrows to look the big-busted teenager in the eyes. "Do you have beer? Serengeti?"

The young lady looked down her nose at Brody then spoke to Gumbao, "Muzungu anataka nini?" she said in a high-pitched nasal voice. *What does he want?*

Gumbao replied, "Anataka Serengeti, iko hapa?"

"Tuna," the bar lady replied. *We have.*

Gumbao looked at his cup, "Lete engine halafu na Kili pia." *Bring another cup and a Kilimanjaro as well.*

Brody asked, "Why won't she speak to me? I understood everything you just said."

Gumbao shrugged his shoulders, "These village girls don't talk to people like you. You're probably the first muzungu to ever sit in her bar!"

The girl brought back a warm bottle of beer for Brody and another cup of mnazi for Gumbao. "You should really try this mnazi," Gumbao said with an evil grin.

"No way, I'm never drinking that shit again, the last time I stank for about a week. I would wake up at night and smell this awful stench of rotting food and wonder where it was coming from. I would get up and have a shower, then come back to bed only to find my bed stank of it too, the sheets, pillows, everything. It took me so long to get that stench out of my place. Never again. I don't know how you do it."

Gumbao laughed, "Just throw your clothes away and move house! It's easy."

Hassan poked his head back inside the hut, "Guys, we don't have time for drinking. I've found out where we go. We'll need some supplies, but there's a shop just behind this bar where we can get everything."

Brody followed Hassan to the duka, or shop, and they bought some flashlights, some biscuits and water and a coil of rope. Brody also picked up a panga, a twenty-inch-long knife for use in the farm.

"I think I'll take this, it could be handy," he said.

They walked back out to the dusty road and whistled for Gumbao. After a few minutes he came strolling out of the bar with a mitungi, a ten-liter jerry can, under his arm. "One for the road," he said jovially.

They made their way along the track and further into Masingini Forest. The tall hardwoods started closing around the deeper into the woods they walked. The only sounds were squawks from the dark crows in the trees and the occasional screech of a red colobus monkey from deep inside the forest.

"There's a path up here somewhere that runs across the forest, and as far as I was told we can walk to about a mile before the house. Then there is a fence and signs saying, 'Keep out,'" said Hassan.

"How much further?" asked Brody.

"The guy in the shop said we walk for about forty minutes until we see the big sausage tree then we head into the forest along the path," answered Hassan.

"Sausage tree?" said Brody.

"Ah, you'll know it when you see it," said Gumbao. "You can make good beer from those trees."

They walked on in silence, each carrying their own thoughts like a sack on their backs. Hassan could not stop thinking about the terrors that had probably befallen his only sister. He knew nothing of the tigiri in the world, he was just a simple fisherman. But his imagination was running riot, he knew the genies were all-powerful on this island and could suck the life out of any person if given the chance. His mind conjured up a thin, dry corpse with ribs showing and bloodless eyes staring up at him. The emaciated body was lying on the floor of the forest with strange-looking creatures surrounding it, all laughing and cackling in the night. The old lady in Kiwayu, with her knowledge, had scared the shit out of him, and now he knew his sister was probably gone for good; but he had to keep trying. He wiped a tear from his eye as Zainab's face hung in the gloom in front of him.

Brody was worried about what lay ahead of them. He had seen things in his army days that beggared belief. The evil of people had never seemed to reach an end. When he was in Uganda, cutting off a person's hand for not showing allegiance to the cause was commonplace. Although he played the brave hero with Hassan, he still harbored horrors in his mind of what might have become of Zainab. And going into a dark forest to find a lost mansion in the middle of nowhere was doing nothing to alleviate his fears. He tightened his grip on the panga, if anything came at him, he would chop it to pieces.

Gumbao took another swig from the jerry can he was carrying. As far as he was concerned this was a shit show. The genies were all just Swahili folklore. This girl had been taken by a rich guy for whatever reason; he did not understand them and never would. But his friend was in trouble, and he was here, so he would do his best. What would be would be and he would do what he could along the way. Although Hassan was a nuisance and complained all the time, he had helped him in the past and this was just returning the favor. He felt the thirst again and took another gulp of the rancid coconut juice.

Brody said, "I see what you mean about the tree. It's unmissable. What do we do now?"

Hassan stood under the large canopy of the stunted sausage tree, the eighteen-inch-long pendulous fruits hanging down on thin lianas that looked like they would break at any second. "This tree is called the mbungati mti to us here in Tanzania," said Hassan. "We use it to cure many skin diseases and gut rot from drinking too much mnazi, eh Gumbao?"

Gumbao just grunted, "So boy, where do we go from here?"

"That way," Hassan pointed at a path that led off between the tall hardwood trees.

"It's getting late," said Brody. "We had better make up some time or we'll be camped out here all night."

The trio set off walking between the roots of the ancient trees heading along the twisted path. Hassan noticed a feeling in the pit of his stomach and started to feel uneasy, but when he looked around, he could see that Brody and Gumbao were fine and seemed to have no such thoughts. He kept looking behind them to see if anyone was following, but there was nothing out of the ordinary. They walked deeper into the forest as the afternoon wore on. Soon the light was fading, and as is usual on the equator the darkness came very quickly. Brody started to quicken the pace, as he wanted to be near or at the fence before it got completely dark, so he could do some recon of the so-called mansion. As they approached the fence Brody tripped on a root lost in the darkness and stubbed his toe on a large rock. He stumbled forward in the darkness and reached out and grabbed a chain-link fence. The fence was new and looked well-maintained. It towered some twelve feet into the evening sky and was topped with razor wire.

Brody said, "This looks more like a fortress than a house. They really don't want people getting in. Strangely, the house in Stone Town had no such fortification and yet the security here looks more like a prison. Maybe we are on to something?"

"Can we get over it?" asked Hassan.
"We just have to walk along until we find a tree we can climb then jump over," answered Brody.

The search was short, as the trees were densely packed around the fence. Brody slithered up a young neem tree and leaned out over the branches until he was on the other side of the fence, then nimbly dropped to the ground. Hassan threw the bags over, then followed suit and Gumbao dropped to the floor soon after.

"We head into the grounds," said Brody. "But keep an eye out for anything that looks odd, like boxes on a tree or wires along the ground. My gut is telling me we are not alone here."

They crept through the growing darkness under the canopy of the spreading trees. Under normal circumstances it would have been a lovely walk in the evening, but the area seemed to pervade a sense of foreboding.

Gumbao nudged Brody in the back and signaled to a tree about twenty feet in front of them. Brody squinted through the darkness and could just make out a red flashing dot about halfway up the trunk. He went down on one knee and signaled for the others to do the same, pointed where Gumbao had noticed the flashing light, then whispered, "That's a camera, we have to go around. Keep your eyes peeled."

The group moved back and then flanked the tree and started moving further into the grounds of the house. Brody was moving from tree to tree, trying to keep them undercover, but the large, ancient hardwoods had turned into smaller mango trees, then young neem trees. It was getting tougher to stay under cover.

The stone house loomed above them in the growing darkness. The ancient masonry had chipped and cracked as the sun had gradually attacked it over the years. The ornate arches and towers made the stately home look more imposing than it was. The easterly corner of the building was different from the rest. There was a central dome surrounded by four minarets, one of which had a loudspeaker attached. Wrapping around the outside of the palace was a twenty-foot-wide verandah with cracked marble flooring that had seen better days. In the center was a massive, intricately carved, mvule Swahili door. Brody whispered, "We can't go in that way. We'll look for a servants' entrance or climb the wall. If we get spotted here, we're dead men."

Brody rolled across the dew-covered grass until he was behind a small acacia bush, then signaled for the others to follow him. Gumbao put his mitungi down behind a tree and followed Brody. Hassan wiped his sweaty hands on his now-dirty kanzu and crouched down as low as he could as he crab-walked across to Brody.

"Do you think there is anyone home?" said Gumbao.

"Who the fuck knows," replied Brody. "Those cartoon characters might turn up at any minute and chop us all to pieces!"

Brody surveyed the house, looking for any sign of life or an entrance but saw nothing. The front of what he now assumed must have been some sort of sultan's weekend palace was blank except for the enormous door.

"We'll have to go around the side and see if there is another way," he said.

The group crawled along the hedgerow until they reached a small dip in the ground, then sprinted to the side wall. Once they were in the lee of the wall Brody scanned the area for any cameras but saw none. After thirty yards, they came to another arch that was not as ornate. The crown of the arch had a red flashing light. Brody stopped in his tracks, "Another camera, that's annoying. It looks like going in through a door is out of the question. Let's go back and try the wall."

They moved back along the wall, Brody surveyed each section with a keen eye, "What you looking for?" said Hassan.

"I need some purchase on this wall so I can get over and then throw the rope back for you guys," said Brody. "There, look, a large piece of plaster has broken off. If I can get above that I can reach the top and have a look." Brody put the coil of rope over his head. Gumbao was already standing with his back against the wall and had cupped his hand. Brody stepped into the cup and climbed up onto Gumbao's shoulders. "I can't reach," he whispered. Gumbao swiveled around so he was facing the wall and said, "Boy, get between my legs with your shoulders and push us up."

Hassan was about to complain, but he saw his beautiful sister's face hanging in front of him so he so he slithered in between Gumbao's legs and the wall and slowly stood up, his legs starting to shake as he took the weight of the two men above him, but he put his hands against the wall and grunted as he pushed up with his thighs.

Brody's nails scratched against the bare stonework as he was lifted the extra two feet into the air. He finally managed to get his fingers into a crack between the blocks where the cement had fallen out. Then his other hand found a small but sharp ledge above and he was able to pull himself up. His feet slapped against the wall as he pulled with his arms to gain some height. The toe of his shoe caught the edge of the broken plaster, and he was able to lift himself up higher and reach for the lip of the wall above him. Once he had one hand firmly on the lip, he could put the other beside it and pull himself up. He peered into the darkness of the courtyard but could see nothing. Then out of the corner of his eye he spotted movement. A man stood off to the right of the courtyard next to a flowing frangipani tree. The man was leaning against the wall. He stared out at the garden but seemed far away as if he was daydreaming. Brody's arms were starting to ache as he held himself, but he dared not move or the man might hear him. The guy straightened up his back and took a step away from the wall then adjusted the belt around his waist. It was then Brody could see the gun holster attached to his belt. The man fingered the handle of the gun with his right hand then lifted the pistol out and looked at it under the light of the moon. He seemed to shrug, then put the gun back in the holster as he started to move off along the length of the courtyard. Brody waited as his biceps and forearms screamed at him to let go. The man finally went out of sight, and Brody was able to haul himself up onto the wall then drop down onto the soft earth next to a cactus that was full of inch-long thorns. He ducked down behind the bush then uncoiled the rope, tied it around his waist and threw the loose end back over the wall. In a few seconds he could see Hassan's dark red hat appear. Brody immediately motioned for him to be quiet and to move fast. Hassan dropped down beside him and toppled into the bush. Brody grabbed him and wrapped his hand around his neck then covered his mouth to stop him screaming from the thorns which had just penetrated the palm of his hand. Brody only had a second as he was pulled back to the wall with the force of Gumbao climbing the rope. Gumbao landed safely beside them and immediately hunkered down.

Brody said, "Are you alright, Hassan?"

"Yes, it is just my hand, nothing else." He held up his bloodied palm to show the wounds where the thorns had been.

"There is an armed guard patrolling. We've got to move quickly and silently."

The dark courtyard stretched out in front of them. It had been well-kept many years ago, but now like a stately home garden, it was still beautiful but unkempt. A dry fountain sat in the center of the courtyard mourning its lack of water. There were gravel pathways leading from the fountain in four directions. Brody said, "Don't walk on the path, try to stick to the soft ground or we will be heard."

They moved along the wall for a few yards then Brody checked for guards and dodged behind another bush about halfway across the garden. In a few steps they had reached the other end of the corridor the guard had used. Gumbao moved ahead of Brody toward a door, then stopped and waited. Brody nodded to him when they were all together, and slowly pushed the handle of the door down and let it swing open. They moved as one into the room. It was large, about sixty feet in length and thirty in width with no windows on one wall. The room had a smooth, polished, terrazzo floor. There was even a scene worked into the stone floor depicting some sort of hunt with men sitting on top of elephants, the men all dressed in reds and whites. They were holding old flintlock rifles up to their shoulders. Brody stepped into the room where the shadows were deeper and moved to the far end. The next room was the same as the first, but in worse condition. They moved from one room to the next without encountering anyone.

Finally, Brody came to a door that was not the same as the others. He placed his sweaty ear against the old, waxed wood then he opened his mouth and stood silently for a few seconds. "There is some music somewhere behind this door, I can just hear it. Sounds like a radio."

"What do we do?" asked Hassan.

"I think this is more of a me-and-Gumbao job, you stay here for a few minutes and keep watch. Make sure you keep an eye out for that guard."

Brody gingerly reached for the door handle, slowly pressed down on the lever and winced as it creaked under the pressure. He pushed the handle down, hoping the screaming he could hear from the lock was just his imagination. When the latch clicked out of the doorjamb, he pulled the door open a couple of inches. The music instantly became louder, but it was still off in the distance. Brody instinctively knew he had to head toward the noise to gain any useful information. He also realized they were unarmed except for the panga and if they were found and dealt with then no one would ever know. But this was for Zainab, he couldn't lose his resolve now. He motioned to Gumbao to follow him then slipped through the door and into the new corridor.

The new hallway had a concrete floor that was much cooler than the other rooms, its ceiling was lower and bare. A light bulb hung from the ceiling about every thirty feet. "This must be where the servants hang out," said Gumbao.

Brody nodded and started heading toward the tinny sound of the radio in the distance. They jogged cautiously along the hallway expecting to be challenged at any second. There were some rooms off the main route, but they were all empty and bare of any furniture. "If I couldn't hear that music," said Brody, "I would swear we were all alone here."

"Don't worry, Boss I'm sure something will crop up soon," answered Gumbao.

"Yeah, that's what I'm afraid of."

At the end of the corridor, a set of narrow steps led down into what seemed to be a pantry or cellar. Brody dropped to one knee at the top of the stairs and let out a long breath, counted to four, and pulled in a new one. This was a breakpoint, a point of no return. He knew that below them he would find the radio and most likely more than one man. As soon as they moved, they were committed to whatever was going to happen. A picture of the guard crossed his mind. The man had seemed happy with his weapon, but how capable was he? This was an unknown, something to deal with. All battles large or small were the same; too many unknowns.

"When we go down, if we find anyone, we move fast. Don't give them a chance. We're way too exposed here to let anyone get us trapped," said Brody.

Gumbao nodded his agreement. He had been in these situations before and knew that the only way out was forward; just get past the person in front of you and keep moving.

Brody danced down the steps silently and entered the room below. He saw the man listening to the radio a split second before the man saw him. Brody launched himself across the small room and landed on the guy as he was trying to untangle himself from his chair. The radio smashed on the floor as Brody threw himself across the table. The guy tried to dodge Brody, but his head smacked back against the solid cement of the wall with a sickening thump, and he slumped onto the table.

Brody slid across the table and tumbled onto the floor. He rolled to get up, but he was kicked in the ribs by a heavy boot. He tried to turn toward his aggressor, he knew he had been blindsided and was in a lot of trouble. The black, polished boot came flying out of nowhere and caught him in the chin, throwing his head back. He tried to roll away, but he was disoriented so he turned in the wrong direction. The boot came again from above, but this time Brody managed to grab it and twist it then pushed back. The man stumbled backwards into Gumbao, who had just reached the bottom step. Gumbao grabbed the man by his belt and ran him into the wall. The guy twisted at the last second, using his shoulder to take the force. He turned to face Gumbao then reached for his sidearm. Brody was still dazed but managed to grab the broken radio and threw it at the man. He instinctively ducked, giving Gumbao a precious second to move in and grab the gun, forcing it up toward the ceiling. Brody staggered to his feet and then lunged at the two men fighting. He landed at their feet and wrapped himself around the guard's legs trying to give Gumbao a chance. The man lashed out with his knee, trying to break Brody's nose, but he missed. Brody swung his fist as hard as he could into the man's crotch. Gumbao saw the guy's eyes bulge and swung his free elbow into his face, smashing his nose, then grabbed the pistol with both hands and managed to wrench it from the guard. The man put his hands up and took a step back. Gumbao motioned for him to turn and face the wall.

"Shit, that almost went very wrong," said Brody.

"What do we do with these guys?"

Brody looked around and saw another door. It was built from heavy gauge metal with hinges on the inside. He went to the door and tried the lock, but it wouldn't budge. "Ask him for the keys," he said.

Gumbao pointed the gun at the man's head and said, "You heard."

The guard said, "Keys are in the back. We only guard the door—only the doctor is allowed to enter."

Gumbao waved the gun, "Show me back there."

Gumbao whistled in the night, "Boss, I got 'em—they were in a cupboard. But I think you should come and look."

Brody went to the back of the square concrete room; he had not noticed the row of lockers in the shadows and next to them a wire cage with a padlock on the front. Inside the cage placed neatly in a row were six AK-47s, polished and clean. The smell of gun oil lingered in the air around them. Beside them were four handguns, two Glocks, and two Berettas. Brody opened the drawers below the wire cage and saw boxes of ammunition and full magazines for both weapons. "Do you have the key," he said.

Gumbao fumbled with the bunch and tried a few until they heard the magic click of the padlock opening. "Yes, Boss."

"Well, that's certainly evened the odds—why would anyone want an armory in a place like this?"

"No idea, all I know is this place gets weirder the more we search."

Brody reached for an AK and slid the oiled bolt back to check the chamber, then grabbed four magazines and clipped one into the gun, tugging at the magazine to make sure it was seated.

He pointed the AK at the guard. "Have you ever seen what this can do to your stomach?" he asked.

The guard nodded.

"Then get your buddy and drag him over here."

Brody forced the men into the small wire cage then bound their hands with some cable ties and taped their mouths. When he was satisfied it would take them a while to get free, he locked the door of the cage.

The metal door reminded Brody of a hospital door; it was heavy and wide. The lock was clean and oiled. Brody stepped into the new corridor; his eyes watered with the pungent odor of antiseptic. He felt sick to his stomach as memories came flooding back of a field hospital in the Congo after they had been bushwacked by some drug smugglers. Fifteen of his men lay in the jungle either dead or seriously wounded. They had been helicoptered out to the nearest aid station, which was just a tented camp. When Captain Williams arrived, the place was in turmoil, they couldn't deal with so many casualties at one go. There were pools of blood on the floor, and it stank of sweat, antiseptic, blood, and shit. He had almost gagged when he entered.

This place seemed the same, but it was no hospital, just a dark corridor leading them further downhill into the bowels of the earth.

They silently moved along a sloping, dimly lit, doorless corridor. Brody gripped the AK tighter in his hands and laughed nervously as he said, "I hope those guys from that house in Stone Town turn up now with their stupid swords."

They came to another door; this one was not even locked. "We don't have much time, those guards will be found soon, and this place doesn't look as if there are many ways out," said Brody.

The corridor ended in another door. Gumbao held his AK up to his chin and nodded to Brody to open it. They rushed into the next room and stopped in their tracks. Brody almost doubled over as his gag reflex kicked in and he vomited on the floor. The smell of excrement, blood, and guts filled the room. He stood up and tried to look around, but it was almost too much. Gumbao grabbed him by the arm. "Boss, we must get out. This is way worse than I thought. I've seen this before when I was a kid. If we don't move now and fast, we're dead."

Brody shook off Gumbao as his senses returned to him. He looked around at what he now knew was a dungeon of sorts. Six people were chained to the wall—he could not tell whether they were girls or boys, but he could see they were young. One of the youngsters had a tube stuck in their arm which led to bags filled with what looked like blood. The next one had a huge bandage around his or her waist, the small frail body was so white he was sure the child was dead. As Brody's eyes became used to the darkness, he could see cells in the back of the room. One had a bed with a person who had his head bandaged. "What the fuck is this?" he said.

"Boss, these guys are organ brokers. I saw them in Mozambique years ago. The kids are being used for their organs or their blood. The rich use it to stay young. That guy in the back has probably lost his corneas. These fuckers probably sell the body parts to foreigners to make money. Kidneys are the most common, then lungs and hearts—even skin sometimes."

Brody looked around the gory room, "We have to see if Zainab's here."

They ran around checking each of the people hanging from the wall, then the beds, then the back cells. Brody broke the padlock on the first cell door and strode into the room. The kids all cowered back from him in fear. He said, "Don't worry, I'm not here to hurt you." But they didn't understand or were too far gone to even know. Brody checked each one as he went through all four cells but there was no Zainab. Part of him was relieved, he would not have known what to say to Hassan. But he was equally horrified about this carnage in front of him. How could people be so terrible to other people? If this was Hassan's religion, then he wanted no part of it. He could see there was no God here in this room, this was just man's evil nature.

Gumbao stood in the center of the room. "Boss, we have to get out of here now."

Brody came out of the last cell. "Look man, you can go. But I can't just leave these kids here. I would never be able to carry on. You go and get Hassan, and head back into the forest. I'll figure something out here and try to get as many out as I can."

"Ah, fuck it, Boss, I knew you would say that bullshit. Now we're all gonna die to save these fucking half-dead people. It's always the same with you muzungus. You can't just get on with your lives."

"Look, Gumbao, I'm not asking you to stay. Just fuck off with Hassan and leave me to get on with what I can try and do."

"You know I can't do that." Gumbao bent down and started to loosen the constraints on the feet of the first person hanging from the wall.

Brody went back into the cells and smiled through gritted teeth. "Look, I'm going to get you out of here to safety. If you get up and follow me then I can help you."

A lone voice came from the back of the group, "They don't know English, sir. Are you really going to save us?"

"If I can, I will. But no promises yet. What's your name?"

"I'm Ngumo, sir."

"How good is your English, can you tell everyone what we are doing?"

"Sir, yes I can, and I will help as much as I am able."

"What's wrong with you?" said Brody.

The boy stood up and lifted his shirt, "They operated on me a month ago and took something. I have been short of breath and feel sick all the time ever since that happened."

"Shit," said Brody. "Can you walk?"

"Sir, if I can get out of here, I will crawl all the way back to my home in Kilifi, Kenya, and see my mother once more."

"O.K. Just help as much as you can, tell these kids to get up and move to the entrance. We'll go from cell to cell and organize as we can."

Brody and Ngumo herded the lost souls from the cells toward the door leading to the corridor. Ngumo said, "We are often left for two or three days with no one coming, so we might be O.K."

"I hope we are lucky as there is nothing here to help us except this," Brody said, holding up the AK.

In total, there were twenty-four youngsters in the hellhole. They all had ailments, some were partially crippled and had difficulty walking, others put their hands to huge scars that cut across their bodies. Ngumo helped the boy with the bandages around his head out of bed and led him to the door.

"We move quietly, no talking at all just kimia, *silence*. Mnaelewa, *you understand*?" Everyone nodded in agreement and shuffled forward.

Gumbao hissed, "Now we are fucked, what are we going to do with all these orphans?"

"We'll figure that out when the time comes. You take the rear, no stragglers."

Brody edged out into the corridor, then moved as quickly as he could to the next door. He peered through the square glass window and could see nothing, so he quickly opened the door and checked the room. The guards were still tied up. Brody ushered the kids into this smaller room. "Now we go up the stairs. Remember, no noise."

Brody ran up the stone stairs three at a time, the top corridor was clear. The first kid poked his nose over the top step a few seconds behind Brody. He moved along the corridor, retracing his steps back to where he hoped to find Hassan.

The kids followed him like the Pied Piper of Hamelin all shuffling along in the hope of surviving. Brody reached the door to Hassan and stopped. He signaled everyone to stop and then he put his hand over his mouth for silence. He reached for the door handle and slowly opened the door and whispered, "Hassan, you there?" but there was only silence. "Shit, this doesn't look good." He motioned to Gumbao to come to the front. "Hassan has gone."

"We can only do what we can do, let's head back and see if we can open one of the doors. These kids won't be able to climb over a wall."

Brody closed the door again, then moved further along the corridor. As he stepped out into the long wide courtyard he was suddenly bathed in light.

"I have your friend here with me. My pistol is pointed at his head. You have entered this house uninvited; you are a trespasser and a thief."

Brody stopped in his tracks and held his hand up to cover his eyes. "Whoever the fuck you are, you are a sadistic lunatic."

"Now that is no way to talk to your superior. I have all of the, as you say, 'cards.' You will lay down your weapon and step out. I will then put my property back where it belongs, and we will decide your fate."

Brody knew this was the end. He was caught from all sides and the kids behind him were dead. He had felt this feeling in combat many times before. His sergeant major in the Marines had often said, *"When you believe you are dead, son, then you have nothing to lose. You fight and you fight until the last breath in your body and hope those around you do too."*

He flicked the AK into full auto—at least he would go defending a good cause. Then he took a deep breath and raised his weapon to fire at the lights around the courtyard, but before he could pull the trigger they just winked out. The whole compound was thrown into almost pitch darkness, even a cloud had covered the moon. Brody instantly moved, rolling across the floor. He trusted Gumbao would do the same and hoped Hassan would survive. All he knew was to kill or get killed. The first guard came racing out of the darkness. Brody didn't want to show his position, so he rugby-tackled the man to the floor, grabbed his head, and smacked it against the stone floor. The anger he felt was so strong he was invincible. The guy could not defend himself against the wrath and hatred Brody felt. Blood started pouring out of the back of his head.

Gumbao came out of the darkness and grabbed him. "Stop, get control or they will get us all."

"We have to stop them," said Brody. "If we can, we will," answered Gumbao, then disappeared back into the shadows.

Hassan had been surprised in the room and caught easily; now he was mad. He should never have allowed this to happen. When the place went dark, he slammed his foot down on the guard's ankle, feeling a satisfying snap. Then he grabbed the Glock from the guard's hand and swiped it across the man's face, leaving a gouge in his chin. Hassan then kicked him in the groin and smashed his head against a wall. Without looking back, he ran into the next room and slammed the door behind him. He moved to the next door, opened it, and started shouting. "Brody, there are only eight of them, I'm free."

Brody and Gumbao had moved along either side of the courtyard in the darkness when they heard Hassan shout. Brody ran a few steps forward with the AK held ready. Another man moved in the darkness and a bolt of light flashed as his weapon released a deadly flow of lead in Brody's direction. Brody dived and rolled across the terrazzo floor, sliding into a wall. He rolled again as the bullets stitched the ground behind him. Then he heard a return fire. Gumbao had watched the man open fire and now returned the favor and tore the man in half.

Brody rolled again and came up into a crouched position, gun at the ready. He saw a movement to his right and swung around, a shadow darted across the courtyard. Brody put a short burst of three into the man's chest. Then there was silence.

Gumbao moved along the wall, passing the man he had shot. He knew this was going to happen, these stupid, bloody mzungus with their do-good intentions always got him into deeper and deeper shit. But now he was here. He entered a darker covered pagoda then lunged backwards as the butt of a gun swung in front of his face. He almost tripped as he stepped back into the garden. Then he felt a stinging in his leg, and it almost gave way. But he managed to fall to one knee as he brought his weapon up and released a full automatic burst into the pagoda. A man stepped from the darkness and toppled forward.

Brody had seen the firefight and Gumbao drop to a knee, but he could not help yet. He knew there were more guards around. He got up and ran forward into the darkness, waiting for the bullet to strike at any moment. A door slammed to his left. He turned and kicked it in as he rushed through the door. As soon as he was across the threshold he parachute-rolled into the room and came up firing. A man screamed from the opposite wall as bullets tore into his chest and across the wall above him. Brody didn't stop, he ran through the room and kicked another door then rolled and rose, but it was empty.

Gumbao felt the liquid running down his leg, but now was not the time to sort out his wound. There were probably more guards searching for him. A click to his left made him spin then dive behind a concrete bench at the front of the pagoda. Gumbao ducked back as concrete shards were blasted into his face. He rolled and wiggled forward then held his weapon over the top of the bench and spewed a whole magazine where he thought the opponent might be. He ducked back and reached for a new one, as bullets stitched the front of the bench. Then there were two clear shots from a different weapon and the machine-gun fire stopped.

"Are you alright?"

"Who is asking?" said Gumbao.

"Old Man, it's me, Hassan."

"Well done, boy. Do you have any news on Brody?"

"He went off charging through the rooms, but I think anyone who is left has gone now. I heard the boss man telling them to get out through the big door."

"Come over here and help me," said Gumbao.

Hassan ran over to his friend and immediately saw the blood flowing from a gash in his thigh. "Shit, man. Give me a second." He tore a strip of cloth from the bottom of his kanzu and wrapped it around the wound then took his belt off and tied it just above the wound, pulling it as tight as he could. "There, can you walk?"

"Of course I can bloody walk," said Gumbao gruffly.

Brody checked all the rooms, but he could feel the place was empty. He was about to return to the main courtyard when he heard a familiar voice behind him. "I told you not to do these things and to go. You don't understand our ways and you have gone too far now. They will kill you for sure."

Brody turned to see the beautiful young girl from the house in Stone Town.

"What are you doing here?"

"I knew you would be stupid, so I followed you through the woods."

Brody was skeptical but had no other explanation. "Do you watch this evil house as well?"

"No. I am normally only in Stone Town; it is my place." The young girl seemed less sure of herself than before.

"Do you know what those bastards were doing here?"

"What has happened here is not the way. It was not written like this. These people have wandered from the true writings of Allah and should never have done those wicked things."

"Was it you who put the lights off?"

"I did not want the children to die, it was all I could do."

"You protected us. Will they blame you for this?"

"I am not to be blamed. I am here because I was born to be here. I can only see the right way to do things. You must go now quickly; they will return. Leave through the side door and go straight into the forest. Follow the path and you will be helped."

"Who will help us? I have loads of injured kids back there. I need an ambulance and the police to shut this place down." Brody spun in the empty room. "What the fuck is going on?" he shouted. "Come back here right now." But the silence continued. He couldn't understand where the bloody girl had gone, she must have gotten scared and slipped out the door. She certainly looked athletic, and he had been distracted by her sudden appearance. Brody shook his head, this was weird, but he could not let go of the prize—he needed to find Zainab and fast.

Back in the courtyard, Brody stood in front of the sick and disabled kids. "We are leaving now. We have to walk through the forest. You must keep up."

Hassan asked, "Where are we going?"

Brody didn't want to talk about his encounter with the young lady, so he gruffly said, "I have a hunch we'll find someone in the forest who'll help us."

The motley group trudged along the track. Gumbao had a kid on his back who groaned with every step and another holding his belt. They stumbled through the darkness further into the woods. Soon the saplings and softwood trees gave way to more mature trees like the bamba coffee and the thick trunks of wild mango trees.

Brody had a young boy on his shoulders, another on his back, and Ngumo by his side. They walked in silence not knowing where they were going or what would happen. Hassan constantly looked over his shoulder, sure that someone would shout at any moment.

As they walked, the moon came out and lit the narrow track through the woods. The further they got from the house the more the trees started changing from the old hardwoods into grey, ghostly old baobabs. The huge trunks of the ancient trees took up more space; soon they were weaving between the grey monsters sitting silently in the night.

Brody was the first to see the glow in the darkness. He instinctively raised his fist and dropped to one knee. If this was a village, would they be friendly?

Hassan came forward, "Can I go and look?"

"Be my guest, but don't get spotted. We can't risk all these kids out in the open like this."

A croaking voice in Kiswahili came from one of the branches above them, "Is that the Alakija boy?"

Hassan was startled and looked up, "That's me. Who are you?"

"We have been waiting for you. Why are you all crouched down like crabs on the shore?"

"Old woman, who are you?"

"Alakija, boy, you know who I am. Look around you—can you not see the trees?"

"How did you know we were coming?"

"Ah boy, Kiwayu told me you were stupid, but I didn't expect this."

Hassan bristled at the insult, "You know the old hag in Kiwayu?"

"Of course, you were sent here by her, and now you are here. We will take the kids; you have done your job."

Brody couldn't understand the quick-fire Kiswahili, so he shook Hassan's arm. "What the fuck is going on?"

"I'll explain later. She's willing to take the kids from us. I'm sure we can trust her."

"So, Alakija, are you still listening to me, or do I have to come down there and beat you with my stick?"

"I'm here, *nyanya?*"

"I'm not your fucking grandmother. Fool. Now bring those kids further toward the light and we'll take them from you."

Hassan stood, "We should walk to the light, the people there will help us."

Brody was unsure; but he had very few options. The police were out of the question, and he could not walk these kids back to *Shukran*, so he shrugged his shoulders, picked up the kid, and planted him on his shoulders once again. "Let's go. This just gets weirder and weirder."

Seated around the fire were six old women, all quietly smoking pipes. As they approached one lifted her buttocks and let out a long, loud fart. "Fucking meat, it always gives me gas."

Another looked up and spat into the fire, "Whatever you shove in your face gives you gas, you old hag." She cackled at her own joke.

The six women were all skin and bones, old as hell with drawn-back grey hair. They wore no shoes as they sat with their legs outstretched toward the crackling fire.

Hassan entered the circle, "I've come, I was told you would help with the kids."

One of the women stirred, pulling her legs in to stand up. She reached for her cane with long, spindly fingers. "Alakija, come over here and help me."

Hassan walked over and held his hand out.

"No, you have to pick me up, under my shoulders."

One of the ladies around the fire said, "Don't touch her titties, though, you're too old for her." The group broke into various groans and laughter at the joke.

Hassan helped the old crone to her feet. She pointed at a polished white cane on the floor. "Now give me my stick, fool."

Once the old lady was up, she looked into the darkness. "Show me the muzungu."

Hassan said, "Brody, she wants to see you."

Brody stepped forward into the light of the fire.

"Heh you are a good-looking devil," the old lady said, as she spat into the fire.

"Who the hell are you?" asked Brody.

"Your fool of a friend Alakija didn't tell you about us? That clan was always weak. The father could have been the head of Pemba by now, but all he wants to do is fish."

"What..." Hassan said.

"Shut up, Alakija, it's about time you learned to speak up. Your sister will need a lot more backbone if you intend to find her. Now, muzungu, we are here to help you this time. We don't always help, we usually just watch, but it seems we have to intervene." The old crone took a box from her shawl, opened it to show a block of black tobacco. She rubbed her finger over the surface then sucked her dirty finger and massaged her gums.

"You will leave the kids here with us. Then you will leave this island. Alakija, your sister is no longer here. She is alive. But you need to move fast. We have been told of a man that can tell you where she is."

Hassan spluttered, "Where can I find this man?"

"Shimba Hills—he knows the tigiris' ways and can tell you where to look."

"Why can't you tell us?"

"I don't fucking know, that's why. Were you dropped on your head as a kid?"

Brody was confused, this was not his world with strange, gross old women in the middle of the forest, which stank to high heaven. He had had enough. "You're telling us that Zainab is in Shimba Hills?"

No, stupid, there is a man there that will tell you where to look. The longer you keep on talking to us the less he will know. Now go back to your boat and set sail for Shimba Hills. You are finished on this island. They are all looking for you. If you get to your destination and meet Achiba Bakari then you must pay a price."

"What's the price?" asked Brody.

The old woman reached into her robe and pushed her hands down between her legs and started rummaging around. Then she pulled out a handful of long, white, sharp-looking teeth. "They are backwards on the mainland. Achiba Bakari will only take this as money." She held out her hand for Brody to see.

"Can I buy those from you?"

"No chance, get your own."

"What are they?" asked Brody.

"Teeth from the biggest fish in the ocean. On the mainland, if you want anything from the Achiba Bakari then you must pay in teeth."

"Where do I get these teeth?"

The old crone pointed to Hassan, "Ask his grandfather. The old fool was always looking for trouble. Now leave. We have work to do."

The older woman clapped her hands together and four younger women appeared out of the gloom. "Get those kids and take them to the huts. We'll sort them all out tomorrow."

Brody, Hassan, and Gumbao were ignored as the kids were taken. Soon they just stood alone around the fire.

"Well, we better go then," said Gumbao.

They wandered back into the forest. Brody was curious and asked, "Hassan, how do those old women even know you and your family?"

"I don't know," he said sheepishly. "I met one on Kiwayu that night I went to see my uncle and she told me to call home. That's why we are here. I tell you, the genies are working here. They have my sister, and they just want us to run around until we are killed. I don't know what will happen. Now we have to go and find my grandfather and some fish teeth. It's all just the power of the genies taking over our lives. They will not let us find Zainab and we will be killed in this stupid chase."

"Now hold on, Hassan," said Brody. "There are no genies here. It can all be explained easily. First the girl in the house."

"What girl," said Gumbao.

"I didn't tell you?" said Brody. "Well, I seem to keep bumping into this strange girl. The first time in the market, then the house in Stone Town, and now in that hellhole we just left."

"Who is she?" asked Gumbao.

"I don't know, she is just following me around. She keeps telling me to leave it all alone and go home."

"Does she float off the ground?" asked Hassan.

"Don't be stupid, Hassan, of course she doesn't float off the ground. She is just a girl. Probably sent by someone to help us or get in the way. I don't know. But anyway, I think she followed us from Stone Town to the house in the woods. She mentioned the house when I met her in Stone Town and said if we wanted Zainab we had to find it. But I think it was her plan to get us to find those kids. Then she must have followed us. She probably knew a shortcut and was there the whole time. I think it was her that switched off the lights."

"And those stinking old women?" said Hassan.

"If you hadn't told me about Kiwayu and your chat, then I would be a bit unsure about that. But now it's simple. The old lady called someone on Zanzibar, and they kept an eye on us. They may have wanted us to go to the house and set those kids free—hell, they could all be working together for all we know. It does seem as if we are being led around by our noses here. You have told me about the bush telegraph loads of times, Hassan. And everyone knows you and your family. I am sure your grandfather was a rogue in his day and is well remembered. There are no genies, we are just being played from all angles, and we have to keep going or we lose Zainab. There are no genies or wizards or whatever here, just people fucking with our heads."

Hassan was quiet, he could understand what Brody was saying but the coincidences that had occurred—and now they were sending them to catch some huge fish where his friend Brody could easily die as the old lady had told him.

Chapter Twelve
Pemba Island

As the dala dala pulled into the parking lot at Zanzibar port the sun was just cutting above the ocean on the other side of the island. The darkness around them was starting to lift as they approached *Shukran*. Hassan called out, "Hodi, hodi," to his uncle. After a few minutes, a petite but round young lady came shyly out and peered into the morning light. "Ah, Hassan, you are back already."

"Yes, my sister, we have to leave for Pemba as soon as possible."

"Sayyid is up and just getting prepared; I can make some coffee before you leave."

Brody intervened, "That would be great, thanks, I'm starving."

"No problem, we have some fish from last night and maragwe with coconut. I will send a boy for fresh mandazi, so you can eat on the way."

Brody said, "Fantastic—guys, we set sail for Pemba in an hour."

As soon as *Shukran* was set on her northwesterly course heading back to Pemba, Brody settled into the cushions at the stern of *Shukran* and was asleep in seconds. Gumbao followed suit; he hadn't even set the fishing lines. Hassan had agreed to take the first watch. He was nervous about the whole trip and wanted to get his head straight. He had decided that as soon as they touched Pemba he would find the head cleric to give him some advice. He was sure there were genies here and he knew he had to get more protection.

Shukran headed toward the mainland across the Pemba channel. At the halfway line he would wake up the others and tack to get them back on course to hit the cut in Pemba. *Shukran* ran the broad reach, smoothly rising and falling on the gentle waves. The occasional pod of humpback dolphins chased the wake for a few minutes then headed for the depths once again. Hassan enjoyed the motion of his beloved boat and started to relax, but he kept getting jolted back by the words of the old lady in Kiwayu.

Then I saw your muzungu swimming in the ocean like a fish. He was under the water far down in the depths where the sharks live. He was fighting a fish that is as big as you and probably weighed more. I have never seen such an animal. He struggled with the creature and seemed to be fighting for his life. He was cut and bleeding and too deep to survive. No person should go and live with the fish, they must stay on the surface. The big grey sharks came out of the ocean, like the ones they bring on the beach here, and started attacking him. Then my dream was finished, but he must have died; no man can live through that. It was awful.

Hassan shivered, even though the sun was pouring heat down on him. He could not bring himself to tell Brody that this old lady had seen him die. So much had come true so far, he was sure that he was now leading his friend to his certain death. But what could he do? Brody didn't believe in any of this stuff anyway. Whenever Hassan tried to explain their ways, Brody would laugh and use his logic to make it all sound like rubbish. His conscience kept tugging at him: Brody was a good man, but was this all written and had to be? As his misery increased, he saw Zainab's face in the clouds above. If he told Brody and changed the story, would he be killing his sister? Or if he didn't, would Brody die and they would never find his sister? He needed help and he knew it.

Shukran pulled up to the rickety jetty near Hassan's village. As soon as they had tied up, Brody and Hassan went off to find his family while Gumbao went to the market for some provisions.

Raahim was standing under the mango tree wringing his hands as the two approached. "Hujambo," called Hassan. His father looked up from his thoughts and Hassan stopped in his tracks. The man he had always known had gone. What stood before him now was just skin and bones. He looked like a dead man walking. His shoulders were stooped forward, and his clothes were dirty. His eyes were merely sunken sockets surrounded by dark circles. On his forehead was a nasty black bruise. Brody said, "Raahim, what has happened to you?"

"My son, I cannot sleep, I cannot eat, all I can do is pray to Allah that my daughter will return."

Brody could see the pain this man was going through and wanted to give him some hope.

He said, "We have some good news."

"You have found her, where is she?"

"Not that good, but we know she is alive, and we know someone who can help us find her. It should only be a few more days and she will be safely home."

Farhana came out onto the porch. "My sons, you have brought my daughter home to us?"

Hassan had tears in his eyes as he said, "Not yet, mother, but we are close. I need to see grandfather as quickly as I can. Where is he?"

"How can he help? He is old and usually drunk by this time."

"We were told he has some information we need. I just need to find him."

"Take the picki picki, he is across on the other side of the island with his old fishermen friends. He usually sits at the fish market in Tumbe."

Hassan pushed the old motorcycle out of the shed on the side of the house. "We'll have to get some fuel at the shop."

Brody grabbed the backseat of the bike and started pushing it up the hill to the local duka about a mile away.

The young man looking after the shop had known Hassan all of his life and knew about the problems with Zainab. He watched them arrive pushing the Chinese motorcycle. "Salaam Alaikum, Hassan," he said.

"Uncle, it is good to see you."

"I am so sorry for your troubles. Who is the muzungu?"

"This is my friend Brody, he is helping us find my sister."

"Well, Allah is watching over us and will help, I am sure. Now you need petrol."

"Yes, uncle."

"Here," he handed Hassan three one-liter water bottles full of a pink liquid. "This will be enough for a day's riding."

Hassan started to dig into his pockets for some cash. "No, my son, this is my contribution to finding our sister, my daughter. I know you will find her and bring her back to us."

"Thank you, uncle."

They set off on the battered motorcycle along dusty dirt tracks. For the first hour the bike would sink into the sandy ruts of the road, or the front wheel would suddenly get twisted in the sand and hit a rock. Brody sat patiently on the back. He had considered taking over the driving, but he felt Hassan really needed to have something to concentrate on right now. They finally reached Kinyasini, where the tarmac started and were able to glide along the new road to Konde and then the branch off at Tumbe town to take them down to the fish market by the beach.

Brody hopped off the bike and stretched his legs. He needed a drink, but this was not the time or the place.

Hassan quickly strode off toward the fish market and grabbed the first person he could. "Where can I find Mzee Jalal?"

The man pointed at a group of old men sitting near where the fish were all displayed. Hassan had no time to waste, half a day had already gone. He walked up to the group, "Mzee Jalal, is he here?"

"I'm sitting right here, my boy; you don't recognize your grandfather? Have you found our daughter?"

"No, Mzee," he answered, then blurted out, "We need your help, you have to help us find the teeth."

Mzee Jalal stood up and said, "Come, my boy, we need some tea, and you have to explain everything."

"No time for tea, Mzee, just tell us, and we will be on our way. I am already late, and Zainab needs me to come as quickly as I can."

"My son, there is no use in running now, your boat cannot leave until tonight on the tide. A cup of tea will settle your nerves and help me understand where to find these teeth."

Hassan allowed himself to be led away to a tea stand at the edge of the market where Brody had sat and taken some mahamry and strong black coffee with sugar.

"You have brought our second son, that is good. Now tell me your story and how I am meant to help."

Brody and Hassan quickly outlined the last few days, ending with the old women in the forest.

Mzee sat and listened intently, not saying a word until they had both finished. "Now my boys, you have to be very careful." He shifted his bright white kanzu and settled his cane across his lap. "You are in a big mess right now. I was once a young and reckless man. The fishing made me think I could go anywhere and do anything. But I was wrong. I was taken by the ocean far into the channel and dropped on a beach on the mainland with nothing but a paddle. I was stuck there for days and days, just living on the beach. Back then there were no dala dala or motorbikes. And I didn't know where I was. I caught crabs and ate them raw, as I walked along, hoping to find some help. After many hot days and cold nights, I came to a small village. They helped me and looked after me. I worked with the men in the ocean and helped build the huts and fix the nets in the evening.

"After a few moons, I felt strong enough to find my way home. But I did not know which way to go. The men of the village took me into the bush for what seemed like miles until we came to a large hill with boulders and rocks all around. Inside a cave was a dirty old man who told me to bring him these teeth and he would tell me how to get home. I searched for many days out in the ocean looking for the teeth he had shown me—long white teeth with one edge jagged and the other smooth. The dirty old man knew their value and would only trade with these pearly white teeth. After spending weeks out on the ocean looking and hunting, I found an island off the coast. It was only very small, hardly above the waves at all. It had very deep blue water on the western side. I knew I would find the fish I wanted here. I dived and dived off the ledge until I saw these enormous silver fish swimming in the depths. I was young then; I could hold my breath for a long time. I dived and speared one of these fish. It swam away, but I had my float and rope, so I was able to surface and drag myself to the boat. Then, after many hours of fighting, I landed the brute. I chopped its head off and took it back to the old man in the cave and he gave me a map back to Pemba and that is why I am your grandfather, Hassan."

Brody asked, "How do we find this island?"

"That's easy, I will take you."

"No way," said Hassan. "You are too old, and we are traveling fast."

Jalal waited for Hassan to finish. "I come with you. She is my daughter too. That's final."

Hassan could not argue, he knew his grandfather and he was also counting the minutes. "When can we leave?"

Jalal stood up and tucked some stray hairs into his turban. "We go now, you take the bike you came on and I will travel with the fish man in his van. We meet at the jetty at sundown and head out."

When Jalal arrived, *Shukran* was sitting at the jetty with her engine purring. The sun was quickly sinking into the horizon, shooting bolts of reds and oranges into the stratosphere. He stood on the jetty. "Hodi, hodi."

Brody came forward. "Come aboard, Mzee, we are waiting for you. Hassan is just saying goodbye to his mum and dad."

"How soon until we leave?" Jalal said, as he set his bag on the deck.

Brody rang the ship's bell three times. "He should be here any minute now."

Hassan was cross-legged on the floor of the mosque in the center of his village. As soon as they had returned from Tumbe he rushed to find the cleric. The older man looked deep into Hassan's eyes and said, "You are troubled, my boy. Tell me what to do and I will help all I can."

"Sir, I am a good Muslim. I pray often, and I know the Koran from front to back. But I have come across things I cannot explain."

"Tell me in your own words, my boy."

Hassan felt very nervous about his story as it seemed so far-fetched. "I think my sister was taken by the Jinn. A few days ago, I was in Kiwayu and an old lady explained things to me that only me and my family know. They keep turning up and helping us. There were old ladies in the forest that stank, but they knew all about us."

"My son, it seems you are meeting some strange beings. You know the Jinn are in our Koran, they are just like us. They were formed from the part of the fire with no smoke, the hottest part where the flames lick into the night. These old women you speak of, I have heard tales, but I must admit I have never met them. It is said they are the Jinn who have taken over bodies that were weak. Jinn are good and bad; they are just like us but invisible. They are born, they grow up, and they die. They have culture and languages—none we can understand but they are almost the same. They are said to be able to move so fast it is as if they travel in time itself. We cannot see them in their natural state, this is why they inhabit weak or greedy people. Their only fault is jealousy. When Allah created them, he made them bow in front of Adam and they always felt lower than us humans. When they come, they pretend to be our friends but really, they want to make us do their bidding. Whether they have good intentions or bad intentions you will always have to do as they say. You must be very careful. If you meet them, you must recite the Bismillah. They will not come near you if you are a true believer in Allah and you say your prayer correctly. Do not bow down to them or let them touch you. I was once told a story by an elderly cleric; I think it is time I told you. Now listen. There was once a place with an ancient tree. The villagers started to idolize the tree and began bringing it offerings. A devote Muslim saw this and decided to cut the tree, as he did not want good souls idolizing such a thing. He went to the tree with his axe, but he met Shetani on his way. Shetani asked him, 'Where are you going with an axe?' The man said, 'To cut the tree.' Shetani replied, 'I can't let you do this.' So, they fought and fought, and the man managed to beat the Shetani until he was lying on the floor bleeding. The Shetani pleaded with the man, 'Please do not cut the tree today. If you don't, I will give you three gold coins every day.' The man thought this to be a good deal and so he went home. On the first day the coins arrived on his mat as agreed, on the second day also, and then on the third three bright gold coins awaited the man as he went to pray. But on the fourth day there were no coins, nor the fifth or the sixth. So, the man picked his axe and went back to the tree. But Shetani was waiting for him. He said, 'You cannot cut the tree, my worshipers are following it.' So, the man fought Shetani again. But this time he lost and was beaten badly.

He lay on the ground and pleaded with Shetani: 'Why do you beat me so easily when last time I beat you?' The Shetani smiled and said, 'Last time you were fighting for your faith. I cannot beat that. This time you are fighting for the gold!' Now, my boy, remember what I have said, and go with my blessings to find your sister."

Chapter Thirteen
Fungu Kizimkazi

When Hassan arrived, Gumbao was at the tiller and Brody and Jalal were holding the lines, ready to cast off. He threw three sacks of food onboard then jumped after them. Brody held the stern line while Jalal pushed the bow out and climbed onto the side rail. Once *Shukran*'s nose was pointing out enough for Gumbao to steer clear of the jetty, Brody leapt aboard. The dhow chugged peacefully away from the dock into the long channel leading them to the open water. Golden sandbars loomed on either side, stretching out from the thick, twisted mangrove roots. The sun was in its final moments of life for the day and would soon leave them. The trees on the banks started to come alive with the shrieking and calling of crickets and cicadas. Before long the loud croak of a frog looking for a mate bellowed out across the water like a foghorn. *Shukran* cruised through the peaceful waters, leaving no wake behind. When they came to the cut in the reef Hassan took over, he steered out into the open ocean then looked at his grandfather. "Mzee, which way do we go?"

The old man was silent for a moment. "Wait, boy, we need the night to show us the way." They sat wallowing in the ocean as darkness fell around them. The ocean took on a new character as the evening pulled in, the water seemed to become oily in the dim light. The gentle sloshing of the ocean against the hull almost seemed sinister as the horizon got closer and closer.

Brody turned on the HDS 10 chart plotter and got ready to set a course.

Mzee stood next to the mast with one hand holding a line to balance while he stared up into the night. "There," he said, pointing above him, "the brightest star, and the first to come at night. We follow that star, and we will find the island."

Brody looked up and immediately recognized Sirius up in the heavens. He went back to the GPS and plotted a course almost south.

Soon the throb of the Yanmar pulsed through the timbers of the deck, pushing *Shukran* toward the island.

When Mzee had settled in the cushions, Hassam asked, "Do you know the name of the island, Mzee?"

"It has many names, son. When I was a boy, we did not have maps and machines to tell us where to go, we had to learn what the ocean looked like and feel the wind and currents. And know the stars above our heads. We found most of the islands by good fortune or following the birds. I think this one is called Fungu Kizimkazi. No one goes there; it is away from most of the other islands and there is nothing there.

"We will sail for two days and nights then hopefully find it. The place is small and can easily be missed."

Brody looked up from his GPS. "I have traced a route taking us mostly south as Mzee has said and all I can find is Latham Island. We'll head there first." He pressed some buttons on the side of the screen and a dark green line appeared, heading straight across the plotter. "It should take about thirty-six hours, according to this."

"Gumbao," Brody shouted. "We can haul the sail up, it will give us a little extra speed."

There was no wind, but Brody wanted the sail up before they all settled down; they would be travelling with the Kaskazi, which was the northeasterly monsoon wind. It would probably kick in during the night and then carry them across the ocean until around noon, when it usually died off. Mzee sat on his cushions as Brody and Gumbao hauled the heavy boom up the mast, then strung the limp flapping sail across the deck and tied it to the samson post on the starboard stern side of *Shukran*. The sail hung in the night above them, occasionally flapping in the breeze created by their forward motion.

Hassan tied off the tiller as the crew settled into their routines. Gumbao let the long fishing lines out behind *Shukran*, watching the lures jump and tumble on the surface until he was satisfied that a fish could not ignore such a tasty snack. Brody settled into the cushions next to the GPS and listened to the rumble of the engine below. His eyelids quickly became heavy as the drum of the engine lulled him to sleep. Hassan sat next to the tiller, his eyes darting from the glowing screen to the sky above then to the ocean and the tiller. He breathed the thick salty air deeply into his lungs. A faint hint of tobacco came from Gumbao, who had lit up his fourth cigarette, while he peered into the darkness behind *Shukran* waiting for the strike. All was at peace, as it is when a ship sails across the ocean. Each person knows their place and lives in their own thoughts waiting for the morning to come.

After forty hours of nonstop motoring, just as the light was coming up, Hassan shouted, "I can see it. The island. I can just make it out."

Brody jumped up from the deck and peered into the clearing morning air. In the distance he could see a faint lump on the ocean, it looked more like an anomaly than an island. He went to the chart plotter and could see the tiny dot in the ocean had grown overnight. It still wasn't much more than a football pitch in size, but it was there and visible. He looked at Mzee. "Does this bring back any memories?"

The old man looked at the island. "When we get closer, I will be able to tell you whether we have found the right place."

Gumbao brought in the lines. He had taken only one small dorado during the trip, which had fed them on the second night.

Hassan slowly approached the island, which was just a 300-yard-long and 100-yard-wide sandy ridge sticking out of the ocean. Not one tree sprouted out of the barren landscape. They approached cautiously along the leeward edge, where there were rocky outcrops and some stunted vegetation. The most striking thing was the birds. There were thousands of different birds covering the small, insignificant patch of sand, and many more in the sky above. Each bird seemed to be screeching and squawking. As they approached the shallows the air filled with the sound of birds taking flight all around them like a thick cloud of flapping wings. Brody could clearly see nests all over the island. Flocks of greater crested terns flew in looping circles. Their orange beaks with the black tuft on their heads shone in the morning light. When they landed, they immediately put their heads back and croaked with their forty-a-day voices for their mates to come. Single, smaller, long-beaked black and white birds sat in the sand guarding mottled black and white eggs, waiting for their partner to return from the ocean.

Brody stood on the bow watching the razor-sharp coral outcrops, they could rip the bottom out of *Shukran* in a second. He shouted, "Starboard, starboard!" as a particularly large brain head coral loomed out of the ocean. As they passed, Brody saw two twelve-foot-long bull sharks meander from under an overhang and lazily swim away.

Gumbao said, "When the tide goes out, we'll be high and dry." Brody had already thought of this and came on deck with four large poles. He threw two over each side and jumped into the shallow, warm water, glancing over his shoulder to see if the bull sharks were showing any interest. Then he pushed one of the poles under the running rail and jammed the other in the end of the sand.
"Gumbao," he shouted, "I'll tie off here while she is still afloat then push the line through to you to tie off the other pole." Gumbao was ready on the other side as Brody ducked under the water and swam underneath *Shukran*, then handed Gumbao the line he had tied to the first pole so they could make fast both poles to hold them in place. Soon *Shukran* looked like she had sprouted four legs as she settled into the shallow water.

"Mzee, are we in the right place?" asked Hassan. "Boy, I am talking fifty years ago when I was last here, but as far as I can say it looks about right. On the far side, the water just drops down forever."
Hassan gulped; this could be where his best friend is going to die. If the old hag in Kiwayu was right, then Brody would have problems here and would drown, maybe even today.
Brody came up, "What's wrong, man? You look like you just saw a ghost."
"Ah, Boss, I'm fine. Can we just catch these fish with a fishing line?"

Mzee cut in, "No way, boy, they're way too smart for that, and they live down deep in the dark. They are huge and have a brain to match. Why do you think the teeth are worth so much?"

"Can I use the scuba tanks?" Brody asked.

"We can try, but it will probably spook them. They are shy and dangerous fish. They don't attack unless they are provoked, but if they do, you have seen the teeth. You have to get close to get a good shot. Right through the heart is best, just behind the pectoral fin. If you hit that spot just right, they go dead in the water. If not, you better move quick as the sharks will be coming."

"Sounds great," said Brody. "Sharks as well."

"We will wait until low tide," Mzee said. "Just as it is changing, we will go and have a look. We can dive right off the far side of the island, the drop-off is right there."

Gumbao staggered ashore with Brody's BCD, the buoyancy control device. Hassan followed reluctantly with the five-foot-long spear gun and floats. Brody was kitted in a three-millimeter shorty wet suit. From what Jalal had said the water was deep with the possibility of an upwelling where the currents hit the bottom of the ridge then flow up the side of the island. This would create colder water where the fish loved to feed. Brody suited up and stood on a small wave-cut platform. There were no waves as the tide was about to turn. He checked his equipment, took three long breaths from his regulator while looking at his gauges, then stepped into the dark water. As soon as he hit, he released the air from his BCD and sunk into the dark.

He peered out into the gloom as he slowly sank into the water. He felt a tightness on his face as the mask fiercely gripped his skin. He tilted his head back and blew out with his nose to equalize the pressure. The cold water seeped into his suit, flushing the sweat from the walk and sending a shiver down his spine. It would take a moment for his body to heat the new water and allow him to stay warm. Brody stared intently at his gauges. As he felt his mask tighten a sharp pain shot behind his eyes. He squeezed his nose and blew as he gently inflated his jacket to stop the downward motion. His gauges read eight feet. He stopped in the water column and looked around. The water was like gin, but all he could see in front of him was a dark blue haze that drifted off to infinity. He glanced above to the lighter blues and could see small brown oceanic crabs with odd back legs swimming in the current. He checked his gauge again and saw he had dropped to one hundred feet. He had to be careful, without any visual markers he could easily go into decompression. A snout suddenly came rushing toward him out of the blue, a six-foot-long wahoo headed straight for him and at the last minute turned and headed back into the ocean. He knew the bubbles were putting the fish off; he would never manage to catch a tuna with all of this equipment. He also knew he would probably have to change location until they found an ideal spot. That would mean surfacing and the surface interval, which would just take too long. He let go of the spear gun and it drifted beside him on its tether. Then he slowed his breathing and just watched the water around him, hoping to spot a glimpse of silver in the depths. But after twenty minutes there was nothing, so he turned back toward the island, finning his way back to the ledge where he had dropped in.

"How was it, did you see any of the big fish?" asked Hassan.

"No," said Brody, "just one wahoo that came and went. The scuba gear is not going to work for this. I need to be able to move around and follow the shoals. We'll also have to try different places. We need bait fish, as any fish with teeth like that eats meat."

They spent the rest of the day walking along the edge of the island, Brody entering the water then freediving with his spear gun. With each dive he was gone longer and longer as his lungs became used to the strenuous workout.

As the sun was just about to slide into the waves behind them, Brody said, "This is the last dive for today. He dove off the island and into the darkening waters. As he floated on the surface to get his mind and body in the right place to duck under the ocean, he saw a shoal of bright yellow fish with thin dark stripes running along their sides. He knew these were bait fish, just like the rabbits at home, an animal whose only purpose in life was another animals' food. He took a final lungful of air then tipped his head down, waited for his fins to sink, then paddled down. After a few feet he started to descend naturally. He quickly found the shoal of grunts and drifted through them. They did not seem to worry about him and parted as he slowly descended through the thick shoal of fish. He glanced up to the surface back through the mass of grunts. Then he looked down. He knew he must be at about eighty feet, which was as far as he was comfortable with. The bottom was nowhere in sight. The current had changed as the afternoon tide had turned and he was being pushed back toward the island. He knew he had a couple more minutes before he had to surface and head back to *Shukran*. He would wait and test his lungs one more time for the day. He felt his chest constrict and flatten as his lungs started to use the oxygen and yearn for more. He was about to slowly fin to the surface when below him a faint outline started to appear, a ledge at about one hundred and twenty feet. The rocky outcrop seemed to stick out from the side of the island, then drop off again, but he could make out an overhang. A bright streak of silver flashed out from the cave and started lazily circling below him. Then another came from the cave and joined in the patrol. The two fish looked enormous against the hazy blue and the fading light. Brody sat in the water as still as he could, as the fish swam around, slowly moving up through the water column. His chest started to pump as his body wanted to breathe, but he wanted to watch these majestic mammoths of the ocean for just a few seconds more. There was no way he could take a shot at this point of a dive. So, he relaxed and waited. The giant creatures did not seem to notice him sitting quietly as they moved stealthily, like a leopard stalking its prey, toward the shoal of bait fish. The silver devils were six-foot-long tubes of muscle and sinew. Brody had never seen such a fish; it just looked dangerous. They swam to within twenty feet of him as they passed, heading for their dinner. Brody watched closely as their mouths opened and closed underwater, sensing prey. He caught a glimpse of pearly white, razor-sharp teeth. This formidable animal was his prey. Now he knew he was looking for the dogtooth tuna; one of the most elusive and prized fish in the ocean.

He looked up, it was a long way to the surface; he had overstayed. His chest was pumping, screaming for him to take a lungful of refreshing air. The reflex in his brain demanding he expel the carbon dioxide and fill his body with fresh clean air was almost irresistible. But he calmed his nerves and swam upward, ever upward; the surface seemed to never get any closer. He glanced down and saw the massive fish circling the grunts and knew that the next day he would return and find a way down into the depths to get one of the goliaths of the sea.

Hassan had been wringing his hands for the last two minutes. "Why is he taking so long?"

"You know the muzungu, when he gets into this he can take forever down there," said Gumbao.

"But this is way too long," said Hassan, frantic that his friend had died and was gone already.

Jalal said, "Look, I think he is coming, he will be fine."

Brody's head burst through the surface, and he took the longest breath of his life. He felt a shooting pain in his chest and his left leg cramped up, so he just lay there in the water as the evening light faded to darkness.

Hassan could not sleep; he lay on his mat looking up at the Milky Way far above him. He wished he had had more time to understand what his cleric had said, but it had all been so fast and now they were here, exactly where the old woman had said they would be, and searching for what Brody said was the biggest bloody fish he had ever seen. He had called it a dogtooth. They had chatted over a long meal of fresh fried dorado, with ugali and a chili sauce. Hassan's brain was spinning, and he was constantly feeling the massive guilt of having to choose between his beloved sister or his good friend. The two faces circled him in the dark, he loved each one and was now being forced to make a decision. What if the old hag was just wrong and nothing happened? But could he live with himself if she was right and Brody died, and they did not get the teeth or his sister. He did not know what to do. He sat up and walked to the bow away from the others and stared into the dark lapping waters.

The morning came way too quickly. Brody was up at dawn looking for his coffee. He felt good, the diving had given him purpose. He felt they were making headway toward Zainab. He looked at Hassan. "Man, are you sick?"

Hassan crouched next to the jiko, making the coffee. "I didn't sleep well, maybe it was that fish."

"You take it easy today, I have a good feeling we'll snag one of those monsters and be on our way."

Hassan looked up from his frying pan, "Look, I have to tell you something."

"What," said Brody.

Hassan could not hold the story in any longer and just blurted it out: "That old woman in Kiwayu. She said you would drown while we were fighting a big fish. Now we are here, and you are going to fight a big fish and you will probably drown. Then my sister will be gone, and we will have nothing. I can't lose everyone, not in just one day."

Brody was taken aback. These kinds of emotions were alien to him and as far as he knew to Hassan as well. They were usually much more stoic toward each other, like men usually are.

"Hassan, I do dumb stuff all the time. I risk my life every time I take a breath and go looking for our dinner. You never know what is going to happen next, or when your ticket is going to get punched. But I can assure you, some old lady in Kiwayu with very questionable credentials, who rang another stinking old woman in Zanzibar, does not have any effect over whether I live or die."

Hassan said, "You don't understand the way of the genies. We have been mixed up with them ever since Kiwayu. They are watching our every move and now they want you dead."

"No, my friend, you are right. I understand what you are telling me, and I will be extra careful today. I won't just dive off the edge of the island, we'll take *Shukran* around and you guys can help me to pull the fish aboard."

Hassan had calmed himself a little and knew his emotional outburst had been way over the top. "O.K., Brody, I will sit and watch you like a hawk until this thing is over."

Shukran sat in the open ocean bobbing up and down on the glassy water. Gumbao had set a new line to Brody's four-foot-long spear gun. They had spent the last hour fitting an extra elastic to the gun with stronger swivels. Brody wanted to get more distance in the water for his spear as these creatures seemed to like the deep.

The first three dives of the day were useless, the bait fish were hanging above the ledge as they had been the day before, but the silver torpedoes had not shown. Brody sat on the deck absorbing the sun, and a shiver went down his spine as he pulled his wet suit down. "That water just drains the heat from your body. Any chance of a cuppa, Hassan?" Within seconds a boiling-hot mug of coffee with loads of sugar was placed in his hand. Hassan had not left his side all morning and when he was diving had hung over the side of the boat. He had even convinced Gumbao to get in and lay on the surface with a spare snorkel and mask to watch Brody below.

Brody got to his feet. "Well, I won't catch one of those buggers up here." He donned his wet suit and weight belt, put his mask on, then jumped into the ocean. As usual he lay on the surface, gathering himself for the dive. His mind had to be just right, almost in a meditative state; just calm and peaceful. He filled his lungs one more time, then tucked his head in and dove for the ledge. He managed to get to within sight of the deep outcrop and hung there. The bait fish were shoaling around the ridge as if it was just another day in the office. Brody hung in the blue; a brown oceanic crab paddled past him. A blue and silver head appeared in the grey distance with a flash of gold as a bull dorado swam back into the blue. Brody tugged at the bag at his waist and pulled out the stomach of the fish they had eaten the night before. He started cutting it into strips and letting them float down toward the ledge. One of the grunts swam out and grabbed a morsel then returned to the safety of the shoal. Brody let some bigger pieces float down and over the edge of the ledge. Then he slowly started to sink a little further. He knew he was at around 100 feet, but he felt at peace and comfortable.

The light had faded as he headed for the ledge. He settled onto the top of the outcrop and put himself into a trance. He could lay there for about one more minute before he had to return. His arm was outstretched in front of him, holding the spear gun steady, the thin line headed to the surface with the old plastic fishing net buoys attached to the other end on the surface. A snout appeared in the gloom, the scent of the bait had raised some interest. Brody tensed in the water and settled a bit lower, pressing himself against the bare rock. The snout turned into a head, then the silver barrel appeared and flowed out of the cave in one smooth motion. A second snout appeared and followed suit. Brody calmed himself as the fish gracefully swam out into the water column then circled to grab at the bait. When the largest of the two glided in front of him, not more than ten paces away, Brody let his shoulders relax and gently squeezed the trigger. The extra elastic threw the stainless-steel spear directly at the tuna. It flinched as the tip pierced its flesh about four inches behind the pectoral fin. Too far back for a dead shot.

The animal spun in the water and raced toward Brody. He launched himself from the bottom and finned madly for the surface. This giant was a prey animal; it did not scare easily. The spear had penetrated the body and come out the other side, but it was not slowing the creature down. Brody tried to head for the surface as the fish chomped at his thighs, tearing off a strip of his wet suit, leaving a cut on his leg. A green slick started to flow from his leg as the blood mingled with the water. Brody's heart started racing. He knew any sharks in the area would pick up the scent in seconds. He twisted in the water, still paddling for the surface, the exertion had not been factored into his swim. Now the glassy blue above him seemed like an eternity away. The fish came round again and smashed into his mask, cracking it and pushing it up on his face. He reached for the mask to clear the water, just in time to see the huge white teeth race at his face. Brody moved as best he could in the water to try and evade the massive, six-foot-long predator attacking him. He knew he was way down the list of predators in this environment; probably lower than the bait fish. Everything down here had time—except him. He twisted once again, drawing his knife from its plastic scabbard. Then he slashed at the fish in the water as he still pushed for the surface. The animal seemed to suddenly feel the pain from the spear and moved off into the darkness. Brody saw the line was still attached and headed away from the injured fish as he desperately swam toward the fresh air. He broke the surface and shouted, "Gumbao, the buoys, don't let them sink." Gumbao jumped into the water and swam to the last buoy sitting quietly on the surface, and as he reached it the fish started pulling for the depths, almost yanking it out of his hand.

"Hassan, give me another spear. I need to get another shot, or it will disappear into the rocks." Hassan threw him the second spear and fed out the line. "Keep that line on the boat," shouted Brody as he ducked back under the water.

The fish was spinning in the blue at about sixty feet. Brody knew he was bleeding into the ocean, this and the panicked fish would definitely bring the big boys for a free meal. He pushed himself, making long kicks with his legs to move him as fast as possible. His adrenaline was spiking, and he had not been able to get a good lungful of air on the surface; he would not last long. He reached the line to the buoys and pulled hard, dragging himself down toward the fish. He got as close as he could then fired the second spear into the animal, much closer to the heart, but it was not done yet. As Brody turned, he saw a dark grey cylinder swim past him in the darkness. *Shit,* he thought, *a bull or tiger shark has come to the party.* Brody spun in the water; there were more important things to think about now. The shark had been attracted by the blood in the water from his leg. It swam toward him but turned at the last minute, brushing its coarse grey skin against his hands. Brody started heading for the surface. The tuna was done, and he could see it being dragged up. The sharks had to be kept away for a few seconds longer. He spun frantically in the water, trying to look in every direction at once. The fourteen-foot-bull shark came racing out of the blue, directly at him with its mouth open, ready to plunge its teeth into his body. Brody forced himself to wait and look straight at the shark. Just before it hit him, he grabbed its snout and pushed up with all of his might, forcing the shark's head upwards. The next lunge came so fast Brody almost lost his hand. He punched the shark on the nose to make it turn in the water. The animal twisted in the water, but it was not happy and swam away. As he finned for the brighter light above, he could see the sharks gathering below. One shot up from the crowd and snapped at his fins, but Brody kicked it in the side of the head, which made it veer off.

Brody broke the surface but kept his head down and breathed through his snorkel. Jalal was shouting, "Get it out of the water fast, or we lose it."

Hassan and Gumbao hauled the line in and pulled the animal to the side of the boat, Brody swam up and stuck the flying gaff into the gills of the fish so they could get it out of the water. But his second shot had hit the mark and the animal finally stopped thrashing around. As soon as the fish was on deck Brody launched himself out of the water and stared back as the fins started circling the boat.

Chapter Fourteen

Achiba Baktari

Shukran had docked in Shimoni, a town Brody was familiar with. Jalal wished them well, but he knew he would only get in the way if he stayed, so he had jumped on the early ferry heading to Pemba. Once the dhow was tied off and safe in the hands of one of Hassan's cousins, they boarded a matatu. Hassan, as usual, slid into the front seat next to the other three passengers, Brody and Gumbao were forced into the backseats with what felt like fifty shouting schoolkids heading to the main road to catch another matatu heading toward Kwale and school. "We ride this one until the Kanana Market, then we take another to Mkomba," shouted Hassan.

"Did your uncle give us any more information on how to find this guy?" asked Brody.

"No, he just told us to go to Mkomba then follow the trail toward Shimba Hills."

Brody sat back and watched as the mud huts with coconut palms for roofs flashed past his window. Kids played in the dirt or kicked a football made of old plastic bags tied with string while the mothers pounded maize, the long pole rhythmically rising and falling, smashing the pearly grains to dust. Gumbao was sitting in the row behind him and as usual was fast asleep. But Brody couldn't get comfortable, his mind had been racing ever since he had managed to clamber onto the boat at Latham Island. The premonition the old woman had in Kiwayu had been frighteningly accurate. When he spoke to Hassan, he was full of logic and reason. However, when he sat with his own thoughts, the coincidences were just building up. How could that old hag have possibly seen him in the water fighting off a bloody bull shark? It was just too much, no one could have guessed that. How the hell had she known he was on his last breath. The girl in Zanzibar had also spooked him. He tried to logically explain everything to himself, but there was a nagging doubt. The girl had always turned up at an opportune moment and managed to save them from certain death. Why, and how, and who the fuck was she? His brain was having problems fighting toward logic. The more he thought about it the bigger the headache became.

When they arrived at the market the next matatu was somewhere between Mombasa and them. There was nothing to do but wait; there were no timetables or an office to ask at. It was just wait and see. If it arrived, then fine, if not then another day would be wasted by the side of the road. They sat with a group of older women heading back to Mkomba after selling their fruits in the market. The ladies chatted, enjoying the break from their long and arduous days. Gumbao quickly became bored and said, "I'm going to look for a drink, make the driver honk the horn and I'll come running."

"But what if he is in a hurry, he's late already?" said Hassan.

"Just make him wait, I'll be one minute away."

Hassan whispered under his breath, "I've heard that before, we probably won't see him for days."

Brody lay on the dirt beside the road in silence. He had managed to get some shade under a young neem tree. But his shirt was soaking, and his eyes were stinking from the salt that constantly ran in rivulets down his forehead. After an hour of waiting, an orange and green bug appeared in the distance with a plume of dust behind it. The ladies began gathering their bags and boxes as the matatu arrived at the marketplace. Hassan got in the front seat and asked the driver to blow the horn. Gumbao's head appeared from a small metal hut, and he jogged over to the vehicle. The conductor ran around the group, trying to organize the boxes and bags. He threw three up onto the roof to a man who tied them down, then settled in between them for his ride to Mkomba. The women pushed their way onto the already full vehicle as Brody and Gumbao stood watching, "There's no way we'll get on that," said Brody.

Gumbao just grinned. "He wants our money. They'll find a way."

The conductor grabbed a large crate of chickens from the back of the vehicle. The owner started to complain but was just ignored. He motioned to Brody to clamber in and take the place of the chickens at the back of the bus. While Brody climbed over bodies and boxes the conductor tied the chickens to the front radiator of the matatu. Then he slapped his hand on the side of the vehicle, which was the signal to get moving. The matatu lurched forward and Gumbao jumped onto the running rail and looped his arm through the sliding door next to the conductor.

Brody half crouched, half stood over the wheel arch of the vehicle. His shoulders were hunched as the ceiling was low. He tried to make himself comfortable, but he had to either press his head against the sealed window or stare down the cleavage of the buxom woman perched on the edge of the next seat. The matatu rattled along the road at what felt like a breakneck speed. Each pothole was keenly felt as the old shock absorbers hit their stops and the van jarred them or bounced them up toward the ceiling. On one occasion, when the vehicle was racing around a particularly difficult curve on a hill, Brody slipped and planted his face in the older woman's chest. She shrieked, then burst into a fit of giggles as she pushed him off. The matatu managed to handle the curve, then raced into a river crossing. Water rushed into the matatu as the engine labored to drag them across the river and up the far bank.

Brody had been hanging on for dear life for what felt like an eternity, and had given up all hope of not invading the woman's space next to him. Sweat was pouring down his face just from the sheer effort of holding on. Then the vehicle skidded to a halt next to a mud house. The conductor appeared and slid the door open and shouted "Mkomba." Brody breathed out and let his shoulders relax as the women closer to the door slid out, then the rest of them untangled themselves and alighted from the bus. Gumbao jumped down from the running rail, releasing a cloud of dust from his clothes. Hassan slid out of the passenger door looking like he had been in first class.

"This is our stop," he said. "From here we walk."
"We ain't going anywhere today man," said Brody. "I'm knackered after that ride, and I need a drink, a meal, and a wash, in that order. I'm

following him." he pointed to Gumbao, who had wandered off toward what Brody hoped was a cold beer. "And I am going to sit and relax. It's already four; the sun will be gone soon. We'll head out tomorrow first thing."

"But we are losing time?"

"I know," said Brody, "and I understand. But if we go wandering around in the bush at night, we will probably get eaten by something and then what use would we be?"

Hassan shrugged his shoulders. "I'll go and pray, then see what I can find out about Achiba Baktari and come find you."

By the time Brody had caught up with Gumbao, he was seated in a cracked, white plastic lawn chair inside a dimly lit bar with a metal roof and a mud floor. A scarred glitter ball hung from the roof, hinting at better times. The place smelled of old beer and cigarettes. At the back of the bar under a separate awning was a pool table with six lean young men lounging and smoking, their picki picki motorcycles parked next to them, ready to go and collect a new fare. A young girl approached the table and asked, "Unataka nyama choma?" *Do you want bbq meat?*

Brody wanted to practice his Kiswahili. He said, "Ndiyo, mnanyama gani?" *I do, what meat do you have?*

The girl looked surprised. Gumbao just smiled and lit a cigarette.

"Tuna mbuzi tu." *We only have goat.*

"Sawa lete kilo moja. Halaful una Tusker baridi?" *O.K., bring one kilo. Do you have cold beer?*

"Hapana, hakuna stima hapa, Tusker moto tu." *No, we have no electricity, we only have warm beer.*

"Sawa, lete mbili kwanza." *O.K., bring two first.*

Brody and Gumbao drank their beer and ate their meat as the chirps and squeals of the jungle started penetrating the bar. Occasionally one of the boys would jump on his picki picki and head off into the dark then return with two or three passengers on the back of his bike. Some would stop for a drink, and others were just waiting for the next matatu to rattle past.

At sunrise, Hassan was pacing on the track outside the three rooms he had booked. Brody pulled open the door, a towel around his waist, wincing as the sun hit his face. "Where's the shower?"

Hassan pointed to a rectangular metal structure about fifty feet away. "Here, take the bucket."

As soon as they were ready, Hassan led them toward a path leading away from the huts. "This is the way. I asked around after prayers last night—a guy told me to head for the waterfalls, and we should find Achiba Bakari. But he said he was mad, and we were probably wasting our time!"

"Sounds like a normal day then," said Brody.

They walked into the morning sun and were soon guzzling on the water bottles Hassan had put in their packs. The five warm Tuskers from the night before were not helping their journey. They gradually climbed out of the small depression that Mkomba called home. The path twisted between thorny, stunted acacia trees, many with the bark ripped off from the elephants passing through. They dodged huge piles of brown, grassy dung still steaming from the night before, busy beetles rolling huge balls of it away to their homes. "How fresh is this?" asked Brody.

"It looks about six or eight hours," answered Gumbao.

After hours of climbing, the broken path came out onto a huge plateau. Spreading out in front of them was grassland all the way to the glistening, sapphire-blue ocean in the distance. Brody stared out into the African plain, "Is that buffaloes down there?"

"Yes," said Hassan. "This whole area is known as Shimba Hills, it's a reserve."

"You mean there are lions and shit around here?"

"I'm not sure. I was told only leopards. But the buffaloes are the ones you have to watch out for."

"Shit," said Brody. "Which way do we go?"

"We carry on upwards, following this path," said Hassan. "Then there is a valley we have to look for."

They trudged up the hill, higher and higher. The sun was beating, and their water was gone. The bush had given way to thick, tall grassland with the occasional acacia tree. Hassan pointed to a ridge about halfway up the next hill. "That looks like what my friend described."

They walked through the thickening tall grass, finding it more and more difficult to follow the broken path. Gumbao stopped. "Look," he pointed, "those are a large cat's footprint. It came along here a while ago. Probably last night."

"Let's hope he got his dinner and is asleep in a tree right now," said Brody.

They left the six-foot-tall grass behind them as they climbed toward the ridge line. When they reached the top of the ridge they looked down on another valley. The grass thinned out as trees covered the floor of the valley below. Elephants wandered around in small groups, the matriarch leading the youngsters on well-trodden paths. Then a small group of young bulls hoping for a chance followed behind. The path twisted and turned between grey rocks and boulders down onto the valley floor. They continued to walk, feeling better as they dropped into the cooler valley where the trees started to give some shade. Hassan said, "Hear that? It sounds like a stream; we can get some water."

Brody and Gumbao quickened their step as the alcohol from the night before had left them feeling groggy. A clear stream burbled over small sandy shale as it flowed along the center of the valley. It twisted and turned as it encountered huge boulders the size of trucks. When Brody saw it, he plunged his head in, feeling the coolness of the water seep into his skull. They sat by the river and ate mandazis while they cooled off. With the water bottles refilled they decided to continue along the side of the stream. Black and white colobus monkeys leapt gracefully from tree to tree above them, watching the newcomers with their sad faces. Each break in the forest had brown and black sable antelopes who stood like statues and stared at them as they walked across the glade. The buck, with two-feet-long horns, would stamp his feet then herd his harem into the trees for cover. Finally, when the sun was heading toward the western ridges of the valley, they noticed the sound of a waterfall in the distance. Hassan said, "We should move quickly, so we are there before dark."

They covered the last two miles and stood on the bank of the now 100-foot-wide river that abruptly stopped in front of them as the water split into six different flows and then disappeared over the edge. In the middle of the river, a herd of elephant had come down for their evening ablutions. A baby played on the opposite bank, rolling in the soft mud. The mother kept a watchful eye on her child as she stood up to her stomach in the cool waters. A bright white bird stood on the matriarch's back and pecked at the ticks.

Brody shouted, "We need to find a way down."

They searched around the edge of the falls. Gumbao shouted over the sound of the water, "This looks good, there seems to be some sort of path here," he pointed at what looked like a sheer cliff covered in bright green lichen heading down beside the falls. "We can climb down this way and use that tree to get the rest of the way." Then he was gone, clambering down the rocks hand over hand. Hassan followed, gripping each handhold as if his life depended on it. At about the halfway mark, there was a ledge that led away from the water. Gumbao followed the narrow walkway until he came to an old bamba coffee tree with thick limbs brushing up to the rock face. "Here, we just climb down this tree, and we are done." Gumbao stepped out onto a branch, then slithered along until he came to the trunk. Within a few minutes they were all on the ground at the base of the tree.

"It's getting late. What do we do now?" asked Brody.

"We follow our noses until we find Achiba Bakari and hope he is around," said Hassan.

A circular pool about fifty feet across sat in front of the falling water. The water was crystal clear and looked very inviting. On the far side of the pool the water overflowed down a series of small rapids then formed a new river heading toward the ocean. The falls were about 100 feet high. The water cascaded down and hit a solid stone platform then flowed into the pool. Brody climbed up on the slimy rocks and put his head into the falling water. Then he stepped through and disappeared. A few seconds later his arm came back through the curtain of water and waved them in. The water cascaded in front of them like a moving curtain, but the path was dry and looked well-worn. "This must be the way," said Brody. "Look, they have even left rubbish." He kicked a plastic bottle. They followed the rough stone path and appeared on the far side of the falls. Hassan took the lead and headed up a slope following the path. It was only a few minutes before they smelled smoke. Hassan pointed: "Look, a fire, up there by that cave."

When they reached the fire, a young woman was sitting next to it with a round piece of dough in her hand which she was kneading then smashing down onto a flat rock. Her hair had been shaved close to her scalp. She was wearing an old pair of jeans and a ragged T-shirt. Across her legs she had spread a brightly colored piece of cloth called a kanga. The young woman didn't look up from her work as she said, "What do you people want?"

Hassan stepped forward, "We have come to see Achiba Bakari, we can pay."

"He's sleeping now, he does not rise until the moon comes out. Why do you want to see him?"

"I'm searching for my sister; we were told on Unguja that he could tell us where to look."

She didn't answer as she threw the dough down onto the flat rock and picked up a dark red clay pot from the ground. "Take this, and fill it with water."

Hassan, stood up again, feeling a little crestfallen, and took the gourd then wandered off toward the pool below the waterfall.

Gumbao had sat on a rock next to the cave entrance. "Girl, are you his wife?"

"No, he is too old and doesn't like women. My mother was sick, and my father had no money but wanted medicine, so I have to work here until he releases me."

"Have you been here long?"

"I don't know. I feel older, I was just a girl when I came," she pointed at her budding breasts. "These were only mosquito bites."

Brody felt for the girl, but he understood that in a country where many of the people survived on less than two dollars a day, situations like this often occurred. At least she had not been forced to be the old man's wife.

Hassan returned with the clay pot and the girl pointed to the fire, so he placed it in the embers at the edge. "He will need his food before he helps you, so you had better get comfortable."

"What is your name?" asked Hassan.

"I'm Kadzo," she said.

Brody said, "I'm Brody and these are my friends, Hassan and Gumbao."

Kadzo lifted her head from her work. "Nice to meet you. We do not get that many visitors out here."

They settled down by the fire. Hassan produced some coffee and flour from his rucksack and started working with Kadzo.

Gumbao took a line and a hook out of his pocket, then lit a cigarette and wandered down to the pool below the waterfall. He settled on a large boulder blessed with the evening sun and watched the waters below. It only took him a few minutes to see some heads dodging in and out of small crevices around the rocks. He baited his hook and expertly landed it in front of the unsuspecting tilapia. One popped out and eagerly nibbled at the free meal, then another chased it away and approached the baited hook. Gumbao waited until the greedy fish was tucking into the worm on the end of the hook then gave it a quick sharp tug and pulled the fish up onto the rock. Within thirty minutes he had six gutted tilapias ready for the fire.

Brody sat away from the group. He was always amazed at how people in this wonderful country he had adopted as his own could settle and share. Kadzo was chatting away with Hassan, a man she had met only an hour ago. He was sharing his flour and making coffee for everyone, and she was busy frying the chapatis. Gumbao had headed off to the pond and now had a string of fish. When he had been in the army, a three- or four-day trek through the African bush would have taken six weeks' prep. Their packs always weighed in excess of sixty pounds—tents, mosi nets, ration packs, water, tablets, medical packs and changes of clothing, to mention only a few items. Now he walked with a two-liter bottle of water and some bags of beans or flour that Hassan had insisted he carried. That was it, and they managed, no problem. In fact, he was looking forward to his meal.

The darkness quickly surrounded them. A long low groan emitted from inside the cave. Kadzo looked up with a smile, her bright white teeth shining in the firelight. "Here comes Achiba, he is not as bad as he sounds," she said. Then she got to her feet and picked up another clay bowl full of water and walked to the fire. She prodded a round stone and deftly picked it up with a forked stick and dropped it into the water, which immediately started to bubble. "He likes hot water to wash with." Then she carried it into the cave. Brody was enjoying his coffee as he watched the fish skin start to split and peel as the rock in the center of the fire got hotter and hotter. The chapatis had been finished and wrapped in a bright green banana leaf. He took another sip of his sugary coffee and felt good for a moment. The thoughts of Zainab were just at the edge of his mind; a moment of peace.

They heard footsteps from the cave, and all looked up not knowing what to expect from this legendary man. Brody had never seen a witch doctor before and thought it would be something like the *Tarzan* films he had watched as a child. He knew they were all over the coast as there were signs on most of the electricity poles claiming spells and magic that could change your business or help you find your loved one. He was not let down: a small, wiry man walked out of the cave wearing a black headdress of ostrich feathers sprouting in all directions. Below that, covering his forehead, was a thick string of brightly colored shells all carefully strung together with what looked like a silk thread. The first thing Brody noticed about the man was his smile. It was bright and beaming, making everyone in the room feel just a little bit better. His nose was flat, leading to a large forehead. He had small eyes that darted around the fire. He looked at them all, then produced a clay pipe from his leopard-skin wrap that hung around his shoulders. He slowly and meticulously packed the bowl of the pipe then lit it with an ember from the fire. He was an old man, probably in his seventies, but he had fared well. His limbs were long and wiry—they had once been strong, but were now sinewy. His skin glowed in the darkness from what smelled like coconut oil he had liberally applied to his chest, arms, and legs. As he moved, the bells on his ankles started to chime. He reached into the darkness at the edge of the cave and produced a long cane. Then he put his tongue between his teeth and let out a loud whistle. After a few seconds he did it again, and then again. He stood waiting, then Brody heard a yapping bark come out of the night behind them. Bakari smiled and said, "Don't be afraid, my fisi comes every night to sit by the fire." A long, brown, dirty, snout appeared on the far side of the clearing. The hyena stealthily walked toward them. Brody held his breath, he cursed himself for not bringing a weapon. Had they walked into a trap? The high-end pack scavenger was known to be lethal, with jaws that cracked femurs with ease. It stalked across the clearing and pushed its head into Bakari's hands like a kitten searching for some love from an old lady. Bakari petted the creature for a few minutes then tapped his cane on the floor beside him. The hyena snarled a few times then lay down by the fire, her brown-flecked fur rising on her back as she eyed the newcomers. "I found fisi when she was a cub. Her mother was trampled by a buffalo. I took her in, and she has been with me ever since." He stroked the lethal animal's head. "She visits me most evenings, before heading off to hunt with her pack. Kadzo tells me you are seeking a sister? But first, we eat and drink, then I will see what we can see in the darkness. Do you have my currency?"

Hassan moved forward. "Here," he said, holding out a small pouch. "We were told by the old women on Unguja that you accept these."

Achiba Bakari tipped the bag of teeth into his palm, then smiled. "These are new, and from an old fish, you must have dived deep to get them. I will help you if I can." Then he tucked the bag into his leopard skin and sat by the fire.

They ate in silence, the old man crunching on the fish bones and chapati as he watched the flames flicker in the fire. The hyena sat at his feet, like a dutiful family pet. When the fish heads were dropped, she eagerly crunched them up, her powerful jaws flexing in the light of the fire.

From time to time, Bakari would look up at one of the group and stare intently into their eyes then go back to his flame watching. Kadzo finished the meal with a gourd of mnazi from the back of the cave. She carried the bright orange gourd on a tray with four plastic cups. Bakari nodded as she approached each of the guests to allow them to drink. When it came to Hassan's turn Achiba said, "You do not partake of the alcohol; I respect a religion and will not force you. Please take some water instead."

Hassan replied, "I thank you, Bakari," and picked up his mug of water then raised his glass to the old man.

"Now," said Achiba, "I see you are travelers"—he nodded toward Brody—"you have traveled very far and wide in this world. You have done and seen many things, but for all of this life you are not a believer, maybe you have seen too much or have lost your way. And you are covered from head to foot in blood. But I might say, the old man is drenched in it. You were both soldiers, but not together. You have both fought many adversaries and are here today only by the grace of any God who smiles on you. The old man, he has traveled too. But only close to his heart. I cannot see his soul—you muzungu wear yours on the outside, but him, he learned long ago to hide his in the depths of his mind. I can see you are troubled, but it is not why you came to see me. I can help you both see the way..."

Brody interrupted, "We're not here for ourselves. We're looking for Zainab."

"Well, you should come back and see me one day, with a big bag of teeth, and I will help you. For now, I will ask our young Muslim why he is here?"

"Sir, I lost my sister some weeks back. Since then, we have been on a journey to find her, from Pemba, to Unguja, then to Kimakazi and now here. I am a good Muslim; I pray to Allah every day and know what I do is good. I even give to the poor when I can. But now my sister is gone. The old women on Unguja said you could help us find her."

"Boy, I can see your soul is pure, you do not have any stains on you at all. You have lived a good life with your God, and he is blessing you. Your journey here is a necessary one, you need to grow and so do your friends. Do you have something of this girl you call your sister?"

Hassan pulled his battered leather wallet out of his kanzu and reverently removed a picture. "This was taken the last time I was at home. Zainab was leaving for the university in Dar. We went to the photo shop and had this taken, so we would never forget who we were."

Achiba studied the photo for a long time. "She is beautiful, no?" He ran his fingers over the outline of the young girl.

"Yes, she has the brains and the looks," said Hassan.

"Ah, you are not too bad yourself, boy. Not my type, too straight for me," laughed Achiba.

"Now, girl, go and get my bag. And fill the cups, we have a lot of work to do here." Kadzo stepped in and refilled the cups with the vile-smelling mnazi. Brody had almost gagged at the first one and now gingerly took the second. Achiba looked at him and smiled at the obvious pain in Brody's face. Then he lifted his cup and toasted them. Brody swallowed his mnazi in one go, it was the only thing to do. He felt the sweet, rotting coconut slide down his throat and hit his stomach; there would be problems later!

Kadzo returned with a cardboard box that had bags and smaller boxes stacked neatly inside. Achiba spent some time fiddling with the insides of the box and muttering to himself, then he produced a small leather pouch. He lifted his head, "They are telling me this is the one to use. I have not used these bones in a long time. I collected them when I was wandering, long before I found this home. I used to walk from town to town offering my services. These bones I found in a small town near this Dar you are talking about. There's a lot of magic in that area, the demons are hundreds of years old. The Arabs brought their own devils to this place, and they married our devils and grew into such a force. They hide in the light, and the dark. Some are good and help us, but others are evil beyond comprehension. The good always fights the bad, which is the same in any world. But these bad spirits, or genies or whatever you call them, suck the life out of any human that lets them in. You have spoken to the good ones, and you muzungu have one watching your every move. Do you not feel it?"

Brody looked up from the fire. "No, I have no idea what you mean."

"Well, the shape comes to you when you most need it. It has saved you on several occasions and still looks over your shoulder, even today, right now it is around. I can sense it. Somewhere up in the trees or hiding behind a rock. But you are a non-believer, your mind was twisted many years ago, so you are blind to these things. But your life will be long, and your eyes will open."

Brody's head was spinning, he had never seen or heard a person talk like this. His life was full of logic and reason. Science explained everything he needed to know. Now, some old gay guy in the bush was sort of hinting at his life and hitting points that only he knew. Was he that easy to read? He had always thought of himself as a tough fighting man. A stoic warrior, fighting for the good in the world. Now, it seemed this old man could read him like a book.

Bakari continued, "Old man, you have no interest in this. You have already lived long and hard. But I can tell you. Your life has not been wasted as you think, there are many good deeds to be done before you end this time around."

He emptied the bones from the bag into his palm and stared at them. "They are from a long-lost soul who died at the hands of the takers. These are the same shapes that have your sister. His head was smashed when I came across him. He had jumped or fallen off a high cliff. I was told to dig into his ears and pull these bones as they would let me hear what the evil ones were saying." He shook the tiny bones in his hand, then he took the picture of Zainab and placed the bones on them then rubbed his hands together above them. A smoke appeared and the hyena growled deep and low as its beady eyes flicked from person to person. Bakari moved onto his haunches, his feet flat on the ground and started rocking back and forwards. The flames of the fire seemed to flick higher into the sky. Kadzo sat forward, enjoying the show.

Bakari looked at the stars and howled into the night. He opened his eyes wide, but they were just the whites. The hyena stood up, its tail flicking this way and that as it peered into the darkness. Brody twisted to follow the animal's gaze, the sweat dried on his skin, there was nothing there but the black of the night. Hassan went to his knees and bowed his head; all he knew to do was pray the Bismillah to his god.

Bakari started chanting and talking in tongues, spitting words into the fire, talking what sounded like gibberish as he rocked closer and closer to the fire. The hyena jumped over the fire and ran into the night. Bakari kept howling, then chanting, then rocking. His fingers running over the picture, he picked up the tiny bones and clenched them in one fist as he arched his back and screamed into the night. His legs suddenly straightened, lifting him up to his full height. He sprang forward, landing in the middle of the fire and kicked at the flames. His skin was glistening as the flames licked at his skin. He stood there for a second chanting and mumbling, calling someone to talk to him.

Kadzo watched with wide bright eyes. She was scared now; she had never seen her master acting this mad before. "Get out of the fire!" she shouted.

Brody came back to his senses and leaped to his feet, but then he heard a low growl behind him and froze.

Achiba stood in the flames, his bare feet on the stones they had used to cook the fish. His naked legs were being licked by the flames.

Brody turned and saw two glowing eyes staring at him; he was rooted to the spot.

Hassan was chanting from the Koran. The old man stood, his eyes rolled back, and he shouted at the new moon as it appeared above them.

Bakari screamed again, then leapt forward once more, pushing Brody over as he ran into the night. A few seconds later he ran back into the camp, then he ran around the fire three times and kicked at the embers, sending them up into the air.

Then he sat on a ledge and shook himself from head to foot. Kadzo stood and took an earthenware pot from the floor and approached him. She dipped a cloth into the pot and started wiping the ash from Bakari's legs. He just sat with his eyes closed and mumbled incoherently.

Brody looked at the old man's feet, expecting to see third-degree burns and blisters, but the skin was pink and soft. He looked into the darkness for the glowing yellow eyes, but they had gone.

Hassan sensed it was calming and lifted his head. Bakari spoke, "Did you know there were elephants at the top of the waterfall?" He pushed Kadzo away, ordering her, "Bring me a drink."

Brody was handed a cup of mnazi and just gulped it down. This evening had been a once-in-a-lifetime event and he needed a drink. Anything would do at this point.

Bakari sat for a long time with his eyes closed. He slowly moved his arms and his legs as if he was feeling them for the first time. When his breathing was back to normal, he looked at Hassan. "I have seen many things tonight that I believed were long forgotten. You are very frightened; I can smell it on you. Your sister is lost, but not lost completely. She is in a very dark place with spirits that are strong, they hold her heart and her soul. It will not be easy to get her back. I do not say this lightly. She was taken by a force that has been growing on our soil for nearly 500 years. She showed how clever she was—they love that and feed from it day and night. She is weak now, they have gorged on her many times, but I can feel her source, and it is still bright. You must go from here when the sun rises and head back to your shiny boat. There is a place she has been taken. A place far from here. You must go south and find a tiny plot of land in the vast ocean, it is five days' travel. You must go to Songo Songo Island, there you will find the big white boat tied to a long jetty. It will be very dangerous for you. If you do not stay together, you will die." He looked at Gumbao. "You know what has happened here, you have seen it in the jungles when you were no more than a child. You will guide these two. That is it. I am finished. I have earned my teeth. Now I will drink to rid myself of what I have seen."

"What—" said Hassan. "That's it? You can't help us anymore?"

"What more do you want? I can only do so much. I have a sight, but you are asking me to look into hell itself. I am a strong healer, but I am not evil; they are. Well beyond your imagination."

He spoke to Brody. "Brody, learn to listen to your friend, it is around and will help to show you the way. It is a warrior like you, and on the right side of this. If you listen, then it will show you. But you must believe."

Everyone fell silent. Gumbao picked up the gourd of mnazi, poured himself a cup then handed it to Bakari, who took a long draft from the gourd, the foul-smelling liquid pouring down his face. He dropped the gourd to the floor and said, "Girl. Another." Then slumped back onto the ground in front of the fire and wrapped his blanket around his shoulders.

Chapter Fifteen
Shimoni Jetty

Brody sat in a bar next to the Shimoni stone jetty. He was on his fourth cold Tusker, a dirty plate with a few beans and half a chapati sat in front of him. It had taken them two days to get back to *Shukran*. Once they were on board, he had plotted a route to Songo Songo Island, which was about 250 nautical miles, but they would have to make several long tacks which increased the distance to more like 500. Hassan had gone to the market to get food and water for the trip. Gumbao was busy shouting at a man stood up in a dug-out canoe with twenty-liter jerry cans full of diesel precariously balanced in his unstable craft. The man's feet were awash with an oily mixture of sea water and fuel, and Gumbao was trying to bribe the man by passing him his half-smoked cigarette as they haggled over the price of the fuel.

It had taken all morning for Brody to go over the dhow and make sure they were shipshape. The tide was changing at three in the afternoon, which would take them out to Pemba Channel where they would thread themselves between the mainland and Zanzibar, before heading out into deeper water and sailing down to Songo Songo right on the southern edge of Tanzania.

The journey would take about four days if all went well. Hassan had been shouting at everyone since they had returned. Brody understood his frustration, but he also knew they were going into dangerous waters which had no coast guard or backup. They needed to be prepared, and at least have food, water, and fuel. He did not know when they would be back, and in fact if they would be back. Achiba Bakari had really freaked Brody out with his matter-of-fact way of being able to read him. Brody had felt naked in front of the man. He was still holding onto his scientific beliefs, but they had been shaken to their bedrock with all the things that had happened over the last week or so. He was beginning to think Hassan was not as wrong as he had thought. There were just too many coincidences that would not add up.

Shukran pulled away from the jetty and headed out toward Pemba Channel. The breeze felt good on Brody's face. Hassan was at the tiller with a stern look on his face. Brody had never seen this side of his friend; it was almost frightening. He stood on the bow watching the land go by, a shoal of tiny bait fish leapt out of the crystal-clear water on the port side. The fish were like tiny silver arrows flying through the air then hitting the water like rain. Gulls hung above the show waiting to dart in and grab one to take back to their young on Wasini Island. Brody stared at the strange island as it passed them by. Huge baobabs clung onto the cliff edge, their twisted roots, like thick sailor's arms, grabbing hold of the coral and clutching for dear life, spindly branches still pushing for the sky laden with dark green seed pods the size of grapefruits. Brody thought to himself that most would fall into the ocean and be washed away to foreign lands where the tree could sprout and start again.

As soon as they were clear of the malango, Brody shouted to Gumbao, "We need to get this sail up. Come help me pull and tie it off."

Hassan turned *Shukran* into the wind while Brody and Gumbao hauled the boom up the mast. It banged and whacked madly in the rising wind, which made the task more difficult. If this had been a pleasure trip, they would still be sitting next to the harbor wall. But they needed to get to Songo Songo as quickly as they could. Brody tied off the line to hold the boom in place and felt the dhow roll as she pitched over a wave. Gumbao tied the end of the boom to the bow cleat and pulled the sail away from the boom, then ran back to the stern as Hassan put them onto a southeasterly course. The new course would take them past Zanzibar, then they would adjust their heading and beat almost due east. Then several more tacks to take them to Songo Songo.

The ocean was dark and ominous as the light started to fade. White caps were starting to form and there was spray on the deck. The engine was turned off. *Shukran* was a displacement hull, with a maximum speed through the water of eight knots. It didn't matter if you fitted a jet engine on the back, she would still only go at that speed. With the wind rising, they had already hit the top speed. Brody stood on the bow with the rising wind blowing in his face; he was worried, the clouds in front of them were gathering high up in the sky. He had learned through bitter experience this was an ominous sign, not to be ignored. He walked like a drunk back to the stern as the dhow ploughed through heavier and heavier seas. "Hassan, do you think we should pull into Zanzibar and let this pass?"

"We have to get to Songo Songo. We have wasted enough time already. These waves will not pick up any further. We'll be fine."

Brody looked at his friend of many years. He knew he was lying and sending them toward more danger, but he also knew the man was fighting for his family, which meant everything to him. "Fine, my friend. If you say so, then we're in. Gumbao, tie everything down, put the cushions in the lockers and break out the lifejackets."

Hassan put on his bright yellow life jacket just as the first drops of rain hit the deck. Gumbao had retired to his engine room as usual, but Brody had opted to stand next to his friend. The rain came in gusts, whipping the narrow Pemba Channel waters into a frenzy. The shallow water became treacherous very quickly as the waves started to mount against the bow. First the rain lashed down on the roof of the stern cabin, but as the wind picked up, it started to change its angle and come directly at them. Hassan was squinting into the failing light, holding the tiller with both hands to maintain their course. The bow of *Shukran* rose out of the water then plunged back into the trough of the wave. Water threw itself over the bow and ran down the gunnels, flooding the stern as it went. Brody tightened his life jacket; this was going to be a roller-coaster ride. The night wore on as they battled the wind and the waves. After the third or fourth wave had broken over the nose of *Shukran* Brody opened the hatch to the engine room. Gumbao was feverishly pumping the manual bilge pump with water washing around his ankles. "How bad is it?" he shouted.

Gumbao looked up from his work, "The electric pumps are not strong enough for this. But I'm sure we'll be fine; she has seen rougher waters." Brody slammed the hatch as he felt the bow rise and then fall into an even bigger trough. He was almost knocked off his feet as the wave sluiced along the deck. Hundreds of gallons of water were flowing along the gunnels and back into the sea. Hassan stood firm at his post for six hours straight as they plunged through the night. At midnight Brody tried to take over the tiller, but Hassan stood resolutely as if he was challenging the universe to stop him finding his sister and refused the offer.

As the eastern horizon started showing signs of life, faint outlines appeared in front of them as the new grey day started. Brody was happy to see the morning coming, but with the light came the sights around them. The ocean was grey and dark, it was showing no mercy. He felt a shiver run down his back as he looked at the growing dawn. It was going to be a hard day. During the night they had managed to alter course and head out into the dark ocean. According to the HDS 10 they were almost twenty miles offshore, nearly time for a tack. Brody opened the hatch to find Gumbao still pumping and said, "Come up, we need your help."

All three of them looked like drowned rats with nothing around them but dark grey waves. Hassan said, "We need to tack. I'll pull her into the wind. Be careful, everything is slippery and wet."

Gumbao took the main sheet as it started to flap in the wind and Brody started pulling the sail into the boom. The heavy wet material cut at his hands as he tried to roll it along the boom. Gumbao joined him, fighting the soaking sail as it flapped in the almost gale-force winds. They pulled and tightened the sail cloth, rolling it with tired hands, wringing out the water as they went. Brody was the first to the bow which was now rising and falling at an alarming rate. Gumbao shouted, "I'll go first and pass it all to you."

"No," Brody shouted over the wind. "You get ready to receive the boom."

Gumbao was not happy, but he knew there was no sense in arguing, so he hung onto the side rail next to the bow and watched his friend slip and slide forward, holding the boom with the sail wrapped tightly in a roll underneath.

Brody gingerly moved forward trying to keep his balance as the boat rode over the waves, pitching and rolling as the troughs and peaks passed under the boat. He managed to wedge himself above the front locker, jamming his feet under the bowsprit. Every time the bow started its downward journey gravity seemed to vanish and his stomach would come up to his chin, as if riding a deadly roller coaster going over the top and plunging down with the crowd screaming. He grabbed the end of the long heavy boom and juggled it in his arms like a baby. It was almost impossible to manhandle it around the top of the mast. But after several attempts he was starting to get the feel of the boat and the long wooden pole in his arms. A wave came and threw him up, so he used the momentum to twist the long pole, and as he watched it banged against the top of the mast once then twice. At that point *Shukran* had mounted the wave and was teetering on the edge as she started to plunge down the other side. Brody clamped the bowsprit between his legs and twisted the slippery wood in his arms, sending the top of the boom over the starboard side. As he released the grip with his thighs the boom twisted and the bottom shot out, lifting Brody into the air and throwing him ten feet into the air. He instinctively curled his body into a ball as he was thrown over the side of *Shukran* and into the boiling waters.

Hassan saw what was happening and immediately threw the stern line overboard and shouted to Brody to swim back.

Brody plunged into the frigid waters and came up spluttering. He immediately looked around. *Shukran* was already twenty or thirty feet away; she was almost disappearing in the waves. He just saw Hassan waving his arms pointing to the back of *Shukran*.

Gumbao ran with the rope to the stern and tied it off then dived into the hatch and started the engine.

As Gumbao came back on deck, Hassan shouted, "Can you see him?"

Gumbao looked all around the boat and ran to the bow looking in all directions. Then he spotted a bright orange jacket, and shouted, "There, to the port. About 100 yards."

Hassan pushed the tiller hard to starboard, forcing *Shukran* back into the heavy ocean waves.

Brody spat out what felt like his hundredth mouthful of water as he was washed along, powerless to do anything against the heavy seas. He had started swimming toward *Shukran* but soon realized it was a waste of his energy. The best thing he could do was hope and wait for Hassan to come and collect him. He would need all of his energy for the rescue.

Gumbao kept his arm outstretched, pointing to Brody in the ocean, as Hassan maneuvered *Shukran*. The seas were too heavy to just pluck their friend from the ocean. If they got too close the hull would probably slam down on Brody and smash his skull to smithereens. Hassan decided to swing around the man in the water and hopefully he would be able to grab the rope that was trailing behind. Brody watched as *Shukran* loomed over the waves. Gumbao was waving at him, but it took him a few minutes to understand what they were doing. It finally dawned on him what the plan was and he started swimming toward where he hoped the rope would be dragging through the water. But *Shukran* had been lifted by a wave surfing fifty feet away from him. It took another twenty minutes before Hassan could line himself up for another run.

Brody was beginning to feel the exhaustion kick in. He had been desperately trying to keep the salt water from this mouth, but as time wore on and wave after wave washed over him he was losing the will to keep up. He watched as Hassan lined up *Shukran* on a course that would pass around and in front of him. This time he had to catch the rope, or he was doomed. The dhow rode a wave which also lifted Brody high in the water, then she surfed past him riding the crest. Brody watched her pass, then broke into a panicked freestyle, heading for the bow of *Shukran*. He knew he would miss the whole boat, but he hoped he would snag the rope. He powered through the water, swimming like he had never swum before, the vital, bulging life jacket making his stroke clumsy and slow. He lifted his head to get a breath and saw the rope slithering past him like a snake in the water, but it was too far for him to reach. He put his head back down and used the last of his willpower to push himself through the water. He felt a lump hit his head and with the next stroke his arm wrapped around the slimy rope. He slid along for a few seconds then hit the knot at the end and held on for dear life.

Gumbao had been watching from the stern and shouted, "He has it. Bring us around."

Hassan immediately brought *Shukran* back into the wind and let the sails flap. They hauled on the rope, dragging Brody back toward the stern of *Shukran*. Brody tried to help but felt exhausted and knew he was going to have to climb the ladder. When they got within ten feet Brody signaled for them to stop pulling. He sat in the water gathering his strength for the final swim. He watched the ladder on the back of *Shukran* as it rose and fell. The waves ran underneath the keel, pulling it up about five or six feet above the water then plunging it back in. Brody slowly swam closer and closer to the steel ladder. If it hit him on a downward stroke, he would be skewered to the bottom of the ladder. He watched as *Shukran* pitched in the ocean. Hassan was feverishly pushing the tiller left and right to try and keep her straight into the wind, but the sail kept pulling the boat off course. Gumbao was leaning over the stern high above Brody's head, willing his friend to clamber up the ladder.

Finally, Brody realized he had to move. He treaded water for a few seconds longer, waiting for the ladder to reach the zenith of its cycle. As it plunged into the waves Brody raced forward, his hands reaching for the slippery rungs. One hand managed to grab one of the treads and he was hauled up into the air, his legs dangling below the ladder. He held on for dear life as *Shukran* rode another wave and he was plunged back into the ocean. He managed to retain his grip and his other hand found the next rung as he was pulled out of the water a second time, coughing up the salty water. This time he was ready and heaved himself up with his hands, feeling the pull of his weight in his already knackered arms. He felt gravity leave him as he was taken back down, but now he had two hands on the ladder and had pulled himself up so one foot could slide into the bottom rung. His lungs were full of water, and he coughed as he was dropped back into the ocean. On the third cycle, he had both feet on the bottom rung and was able to move up several steps before he had to hang on for dear life and was dunked in the water again. As *Shukran*'s bow dipped and he was lifted once more he moved four steps up and reached out. Gumbao grabbed his wrist and yanked him up the last three feet and they rolled on to the deck.

Hassan shouted, "Gumbao, untie the sheet, we need to get back on course."

Brody just lay on the deck shivering and coughing up sea water. Once they were back on course Gumbao gave him a blanket and Hassan said, "Sorry, no coffee until these swells stop."

They sailed on through the rest of the day, heading back toward the mainland. Brody sat motionless on the hard wooden seats at the back of the dhow. He had seen death, and felt it; none of the battles he had fought as a soldier had prepared him for the massive strength of the ocean. It was merciless. He kept replaying scenes behind his closed eyes, where he missed the rope, or the ladder crashing down on his head.

As the day wore on and the waves finally started to abate, *Shukran* began to feel like her old self again. The clouds parted and wonderful rays of warming sun hit the deck. Brody stood up and stretched his sore arms and legs then unzipped his life jacket and walked out into the life-giving sunlight. The warmth hitting his skin made him feel human again, he stood absorbing the heat, feeling the deck planks' warmth through his feet. Gumbao came up from below. "Are you feeling more alive?"

Brody smiled at his friend. "I owe you guys my life. That was some maneuver you pulled back there. I really thought I was gone for good. Hassan, that was some brilliant seamanship."

Hassan just nodded. "Gumbao, take the tiller, I need some coffee, and I think I have a few mandazi left."

They tacked *Shukran* again at the end of the day and headed back into the ocean. According to Brody's calculations they had one more ocean tack to make, then they would head directly for Songo Songo. The ocean continued to calm as the evening wore on into night. They were alone in the sea, not another light or ship anywhere around them. The stars finally came out as the clouds cleared. Brody stood watch, holding the tiller and keeping them on a steady southeasterly course. He looked up into the now-clear sky. The Milky Way sat above, he could almost reach out and touch the individual stars. The sky always seemed clearer and brighter after a storm, the air was fresher, the breeze cleaner. He took a huge lungful of air and held his breath for a moment then let it all out. His body relaxed and allowed him to think. Songo Songo was an unknown. The people he was up against were also unknown. He was outmatched in this fight, and he knew it. Achiba Bakari had said the way would be difficult. Brody did not doubt this for one second. What they had seen on Zanzibar with the kids in the dungeon was beyond ruthless. And the white boat had managed to stay at least two steps ahead of them for this whole trip. What if they knew they were coming and had already prepared an ambush? Then all of this would have been in vain, and Zainab would surely die. He started formulating plans in his head but ultimately knew they would not know what to do until they saw the island and assessed the situation.

The following morning *Shukran* was slowly pushed toward Songo Songo, now just visible in the early morning light. Gumbao stood on the bow and looked at the island though the binoculars. "There are loads of dhows fishing just off the leeward side of the island."

"Great," said Brody, "We can use them as cover. Get the lines out and let's look like we're fishing."

The boats seemed to spread out about two miles offshore. Hassan slipped *Shukran* into the line as close to the beach as he dared. Gumbao dropped in some bottom lines and soon had a decent brown grouper. Brody stood on the port side of *Shukran*, idly jigging a line, but he was studying the island. "Where do you think these boats go in the evening?"

"There is probably a small harbor along the coast, we can follow them when the tide turns and see where they end up," said Gumbao.

Chapter Sixteen
Songo Songo Island

They arrived in a large, curved bay at the southerly end of Songo Songo. All the smaller dhows had gone straight to the beach but there were some larger ones sitting at anchor in deeper water. Brody said, "We'll stay out here with these dhows—it'll look less conspicuous."

"From what I've heard these people sell most of their fish to the mainland. These boats are probably buying the catch," said Hassan. "These people are the Matumbi, they are a tribe that only lives on these islands. They don't let us Swahili in, so I have no family here."

Gumbao said, "I'll go into town and see if I can get some ice for these cooler boxes then ask when I can buy the catch. That should keep them off us for a couple of days."

"What happens here, Hassan?"

"They found gas years ago. The government came and drilled. These people are rich, that's why no one is allowed to live here unless you are Matumbi. But they still fish, as the waters are full."

"How will we get ashore," asked Brody.

"We just wait," said Gumbao. "I'll tie a flag to the mast, then they'll know we are looking for a lift."

"Keep everything stowed away," said Brody. "She looks a bit of a mess after the storm. Gumbao, get some ropes from below and hang them around to make us look more like a working dhow."

When they were done the dhow looked a bit shabby, the sail was half hanging from the boom. A small skiff pulled up next to them, the young boys smiling up at the crew. "You want us to take you to the beach?" they shouted.

Gumbao looked down at them. "How much?"

"Old man, we charge 500 shillings each way."

"I'll pay you 200 and you'll be happy."

"No way, old man, you can just sit here and watch the other boats fill with fish. Or maybe you want to swim!" the boys laughed.

"Ah, come on now, let me pay you 600 for two trips."

"We'll take 700 for two trips, but you can't come back late."

Brody nodded, and they jumped into the rocking skiff. The boys immediately started paddling for the shore. Brody looked at the idyllic beach scene in front of him. There were no high-rise buildings as far as he could see. No rubbish or piles of plastic adorned the beach, and the water was as clear as gin. He could see rows of smaller dhows lined up along the beach waiting for the high tide to return. Nets were spread out on the white sand, as men got to work sewing up tears from the sharp coral. Others had spread sails out and were renewing lines or patching holes. There was a hammering coming from one end of the soft white sand as fundis took the opportunity to fix any leaks in the ancient boats that went out each day to fish the rich waters.

Behind the boats were rows of thatched huts with women sitting outside in the afternoon glare. They were sorting the fish their husbands and sons had caught. Some of the fish were gutted, then split along their length with razor-sharp knives, and hung to dry in the salty wind.

A stone-built market with a metal roof stood at one end of the beach. Men dressed the same as Brody, in long kanzus, all seemed to have beards coated with henna and small round hats with a flat top called kofir. Brody adjusted his dirty kofir that Hassan had made him wear to cover his hair.

They landed, and the boys showed them where to come for the return journey.

Hassan said, "I'll go and pray, then see if there's any information. You two wander around and find out what you can. The Matumbi are very strict Muslims, so you won't find any alcohol here."

Brody left Gumbao smoking with some men fixing a net and wandered further into the village. He had already decided that they would visit this place again under nicer circumstances, it was just beautiful. A young boy approached him. "Unataka nazi?" he said. *Do you want a coconut?*

"Bei gani?" said Brody. *How much?*

"Shilingi mia moja," replied the boy. *One hundred shillings.*

"Sawa lete." Brody sat on a tree stump and watched the young lad nimbly climb the nearest coconut tree. When he got to the top, he sorted through the nuts, choosing the best, and with a quick twist of his wrist the nut fell from the tree. In seconds the lad was down again and expertly sliced the bottom then the top from the nut. When the white meat was exposed, he slid his knife around through the meat, cutting a neat hole and presented it with both hands like a gift from the gods.

Brody drank the sweet warm coconut milk as he walked further along the track, moving inland until he came to a tarmac road. There were no cars, but a sign pointed into the interior saying Songo Songo Airstrip. He turned, as the sun was still hot, and headed back to the beach.

Hassan took off his shoes, washed his hands, feet, and finally his face then walked between the thick walls of the ancient mosque. He was early to pray, the main hall was still filling up with men. He took a place near the edge where he knew newcomers were allowed to kneel. Then he spread his mat and knelt, waiting for the cleric to come and lead him through the daily ritual. As he prayed, he watched the other men in the group. The mosque was small and ancient. He could smell the age leaching out of the cool stones, but it had been well-kept and was freshly painted. He waited until the end of the salat then approached a younger man as he was leaving. "Brother, where would I buy fish here?"

"You are new to this place? I haven't seen you before," said the man.

"Yes, we're from Dar, we're thinking of starting a regular route buying your fish and taking them to the markets in Dar and maybe even Mombasa."

"Many boats do that already, but if you can pay, then it's your risk."

"Do I have to get a license?"

"No, just head to the market and see what you can buy. The fishing has reduced over the last few years. When my father was here, he had three boats and the bay would be full of you people coming to buy our fresh fish."

"What happened?" said Hassan.

"When the gas came, we got rich!"

"Eh, how is that?"

"If you go inland, you'll see the new city the government has built. There are pipes everywhere, all along the ground. They even built a brand-new stone jetty for the big metal boats. Not us fishing boats, though. But they give us free electricity, gas, and water. There is even a free clinic if we get sick."

"How far is it to this new town?"

"We have no cars, so you must take a bike or walk. But it's only a few miles, you can walk it in an hour. But there is nothing there, and you are not allowed in through the gates. They say it is too dangerous for us."

"O.K., thanks. Maybe I'll go and take a look. But first I'll head to the fish market and see what's around."

Hassan headed back to the beach where he found Brody and Gumbao talking to some fishermen. He walked into the market and started haggling over the price of fish. When he was finished, he had bought six large kingfish and four blocks of ice. He waved to Gumbao. "Let's take this back," he said in a loud voice. "We'll come earlier tomorrow for more."

Gumbao loaded the fish and ice into some baskets and lugged it back to the beach. The boys were waiting and quickly stowed it on their skiff.

When they got back on *Shukran*, Hassan said, "There is a new town a few miles from here, we have to go and look tonight."

"Fine," said Brody. "We can move *Shukran* a bit closer to the beach, then swim ashore once it's dark. I found a road just after the village that must lead to the new town."

As usual on the equator the sun can be relied upon to go down right on time. By eight p.m. the village had settled in for the night. There were occasional fires dotted along the beach, and a few light bulbs helping the children complete their homework.

They slipped into the water and silently swam the short distance to the shore. When the water was too shallow to swim, they pulled themselves along hand over hand until they were in front of the market. The stone fish stalls were empty and dark after the hustle of the day, water tricked down a rough center gutter of the building and poured out onto the beach. Brody unpacked their clothes from the dry bag he had carried over his shoulder. They quickly walked through the coconut grove and out to the road. "Do you think anyone will be driving at night?" asked Hassan.

"It looks dead, but if we see any lights, we just hop in the ditch and let it pass," said Gumbao.

They half walked and half jogged along the smooth warm tarmac until they could see bright lights in the distance.

Brody said, "Let's get off the road. There'll probably be guards."

They skirted the road, walking through more coconut groves, the soft sandy soil making no noise as they passed. The road to their right came to a junction and turned left toward the beach. Brody signaled for them to go deeper into the shadows as he moved forward. The main compound loomed ahead. It was lit up like a Christmas tree. Brody took a knee and peered ahead. In front of them was a twelve-foot-high chain-link fence topped with razor wire. Massive, blinding halogen lights glared down from the fenceline. Brody guided them back into the darkness before saying, "We'll have to get closer and figure out a way over that fence."

Hassan whispered, "Let's move along a bit, this just looks like industrial stuff. If anyone is here, they will be in the living quarters."

They dodged along the fence, using the trees as cover, until they came to a corner with a guardhouse planted twenty feet above them. A guard swept a searchlight out across the coconut grove as if he was looking for something. They ducked down and crept further along the perimeter, looking for a way in. Finally, they found what looked like a bar or restaurant set a few yards back from the boundary. Groups of people milled about in the moonlight, chatting and drinking. Waiters with silver trays above their heads moved nimbly between the guests. Brody said, "This is no good, we're not going to get over that fence. We need to find another way."

Hassan grabbed his arm, "Look, there, a man standing with that group." He pointed to a group of men in bright-white kanzus. "They don't look like the others." One of the men moved away from the group and lifted his arm to wave across the crowd. "Look, he has a big golden watch," said Hassan.

Brody pulled Hassan back into the gloom. "That's true, but loads of people have those watches. It could be anyone. Did the guy from the village tell you anything else?"

"He said there was a new stone jetty."

"Let's take a look," said Brody. "We can come back later when it quiets down."

They slunk away back into the shadows then altered course toward the sound of the waves on the shore. Gumbao took point, he was thinking about what the witch doctor had said and felt he should be the one to lead. Achiba had made it clear he would know what to do.

They lay on a sand dune and surveyed the concrete jetty sprouting unnaturally out into the ocean below. Gabions full of gray river rocks supported the structure as it left the sandy beach, and lampposts were strung along the length, keeping the whole place brightly lit. A guard sauntered along the pier, smoking a cigarette as he walked. He adjusted the small black machine gun hung around his neck. Brody gasped, "That looks like an MP5, Heckler & Koch."

"So what?" said Hassan.

"Those things are lethal; the clip looks like the thirty-round version."

"Does that mean something to us?" asked Hassan.

"It means this place has a lot of money; those things are not cheap. You don't just go to the market and buy a top-of-the-line, automatic military weapon. These guys have some serious connections.

Why would they be guarding a jetty with so much firepower? You said this place is legit, right?"

"The guy in the mosque didn't seem that interested as long as he got the free stuff," said Hassan.

Brody said, "Let's take a closer look," and moved off into the darkness.

At the base of the jetty, tied to a hook was a battered rowing boat that looked like it was used for maintenance. Brody and Hassan climbed in, and it almost sank to its gunnels. "You stay here, and keep a watch," Brody said to Gumbao. He nodded and moved back toward the beach.

Brody pushed the boat away from the jetty wall and gingerly dipped the oar into the dark, oily, water, then silently pulled the ore back and slipped it out for another stroke. Hassan sat in the bow and looked ahead. Several dark support ships hugged the pier, their generators humming in the night. They paddled between them and the jetty, trying to keep undercover. Brody kept them moving while Hassan looked for guards or anything that could help them find his sister. They rowed to the last support ship and almost the end of the jetty when Hassan reached back and grabbed Brody's hand, then put his fingers to his lips. Brody peered out from the stern of the ship they were holding onto and was shocked to see a bright-white hull sitting in the water. It was bow-on, but it was unmistakably a luxury boat. The polished fiberglass lines of the hull shone under the moon. The boat had lights set all along the hull, lights even shone from under the water. They sat in the darkness and watched the sleek craft in front of them. Hassan whispered, "That could be the boat my father saw in Pemba."

"Could be. We have to get a closer look."

Brody slipped into the water and dove down into the darkness. He could see the lights from the new boat shining in the water and swam along just underneath them. When he got past the last light, he surfaced and looked back into the stern of the boat. A hydraulic swim-platform jutted out from the rear and a black jet ski sat in a storage locker waiting for the following day. Brody swam silently over to the platform and waited. The boat remained quiet. When he was sure no one was around, he pulled himself up and onto the wooden platform. He quickly climbed a few steps and found himself in the rear salon. A beautiful dark oak inlaid table with six chairs sat in the center of the rear deck. Six cut-crystal glasses were strewn across the polished wood and a carafe of what looked like very expensive brandy sat in the center. One of the glasses was half full—was there anyone around? Or had they just left the glasses and gone to the party?

Brody entered the rear of the boat through the sliding doors, it smelled of polished wood, cologne, and expensive cigar smoke. He glanced around at the stainless-steel fittings gleaming under the overhead lights. The deep carpet muffled his footsteps as he ran to the stairs leading to the lower cabins. At the bottom of the stairs, he went forward to the captain's cabin. It was beautifully appointed with a massive king-size bed, but there was no one home. The other three cabins were the same. No sign of Zainab. He had hoped that it would be an easy in and out, that Zainab would just be tied up in one of the cabins and he could grab her and run, but life just didn't happen that way.

He went back up the stairs to the main salon then moved up to the fly deck, but again it was empty. He could see the disinterested guard wandering back toward them. Brody slipped silently back to the main deck. Then he walked to the stern where he found a hatch that led to the engine rooms. He pulled on the hatch cover, and it silently purred open. An automatic light went on, filling the space below. He slid down the ladder and found himself in the crew quarters. There was an alcove kitchen in front of him and three doors, one with a large window. He looked through the windows and saw two massive engines. A generator blinked at him from the corner, but there was no sign of anyone. The first crew cabin was spotless and empty. He went to the final cabin hoping Zainab would be inside, but there was nothing. Then he looked again. At the head of the tiny bunk was a metal loop screwed into the wall. He looked closer and there were scratch marks around the loop and the bed smelled of sweat. Could she have been here? He started a methodical search of the room looking for anything that might lead him to Zainab. In a cupboard under the sink, he found a length of chain and some handcuffs. He went to the wardrobe and searched for any clues then pulled open one of the drawers and came across a cheap, plastic, ladies' purse. He opened it and a folded picture slid out and fell onto the floor. He picked it up and immediately saw Hassan's face staring back at him. His heart flipped; this was the first real clue they had found. Zainab had been here at some point. He quickly searched the rest of the cabin and found a pair of black leather sandals, the type the girls wore on Pemba. He put those back, but he kept the purse. Then he made his way out of the crew quarters and back onto the deck.

As he slid the salon door closed, he heard loud voices coming along the jetty. Maybe three or four men were all talking and laughing. He listened as they spoke to the guard: "Hi, my friend, anything happen while we were gone?"

The guard said, "Sir, all is quiet, no one has been along this jetty during my watch."

"Here, take this for your trouble. It must be lonely out here, go buy your wife something nice."

"Thanks, Sir. Enjoy your evening. Can I escort you to your beautiful boat?"

"No problem, we're here."

Brody ducked back to the swim platform and crouched in a shadow under the stern railing. The men noisily clambered onto the boat and made their way to the rear salon and the waiting drinks. Brody listened from his hiding place. He had been chasing these guys for a long time and wanted to get a feel for who they really were. He might also get some information on the whereabouts of Zainab. A plume of rich-smelling tobacco drifted over the stern of the boat as glasses clinked together. Someone said, "These cigars are from Cuba, you know. Apparently, some old lady rolls them on the island. She has been doing it for fifty years. They're called Padron, they even won an award."

"You really know your cigars, Tariq."

"Faaiz, I have traveled the world. I have many skills in the finer things life has to offer. This brandy is the best money can buy, it's a Rémy Martin. I have it flown in especially for me. Here, pour yourself some more. When my father was offered the partnership with this gas company, we did not know the riches that would flow. This place just pumps money, and all we have to do is collect it. The locals are happy with some power and fresh water; they have no idea what we make here."

"Your father was a very shrewd man, Tariq, he saw profits where others did not. But we must not partake too much. We must remember our faith," said a third voice.

"Now here comes the prude. Why must you always spoil my fun?"

"Tariq, you have already drunk at the party, now you come home to drink. You know how our religion feels about such things."

"I was born to this; I have been here dealing with this religion and all the curses that it brings for a very long time, and my father before me. You think my pious father never drank a good brandy?"

"Tariq, I am here to guide you on the path. And drinking and smoking while living on this luxury yacht is not going to appease who we have to appease, and you know they are always watching us. They are the ones that put these riches at your families' feet. For centuries your family has looked after them and they have reciprocated. Your great grandfather was led to this vast and wealthy country by them. You must not upset the Jinn, or we will all be sorry."

"Zaeem, I will drink if I choose, and I will smoke and have sex with whoever I like. As long as I bring them their prey, they are happy."

"Your sister thought that and look at her now. In chains, locked in her room in Dar. Forever in turmoil as they spite her."

"I am not my sister, Zaeem. I am much cleverer than her, and I can outsmart the Jinn easily, I will play them as I wish. Look, I travel these islands to bring them what they need. Even a doctor."

"You are correct in all things, Tariq, that is known. All I am saying is we must be careful. They are whispering that all is not well. And our Unguja property was raided."

"That has nothing to do with any of this. We had left hours before that happened. From the report it was just some mercenary, probably a father of a lost child. We will leave that place empty for now and use the property on Mafia. Faaiz, did you call the chief of police on Zanzibar?"

"Yes, Tariq, and he said nothing had been reported and if it was he would make sure it disappeared."

"You see, Zaeem, we are bulletproof. No one dares to make any waves in this country. The chief of police is happy he has a nice car and a beautiful house in Stone Town to share with his wife and family. He will not risk that over some orphan street kids."

"As you wish, Sir. I am here at your mother's bidding. I will take my leave now, as I want to rest. I need to visit the cavern early tomorrow, then we have to leave for Dar."

"You go, I will sit here and enjoy my cigar."

Brody slipped silently off the rear of the boat, took a deep breath, and allowed himself to sink into the dark water. He pushed off the soft mud on the bottom and swam toward the pier with his hands reached out in front of him. He searched around, feeling for one of the piles that stretched along its length. The rough, barnacled concrete was easy to find, he felt his way around the column and into the recess of the pier. When he was sure he would not be heard he surfaced then swam back to Hassan. Brody signaled to him to stay quiet, then pushed the rowing boat back between the other maintenance ships. Gumbao materialized out of the darkness as they tied the boat back to the hook. Brody signaled for them to head back into the dunes. Once he was certain they were safe, he lifted his shirt and gave Hassan a tightly packed plastic bag. "Look inside," he said.

Hassan unwrapped the parcel and immediately a tear formed in his eye. "It's hers," he whispered. "Where was it?"

"I'm pretty sure she was recently on that boat. I found it in a crew cabin below decks."

"Why were you so long? I heard them coming back and thought you had been caught."

"I was listening, the head guy is called Tariq. He is a bit of an asshole. But he is pulling the strings."

"What did they talk about?" said Hassan.

"Zainab is around—they spoke of a doctor, and some caves or caverns. Do you know anything about them?"

"I've got nothing," said Hassan. "And we can't go around asking questions like that."

"There was another guy called Zaeem—he seems to be there to make sure Tariq doesn't get in too much trouble. He said he had to go to the caves in the morning. So, I guess we hunker down here and set up a watch."

"I'll take the first shift. Anything happens, and I'll let you know," said Gumbao.

Brody woke from an uncomfortable sleep; his clothes were still damp from the night before. He stretched his back and felt the bones snap into place. Gumbao sat leaning against a tree idly chewing on a blade of grass. The sun had not started to warm the day, so Brody stood up and started doing some star jumps to get his circulation going. A faint whistle carried in the still, early morning air. Gumbao jumped to his feet. "That's Hassan. We better go."

They walked through the grove, then crawled to the top of the sand dune. Hassan was intently watching the jetty. He pointed, saying, "Look at those two guys. They're too well-dressed to be workers, and it's early."

"You're right, let's see if we can follow them."

The two men strode along the jetty, then turned before they reached the main gate. They followed a paved walkway that led around the perimeter of the fence. The gold braid in their kanzus shone in the early morning light; each wore a heavy gold chain on his wrist and an even bigger one around his neck. Brody could smell the cologne from above them in the dunes. The men easily loped along the path, both looking athletic and powerful. Gumbao signaled for Brody and Hassan to drop back lower on the dune as he tracked the two men from above. When they reached the end of the compound they turned left and walked along another path leading them toward an inlet covered with mangrove trees. Gumbao kept up with the guys by jogging along in the coconut grove. The men were chatting easily, as if nothing was amiss, and the taller of the two let out a laugh as they came to a bend in the path. They stopped and pushed open a metal gate, then disappeared into a tunnel. Gumbao waved for the others to catch up, then he also went into the dark tunnel. Gumbao felt the dampness as he entered, occasional dim light bulbs hung from the ceiling. A large metal pipe ran off into the distance. Gumbao stopped and stood still, there was a throbbing noise like a large pump somewhere in the distance. He couldn't see the two men, but he could clearly hear their voices bouncing off the walls. His bare feet slipped on the cool polished concrete. The tunnel led, in a slight incline, back toward the center of the island. Gumbao waited, and when he was sure he was not being watched he headed further into the tunnel. The two men continued to chat away in

Arabic as they walked along the corridor, they seemed completely at ease. Gumbao kept a safe distance behind, always making sure a curve was between them. He had a basic understanding of Arabic so was following along with their conversation. They stopped next to a large metal gate. Faaiz took out a bunch of keys and opened the lock, then he pushed the gate which swung open on well-oiled hinges. He beckoned for Zaaem to go through first then closed the gate behind him. Gumbao was there in seconds and slipped through the gate to follow them. This part of the passageway was much darker, there were only a few low-wattage bulbs set into the rock. Faaiz said, "Why do they like it here?"

"I have no idea, brother; it is just what they ask of us. They are old and have strange ways."

Faaiz said, "We are near the pool, it's just up ahead."

"I am happy this place is private now. Since we started giving the Matumbi free water they are too lazy to even come here."

"Well, that and the deaths," said Faaiz.

"Ah, a few sacrifices are fine," said Zaeem. "Fear always instills respect."

"The old people complain. They say this water heals," said Faaiz.

"I'm sure that is why the Jinn want it. They had this island long ago and told Tariq's grandfather to buy it. They can see things we cannot understand. But the gas has made the family the richest in Tanzania. So, what they want they will get. The old women of the village will die off soon and then this place will be forgotten."

Faaiz unhooked a flashlight from the wall and continued along the path. Gumbao crab-walked, keeping low as he followed. The smooth concrete was replaced with roughhewn slabs of rock covered in green and brown stains. Gumbao's feet naturally found the center of the path which was worn smooth from centuries of people coming to collect the life-giving water. The beam from the torch flashed left and right ahead then was gone. Gumbao moved forward and crouched behind a cold slimy rock. He found a vantage point, then lifted his head to get a better look. In front of him was a wide-open chamber with dripping white stalactites hanging from the ceiling. In the center of the cavern was a raised pool of clear water. Several streams flowed out of natural tunnels in the rock face. The room was ethereal, the polished white walls seemed to emit their own light. Gumbao could make out several tunnels leading off into the dark. Zaeem was standing in the corner, next to one of the entrances as if he was looking for something.

Faaiz said, "Have you ever actually seen one?"

"No," answered Zaaem. "And I don't want to. If you are looking at one of them then they want you, and I have no inclination to be in that position."

"The girl is strong," said Faaiz. "But I don't think she will last much longer. Then we will have to find another."

"Let's not worry about that now. That's Tariq's problem."

Both men walked into one of the tunnels, shining the light in front of them. "He hasn't moved an inch, they must have just come and taken from him here," said Faaiz as he shone the torch on a crumpled form in the darkness.

Gumbao moved closer and strained to see the person on the floor. Was this what he had been told by Baktari? Was this the moment?

He jumped as he heard a noise behind him. Brody's head appeared behind a rock further back. Gumbao motioned for him to come closer. They both watched as the two men dragged the lifeless form out of the tunnel and checked for any pulse. "He is still alive," said Zaeem. "We'll hook him up to an IV, so he lasts a few more days. You go and get some water."

Zaeem unzipped a small pouch he had been carrying in his kanzu and took out a bag of fluid attached to a pipe. He grabbed the young boy's arm then pushed the needle into a vein. The boy didn't even flinch.

Brody was shocked, he did not know what was happening. Why would they keep some poor kid locked up in a stone chamber under the ground? He looked at Gumbao and raised his hands as if to say "Why?"

Gumbao crouched down below the rock and whispered in his ear, "They say there are Jinn in the tunnel that help them. I guess they are feeding them."

Brody could not believe his ears. "We have to do something about this, man," he whispered back.

"There are more people running along the corridor outside," said Hassan. "I think there must have been cameras."

"Shit," said Brody. "We have to get that boy and get out of here."

Brody leapt up and crossed the chamber in three strides. He slammed his hands into the back of Zaeem, sending him sprawling across the smooth rock. Faaiz was quicker and spun around to face his opponent, raising himself onto the balls of his feet. Brody stepped in quickly and kicked Zaeem in the ribs then turned as a right hook slammed into his jaw. This guy was strong and fit, he was going to earn his pay today. Brody dodged back as another uppercut came looping in toward his stomach.

Gumbao had rushed out and grabbed Zaeem then threw him against a wall, splitting his nose. Zaeem yelled, "Guards! Guards!"

Hassan saw his chance and ran out from his hiding place straight to the boy. He grabbed him and tried to stand him up, but he was unconscious, his skin as white as Friday's kanzu. Hassan pulled him up as far as he could then threw him over his shoulder.

Faaiz was a rich kid, but he had skills and knew how to use them. He circled Brody, twisting on the balls of his feet, rotating his stance. Brody watched his opponent's eyes like a hawk, he saw the tell just before the fist lunged out in a perfect straight punch aimed at Brody's throat. Only experience stopped the punch from landing. Brody's instincts and training kicked in and he knocked the fist away inches before it made contact. Then a roundhouse kick came out of the blue and landed in Brody's kidneys. He staggered, but he managed to stay on his feet. Faaiz was enjoying himself now, he felt he had the upper hand. Brody flicked his eyes toward the entrance, he knew it would be only seconds before the guards arrived, and from what he had seen last night they would be well-armed and probably well-trained.

Hassan had the dead weight of the boy on his shoulders as he staggered off into one of the tunnels. The floor was still paved, and he could see light up ahead.

Gumbao put one final kick into Zaaem and then turned. Was this his time to help? He had no idea. He was about to grab Faaiz from behind when he heard shouts from the entrance. He ducked into the tunnel as two guards came racing over the rough path with their guns up and ready.

Brody knew he had to finish this quickly and follow his friends, so he ducked low and came up fast with a right hook into Faaiz's chin. He staggered but amazingly kept his ground. Then he dodged forward and slammed a double-handed punch into Brody's chest which sent him flying back into the pool. The guards reached the chamber and started shouting for everyone to get down. Gumbao slipped into the tunnel. He knew he was of no use to Brody right now. He would get Hassan and the boy out then decide what to do.

Brody stared into the two MP5s as he sat at the edge of the pool.

Zaaem got up, holding his nose. "Take him to the boat," he told the guards.

One of the soldiers expertly flipped the gun in his hands then slammed the butt into Brody's forehead.

The soldiers dragged Brody out of the pool and rolled him onto the floor. They roughly handcuffed him and dragged his limp body back the way they had come.

Faaiz gave Zaaem a handkerchief. "We had better sort out your nose."

"Forget that," he said. "We need to get that boy back. Where do those tunnels lead?"

"I have no idea."

"Go back and call for backup. We need to search this place and find those other idiots. I want the old man here in front of me, I have a debt to settle with him."

Chapter Seventeen
Songo Songo Caverns

Hassan tried to run, but with the dead weight of the boy on his shoulders he was quickly just staggering along the passageway. He winced at every step, expecting to hear shouting or feel a bullet smack into his spine at any moment, but he was alone for now. The boy was just too heavy. He heard a scuff on the ground and spun around, only to see Gumbao appearing about 100 feet behind him. He stopped and leaned against the wall. "What happened?"

"They got Brody," Gumbao breathed. "I had to leave him, or we would both have been taken. Now we have to move."

Gumbao took the boy and started trotting along the passageway. They soon came to a junction with a large pipe running along the floor. "Do we head up or down?" asked Hassan.

"I'm sure the entrance is locked and guarded by now. Did you see any cameras? How did they know we were inside?"

Hassan looked around, "There's nothing down here, maybe they caught us at the door when we came in. Or while we were on the path outside."

Gumbao stood, not sure which way to go. A siren suddenly blared out, echoing along the tunnels. A voice boomed after it: "You are on government land. Surrender yourselves immediately, we will shoot to kill."

Gumbao said, "This way." And started running.

Brody's feet dragged along the tunnel. He had quickly regained consciousness but had decided to just go with the flow for a while until an opportunity arose. The soldiers seemed very well-trained and were holding him as if he was awake. The cuffs had started to cut into his wrists as he was dragged along the sandy path. He tried to calm himself; if they had wanted him dead he would have been shot in the cave. So, right now his life was safe. How long that would last, though, was anyone's guess. Once he was on the boat the guards put a hood over his head then bundled him into a very small cupboard. Brody knew the best thing to do was sit and wait. He was sure there would be a guard standing outside the door. He needed to conserve his energy if he was going to get out of this. The hours wore on, occasionally he could hear muffled voices, but no one came and opened the cupboard. His arms ached and his wrists were itchy like hell, his legs were full of pins and needles from not being able to stretch out. But he managed to relax and control his breathing. After a while he began to doze in his tiny box. He stayed in that weird place just between being awake and asleep, where his mind kept wandering. Back and forward, strange images started forming in his head. He couldn't grasp the complete idea, he felt the idea was just out of his reach. His awake brain kept trying to grasp the idea but it flitted away as his head nodded forward. He was searching, always searching for something, but he could never actually lay his hands on it. The girl's face from Stone Town appeared. She frowned at him with those cold, heartless eyes. She was whispering something he couldn't get, so he leaned forward to get closer and maybe hear. The girl stood next to a grave and was pointing at the name, but Brody could not make it out. He took some faltering steps forward in his dream. The girl appeared closer, "You have really messed up this time. I don't think I can help you anymore."

Brody sleepily said, "She is Zainab. I can't give up."

"You are in a place you do not understand."

"Help me understand."

"You must believe before I can help you. Only then will you be able to find your friend."

"How do I believe?"

"You have a good friend who knows the way. Just follow him."

He reached out in his dream, but the girl slipped away. His tongue felt swollen and his head hurt like hell.

Zaaem and Faaiz arrived at the boat to find Tariq sat at the stern with a large cup of coffee in his hand. "What has happened?" he asked.

Zaaem stepped froward, still holding the handkerchief to his nose. "We were in the tunnel, sorting the boy we put there a couple of days ago and we were jumped. A muzungu and two locals came out of nowhere."

"Do you think they were connected to Unguja? The report said a white guy was there."

"Probably," said Faaiz. "He was tough, probably some merc that a pissed-off family went and found."

Zaaem said, "What do we do now? We can't have people interrupting this business. Your mother will want to know what is going on."

"We keep the rest of the family out of it for now. I need to find out what this guy knows, and who he's after. Let me think. This cannot get out of hand; we need to keep everything quiet. This gas gets sold all over the world—if a scandal breaks, we could lose everything."

Gumbao pushed Hassan into a side tunnel then followed him. They pressed themselves against the wall and held their breaths as four guys ran past the entrance. After a few seconds, Hassan stuck his head out and said, "All clear." They hurriedly walked along the tunnel, constantly glancing behind them. Twice more they had to duck into a tunnel as men ran back and forwards. Gumbao said, "I'm tired, we need to find a safe place to hide and rest."

They came to another junction; one corridor ran on with lights, but the second was much darker. They stumbled into the darkness and soon bumped into a heavy metal door. Hassan twisted the handle and managed to drag it open. They entered a large room with a humming generator in the center. Gumbao pushed past him and put the kid down on the floor. "Check his pulse, make sure I'm not carrying a corpse."

Hassan started working on the boy while Gumbao wandered around the room. He was out of his depth, and he knew it. A firefight was fine, but this was way above his paygrade. He paced back and forth trying to think of how they could get to the surface. But when they did, where would they go? He was sure *Shukran* was swarming with people by now—it would not take long to connect the dots.

"Is the boy alive?" he asked.

"Just, but we need to get him out of here and to a hospital as quickly as we can."

Gumbao said, "Quiet." Then motioned toward the door.

They stood in silence for a second hoping they had been lucky. Hassan felt a trickle of sweat run down his face, as he heard muffled voices. Gumbao ran to the door and stood beside it, he motioned for Hassan to drag the boy behind the noisy generator. Gumbao watched, willing Hassan to get into cover as the door handle started to move. Hassan just managed to drag the boy out of sight as the barrel of a gun entered the room. Gumbao stood still, holding his breath as the man moved cautiously forward, then quickly pushed the door back and stepped into the room. His partner followed. Gumbao stepped in behind both men, and in one fluid movement he grabbed one of the MP5s and twisted it. The sling was around the guy's neck. He was pulled forward right into Gumbao's forehead. The man staggered backward and lost his grip on the weapon. Gumbao pulled the trigger and bullets spat out at point-blank range into the second man. The staggering man tried to move back into the fight, but Gumbao rammed the butt of the gun into his face. The guy couldn't help stepping back again and tripped over a conduit on the floor. The strap of the MP5 was still looped around the man's neck, which pulled Gumbao down on top of him. Gumbao held the weapon as he fell and rammed it into the man's chest, forcing the air from his lungs. They both knew they were fighting for their lives. The soldier rolled Gumbao off him and kicked out hard with his heavy boots landing a blow on Gumbao's thigh. The man then twisted to try and move away, but the strap was around his neck. Gumbao pushed himself up on one arm and pulled the gun toward him, tightening the strap. The man swung around to hit Gumbao in the face, but he was too slow. Gumbao bunched the strap in his hand and pulled as hard as he could. The man slid up between Gumbao's legs like a child being comforted. He squirmed as the strap started to bite into his neck. His arms flailed above his head, reaching for Gumbao, but nothing worked. Gumbao held on pulling with all his strength, his muscles strained as the man twisted. Then the movements became slower and slower as the life drained from the guard. Gumbao kept pulling until he was sure there was no movement. Then he reached down and pulled a Glock from the guy's holster and rolled him away.

Hassan came out from behind the generator, "Are they dead?"

"Yep, and they will be missed very soon. We must keep moving."

"There's another door back here, but no lights," said Hassan.

"O.K. We have no choice."

Hassan opened the metal door and they found themselves in an older part of the tunnels where water dripped from the damp ceiling. Hassan peered into the pitch blackness. A shiver slipped along his spine. "This feels different," he said.

"Just keep moving."

Hassan walked tentatively along the new tunnel with his hands sliding along one wall. The rock under his fingers was rough but the floor had been worn smooth. They walked further into the tunnel knowing going back would mean certain capture. The boy hanging off Gumbao's shoulder started to groan as if he was in pain. The floor started to incline toward the surface. They kept walking for what felt like hours, just stumbling along in the darkness. Hassan walked ahead with one arm sliding along the wall and the other outstretched in front of him. He was beginning to feel exhausted, as his eyes strained into the darkness. His right hand was cut and bleeding from sliding over the roughly cut rock. He stumbled over something on the floor then he yelped as his left hand hit something solid. He frantically slid his hands over the rock face looking for a way forward. Then he turned and did the same to his left and his right. His eyes started stinging and he could hear his heart thumping in his chest.

Gumbao's voice called out of the pitch black behind him, "What's wrong?"

"It's a dead end. We're stuck. We're going to die down here!"

Gumbao felt around, then lay the boy on the ground and sat beside him. If this was it, then he was going to have a smoke.

Hassan continued to run his hands along the edge of the tunnel hoping he had missed the exit. He went around again and again, but there was nothing. He sat down beside Gumbao, "What do we do?"

"I've no idea right now."

"We can't go back, that place will be swarming with people. And we can't go forward. We're stuck down here and lost."

Gumbao sat on the floor, he had no idea what they would do next, one thing he did know was that panicking was never a good idea. He fished his cigarettes out of his pocket then dug around for the matches. The match box was damp from the sweat of his clothes, he just hoped the matches would light. He twisted the box in his fingers and struck the first match, but the damp phosphorous sulfide crumbled as it was scraped along the side of the box. The second one was the same. He was down to his last three matches. He carefully held the match as close to the head as he could and rubbed it on the side of the box. It smoked, then burst into light. They both shut their stunned eyes, and when Gumbao opened them, he watched the light flicker for a second then lifted it to his cigarette and took a grateful lungful of the tobacco smoke. They sat in the match light, their eyes slowly focusing on their surroundings. Hassan looked at the blank walls around him, it was hopeless. The wood quickly twisted and split in Gumbao's fingers then went out. Hassan sat for a second, "Have you got another one?"

Gumbao felt in the box, "Two more."

"Light one."

"Why?"

"Just do it, old man."

Gumbao fiddled with the damp box, he knew the paper on the side was worn and the match probably wouldn't light, but he gripped it very close to the head and tried. As he struck it across the worn abrasive paper the head of the match snapped off and fell into the darkness. "Shit, I've only one left," he said.

Hassan jumped to his feet, "We have to try."

Gumbao did the same with his last match and struck it against the side of the damp box; the phosphorous sulfide spluttered, but then it took. Hassan said, "Hold it up high." He ran back to the rock face and jumped up off the ground, sliding his hands on the wall. "Here," he shouted. "Look."

Gumbao watched him jump and was amazed as he just hung in the air. "I've found some sort of ladder."

Gumbao just managed to see an old iron rung sticking out of the wall as the match started to burn his finger. They were thrown into darkness again. Hassan leapt into the air and dangled off the rung, "Come, old man. Push me up."

Gumbao came over and pushed Hassan up onto his shoulders.

"I can feel another one," Hassan said, struggling up again until he was standing on Gumbao's head. "There are more, I'm going up. You wait here with the boy. I'll be back as soon as I can."

Hassan fumbled upward in the dark as he climbed one rung of the old rusty ladder at a time. His legs ached as he pushed himself up; he was careful to be on at least three rungs at any one time. But the ladder just kept going and going. He estimated he was about forty feet up when his hand touched the ceiling. His body tensed. Was this the end, just a ladder up to a roof?

His hands frantically felt around in the dark and touched a metal handle directly above him. He brought his legs up another rung then bent his shoulders against the panel above him and pushed with all of his strength. The hatch was stiff, but a sliver of light appeared. He rested, then did the same, forcing the lid up another inch. Then his strength gave out and it slammed shut. He doubled up on the ladder, folding his legs underneath his body, then bent his head and pushed with his thighs, forcing the hatch to rise six inches. Once it was moving, he shoved it with his hands, and it slammed back behind him. He poked his head out of the entrance and looked around. He was in a dusty storeroom; it looked unused and forgotten. He climbed out and went to the door, opening it cautiously looking out into the early evening light. Next to the hut was an enormous baobab tree. The grey bark seemed to glow in the night. At the bottom of the tree was an old lady sitting next to a fire, a black dog with bright eyes lying next to her. She looked up. "Kadijah, that took you ages. I've been waiting for you all afternoon. Why are you so stupid?"

"Who're you? Hassan asked.

"Are you going to get that boy out for me? Or just chat?"

Hassan looked around helplessly.

"Kadijah, your family always needs our help. You have never amounted to anything, not you nor your father or grandfather. Don't just stand there, I'm waiting for the boy. I have places to go."

Hassan ran back into the hut and found several lengths of rope. Then he went back to the fire and plucked a burning stick from the fire. The old crone said, "Hurry up. I'm hungry." She took a silver box from the folds of her dress, opened it, and rubbed her finger over a black substance inside, then rubbed her finger on her gums. "Go on then. Get on with it."

Hassan took the burning stick to the hut and found some tattered clothes on the floor. He fashioned a torch and dropped it into the hole. Then he tied the rope off at the top and clambered back down. Gumbao was waiting when he returned, holding the burning torch.

Hassan just said, "Let's go."

They tied the rope around the boy, Gumbao climbed the ladder and started hauling the lad up rung by rung with Hassan pushing from below.

When they got back outside, the old woman said, "Lay him here. Now you go on your way."

Gumbao asked, "Where are we?"

"You walk west, and you will find the shore. They have your boat, by the way."

Hassan said, "Old woman—" but stopped as a low menacing growl came from the jet-black dog, its eyes seemed to shine in the evening light.

"Ha," she said. "Kadijah, just go on your way. Don't ask any more questions, just follow that fat nose of yours. You will need to grow a backbone before this is all over."

As they walked off Gumbao said, "Who are these people you keep finding?"

"I have no idea. Ever since Kiwayu, they keep turning up. We better head back to the jetty. We need to find Brody."

Chapter Eighteen
Sun Seeker

Brody's hands tingled with pins and needles, his arms throbbed from being tied behind his back, and his legs were numb from being folded into the cabinet. His head felt thick and fuzzy like he had been on a heavy night and his damp clothes had taken all of his heat. He crouched in the darkness of the cupboard and tried to keep his mental strength. He knew there was nothing he could do. He had to conserve his energy and wait. But the discomfort started to affect his thought process. He had been trained to suffer; in the SBS (Special Boat Service) there had been a whole month's course on being taken captive. He had been beaten and psychologically tortured then questioned over and over. He had come close to giving in but always managed to draw on some special reserve or just plain bloody mindedness and not given in. He had been younger then, and knew it was just an exercise. This was different. The soldiers that had taken him were well-trained. If he started anything in his current condition, they would just beat the crap out of him.

He heard a click and footsteps, then the door was thrown open and he was dragged out onto the floor. "The boss wants to ask you some questions." He could sense one man standing over him, and was sure another was at a safe distance watching, ready to jump if he did anything they didn't like. "You mess with us and we shoot you and throw you overboard."

Brody rolled over onto his side and tried to get up. "I can't feel my legs," he said.

"You'll manage," sneered the guard and kicked him in the ribs.

"Hold on—the boss wants him in one piece," said the guy by the door.

Brody got to his knees then managed to stand. "Where are you taking me?" Brody pleaded. He wanted these men to think he was frightened.

"No questions. Just do as you're told, and you might live through this."

The first guy turned Brody around and grabbed the handcuffs to make sure they were still tight. "You walk in front. I only need one excuse to put a round through you. Understand?"

"O.K. O.K. I understand, I don't want any trouble," said Brody. He shook his legs out like a runner getting ready for a 100-yard sprint. Then he started limping toward the door.

He was walked through what felt like narrow corridors, then up some stairs. Thick carpet cushioned his bare feet. As soon as he had climbed the stairs the hood became claustrophobic, stifling his breath. The guard nudged him forward with the barrel of his gun. He felt the sun on his arms before he was pushed down into a straight-backed chair. He knew he had no control, so he just waited. There was a clink of glasses. The rich, mellow, oaky smell of tobacco drifted over his hood.

"Are you the man who attacked us in Zanzibar?" said a cultured voice with a mid-Atlantic accent.

"No, I'm just a tourist who got lost. Then your goons decided to beat me up. I want to call my embassy right away. I'm a British subject and deserve to be let go immediately."

The voice chuckled, "A British subject, eh? I am so sorry we disturbed you on your holiday. Which hotel are you staying at?"

"I was just visiting for the day. I'm a backpacker. I got lost. You have no right to keep me here."

"How did you get to Songo Songo?"

"I jumped on a fishing boat. They dropped me at the beach, and I followed a path to the road and wanted to explore. There is no law against that."

"You are starting to try my patience. Why were you following my friends?"

"What friends?"

Brody winced as the barrel of a gun was forced between his shoulder blades.

"Why were you in the caves snooping around?"

"I told you, I'm on holiday. I didn't see any signs stopping me. It looked like an interesting place to poke around."

"I think differently. I am sure you were there with your friends. And you were up to no good."

"What friends? I already told you; I'm traveling alone." Brody stuttered, "Look, you have no right to hold me. I've been cramped up in that cupboard for hours. You need to let me go right now or…"

"Or what? You are alone here in Africa, who do you think is going to help you?"

The man standing behind Brody forced the barrel of the gun between his shoulder blades, making Brody lean forward. The hood was hot and claustrophobic, and Brody was feeling exhausted after his stay in the cupboard. But he knew his only chance was to keep up the charade and hope either his friends were still alive, or that these people would not risk killing a foreigner. He was outnumbered at the moment. He had to wait for an opportunity.

The mid-Atlantic voice purred at him once more, "I am a very powerful man on this island, I suggest you talk now, or your life will become very uncomfortable and extremely short. We will take you out for a ride in my lovely boat and then you can decide to go swimming."

"Listen," whimpered Brody, "I really don't know what you are talking about. I just want to go back to Dar and carry on with my trip around Tanzania."

"My friends say that you are looking for a girl. Is that true?"

Brody was suddenly happy he had the hood over his head. "What girl are you talking about?" he said.

"Now you sound more interested," said the mid-Atlantic voice.

Brody received a rap on the end of his kneecap which made him cry out in pain. Then another voice joined the conversation, "You certainly don't hit like a tourist, you know we have been following your movements since you invaded the house in Stone Town. Do you think we are idiots? We have been watching you ever since you spoke to the harbor master."

Brody knew he was in trouble now. They had been wandering around causing trouble in such a hurry to find Zainab they had left a trail a blind man could follow, but he decided to continue his bluff. "I've never been to Zanzibar. I came from Dar on a fishing boat. You must have me confused with someone else."

"The girl you seek is gone. You might as well tell us what you know, and we will let you go. Hell, I will even fly you back to Dar and put you up in a fancy hotel for a week."

"I don't know anything about a girl. If I knew I would tell you. Look, I'm telling the truth. All I want is to be let go and I will be on my way."

"Was she your girlfriend in Dar, or did the parents pay you to come looking?"

Brody needed more information from these guys. This was confirmation they had Zainab, but he couldn't let on he knew her.

"Dar is full of beautiful girls; I knew many when I was there. Maybe you have me mistaken with someone else. Look I am just a back packer..."

"Shut up!" said the second voice, "We know you have been following us with your two friends and we also know you want the girl from Pemba back. But it is too late for her..."

"Be quiet!" said the mid-Atlantic voice, "You have said too much."

"Sorry, Tariq. I was not thinking."

"And now you use my name! How stupid are you."

"Put him in the crew cabin and shackle him, both hands and feet," said the mid-Atlantic voice Brody now knew as Tariq's. "Make sure there is a guard on duty around the clock. We will be out of here in forty-eight hours. Then the sharks can deal with the muzungu."

Brody was happy he was not being put back into the cupboard, but he knew escaping from the crew cabin was not going to be easy. He also knew that Zainab must still be alive for the moment.

Chapter Nineteen
Alone

Gumbao and Hassan crept through the coconut grove toward the jetty. The words of Achiba Baktari were ringing in Gumbao's ears. He knew he had to take command, but he was not keen. During his days in Mozambique, he had fought against the government and local gangs vying for possession of this or that, but he had never taken command. He had always been in the group that was told to run at the enemy and start shooting. This was totally new to him and he hated it. What if everything he did was wrong, and they all ended up dead? He had seen the guards take Brody and they were well-trained and well-armed. All he had was Hassan, no weapons, and no idea of what to do.

Hassan broke him from his thoughts, "What do we do now? We're lost, we have nothing, how do we get out of this? I'm sure my sister is lost and now we have lost Brody too. I don't know what I will say to my mother."

Gumbao knew Hassan was scared. And he was just venting, but it didn't help the situation. He turned to Hassan. "Look! We have to try our best. The first order is to get Brody back. If we can't get him, then you can just forget your sister, she will be dead and gone. I don't know what to do!" Then he stormed off through the coconut grove heading toward the beach.

Hassan raced to keep up with him, he was distraught. They had nothing, and he knew Zainab would not last much longer with the Thuwainis, but his only hope now hung on a drunk old man with a very checkered past.

Gumbao walked out onto the beach and stared at the ocean. This must have been what Achiba was talking about. This must be his time; he had followed Brody and even Hassan ever since they had met back in Pemba. He had always played the fool and relied on them to get him through everything. Now, according to Baktari, it was his turn to stand and do the right thing. But what was the right thing? Suddenly he had to make decisions. He absentmindedly reached down and scratched the dirty bandage on his leg. The stray bullet had left a deep furrow, the wound itched like crazy, and his thigh was starting to ache, but this was not the time to worry about a little scratch. His whole life he had wandered around allowing life to push him this way and that and now that had all come to a grinding halt in a cave on Songo Songo. He was torn. He could just as easily walk back to the main beach, find a fishing boat, and head off to a new life, but this time it was different. His little group of friends had really gotten under his skin. He loved the life he had found, or had been given to him; he was never sure. He wanted it back and felt cheated that he had been put in this situation. He had a choice to make; he could turn left and head to the beach and disappear as he normally did, or he could listen to what Baktari had said and risk his life to save another. He reached into his pocket for his cigarettes, then remembered he had no matches.

Hassan was sitting on the beach a few yards away with his head in his hands. He was no soldier; he was just a fisherman. If they had not had Brody, then they would not have even made it as far as Zanzibar. And he was scared, the old woman had not said anything about this. But they had said to him over and over again how stupid he was and that by the end of this he would have to find some backbone. Was this the time? Was it now that he had to do something and get Brody out of the shit, and then maybe, if Allah smiled on him one more time, they could somehow find Zainab and get away from this awful place?

Gumbao walked over to him, "Have you got a light?"

"You know I don't smoke, old man."

"Yes, I do, but I always live in hope." Gumbao said with a grin.

"I don't know what to do," said Hassan.

"Me either, but I do know someone who does. The only problem is he is inside that big plastic boat."

"Do you have any idea how we can get him out?" asked Hassan.

"We won't do it here crying to ourselves that's for sure. We have to get close and have a look, then see if we can come up with a plan. Come on, get up, let's head back to the jetty and see what we can see."

Gumbao crept up to the top of the sand dunes and peered at the white boat at the end of the jetty. He could only see the bow, which was empty. He did notice a couple of guards standing at the end of the gangplank, which was new. Adding to the new security were two armed guards at the entrance to the jetty. He slithered back down the sand dune and asked Hassan, "Do you have any matches?"

"I keep telling you no."

"Ah, yes, sorry. I forgot I asked you. There are loads of guards all around that boat now. If we are going to get onboard, we have to come up with a smart plan."

Hassan said, "Let me look, maybe I can see something."

He crawled to the top of the dune and looked down on the scene below. He knew that doing what Brody had done was out of the question. But there had to be a way. As he watched, a man came out of the gate to the refinery and signaled to a group of locals who were sitting by the fence. They ran forward eagerly, obviously looking for work. The man picked eight of the men then gave them buckets and mops. He unlocked the gate to the jetty and took them to the first maintenance ship.

Hassan slid back and went to Gumbao. "There are cleaners that go to the maintenance boats, maybe we can get into one of the crews and get onto the jetty."

"What then?" asked Gumbao.

"I don't know. Brody always says, *'One step at a time.'*"

A couple of hours later, Gumbao and Hassan sat in a group of locals all hoping for an afternoon's work cleaning one of the ships. The gate was opened, and the man came out. Gumbao was used to this type of work, so he knew that he had to push forward to be chosen. He dragged Hassan with him as they vied for the attention of the foreman. The man chose his favorites first and was looking at the rest of the motley crew in front of him, undecided on who to take. Gumbao stepped forward and said, "Do you want a cigarette?"

The man took the whole packet and waved Gumbao forward, "and my friend he needs the cash for his wife, she needs to go to the mainland." The man frowned, but then waved Hassan forward. They were given a mop, bucket, and a broom each then sent to the jetty. Gumbao nudged Hassan and whispered, "Look out to sea. That's *Shukran*, they're bringing her to the jetty. Let's hope they didn't search her too well."

The foreman came and told them what to do, then lost interest and wandered back toward the refinery. Gumbao set to mopping the decks of the maintenance ship and Hassan swept and cleaned the cabins inside. Gumbao kept a watchful eye on *Shukran*. The temporary crew pulled her alongside the jetty opposite the big white boat, then tied her off and left. The sun began to set and the cleaning crews started to pack up their things, getting ready to be paid for the afternoon's work. Hassan and Gumbao hung around at the back of the group and waited for their chance. The foreman strode along the jetty, but was stopped by one of the men, who said, "I have done a double shift today, I was here in the morning then in the afternoon. I need double the pay."

The man looked at him and said, "I will give you what I feel, you come begging for work and get what you are given. Now stand in line." But the worker was not happy and shoved the foreman, "You can't speak to us like that. This is our island!"

The foreman signaled to the guards watching the big plastic boat and they ran over to help him.

Gumbao said, "This is our chance. Jump on *Shukran* and go below. I will be right behind you."

Hassan stealthily moved across the jetty and slid behind an oil drum. Then he jumped onto *Shukran* and ran to the stern hatch, lifted it and was gone. Gumbao followed suit and they were soon both in the hold.

Hassan said, "What now?"

Gumbao grinned, "Now we hope they didn't find the weapons."

They waited until dusk had settled into the night before they slipped out of *Shukran*'s hold and onto the deck. Hassan had refused a weapon, as he had no idea how they worked, but Gumbao had an old Glock 19 with a full clip. His intention was to surprise and threaten though, as using the gun would bring hordes of guards from the refinery.

Hassan crept over the side of *Shukran* and onto the jetty then hid behind a diesel tank. When Gumbao had caught up Hassan whispered, "What do we do now?"

"We wait for a chance," answered Gumbao.

Gumbao wiggled his leg into a different position to try and reduce the cramping, the stained bandage would need changing soon. He was not happy; this was the crux of the whole operation. What if he got it all wrong and they were captured before they even got close? He hated command; a simple soldier's life was more his style, where others made the decisions so he could not be blamed. They knelt behind the diesel tank and watched as the night slowly wore on. Gumbao was getting fidgety; he knew a decision was due, but he just couldn't bring himself to make it. Then there was a commotion on the big white plastic boat. Three men dressed in beautifully embroidered white kanzus, with gold embroidered collars and cuffs, came to the stern and sat for a drink.

"Shall we go up to the restaurant?"

"Tariq, you are always hungry for comfort. I think it is those ladies in short dresses more than the food."

"Faaiz, you are worse than me. Last night, we had to drag you away from that young girl. She was half your age!"

Another more mature voice said, "You both need to stay away from the booze, we have an important night tomorrow. Everything we have worked for over these last few years will come to fruition. Now we have found the perfect girl, and the perfect spot, they will give us the power we have asked for. Tariq, you will be president of this country and this little oil refinery will seem like small change."

"There is no moon tomorrow, it will be the perfect night. The ruins are on the far side of the island, so we will not be interrupted." Glasses clinked together and the smell of rich tobacco smoke filled the air.

"You are right, my friend," said Tariq, "We just need to stay the course. Now let's go and eat and drink and stare at the girl's pretty legs!"

The three men mounted the gangplank of the *Sun Seeker*. When they were on the jetty, one of the guards led them toward the exit.

"Now," said Gumbao, as he moved from behind the diesel tank then followed the shadows until he was behind the remaining guard. He didn't even check if Hassan was behind him before he reached up and grabbed the man by the neck and dragged him back into the darkness. Hassan was waiting for him and put his hand over the guard's mouth before he could shout. Gumbao squeezed as hard as he could. He was terrified there would be a noise, and everyone would come running with guns blazing. When the man went limp in his arms, he laid him on the jetty.

"Take his jacket and hat and stand where he was standing," said Gumbao. "I will tie and gag him."

Hassan quickly put on the clothes and awkwardly grabbed the gun then moved back onto the jetty as if nothing had happened. He stood looking bored with his hat pulled down over his face. The other guard sauntered back along the jetty smoking a cigarette. As he approached, Hassan moved further back into the shadows. The guard came forward, sensing something was wrong, but before he could do anything Gumbao reached out of the night and pulled him behind a big pile of ropes. Hassan quickly walked in behind and hit him on the back of the head with the rifle.

"You go back and stand guard," said Gumbao. "I'm going to find Brody. Then we can get out of here. If anyone comes let out a whistle."

Hassan nodded and went back to his position.

Gumbao jumped the four-foot gap and landed on the *Sun Seeker*'s deck. He moved as quickly as he could and went inside. The place was silent, but he knew if Brody was onboard then there would probably be another guard or two. He sneaked into the main saloon and walked across the deep pile carpet toward the stairs to the lower deck. A generator hummed almost imperceivably in the background. He moved as quietly as he could down the spiral staircase and into the living areas. He went from cabin to cabin, but the place was empty. Gumbao had never been on such a ship. It was like a king's palace, so much luxury. He was used to dhows where you were lucky if you found a few square feet to lay out a sleeping mat. He found the kitchen and saw some matches next to the stove, so he pocketed them. Then he went back upstairs to the main salon. He was lost—*where could they have put Brody?* From the outside the place looked enormous but now that he was inside it wasn't that big at all. He went up to the fly bridge and looked around but saw nothing. There were no guards or any signs of life. Hassan peered up at him from the jetty, but all Gumbao could do was shrug his shoulders. He rubbed his sweaty palms on his shorts; this was their only plan. He looked around the main saloon and noticed a large picture of the boat on the wall with tiny pinpricks of light spread across its length. Gumbao peered at the picture, then noticed that he had missed a whole section below where the engine was. He traced the line of passageways to the stern where there was a hatch. When he found the hatch at the rear of the boat he paused and checked his Glock. If there was going to be trouble, then this was the place. He had to get in and get Brody as fast as possible. Once Brody was back, he could hand over command once again and sit and have a quiet smoke. He twisted the D-ring handle and slowly pulled the hatch toward him. He was expecting a shout at any second, and the wound on his leg from the house of horrors on Zanzibar started to throb. Once the lid was a couple of inches open it surprised him and whirred the rest of the way on electric motors. The light was on below. He looked into the space, but it was empty. All he could see was a small kitchen and some more doors. He remembered from the plan that there were two more cabins in the crew section and a door to the engine room. He slid down the companionway ladder and landed with a soft thud on the lower deck. He pulled the pistol and checked the corners of the kitchen then he looked into the engine room. It was spotless, but empty. Then he tried the first cabin door, but it was locked. He went to the second door and gently pushed it open. A man was lying on the single bunk reading a magazine. Gumbao stepped into the room to take the guy by surprise, but it didn't happen that way. The man leapt off the bed in a spilt second and threw himself at Gumbao. They rolled back into the main crew quarters' living area. Gumbao tried to knee the guy in the groin, but the man twisted away. Then the guard threw a wild elbow at Gumbao's head. It missed, but the blow caught him in the chest, sending waves of pain up through his body. The man jerked himself free and tried to slide across the floor, but Gumbao grabbed his bare foot and pulled him back. Then he launched himself onto the man. He rained punches down on the man's head, but he twisted and turned and covered his head with his arms, so Gumbao could not get a punch to land. It was like sitting on a wild animal. The man fought to throw Gumbao off. Finally, the guard twisted and threw a left hook, which landed squarely on Gumbao's chin, sending him sprawling backwards. The man kicked himself away toward the kitchen area. Gumbao looked around for the gun—he was desperate now and needed to get this done. If there was too much noise, then so be it. Before Gumbao could find his weapon, the man came racing out from the kitchenette brandishing a knife. He looked at the ladder with greedy eyes, then darted forward, thrusting the knife toward Gumbao's chest, but missed by a few inches. Gumbao grabbed the man's wrist and started twisting the knife away from himself. But the man was very strong and forced the blade back toward Gumbao. The guard felt he was getting the upper hand and tried to twist, but Gumbao had seen this move before and slammed his bare foot down on the man's ankle. He grunted but did not lose any purchase on the knife. The man twisted again in the other direction, which caught Gumbao a little off guard, so he lost his grip on the man's wrist. He broke free, then swung around, slicing the knife through the air. Gumbao danced back and let the knife pass in front of him. He dodged another attack as the man started moving toward the hatch. The two men stood, panting and staring at each other, knowing this was probably the last thing they would do in their lives. The man raced for the steps. Gumbao grabbed him and slammed him into the stainless-steel ladder. The man tried to spin around, but his arm had gone through one of the rungs in the ladder. Gumbao reached around and grabbed the arm then bent it back on itself against the metal rung. He heard a terrible snapping sound as the man's shoulder popped out of its socket. The soldier slumped and Gumbao threw a punch at his head. The guard screamed in pain as his head was smashed against the ladder once again. Gumbao grabbed the man and threw him back onto the floor. His left arm was dangling and useless, and he had lost his knife, but he was not dead yet. He kicked out at Gumbao's bandage that was red with blood from the seeping wound. Gumbao staggered as lighting strikes of pain went from his leg to his head. He lost his senses for a moment, then brought his other foot down on the man's other ankle and swiftly kicked him in the head.

Then all he could hear was his own heart beating like a drum. He stood for a second trying to compose himself. He looked down as blood pooled on the floor at his feet. Then he staggered back to the locked door and searched for the key. But it was nowhere to be found. He was starting to feel desperate, then went to the prostrate guard on the floor and checked his pockets. He found a clip of keys, a wallet full of money, and a packet of cigarettes. He stuffed the money and cigarettes into his pockets then tried the keys one at a time on the door. The fourth one clicked in the lock, and the door swung open. Lying on the bed wide-eyed, gagged, and chained hand and foot was Brody. Gumbao ripped the gag from his mouth.

"How do I get you out of these chains?" he panted.

"That guard you were smashing the place up with has them."

Gumbao held out the bloody keys. "The small silver ones. Come on, we haven't got all night. I'm sure someone heard that commotion and will be coming soon."

Once Brody was free, he put the guard on the bed and gagged him then chained him up. Then he shut and locked the door. Gumbao was sitting on a bench seat holding a dishcloth against his leg. Brody went to the kitchen and grabbed the first aid box. He ripped it open and quickly wrapped Gumbao's leg and then helped him to the ladder. They were on deck in a few moments. Brody helped Gumbao limp across the gangplank and onto the jetty.

Hassan reached out and helped Gumbao the last few steps. He blurted out, "It's great to see you, Boss. The old man was missing you so much."

Gumbao said, "Shut up! I was doing just fine. You were the one crying for your mother."

Brody said, "There's no time for this now. How do we get out of here?"

Hassan looked at Gumbao who looked at Hassan, then said, "Our plan was to get you out and we did just that."

"Shit," said Brody, "We have no idea how we are getting off this jetty?"

"We are playing it by ear. One step at a time, as you say."

"O.K. What have we got?"

Gumbao pointed at *Shukran*, "Well we have her."

"That would be nice, but we would not get far at eight knots."

Brody was starting to get his senses back. He knew they had to get off the jetty as quickly as possible and into the sand dunes where they could hide. "Gumbao can't swim with that leg. Our only choice is the gate," he said.

"But how? There are two guys there with guns."

"Gumbao, put the other guard's clothes on and try to hide that limp. Hassan, get some rope and tie my hands behind my back. You have been ordered to take me into the refinery."

Hassan looked the best as a guard, so he went in front, then Brody, who kept his head down and looked miserable, then Gumbao, trying not to limp.

They approached the gate, and Hassan stopped, "Hey, let us through. The big boss has asked us to bring up the prisoner."

The two guards had been playing cards on a stool they had set up next to the gate. One looked up and said, "We haven't heard anything."

Hassan froze until Brody nudged him with his shoulder. "O.K. We'll take him back then, no problem here. You can explain to those tigiris that you said we couldn't go through."

"What do you mean?" said the second guard.

"Those rich guys, in their Friday kanzus. The ones that pay us all. You can explain to them why we didn't bring this muzungu when they asked."

The two guards looked at each other. They both had families, the salaries enabled their kids to go to school and their wives to be happy. Fear of losing their jobs overrode common sense, so they opened the gate. Hassan walked through and Gumbao gave Brody a push for good measure. Then grunted at the guards, "Asante."

The three marched purposefully toward the gate to the refinery. As soon as the guards went back to the card game, they darted off the main path and into the dunes.

They ran across the dunes until they were all out of breath, Brody half-dragging Gumbao along. When they reached the beach, they were all knackered. "We have to rest for a bit," said Brody.

They walked into the coconut grove and found some cover. "How long before they find out what has happened?" asked Hassan. "No fucking idea," said Brody. "But thanks for the rescue. I would have been food for the sharks without you."

Gumbao grinned in the darkness, then reached into his pocket and found his crumpled pack of cigarettes and the matches. "Ay, Boy, we did good." He leaned back on his elbow and took a long drag, filling his lungs with smoke."

"What do we know?" asked Brody.

Hassan said, "We heard them talking on the boat before the rescue. There is something happening tomorrow night at some ruins on the other side of the island. They said they needed Zainab for whatever they are doing. We have to be there and get her out then get off this island as quickly as possible."

"What exactly are they doing tomorrow?"

"We didn't hear that bit. They only said it was some kind of way for that guy Tariq to become the president of Tanzania," said Gumbao.

"We have to get sorted, we need some food and to dress his wound. Then we will have to find this place and get ready. Any ideas?"

"When we first arrived, a guy told me there was a clinic around here. That will be the only place to get medical supplies," said Hassan.

"Fine, let's head back to the village and see if we can find this clinic," said Brody.

Hassan found a stick that could be used as a makeshift crutch for Gumbao and they started walking toward the road. It took most of the night, but just before dawn they arrived at the outskirts of the village on the beach. "Hassan, go in and find the clinic," said Brody.

Gumbao was lying on the ground, his face was pale, and his leg was drenched in blood, which dripped into the soft sand.

Hassan came jogging back in the early morning twilight. "I've found it, we have to go around the outside of the village first. Can he make it?"

"I will carry him if I need to," said Brody.

They staggered around the village and entered from the southern end. Hassan said, "The block building up ahead."

"We go 'round the back, no one can see us. This place lives off that refinery, they will hand us over in a second," said Brody.

Brody leaned Gumbao gently against the wall of the infirmary then picked up a rock and smashed the back window. He climbed through the broken window then opened the door for Gumbao and Hassan. "Quickly, we have to be in and out. Hassan, go look for food and water while I deal with Gumbao."

They split up. Brody dragged Gumbao into a cubicle and put him on the bed. Then he sorted through the medical supplies. He found a saline drip which he hooked up to Gumbao. Then he started checking the wound. Hassan came rushing into the room, "There's someone coming."

"Shit, that's all we need," said Brody.

He looked out of the front window and saw a pretty nurse in a bright white uniform, with a headscarf wrapped tightly around her head. She was trudging through the sand toward them, with a determined look on her pretty face, holding a large woven bag in one hand and a bunch of keys in the other.

Brody said, "Get back with Gumbao. Keep him quiet." Then he stepped behind the door and waited. The young nurse took her time opening the door, then shoved the door open with her butt as she lifted the heavy bag and dropped it on the floor. Brody silently stepped in behind her, closing the door and putting his hand over her mouth. She immediately screamed and twisted in his arms, but he held on tight. Then Hassan came back into the room and started whispering in rapid-fire Kiswahili. The girl stopped struggling and Brody slowly let go of her. She turned and frowned at Brody then walked toward the cubicle where Gumbao was.

"What's happening," asked Brody.

"She will help Gumbao. Then I have no idea," said Hassan.

The young girl took one look at Gumbao then started working. She lifted his leg and opened the wound. Gumbao was so far gone he didn't even moan. She took a pair of tweezers and fished inside the opening and pulled out what looked like a splinter of wood. "He probably has blood poisoning," she said.

She washed the wound with antiseptic and poured antibiotic powder into the hole. Then she wrapped a white bandage tightly around his leg.

"The doctor will not be here until the afternoon. But I will give him some antibiotics anyway."

"Listen," said Brody, "we mean you no harm. We are here just looking for his sister."

"That looks like a bullet wound in his leg," the nurse said.

"I can explain," said Hassan. "Just give us a chance."

The nurse pointed at Hassan and said, "I will listen to you because of your faith. But any tricks and I will scream until the whole village comes, and they will beat you to death."

"I understand," said Hassan, "Let me explain. Then you can make your own mind up and we will not stop you. Do you have any food in your bag?"

"Yes, and we have a water machine in the back office."

Brody gulped down the first liter of water and almost vomited it back up.

Then he sat and hungrily ate the samosas.

Hassan explained the whole trip to the young nurse, concentrating on his sister Zainab and her wanting to be a doctor. The nurse listened quietly as she continued to help Gumbao, who looked like he was unconscious.

When Hassan had finished, she said, "This island is known for the Jinn. We have some of the oldest ones ever to be found on this coast. They came with the Arabs many years ago. It is even said there is an Ifrit that belongs to this island that is more than five hundred years old. The old women of the village talk about them often. They say that the Ifrit found the gas and then brought the Thuwaini clan here to collect it all. Many of our young men and women have disappeared over the years. They just seem to vanish one day and are never heard of again. We always go to the chief and the refinery to report them missing. They usually do a big search of the island; they even use helicopters sometimes. But they never find anything. The chief reports back that they must have just run away. Then the case is closed. But I was always sure that something was wrong."

Hassan said, "I am looking for my sister, but if we can work together, maybe we can help each other."

The nurse looked at Hassan, I can see you are a good Muslim. But your friends I do not trust. Muzungus always tell lies—when they came to the island to drill, they said nothing would go wrong but our fish are disappearing. And the old man; he is not of the faith."

"Sister, we are both Muslims. We are here to help whoever comes across our path. We must be kind and care for the sick and injured."
"Yes, I know, that is why I have helped you. But that does not mean I trust you. You can stay here until midday then you have to leave. I will feed you and help the old man. If any guards pass by when you are gone, I will tell them the truth."
"That's fair," said Hassan. "Have you heard of any ruins on the island?"
"The only ruins are an old Swahili Arab settlement at the top of the island. They are known as Songo Mnara. There is very little there, an old broken-down mosque and some houses."
"How do we get there?"
"It is too far to walk. You'll need some donkeys to help you, especially with the old man."
Hassan took off his kufi and wiped the sweat from his face. "Do you know where I can get a couple of donkeys?"
"My brother has six, he uses them to carry stones from the boats."
"Do you think he would hire them to me?"
"You will have to go down to the beach and ask him. But he works for the refinery so be very careful."

Chapter Twenty
Songo Songo Jetty

Tariq threw the cut-glass brandy decanter across the deck. It hit a stainless-steel Samson post, and smashed to smithereens, spilling the dark expensive liquid all over the teak deck. A guard stood in front of him, his useless arm limply hanging by his side. He stared at his feet knowing he was in deep trouble.

"I told you to stay alert and keep the muzungu tied up! What happened?"

"Sir, I was standing on guard in the crew area when a highly trained man slipped into the room from somewhere and took me by surprise. He must have been a special ops soldier. I did not see him coming."

"Shut up. You are a fool. You were sleeping on your post. The crew quarters is the most secure place on this boat. And I ordered you to keep all of the doors locked. What happened?"

The guard lifted his limp arm as if to show Tariq that he deserved some kind of mercy, "Sir—sir—I fought as hard as I could. The attacker was so highly trained I had no chance. Look he nearly ripped my arm off. I need medical attention."

"You will be lucky if you stay alive after the damage you have done tonight. Now get out of my sight."

Tariq sat heavily into one of the wooden deck chairs surrounding the teak table. "Faaiz, get another bottle of brandy. Zaaem, what do we do now?"

"I have already sent out search parties to find these people. They are more dangerous than we thought. They sound highly trained. Our askaris are all ex-military and trained in hand-to-hand combat. I ordered the helicopter from the mainland, it left twenty minutes ago and will be here soon. We will comb the island until we find the infidels. The guards have a shoot-to-kill order."

"We can't let these people interfere with our plans," said Tariq.

Faaiz passed Tariq a glass of brandy. "Sir, don't worry, we will have them long before tomorrow night. This island is only small; there is nowhere to hide. I will go with the patrol to the town. There was blood all over the cabin, the attacker must have been injured. I am sure he will head for one of the clinics. We will start in the northern one then clear the other villages one by one."

"Good, then go! We have no time to waste. Keep me informed. I want that muzungu dead before lunch. Zaaem, where is the girl?"

"She is safely in the caverns. I have doubled the guards with orders to shoot on sight."

Chapter Twenty-One
Escape

Brody looked out of the window as a bright red helicopter flew over the village. "Where the hell is Hassan?"

The nurse looked up from Gumbao's leg. "You must leave here," she said. "This is the first place they will look. Go to the edge of the village. There is a track that leads from the back of the clinic and heads to a thick bamboo grove. Hide there. I will send Hassan when he returns when the soldiers come. I will tell them you threatened me and made me help your friend and then you left."

Brody was not sure; this was probably a trap to get him away from the girl so she could send the guards to kill them away from the clinic. But he had no choice.

"O.K., let's get Gumbao on his feet, then we'll make a run for it."

Gumbao was awake, but still feeling very groggy. He moaned as Brody sat him up straight. "Listen, we have to go. This place is not safe anymore. The guards will be here soon. Can you walk?"

"Yes, just give me one of the crutches by the door and I'll be fine," said Gumbao.

Brody opened the rear door, expecting shouts at any moment. He was sure as soon as they were gone the nurse would run into the village and tell the guards exactly where they were. In front of them was a small, sandy field with a well-trodden path going across the center, leading to a coconut grove that was over a slight rise. The nurse peered over his shoulder, telling him, "Just follow that path. When you get over the hill you will see the bamboo forest. It is very thick; you will be able to hide there. Take these extra bandages and antibiotics." Then she pushed them out of the door and slammed it shut.

Brody grabbed Gumbao around the waist as they hobbled across the open sandy rise following the path. They stumbled up and over the first slight rise, then the village disappeared behind them, which was a blessing. The drugs were taking effect on Gumbao, and he was improving with every step. They soon saw in the distance the bamboo grove. Densely packed, deep green shoots, as thick as a man's arm, shot up into the air. Brody pushed Gumbao along as fast as the crutch would allow. When they reached the bamboo grove, he shoved his way inside and soon they were hidden. "We just have to hope that girl believed Hassan," said Gumbao.

Hassan had met the nurse's brother on the beach and paid a heavy price for three donkeys. He was about to leave when a four-wheel-drive pickup screeched into the village and raced onto the beach. Four men with guns jumped out and started moving through the early morning crowd of fishermen. The men pushed the fishermen into a group on the far side of the beach then started shouting at them. The donkey renter said, "What is all that about? Do you think they are looking for something?"

"Do they do that often?" Hassan asked, feeling the trickles of sweat start to pour down his spine.

"Sometimes, when the fishermen go too near the jetty or one of their boats, they get angry. They say it is for our own good."

"I'm leaving, how do I return the donkeys to you?"

"Just let them go and they'll find me. This is a small island."

Hassan walked away from the beach heading for the dunes. As soon as he was out of sight, he followed the path leading to the clinic. He jogged along with the donkeys in tow behind him and was about halfway there when the nurse came running down the path toward him. "I had to send them away," she said. "I was frightened the guards would come and take them. You have to get off the island as soon as you find your sister, it is too dangerous. If you go as far north as you can, past Vilena, you will find a Christian church. I am sure they will help the muzungu."

Hassan said, "Where are my friends?"

The nurse pointed toward the dunes behind the village. "Follow that path until you see the bamboo. I told them to hide there."

Hassan said, "Shukran, my sister. You should go home. Do not go to the clinic—say you were sick and did not go to work."

"Brother, if you find Zainab, please stop these men from bringing the Jinn to our homes. I beg of you. We have lost too many of our young people."

Hassan turned and pulled his stubborn donkeys onto the new track. As he was leaving, he shouted back to the nurse, "In Allah's name, I will find my sister and stop these evil men. Even if it kills me."

Hassan quickly found the bamboo grove.

Gumbao was sitting on a tree stump smoking a cigarette, and Brody was pacing in front of him. "I'm here," said Hassan.

Brody breathed a sigh of relief. "Thank God, you made it. What's happening in the village?"

"When I was on the beach a truck came full of men with guns, but I managed to keep away from them."

"Did you see the helicopter?" asked Brody.

"Yes, I did. We'll never manage to cross the island now," said Hassan.

"Before we left *Shukran,* I checked this place out on the map. From what the nurse said the ruins are in the far north. I would estimate we are only about four miles from them. That would only take a couple of hours normally—with the donkeys maybe even less. Our only issue is staying off the roads and hiding in the sand dunes as much as possible. We just move inland away from the roads and the airstrip and move as quickly as possible. It will be a breeze, Hassan."

"What about the helicopter?" asked Gumbao.

"That's luck, as long as we try and stay undercover, we should be O.K."

They loaded Gumbao onto the biggest donkey then set off through the coconut groves moving inland. Brody put Hassan in the lead with Gumbao in the middle and he took up the rear. He checked the Glock and put a round in the chamber. He was not sure about his plan at all, but he had to give the guys some confidence to move. What they were doing was a suicide mission. Everyone was looking for them and he was sure, after last night, that if they were caught, there would be no trial or police involvement; it would end very quickly and very badly.

For the first hour, they moved across the island, staying away from the only road. The place was covered in tall coconut trees as far as the eye could see, interspersed with deep green bamboo thickets and the occasional thorny acacia tree. Not great for cover, but good for speed.

As the sun was reaching its zenith, they met the road again. "We have to cross here—let me go and have a look," said Brody.

He left the donkeys in a bamboo thicket and crept up to the road. It was empty in both directions. His only problem was that on the other side of the road, it was just scrub and low-level vegetation—no cover at all. If they were caught out in the open, they were dead. He sat watching and thinking. They couldn't go any further north on this side, or they would meet the refinery. This was the only real place he had seen where they had enough cover on this side of the road. He heard a vehicle in the distance and slid into the drainage ditch running alongside the road. The pickup truck had four guys in the back, all armed with what looked like stubby machine guns, probably MP5s. The men drove along, scanning the surrounding countryside. Then he heard the *whoop whoop* of a helicopter approaching. The guys in the pickup started waving at the chopper. Brody knew it was hard to spot anyone hiding from the chopper, but he dug himself into the earth of the drainage ditch a little more. The car passed him with the helicopter overhead; the driver and the pilot were obviously talking. Then the vehicle stopped and the four men jumped out. Brody could just make them out about 100 yards further along the road. He was at an impasse; he had to cross the road and get to cover. But how, with the truck and the helicopter. Creeping up on four armed men and taking them out with just his Glock and an open road was suicide; he would not get to within fifty yards of them before he was cut down. And now he couldn't even retreat to the bamboo grove. He lay in the dirt thinking. The helicopter rose in the sky and headed back toward the north of the island. That only left the guards. He noticed they were stationed by the side of the road and seemed to have set up a roadblock. This seemed stupid to Brody, as he was hardly likely to walk along the only road on Songo Songo when he was being hunted by everyone. He slid along the bottom of the drainage ditch, closer and closer to the men. He was not sure what he would do, but doing nothing was not worth doing either. Maybe he could hear something useful. He pushed carefully though the thick bushes growing in the ditch as he crawled to within ten yards of the truck.

He listened to the men but could not understand anything they were saying. Then one shouted, "Hey, girl, come here." Brody lifted himself up to get a better look and saw the four men's backs. He made a move, stealthily climbing out of the ditch and crouching behind the pickup. He took a chance and peeped around the edge. A girl was riding a bicycle along the smooth tarmac toward the men. He did a double take, what he saw was not possible. The girl was smiling and waving at the men. He could not have made a better distraction if he had tried. The girl looked young with jet-black hair and a wide smile. The hairs on the back of his neck stood on end as the men started jostling for a position to talk this young lady. She stopped her bike in front of them and said, "What is happening? Why are you men here?" Brody froze in position; how could this be? He knew that voice very well. The last time he had heard it was in the horror house on Unguja. But this was impossible. He peered out around the side of the pickup and saw the young girl from Zanzibar standing in front of the soldiers. Her blue eyes had them mesmerized; she seemed to be talking to them, but it was more like a snake charming its owner. She smiled and talked, but the words didn't register with Brody, nor the guards. Baktari's words flooding back into Brody's brain: *The shape comes to you when you most need it. It has saved you on several occasions and still looks over your shoulder, even today, right now it is around. I can sense it. Somewhere up in the trees or hiding behind a rock. But you are a non-believer, your mind was twisted many years ago, so you are blind to these things. But your life will be long, and your eyes will open.*

For a second Brody was spellbound; all of his beliefs flashed before his eyes. Had he been blind his whole life? He was born a Catholic, his father had taken him to church for every Sunday Mass. But he had never really believed. Then the army had beaten any semblance of relying on a friendly deity in the sky right out of him. Now, he was seeing the impossible. The girl kept charming the men, they stood and watched her.

All of their senses seemed to be focused on the girl. Brody snapped out of his mind-altering trance. He pulled the Glock from his pants pocket and walked up behind the first man. He shoved the pistol into his neck as he grabbed his arm and twisted it up the man's back. For a second, time seemed to stand still. The guard did not notice or feel what Brody had done. Then his senses snapped back into focus, and he yelped. This made the others wake up and turn. Brody said, "Drop your weapons or I blow his head off."

The men fumbled for a few seconds as if they had been asleep, then they just dropped their weapons on the ground. Brody marched them to the side of the road and checked the cab of the vehicle. Nobody moved. The young girl just stood in the road holding her bicycle. Brody found a bag of tie wraps and threw them at the men kneeling on the ground. "Here, put these around your hands and feet." The men complied, then Brody went behind them and tightened the ties. He then got each man up and put him in the back of the truck. Then he turned to talk to the girl. "Are you here to save me again?"

"You are the first muzungu I have ever met. And I see you are very silly people. You are trying to save us all from more than you know. I have been watching you. I am surprised you have made it this far. But it seems you and your friends are the only ones around that might stop what is to come tonight. So, I have to aid you."

"What is happening tonight?" asked Brody.

"If I explained, you would not go. What will happen is already written. You must follow your path and we will all see what comes of it all."

"That's not very useful," shouted Brody. "I'm trying to help. I need more than that."

"I cannot give you more. Follow your heart and do what you do. It is already written."

The girl got on her bicycle and rode back the way she had come.

Brody waved frantically at the bamboo grove. Hassan saw him from their hiding place and came running over. "What happened? How did you manage to get all of these guys into the back of this truck?"

"Weren't you watching?" asked Brody.

"Yes, of course."

"Did you see the girl?"

"What girl? You crept up behind them and they all just gave up and sat on the floor. We were sure you were dead."

"There was a girl here on a bicycle."

"Boss, we were watching from just over there. Nobody has been on this road."

Brody wiped his forearm across his face. This was too much. Way too much. His life of science and technology that he was so proud of was crumbling in front of his eyes. He stared along the road hoping he would see the bicycle moving off into the distance, but all he could see was the waves of heat pulsating from the hot tarmac.

"Are you alright, Boss? I don't think we should sit out here in the road all day."

Brody snapped back, "Yes, I have a new plan." He jumped into the pickup and fired up the engine then drove it across to the bamboo grove. He bundled the guys out and stripped them of their jackets, trousers, and hats. "You two, put these on. From now on we work for the refinery and travel in style."

Songo Songo
Songo Mnara

With the guards gagged and safely tied to the thick bamboo branches, Brody jumped behind the driving wheel and they headed for the road. They flashed past the refinery gate and headed north. As soon as Brody could, he turned off the main road and onto a dirt track leading back into the coconut groves. He raced the car across the sandy, coarse grass, heading as close to north as he could. The day had gone by so fast. The sun was starting to head toward the horizon on the western side of the island, as they followed the old tracks always heading north. They came to a junction and Hassan said, "Look at that sign." A battered, old wooden plank had been nailed to a tree. Painted on the plank in large faded letters was *"Songo Mnara"* and an arrow. Brody turned the car onto the rutted old road, and they bounced down toward the ocean once again. The road passed through a thick forest of old, gnarled neem and mango trees, their branches intertwining above the car, closing off the light from above with their heavy fruits hanging from the laden branches. They came to a ford in the road with crystal-clear water flowing toward the beach. Brody raced through, wanting to find the ruins before anyone else arrived. When they came out of the forest they were on the most northern part of the island. The tip seemed to protrude out into the ocean, like a hooked nose from a face. It created a perfect harbor on the leeward edge and on the very top they could see the remains of a mosque dome. "This must be it," said Hassan, pointing at the crumbling minarets.

Brody raced up to the old mosque then drove the car along a side road that headed back into the forest. He pulled up after a few yards and reversed the car under an ancient mango tree. Once he was satisfied it was well-covered, Brody cut some branches and hid the vehicle. He then tucked the keys behind a low-hanging branch. "Hassan, If I can't drive you know where the keys are. Just make sure you get as many out as you can."

The ruins spread across the top of the rise; they had a perfect view in all directions. The slope ran down to a sandy beach and the long ridge of land made a perfect harbor. "The people who had lived in this town were in a great spot for all of the traffic from India or from further along the coast in either direction," said Brody. "It's amazing—they could see for miles in all directions. What is that building in the far distance?"

"The nurse said there was a church here, maybe it's that," said Hassan.

The buildings were set in neat orderly rows running down toward the beach. At the top was the ancient mosque, its bright white limestone walls shining in the afternoon sun, crumbling minarets hanging onto each corner, and then some larger buildings stretching across the very top of the hill. Next to the mosque was a tall arched doorway leading to what must have been a palatial room. Next to that was a stone building with an unbroken stone door on the front and a tower protruding about sixty feet into the air. Brody patted the stone door. "This hasn't moved in a millennium, I wonder who is buried in here?"

Hassan said, "They even have a well, and it still has water."

"I wonder why everyone left. It seems like an ideal place to live," asked Brody.

"We don't have time for a history lesson," said Gumbao. "We need to find some cover and get ready for the guests."

"True," said Brody. "Gumbao, you take one of the MP5s and find some height. You aren't up to a fight right now, but you could save my ass with a few well-placed shots. Hassan, we'll find some cover and see what happens. I'm sure I don't have to tell you, but we are outgunned and outmanned. We'll be very lucky if one of us leaves here alive."

Hassan gritted his teeth, the words of the old ladies were ringing in his ears. "Brody, I'm here for my sister and will either take her home or not go home myself."

"I understand," said Brody. "And we haven't lost until the last man is down."

Gumbao climbed up one of the ruins near the mosque and settled himself on a broken roof. He could clearly see the entrance to the town and most of the other buildings. He checked and rechecked the automatic weapon. He had never fired one of these guns before but guessed it was just point and press. At least now they were matched with the guards in firepower. And Baktari had said he would live to fight more battles.

They sat and watched the sun go down. Hassan whispered, "There is no moon tonight."

"That's good for us, we need all the help we can get," said Brody.

As the sun dipped below the horizon in the west, they saw the first headlights coming through the forest. Brody ducked down as the four pickups drove in through the entrance to the village and parked in a semi-circle in front of the mosque. Brody watched as eight men jumped off the back of the first pickup. He let out a low whistle. "That's the guys from Zanzibar. The Walt Disney team."

The men adjusted their swords and turbans and started walking around the perimeter of the buildings. Brody and Hassan crept further back into their ruined house and held their breath as the guards searched the empty houses. The other vehicles had refinery guards who fanned out into the perimeter. Brody guessed they were on the lookout for him.

Once the Walt Disney gang were done, they moved to the mosque and stood at attention in front of the dilapidated building.

A *whoop whoop* sound suddenly filled their ears. Gumbao ducked down in the darkness as a helicopter came in low, skimming the trees. It swooped to a halt then hovered before it landed just outside of the town. Tariq, Faaiz, and Zaaem all jumped out. Faaiz reached back in and pulled a slim person dressed all in white from the chopper. She immediately stumbled and fell forward. Faaiz grabbed the woman and roughly pulled her up straight again, her cuffed hands were tightly held behind her, her long black hair blowing in the downdraft. She looked up at the sky, her face pale with dark rings around her eyes. Brody grabbed Hassan's arm as he leapt up to go get his sister. "Wait, my friend. We know she is here now. We must pick our time, or we won't get within ten yards of her."

Hassan knew Brody was right, but he couldn't bear to see his sister like this. She used to be a bright happy soul who always had good things to say, now she looked like a walking corpse. "What is she wearing?" asked Hassan.

"Fucked if I know, these guys get weirder and weirder. But we are in the right place, and we have surprise on our side. So just wait. I will not let anything happen to Zainab."

Brody watched as Faaiz dragged Zainab toward the mosque. He had observed many strange rituals when he was in the army, and he knew the ones with girls all dressed in white never ended well. He had to get to Zainab quickly.

Tariq led the group toward the large, smooth stone below the obelisk. "Tie her to the ring!" he shouted.

Zainab lay on the ground; she was obviously exhausted and weak from whatever they had been doing to her. She seemed resigned to her fate.

The men in turbans all stood to attention and drew their swords, holding them in front of themselves. Their eyes seemed to burn in the night. Tariq stood next to Zainab, his bright white and golden kanzu glowed in the light from the torches, his black bejeweled slippers seemed to float just off the ground.

Zaeem and Faaiz stood back from him as he stretched his arms out to the tomb. Tariq began chanting in some foreign tongue. The turbaned men moved forward, creating a closed circle around Tariq. He seemed to grow in size as he chanted and cried out. His body started to convulse, then he threw his arms up into the sky and shouted, "Ifrit, I call on you. As promised, I bring the chosen one for you to feast on."

Brody was taken aback by the show, but he had seen things like this before when he was in the army. Lunatics could always take over the locals if the theatrics were good enough. But when Hassan heard the word "Ifrit" he grabbed Brody's arm. "That is the head Jinn. He is calling on the devil himself."

Brody said, "Don't worry. Nothing is happening, he is just putting on a show for his buddies. Let them get all excited, then we will go in and grab Zainab."

Hassan was very frightened. This was the worst Jinn to ever be seen, they were evil incarnate and could not be stopped.

Brody watched in fascination as Tariq continued to chant and speak in tongues at the stone slab.

Hassan almost leapt out of his hiding place as the stone slab started to slide back. Tariq screamed and his eyes grew brighter, his black sweaty hair covering the maniacal look on his face.

Brody knew this was the do or die moment; he had to move. He touched Hassan's arm, "Follow me."

They crept around the edge of the compound, keeping low in the shadows. Brody just hoped that Gumbao was still in his position and could help with the guards on the perimeter.

Hassan grabbed him again. "Look, the stone is moving. We have to be quick, or my Zainab will be gone."

Brody raced across the small clearing, cleared the steps to the mosque in one jump and landed on the platform in front of the tomb. He slammed one turbaned man against the walls of the ruins and kicked another, sending him back down the steps. Then he grabbed Tariq by the back of the head and thrust the MP5 into his back. The other guards just stood spellbound watching Tariq with glazed eyes. Hassan ran to Zainab and cut the rope. Brody could not understand why, but Tariq was not struggling, so he shook him but all he got was a low, sort of animalistic growl. Hassan screamed as the stone slid back. The space behind the stone was pitch black, then a shadow seemed to flit across the doorway. They were all spellbound. Brody hung on to Tariq, who just seemed to be in some sort of trance and staggered back onto Brody.

The shadow seemed to take a form, but it was more of a vague shadow with no real outline. Brody was being drawn into the scene and knew he was losing control. He shouted, "Everybody back or I kill him. But nobody was really interested in him anymore; all eyes were on dark space where the door had been."

Hassan grabbed Zainab and tried to pull her back, but there seemed to be a force holding them both in place. He looked into the darkness and saw two bright red eyes glaring back at him. All he could think to do was start chanting "Bismillah Hir Rahman Nir Rahim" (*In the name of Allah, The Most Gracious and the Most Merciful*). It was what the cleric in Pemba had told him. He could not bow his head, so he stood in front of the doorway facing the evil, his arms by his sides, his hands held out with the palms pointing up. He seemed so frail to Brody as he stood facing what he believed to be the evilest thing that could ever come to this world. Tariq twisted and turned in Brody's arms, still following the ritual.

Hassan knew he had to stay in front of Zainab. He called out, "Bismillah Hir Rahman Nir Rahim" over and over again. But the red glowing eyes began to glow brighter, and the form seemed to be taking some sort of animal-type shape. One second it seemed to resemble a large dog with dripping fangs, the next the head of a snake. Hassan felt the energy being sucked from his body as he chanted the Bismillah at the Ifrit. The creature was growing in size in front of him. Not quite a real thing yet, but it was searching for its prey. Hassan knew the prey was his sister and he could not let that happen. His only weapon against this evil force was his faith. The creature grew in size again, but it was still only a shadow. Hassan felt a force around him so strong it pushed him back one step, then another, then another. He was chanting and praying for the life of himself and his sister, but he knew he was weak, and the Ifrit would push him down then beat him. His clothes were wet with sweat and his head ached, but he continued the losing battle. He started to say, "Bismillah ..." But he heard in his head, "Be silent!"

The creature was talking to him as it grew in strength. He was lost; he did not know what to do. His faith was just not strong enough to beat such a creature. He knew he would lose his sister to the other world and never see her again. He asked, "How can Allah desert me now? I have never asked for anything from you. Now I will gladly give my life if you spare Zainab's." He knew not to bow or kneel, but he felt his knees buckling under him. His eyes were lowering as the shadow grew in the depths of the tomb. He fell to his knees in front of the gaping black hole, his eyes fixed on the red dots he could see in the depths of the darkness. Now he knew he was going to be swallowed up by the evil that was waiting to escape into his world and Zainab would be lost forever.

Brody was trying to grapple with Tariq, who did not seem to notice he was there. The turbaned men all stood staring at the tomb entrance, their swords shining in the night. Brody let off a short three round burst from the MP5, but nothing happened. He didn't know what to do—if he let go of Tariq, there was nothing to stop the guards from killing them on the spot. He dragged Tariq toward Hassan and Zainab, and shouted, "Hassan, grab her, let's go!"

But Hassan just stayed on his knees. He was mumbling Bismillah, but his strength was ebbing. As Brody watched he fell forward onto his face. Brody looked into the darkness of the tomb but could see nothing. Then Tariq screamed, "He is here, he joins us. We are free."

Hassan lay with the cool stone seeping the heat out of his face, thinking, *How could my faith not have been strong enough? Why is Allah deserting us? Why is this happening? How could I let my parents down so badly? Why can't I move?* His head swam as he felt his consciousness leave him. He drifted into a darkness that seemed full of red eyes and formless creatures. One of the old women popped up. "I told you that you could not do this, you spineless creature," she taunted. In his semi-conscious state he swept the old hag away. He knew there was something, but every time he reached for it, it flitted away from his grasp. His energy was being sapped by the mass in front of him. It would not be long now and Zainab and he would be gone forever. No more laughing and joking. No more Brody or Gumbao, just darkness and evil. He mustered one more try and started, "Bismillah Hir Rahman Nir Rahim," but it was just mumbling, and he could tell there was no strength to the words. His brain wandered again, back to the mosque on Pemba. He could see the cleric, the man he had respected his whole life, a true believer. The man was talking, he was teaching, then from his pocket he produced three gold coins. Hassan's eyes focused on the gold coins, and he heard the cleric saying, the devil won because you were fighting for the gold, not for Allah. The thought hit him like a bolt of lightning, he felt a small amount of strength seep into his veins. Allah had been giving him the answer all along, he was just too stupid to listen and understand. He had taken his faith for granted, he had been arrogant, he had been stubborn, he had let his emotions turn his faith like the three gold coins. He felt more strength enter his body as he knew the way. The light was upon him, he now knew the only way forward was to be a true believer. His fear for his sister and his own life had made him weak. If he fought for the faith and only the faith, then no Shetani could stand before him. He raised himself on his arms and pulled his legs under him. He looked into the abyss of darkness and shouted, "Bismillah Hir Rahman Nir Rahim," then again, "Bismillah Hir Rahman Nir Rahim." He felt the faith of Allah flood though his arms and legs as he stood strong in front of the Ifrit. He continued to chant, his head held high, his arms out in front of him. The faith flowed though him and pushed the darkness back. He could feel the Shetani leaving. The door started to close and the darkness around him started to lift.

He grabbed Zainab and threw her over his shoulder then raced back toward Brody. As he moved the spell was broken. Tariq slumped in Brody's arms as Hassan staggered toward him.

The turbaned men suddenly noticed Brody and Hassan among them. Faaiz started to rush toward them, reaching behind him as he ran. Brody saw the pistol as it cleared Faaiz's hip, but it got no further as a short burst from the rooftop tore him in half. This galvanized the turbaned warriors; they leapt toward the fight, brandishing their sabers. Brody shot the first one in the throat, and hit the second one in the thigh, but the third one managed to break through. Brody dropped Tariq and held up his MP5 to take the blow from the saber. Hassan dragged Zainab back along the wall toward the crumbling mosque. Brody parried strike after strike from the determined attacker, his sword flashing in the night. A second warrior ran up the steps and tried to join the fight, but he was clumsy and Brody was able to kick him in the groin before he could get a sword blow in. Brody took a chance and rolled away from the group. He came up and fired at the two men, who staggered and fell. Hassan grabbed his arm. "We have to go now." They stumbled down the steps from the tomb and made it to the door of the old mosque. Hassan could feel that his faith was stronger inside the old building. He grabbed Zainab. "Talk to me? Are you O.K.?" She seemed half-conscious, but mumbled, "Hassan, I knew you would come."

Brody ducked behind the first column of the mosque and let off another three-round burst at the attackers. The guards from the perimeter were running toward them, and as they got close the ground erupted with bullets from above, stopping them in their tracks. Gumbao stood above them and shouted, "Anyone move, and I cut you down."

Brody smiled. His old friend was always there when he needed him. "We need to get away from here and fast."

They raced back through the mosque and into the night, following the track into the forest and down to the car. Brody was first to the car; he grabbed the keys from the tree and jumped into the driver's seat. "Let's go," he shouted. "We have to get Gumbao before they overrun him."

Hassan bundled Zainab into the front seat then jumped onto the flatbed and banged the roof with his fist.

Brody gunned the engine, spinning the wheels on the soft soil, then sped along the track heading back to the ruins. He kept the lights off as he raced into the clearing, scattering the men who were milling around trying to get their bearings. Bullets started pinging off the side of the car as they raced in circles trying to disorientate the attackers. Brody saw flashes of light from the top of one of the buildings and headed in that direction.

Gumbao was pinned down—several of the guards had attacked his flank. He was kneeling in the corner of the rooftop. Chips of stone seemed to fill the air as bullets came from every direction. He knew if something didn't happen soon, he was dead. But he kept Baktari's words in his head: He would survive to fight another day. Brody bounced the pickup between the houses and approached Gumbao's building from the rear. A guard jumped out in front of the car, but Brody gunned the accelerator and mowed him down. Brody could see the flashes above him. He jammed on the brakes and jumped out, then grabbed an MP5 and ran toward the building. Hassan stood in the flatbed hoping he would not have to fire a gun.

Brody raced forward, he was in full battle mode now, a thing he thought he would never do again. The images of ruins in Iraq flashed before his eyes as he dashed toward his comrade in arms. The first man dodged out from behind a pillar and Brody shot him in the head without even slowing down. He moved forward, never slowing, always moving. The next came at him from a corridor but didn't even get a shot off as Brody put two in his chest. Then Brody mounted an old staircase. The next man appeared at the top, but Brody fired on instinct and the man tumbled down toward him. He dodged the body and mounted the last few steps. On the rooftop he sprayed the rest of his magazine then ran forward. Gumbao stood up and stepped forward. Brody grabbed him around the waist and pulled him back to the steps. Gumbao had his MP5 up and ready. Brody said, "How many rounds?" Gumbao answered, "One full clip."

Then they stumbled back to the stairs, a bullet tearing at his shorts as he pushed Gumbao toward the top step. He spun and fired at a man running toward them. The gun in his hand clicked empty. Gumbao turned and sprayed the guard, stitching bullets across his chest. "We have to go," said Brody.

They tumbled down the stairs and out into the road between the ruins. Brody had the Glock out and ready. He lifted Gumbao up and chucked him into the flatbed then jumped into the driver's seat and rammed the car into gear. He shouted, "Hold on!" And they sped out of the ruins and back toward the forest. Bullets pinged off the body of the car, but they were soon free and clear. Brody raced along the forest track, trying to get some distance so he could think. They needed to get off the island, and quickly.

Brody was driving with the lights off as they came out of the forest and back into the coconut groves. He bumped along the track, keeping the speed above fifty. He constantly looked in the mirrors, expecting to see lights coming after him.

He turned onto the tarmac then took another turn just as he saw the bright lights of the refinery. He knew they had to get off the island before Tariq could get himself organized. They bounced down a rough track toward the beach. Once the truck hit the beach, Brody took a left and raced along just in front of the waves. He bounced up through the dunes then sped along a rough track heading to the back of the gas refinery. The car bucked and jumped as it hit ruts in the old track, then they hit a sand dune and almost got bogged down but the four-wheel-drive pushed through. Brody saw the gate to the jetty approach and gunned the engine. He raced at the two bored guards standing duty. When they saw the lights approaching, they raised their guns but a *rat-a-tat-tat* from above Brody's head sent the guards flying for cover. He smashed into the gates, blasting them open, then hammered the car to the end of the jetty. "Get Zainab aboard and get the engines running—Gumbao, stand guard. I will be two minutes."

Brody jumped onto the sleek *Sun Seeker* and ran to the stern. He lifted the hatch to the crew quarters and slid down the ladder. He slammed open the door to the engine room and went to the bilges where he spun the sea cocks open and slashed at the cooling pipes for the engine. Water started to sluice into the bilge. He ran around in the engine room, randomly cutting wires and slashing at anything that looked like he could break. By the time he was finished the floor was awash with water.

When he got back to *Shukran* the engine was running and Gumbao was standing at the stern with a rope in his hand. "That should slow them down a bit. We need to get as many miles as we can from this place before it's light."

Brody untied the bow rope and pushed with all of his strength. *Shukran* pulled slowly out into the channel. Gumbao jumped onboard then Brody followed. "Keep all the running lights off," said Brody. "Now head for the open sea."

Epilogue
Kiwayu

Zainab sat in the stern cushions, her eyes bright as she watched Gumbao pull in his fourth fish of the morning.

Hassan leaned against the tiller, holding *Shukran* on a steady course between the small islands that lay ahead. They were some 500 miles north of Songo Songo. *Shukran* had motor sailed non-stop 100 miles offshore until they reached Lamu. Then Hassan had stocked for a month and they had headed into the wilderness. Brody wanted to keep as much distance between *Shukran* and Songo Songo as possible.

Zainab had lain on the cushions in the stern of *Shukran* with Hassan feeding and caring for her. After two weeks, she had slowly started to improve. That was ten days ago and now she was up and walking the deck. She had even been swimming with Brody.

Hassan had sneaked back to the doctor's office with Zainab and called his parents. They had decided the best thing to do was keep Zainab away from Pemba and Dar for the time being. They would enroll her in at the University of Nairobi in a few months under a new name.

Brody was sitting on the bowsprit of Shukran. His life in Africa had changed him in ways he could never explain. His friendships were stronger; he felt like he was part of a community: a tribe. Sometimes he longed for the order of the Western world, where everything worked and was on time. But then he would think of his long days sitting on his beloved *Shukran*, his friends who would follow him into the abyss without a question. He had spent many hours brooding over their time chasing Tariq. He had tried to rationalize the events, but his logic always left him. He always ended up with questions starting with, But how could…? His science had left him, and he felt lost and alone. His life beliefs had been called into question. Once again, his mind drifted back to the old mosque on the hill. Had he seen anything inside that tomb? Had he really felt the presence of what Hassan called an Ifrit? Then there was the girl—she had shown up on numerous occasions just in time to get him out of the shit. Was it just luck? Had she been sent by someone to help them? It was more than he wanted to accept in his life.

He had always been logical and practical; everything had an answer. But the trip to Songo Songo had brought more questions than answers. He felt in his heart he had seen something and been part of something that could not be easily explained with science and logic. He now knew there was something that he just did not understand. He felt different in a way that he had never felt before. The haze of his life had lifted; revealing clarity and peace with his past. He stared at the twisted branches of the mangroves as they came closer. Hassan had found another spot for them to hide for a few nights, away from civilization, on a bright white sandy beach with coconut palms laden with sweet juice. He could taste the white snapper he had speared earlier in the day.

The beautiful lines of the lime-green mangrove leaves, hanging on the twisted and knarled intertwining branches, as they folded their way to the crystal-clear waters, seemed sharper. A white-headed egret ignored them as it stalked in the shallows looking for any unsuspecting fry that popped its head out. The sun continued on its journey, tomorrow it would appear breathing new life back into his world. A bright orange shaft of light lit a lazy stretch of low clouds hovering in the darkening sky.

Shukran nudged the sandy bottom of the latest lagoon as darkness began to fall around them, the first stars glinted in the twilight sky. Brody leaped down from the bow into the thigh-deep warm water, as the sun dipped behind the top of the coconut trees. The noises of the night animals erupted around them. Frogs croaking, shouting for a mate, screeches of night birds coming from the dense canopy spreading out into the darkness. Brody stood in awe of the wonders in front of him. Really, could all of this be explained with science? Everything around him seemed so right. He knew he should be right here, right now; but why?
Was there another hand at play here that was so far beyond him all he could do was believe and let life take its course? He dragged the anchor through the water

to the pristine beach, then turned to *Shukran,* and smiled, as he heard Hassan start singing his madrassa for the evening prayer.

The End

I hope you enjoyed this mystical adventure into African culture and folklore. As an indie author I do not have the benefits of a publisher, cover designer and marketing department behind me. I do all of the work myself. Amazon, as I am sure you are aware, are very keen on reviews. Every single review is very important to me. I would be very grateful if you could just end this book by clicking on the stars that Amazon present to you and it would be absolutely awesome, as my daughter says, to leave a short or long review. Anything is better than nothing, so just a "Good read" or "I enjoyed African Jinn." Or whatever you like. Of course, if you would be in a position to write more then all the better and please go for it.

If you do find any mistakes, please let me know. I pay for an editor, but again as an indie author I cannot afford a line editor yet. So, if you see anything, just send me an email at steve@stevebrakerbooks.com and I will not only thank you profusely. I will also put you on a list and you will get the next book free!

Thanks for reading African Jinn.

Find out more and get more background on the character at http://www.stevebrakerbooks.com.

Tutaonana badaaye

Steve

William Brody—African Jinn